EDDY ROSE

BEAST OF ZARALL

<TWILIGHT OF BLOOD, BOOK TWO>

www.eddyrose.com

Published by: Phoenix Hollow Publishing

ISBN: 978-1763734135

Edited by: GCD Editorial

Cover design: Miblart

Map design: Eddy Rose

Chapter headers and scene breaks: Eddy Rose

To happy, healthy, crazy German Shepherds

GLOSSARY

THIS BOOK HAS BEEN crafted so that most terms and concepts are either self-explanatory or clarified through the context. However, for further explanation, feel free to consult this glossary. Please note, some entries may contain spoilers. If you choose not to read the glossary and dive straight into the story, I promise you will not feel lost.

Acts of Defiance – Forbidden or taboo behaviours for slaves.

Beast – A type of slave used for combat in the arenas.

Blues/Chinderian Blues – The currency of Chinderia. One Blue is equivalent to ten Greys, and one Grey equals ten Reds.

Chamber of the Twelve – Places of worship dedicated to the Twelve Riders.

Darkhome – One of the three realms created by the Twelve Riders after the Dividing of the Homes. It serves as the prison for Fiends.

Dividing of the Homes – The event following the defeat of the High Fiends, where the Twelve Riders divided the realm into three parts to imprison Fiends and protect *rhoas*.

Earthome – One of the three realms, Earthome is where humans reside, protected by the Twelve Riders.

Farhome – Another of the three realms, where the *rhoas* of the deceased are sent.

Fiends – Mythical beings of fire and darkness, now imprisoned in Darkhome.

First Word – A unique magic word used to temporarily paralyse a purebred slave. Each purebred has their own individual First Word.

Flame – A type of slave trained for sexual services and entertainment, also known as pleasure slaves.

Freeborn – Slaves who were born free but later enslaved.

House slave – Slaves responsible for household tasks and labour.

Kill Word – A unique magic word that triggers the Rage in a purebred beast.

Lor'qas - An angled type of sword with a serrated blade.

Pain Word – A magic word that causes temporary, intense pain in any pure-bred without leaving a trace or causing damage. Each purebred has a unique Pain Word.

Purebred – Slaves specifically bred and raised for servitude, often trained from childhood in obedience and various skills.

Pyre – A religious figure who serves the Twelve Riders.

Pyrearch – A senior religious figure overseeing Chambers of the Twelve in larger cities.

Rage – A state where a purebred beast loses control, fighting with mindless ferocity until either their target is killed or they are incapacitated.

Rhoa – The essence of a person, believed to contain emotions and everything that makes a person human.

Twelve Riders – The twelve deities who govern the three realms, each riding an ancient dragon. They maintain balance, protect the realms, and oversee the laws of life and death.

Unrage/Bare – When a purebred beast fights without entering the Raged state.

Words – Magical commands used to control and bind purebreds.

CONTENT WARNING

BEAST OF ZARALL IS an adult dark fantasy novel and it deals with some heavy subject matter such as ongoing trauma, abuse, torture, graphic violence, gore and non-con. Some parts of the writing is explicit and will draw you into the characters' minds and let you experience their feelings. If any of these things are triggers for you, Beast of Zarall may not be the best book for you. I can't guarantee the below list is exhaustive, but I've done my best to be thorough.

- Amputation

- Bodily harm

- Captivity

- Childhood abuse and trauma

- Coercion

- Death threats

- Descriptions of violence and death

- Depression

- Dissociation

- Emotional abuse

- Gore

- Injury

- Imprisonment

- Mature language

- Mature sexual themes

- Murder

- Mutilation

- Physical abuse

- Profanity

- PTSD

- Self-harm

- Sexual assault

- Slavery

- Strangling

- Suffocating

- Swearing

- Torture

- Violence

If you or someone you know is in crisis, help is available. Get in touch with your GP and/or mental health professionals in your area, or call a helpline.

Australia: Call 13 11 14 or text 0477 13 11 14 or go to lifeline.org.au

New Zealand: Call 0800 543 354 or text 4357 or go to lifeline.org.nz

US: Call 800-273-TALK or text 988 or chat 988lifeline.org

UK: 0800-689-5652 – the National Suicide Prevention

Canada: Call 988 for the Suicide Crisis Helpline

TRIBELANDS
ALATELL SEA
WASTED SEA
CHORHAMST CRAG
MIREVALE
BLIGHTRIDGE MOUNTAINS
SOLKARA FLATS
SEA OF ASKAR
KALDORIA
KARSONDEL MARCHES
DEEP ISLAND
LOABREN ISLANDS
SALIGIAN SEA
BAY OF BATHUS
CHINDERIA

PROLOGUE

THE SLAVE MERCHANT HATED the *Mad Lion*.

The tavern was located in Swuglus East, a lower-class section of the city of Coldpost. The street stank of vomit and piss. The single-story building was old, its stone walls weathered and cracked, with moss creeping through the mortar. And the regulars of the establishment — including the person whom he was going to meet — were the kinds of people he wouldn't see out in daylight.

But none of these were the reason he felt antsy as he approached the place. It was the name.

Soft light spilled onto the street from the *Mad Lion*'s front windows. Music and raucous voices carried farther than the light. There was a bard singing inside, but the lyrics were lost beneath the slurred attempts of drunken men trying to sing along.

A large man slouched on a stool just outside the doors. His head fell on his chest as if he was asleep, but the slave merchant doubted that. Swuglus East wasn't the sort of place you could nap with both eyes closed. The bouncer at the *Mad Lion* watched the street through narrowed eyes, fully awake and alert.

The slave merchant tugged at his heavy coat against the cold. Beyond the dark hills that overlooked the city, he could see dark clouds swallowing the stars. He was hoping to strike a good deal with the supplier and get home before the storm hit. He shivered at the idea of walking all the way to the other side of the city through rain and mud.

The bouncer didn't stir as the slave merchant climbed up the stairs to the porch and walked into the *Mad Lion*. The mixed smell of sweat, tobacco and oily food greeted him. He stood by the open doors, waiting for his eyes to adjust to the dim light.

Once again, he was reminded how much he didn't like this tavern.

The common room was filled with rows of tables, benches and stools, all occupied by eating, drinking, singing and gambling men. A stage the size of a bed was built on the corner where a bard played his lute and sang an obscene version of a popular folk song. The *Mad Lion* didn't look all that different from an ordinary, lowlife tavern, with the only exception being the ugly, rebellious decor.

Every wall and column were adorned with gold and black banners. Behind the bartender, there hung an elaborate tapestry that portrayed Lion of Zarall's battle against the Bear of Vogros. A round, wooden shield with House Zarall's coat of arms was displayed proudly above it.

Sarte 'Lucky' Hamgard, owner of the *Mad Lion*, was a veteran house guard who had served the late King Leonis Zarall and had the luck to retire several years before the coup. The man's blood ran golden and black and he was not shy about showing his colours, despite the fact that another king with different colours was now sitting on the throne of Chinderia.

The slave merchant could never understand the blind loyalty free men felt for each other. It was a good quality on a slave, but was not useful otherwise.

He wondered if Lucky would still feel lucky enough to openly show Zarall colours if it wasn't for the ongoing riots.

Kastian Vogros was sitting on the throne, and he even had the support of all the noble families, but Vogrosses did not have a solid grip on the country yet. At least not in the Northern Chinderia, where people had been louder and more reluctant to accept the change.

The slave merchant didn't think the instability would last for long. Zaralls were gone and there wasn't anyone else well-connected enough to have a claim on the throne against Kastian Vogros. People could whine all they wanted; Kastian Vogros was still the head of the strongest family in Chinderia. His line still went all the way back to Merduth the Axe, founder of the country. And he still controlled the largest army of slaves and free men.

Riots would go on until the common folk started to realise Leonis Zarall wasn't coming back from Farhome to feed their throats, so they would go back to worrying about themselves. People like Lucky would continue to rant about how Kastian Vogros couldn't even defeat Leonis's slave, but he would lose ears every day until one morning he'd wake to find those Zarall banners burnt down, along with his piss hole of an establishment.

It took the slave merchant a moment to spot the man he was going to meet. He started towards the table at the back of the room. It was a time of uncertainty for most businesses, but not for his. Times like these were when the slave business thrived most.

Public disorder meant people went unaccounted for, leading to a fresh wave of tattoos on the market. Kastian's soldiers were busy securing Brinescar and the main roads leading to it, leaving the lesser-used routes dangerous. Travellers vanished, and the slave merchant was about to meet one of the men responsible.

Tonight's deal could potentially double or even triple his investment.

"Master Kallis," the man at the table said, gesturing for the slave merchant to join him. He was a large man with streaks of grey in his beard. The heavy leather armour he wore was faded and creased at the joints. It looked old, but bore no scars. Kallis wasn't sure if that meant the man was skilled enough to avoid being hit, or if he simply avoided fights altogether.

But you didn't become the bandit king of the Kilrer region by avoiding fights, so Kallis assumed it was the former.

"Master Vurkom," he greeted, offering the criminal a deep bow. He shrugged off his coat before lowering himself onto the bench. A massive fireplace burned fiercely in the centre of the room, and the windows had been blocked against the night breeze. Kallis would be sweating soon, and he didn't want the man getting the wrong impression.

Vurkom grabbed one of the serving girls by the arm and ordered two ales. Kallis didn't even like ale, but he didn't make any comment. He'd rather let the bandit think he was in control. For the same reason, he kept his silence until Vurkom decided to talk.

"I understand you're interested in my merchandise," Vurkom said. He was sitting sideways with one elbow at the table, the other hand on his knee, appearing to watch the bard across the room.

The serving girl brought their drinks quicker than Kallis would have expected at a seedy place like this. Kallis sipped his ale before speaking.

"With all due respect, Master Vurkom, I wouldn't call them merchandise."

Vurkom glanced at Kallis, his lips curved with amusement. "And what would you call them?"

"Raw materials." Kallis imitated Vurkom's body language by facing towards the bard. He was vaguely aware the bard switched to a song about a fierce lion and a fluffy bear. Enough of the lyrics were caught in his ear to know this was another song about the mighty Lion of Zarall. He pushed his dislike aside and prepared himself to make the speech he'd done to others before.

"Go outside the city, Master Vurkom, and you'll see trees everywhere. Anyone with an axe can cut one down, but not everyone can turn it into good furniture. It takes time, skill, resources, and connections to craft merchandise from fallen logs."

Vurkom took a sip from his drink and stayed silent for a while. Kallis didn't break the quiet.

"Let me guess," the bandit said. "This is the part where you start haggling about how hard it is to find a good inker with steady hands."

"Finding a tattoo artist who can forge a genuine slave tattoo isn't the hardest part, Master Vurkom. At least not for me. Training is the most expensive and time-consuming part."

Vurkom's brows drew closer. "I can train them," he grunted. "Cut their tongues so they won't talk back, beat the shit out of them until they learn to do as they're told."

Kallis tried not to grimace. "Mutilated slaves lose at least a sixth of their value, Master Vurkom. Not everyone wants a mute. And training isn't just about beating the shit out of them. If you've believed the sky is blue your whole life, it takes more than pain to convince you the sky doesn't exist anymore — no matter the colour."

He paused, watching for a reaction. Vurkom's scowl faded into a vague grin. Kallis suspected the bandit already knew what came next, but he said it anyway.

"I have connections with breeders at slave ranches — people who can turn freeborn men and women into good slaves, regardless of their age. But time,

Master Vurkom, time is my enemy. Every day they spend in those ranches costs me money. And they lose value as they age. It takes at least two years to break a man properly, if he's over twenty. Even then, some wills won't bend. It's hardly worth it."

Kallis stopped speaking. Vurkom's grin had spread into a smug smile. That wasn't the intended effect of his speech. He waited until the bandit spilt what he had.

"I've got kids," Vurkom said, leaning back in his chair.

Kallis took a long sip to cover his smile. He glanced around the room, hoping the bandit hadn't caught the eagerness in his eyes.

"How old?"

Vurkom pursed his lips. "A couple about this size." He held his hand at the height of the table. "Three more a bit older. That should reduce your costs, huh?"

"Indeed." Kallis licked his lips, finished the rest of his ale, and ordered some wine from one of the serving girls. He didn't expect them to have *Serpentblood*, and was pleasantly surprised to find they did. This business meeting had just proved worthy of a bottle of the most expensive wine.

Moreover, Kallis had noticed Vurkom was holding something back, and he had a good guess at what it was.

"Too bad they're not young enough for Wording."

Vurkom grinned. "One of the bitches is due next month. Could find more."

"Mother should have proper paperwork in place, of course."

"Which I'm sure you can handle, being a registered trader yourself."

"Finding a mage who's authorised to do the Wording is going to be expensive. Casters Board of Chinderia is extremely strict with their regulations."

"I bet you already know someone." Vurkom leaned forward at the table. His mouth was still smiling, but his eyes were sharp and cold as steel. "Let's cut the bullshit, shall we? I already know you have all the permits and the connections I need. I could swing my dick and hit another slave merchant in this city. Why do you think I'm meeting you? You wanna do business, or not?

"As they say, Master Vurkom," Kallis said. "Children are the future of this country."

They started negotiating before their wines were served. It wasn't the fastest service Kallis ever had, but they were lucky to be served at all. The serving girl stumbled, nearly dropping the *Serpentblood* as she approached their table. If it wasn't for the quick reflexes of a patron sitting nearby, Kallis's expensive liquid gold would have washed the mud and sawdust off the tavern's floors.

But even the clumsiness of the serving girl couldn't spoil Kallis's mood. He was going to leave this meeting already feeling like a richer man.

By the time the slave merchant poured their cups, they had already agreed on the rough terms. Details were to be discussed next morning at Kallis's office. Vurkom accompanied him for another cup of wine, then left. Five brutes, armed to the teeth, who had been blended in other tables, stood and left with the bandit leader.

The bard started another repetition of "The Lion and The Bear". Kallis made an annoyed sound from the back of his throat, which turned into a cough. He rolled his eyes at the patrons joining in with the chorus. He didn't understand the passionate admiration these people felt for a non-compliant, broken slave.

It wasn't the slave himself that people cheered for; it was the idea of a worthless piece of property making fun of the strongest man in the country. They found it amusing. It *was* amusing. But also disturbing for a man who made his living from selling slaves.

Kallis picked up the bottle of *Serpentblood*. There was still enough left for two more cups. He decided to finish his bottle before heading back home.

He was just starting to notice the persistent itch on his throat when a stranger sat down at his table.

A frown creased the slave merchant's brow. He glared at the man, his displeasure at the invasion of his privacy quite evident.

The stranger wore an expensive shirt and vest, though both were creased and dusted with the grime of travel. A short sword hung from a plain belt at his hips. His blond hair was cropped short, his features sharp and youthful — early twenties, at most. Bright blue eyes scanned the room with confident, effortless charm. An arrogant grin curled at the corner of his mouth. Something in the way he carried himself — relaxed, assured — unsettled Kallis.

The song finished and the patrons cheered for another repetition. The bard, enjoying the ecstasy of a powerful crowd, climbed up on a table and started his tune again. Kallis straightened and stared at his uninvited guest.

"I don't remember—" the slave merchant started, but his throat spasmed and choked the rest of his words. He coughed on his hand, cleared his throat, and tried again. "I don't remember— inviting—" He coughed, glaring at the man. To quench the itch in his throat, he drank a large gulp of wine.

That's when he saw the little green vial between the stranger's gloved fingers.

The young man was looking at Kallis, his head tilted slightly, turning and twisting the vial in his hands. His arrogant grin widened when comprehension dawned on Kallis's face.

The slave merchant gawked at his cup of wine. He knocked it down, the red wine spreading on the table like blood. The sound was lost beneath the bard's tune and the voices of the patrons. Kallis moved to stand.

A hand clamped down on Kallis's shoulder, forcing him back into his seat. A second man slid onto the bench beside him, sitting with his back to the table, eyes scanning the tavern crowd. He was as young as the first — mid-twenties, maybe — with light brown hair, an amused grin, and the faint scatter of freckles across his nose. His features marked him as foreign. Kallis had dealt with enough foreign-born merchandise to recognise the long, narrow facial lines of a Kaldorian.

Unlike the first man, this one wore armour — a strange, overlapping kind that looked like layered plates — and carried more weapons: a short bow, a pair of daggers, throwing knives. Kallis made another attempt to rise, but the Kaldorian's hand stayed firm on his shoulder.

"You'd rather be sitting," the blond young man said, his voice calm and confident. "Take five steps and you'll drop dead." He shook the little vial at Kallis. "This is the only antidote within your reach."

Kallis's eyes grew large at the statement. "What do— Who are—?"

A surprised shout turned a few heads toward the back of the room. Kallis saw Lucky Hamgard rushing through the tables, shoving patrons aside. He knelt down, briefly vanishing among the curious crowd, then stood with the serving girl in his arms. The patrons had already turned back to the bard as Hamgard carried her toward the back of the bar.

While Kallis watched the tavern workers gather around the girl, he noticed a third man. He knew at once this one was with the other two at his table. The man stood out from the others, with the large build of a seasoned fighter. He had the kind of size that turned heads; the kind bred for war, not work. Older too — mid-thirties, judging by the lines beginning to settle around his eyes. He had dark, short-cropped hair, a somewhat flat nose, and a serious expression that didn't waver. Kallis could make out the bulging outline of a heavy breastplate beneath the man's baggy tunic. A long sword and a short sword hung at either hip, and the hilt of a massive two-hander jutted over his shoulder. He stood several steps away, casually leaning against the wall. A beer mug in one hand, eyes on Kallis's table. He didn't look away when Kallis noticed him.

The blond young man took the bottle of *Serpentblood*, poured some into Vurkom's cup, and raised it to his lips. Kallis blinked, confused. He didn't understand — then he did. His eyes flicked to the bottle, to the man's gloved hands, to the unmoving body of the serving girl, and finally to his own fingers. The faint discolouration was already there.

"The bottle," he said and coughed again.

The blond man smiled and took another sip of wine. "There's no reason to spoil a good wine like this."

"What—?" Kallis gasped between his coughs.

The blond man put the cup aside, indicating he was ready for business now. "You are hard to track down, Master Kallis. Or would you prefer Master Glad-wiel?"

Kallis blinked. "What do you—" he once again attempted to ask their intentions and failed.

"I'm looking for a slave," the man said, leaning forward on his elbows. "A purebred beast."

"Come to— come to my office. Take— take what you want."

The Kaldorian took his hand off Kallis's shoulder and crossed his arms over his chest. He still didn't look at the slave merchant and continued studying the crowd, but his mouth was twisted as if he'd tasted something nasty. The larger man with the heavy armour hadn't moved from where he stood. It was clear this conversation was going to be resolved between Kallis and the young blond man.

The man's smile had nothing to do with pleasure. "You misunderstood me, Master Gladwiel," he said smugly. "I'm not buying a slave. I'm searching for a specific one; a purebred beast with a certain fame."

Kallis's eyes widened with understanding for the third time since the blond man sat at his table. He shook his head. "I don't— know what—" Kallis coughed so hard, he couldn't breathe for a few long seconds. "Please…"

The blond man's smile disappeared from his face and he was silent for a while. "I know you had him," he said impatiently. "We've found the thugs who'd intercepted a convoy of disguised Vogros soldiers. I know they sold you a dying purebred beast for twenty Chinderian Blues."

Kallis was shaking his head violently. "I don't— I don't do business with—" He shook with another violent cough.

The blond man rolled his eyes, then rubbed his temples. "I don't care about the legitimacy of your business activities, Master Gladwiel. I'm not here to report you to the Domestic Assets Trade Union."

The Kaldorian scoffed softly, but the blond man continued without skipping a beat. "Give me a name, Master Gladwiel…" He pulled the cork off the vial with his teeth and set the antidote at the edge of the table. He placed his hand right behind it, ready to push it off the table and spill Kallis's life on the floor.

Kallis attempted to reach for the vial, but the Kaldorian grasped his wrist without looking and twisted it until Kallis buried his face into the crook of his elbow and whimpered.

The bard riled the crowd to join him on the last chorus of "The Lion and The Bear". Several mugs rose to the air as the drunken patrons sang to the obnoxious things a lion with a long spear did to a soft, fluffy bear. Kallis's coughs were lost in the noise.

When the Kaldorian let his wrist go, Kallis cradled his arm in his lap.

The young blond man leaned forward on the table. He didn't bother raising his voice to be heard over the crowd. Kallis read his lips clear as day: "A name, Master Gladwiel."

Kallis closed his eyes. "Olira… Aryanna…" he coughed.

"And where can I find this Lady Olira?"

"Farm… West Kilrer…"

The man's eyebrows twitched upwards. "You sold King Leonis's Lion of Zarall to a farmer girl in West Kilrer?"

"Please…" Kallis's face had turned purple from gasping and coughing. "Tell King Kastian… I didn't know."

The man's grin disappeared, and danger sparked in his eyes. "I'm afraid I can't do that, Master Gladwiel." He leaned further. "When I see Kastian Vogros, there won't be much talking."

With that, he stood. Kallis reached for the vial, but the Kaldorian snatched it off him.

The blond man walked out of the *Mad Lion* with not so much as a one last glance at the slave merchant. His heavy armoured companion followed him closely. The Kaldorian lingered long enough to walk over to the bar and leave the vial there, before following the other two outside.

Kallis looked at the vial with longing. He pressed his fist in his mouth, forcing himself to stop coughing and breathe. Five steps, he thought. According to the blond man who'd poisoned him, that was all he had left.

Lucky Hamgard, who was towering over his unconscious employee, his face creased with concern, straightened up and noticed the mysterious vial left at his bar. He narrowed his eyes.

No, Kallis thought with panic. *That's mine.*

Five steps.

He stood and took the first.

1

DIENUS

Dienus always knew when the need was coming.

It was a craving like hunger, though it didn't come from his stomach. It resembled thirst, but not for water. It occupied his mind, poisoned his thoughts, and never left until he satisfied it.

He was never quite sure how. Sometimes it felt like the need spoke a different language. But he knew it had something to do with their eyes.

"Oh boy," Lotheris said as he reached for his wine glass. "You'll do it again, won't you?"

Dienus was ashamed of how powerless he could be against the need. So he'd learned to hide it — at least from others. But he could never hide it from his brother.

Lotheris watched him with that signature smirk, eyes gleaming with patronising amusement. Dienus struggled to control the blush creeping up his cheeks.

"I don't know what you're talking about, brother."

The Banquet Hall was one of the largest rooms in Castle Brinescar. The walls rose high, making anyone feel small, and staring up at the vast ceiling could make a person dizzy. Four long tables of solid wood ran the length of the room, with a smaller fifth table positioned to overlook the others.

It was slightly chilly; the two large fireplaces on opposite walls did a poor job of heating the space, though both held blazing fires and slaves worked steadily to keep them fed with wood. Despite its size, the hall was generously lit.

The chandelier above the tables drew the eye of anyone entering the hall. Designed and crafted in the distant Stoneheart Mountains, it was made of a rare metal rumoured to be mined by mountain nomads — though Dienus had never seen one himself. Each metal arm held ten candles, and there were fifty arms in total. Dienus had counted them the first evening his family arrived as the new rulers of Castle Brinescar.

Queen Inoeveth had ordered the chandelier cleaned and lit every evening. Just as she had ordered forty-one dishes to be displayed on the tables each night, and all house slaves to appear in pristine uniforms. She also insisted on some form of entertainment each evening. Tonight's performance, occupying the empty space between the two centre tables, was a dance by half-dressed purebred flames.

Dienus couldn't take his eyes off one particular slave with a flame tattoo on her neck. She moved with the other dancers, arms raised, hips swaying to the rhythm of light drums and flute. Her honey-coloured hair spilled over her shoulders in a wild tangle. Her body looked sculpted by Aeyar himself, the God of Art and Passion.

"Why can't you just fuck them like a normal man?" Lotheris asked. There was a trace of disgust in his otherwise wry voice. At least he had the courtesy to keep it low.

"Why can't you mind your own business?" Dienus lifted his empty glass, and a house slave appeared behind him to refill it. He took a sip, his eyes never leaving the pleasure slave. She was a purebred, as all the best ones were. She flung her hair back, thrusting her chest forward. Her eyes were closed. She bit her lower lip as her hands traced her face, then slid down her neck, over her breasts, her stomach, and lower.

Lotheris pushed his half-full plate away. His features were a poor imitation of their mother's — his hair a darker chestnut, his eyes near black. Dienus took after their father instead, inheriting King Kastian's black hair and sharp green eyes, along with his unforgiving temperament. The only thing the brothers shared was their height, which allowed them to look down on most people. Lotheris's knack for making others feel small rarely worked on Dienus. This was one of the rare times it did.

"Mother doesn't like disappearing purebreds," Lotheris said, fixing his brother with a hard stare.

"She won't disappear," Dienus scoffed. He hated the heat creeping into his face. "I'll be careful."

"You will," Lotheris said, dropping his voice to a breath. "Because she already has enough on her plate. Lord Heltez is leaving."

Dienus turned away from the flame. Thirty-five houses that had pledged loyalty to House Vogros were formally invited to dine with the royal family every night. Sixteen lords were present in person, thirteen accompanied by their ladies or mistresses. Nineteen others were represented by immediate family members. Not one had declined the invitation. Not yet.

Lord Heltez, a middle-aged man with a bald patch at the back of his head, sat midway down the table on the right. He smiled and nodded at Lord Deihlan across from him, though his eyes kept drifting to the royal table.

Dienus glanced at his mother, seated to the right of his father. He and Lotheris, crown princes of Chinderia, sat on the king's left. The seat beside them remained empty — Princess Lareani was never allowed at loud, crowded events. It wasn't good for her. Yet every evening, King Kastian insisted a place be set for her.

Queen Inoeveth, along with half their advisors, believed this was a mistake. An empty chair only reminded everyone that the king had an eccentric daughter. To the queen, it was a weakness. Better to pretend Lareani didn't exist. It was the only matter on which she and the king openly disagreed. Unfortunately for House Vogros, the entire kingdom knew Kastian had a soft spot for his daughter.

Tonight, Lord Thalborn and his son were invited to dine at the royal table. Queen Inoeveth listened intently to Thalborn, laughing appropriately throughout whatever story he was telling. Petite and ageless, Inoeveth's smooth skin and cropped hair suggested youth, but the faint creases around her intelligent eyes hinted at least thirty summers. She touched Thalborn's arm now and then, her wide-eyed attention lending her the look of a naive maiden. Thalborn's son — no older than Dienus — watched the queen without blinking.

The music stopped, and the flame-tattooed pleasure slaves drifted toward the servant doors. Dienus realised he'd missed the end of the performance. He clenched his jaw, cursing Lotheris and Lord Heltez for the distraction. His eyes moved to the far side of the hall, where Bronkin, the Master of Slaves, oversaw the service, making sure every table was tended and every cup full.

"Don't do it, brother," Lotheris mumbled.

Dienus caught Bronkin's eyes and gestured him to come over. Lotheris sighed.

"Blonde purebred from the middle," Dienus said when Bronkin leaned over. Bronkin's face twitched, then his mouth parted with a forced smile.

If there was anyone who hated disappearing purebreds more than the queen did, it was the Master of the Slaves.

"As you wish, Your Highness." Bronkin adjusted his posture and went after the flames. His back was stiff as if he had just swallowed a stick.

Dienus glanced at his mother. Queen Inoeveth was still listening to Lord Thalborn with rapt attention. There was no indication that she even noticed Dienus's conversation with Bronkin. Dienus could almost believe he imagined the tightness around her jaw.

"You're hopeless," Lotheris said, rubbing circles into his forehead. Dienus didn't bother with an answer.

The next entertainer was a seasoned bard with a miniature harp. He was joined by a younger version of himself — likely his son — who played the flute. Their first song caught the attention of half the guests; by the second, the mood in the hall had lightened.

Their third song was cut short when King Kastian tapped his knife against his wine glass. The musicians lowered their instruments. Heads turned toward the king.

"I'd like to thank you all for joining me and my family this evening," the king said. "Your presence means a great deal to my house." His voice was deep and steady, not raised, but carried easily across the hall with a natural air of command. Dienus's father had always possessed that quality, even before the crown. The strength of a born leader.

"To House Vogros!" a guest called from the back, raising his cup.

Others followed, and the Banquet Hall echoed with salutes.

Kastian's smile didn't soften the hard lines of his face, neither did it bring any warmth to his green eyes. He raised his glass in acknowledgment. Queen Inoeveth and the princes joined him.

He let the commotion roll for several seconds before quieting the hall with a small gesture. "I would also like to thank Lord Heltez for honouring us with his presence at Castle Brinescar, and wish him safe travels back to Fort Heltn."

Lord Heltez stood. "It's been my honour, Your Majesty. Thank you for your kindness and hospitality." His expression revealed nothing, his posture loose, but Dienus noticed the joints of his fingers whitening around his wine glass. "I hope to return home before the weather worsens. Winter is harsh in Fort Heltn, and I cannot leave my wife alone at a time like this."

King Kastian nodded. "As our elders say, a man's first duty is to his wife." He lifted Inoeveth's hand and kissed it. Her face lit with affection, and she brushed her fingers along his.

Lord Heltez's smile flickered. "Our elders are wise. They also say a man's loyalty to his wife is a good indicator of his loyalty to the crown. May House Vogros reign until the end of our days."

"Your commitment to your family warms my hearth," Inoeveth said. Her speech had a foreign accent that neither Dienus nor Lotheris inherited. Oddly, it could be heard in Princess Lareani's speech, when her mind was clear enough to talk.

"Family means everything," Inoeveth continued, tilting her head and watching Lord Heltez with the softest eyes. "We always want the best future for our family. I think your young son could have a great future squiring for Prince Dienus. Norrol, wasn't it?"

Lord Heltez's face paled a tone while Dienus's darkened. They both managed to keep their composure.

"I could not even describe the honour it would bring to my family," Lord Heltez said. "But Your Highness, I'm afraid I already gave my word to Lord Thalborn. A man cannot break—"

"Oh, I would never ask you to break your word, Lord Heltez." Inoeveth waved a hand as if swatting a fly. "Lord Thalborn, would you release Lord Heltez from his word?"

The question raised many eyebrows in the Banquet Hall. Lord Heltez blinked at the audaciousness of the request. Lord Thalborn, falsely assuming the queen was joking, let out a chuckle, which he contained promptly after noticing she was not laughing.

"Ehm..." Thalborn's eyes went from side to side. He even glanced at the king, hoping he would acknowledge the improperness of the request, but Kastian simply watched Thalborn with a tilted head.

"Ehm," Lord Thalborn repeated. Inoeveth encouraged him with a charming smile and Lord Thalborn realised what she asked was not really a question. "Anything for my queen," he said, raising his cup.

"Fantastic!" Inoeveth approved. "All of Chinderia knows, Prince Dienus is an excellent swordsman. Young Norrol has a lot to learn from him. Isn't that right, my darling?" As swiftly as she took over, Inoeveth returned the conversation back to her husband.

"I couldn't have thought of a better arrangement," Kastian said. "I expect young Norrol to report for duty as soon as possible. You have a safe journey, Lord Heltez."

"Thank you, Your Majesty."

Lord Heltez sat back down, and King Kastian gestured to the musicians to resume the entertainment. The bard and his son started playing "Season for You and I" — a fast-paced song that's popular in the Heltn Hills, but the song wasn't enough to bring life to Lord Heltez's movements, which suddenly seemed to lack energy. The man accepted other guests' congratulations with a bleak expression.

"It's like his son was just sentenced for execution," Lotheris snickered. "His son will squire for a prince. He should be honoured."

"They all know what squiring, being a lady-in-waiting, or being under ward means," Dienus mumbled. "Do we really need a hostage from every house?"

"Do you really need to ask that?"

"I already had one snotty squire."

"Now you have two. You really shouldn't have annoyed mother."

Dienus glanced at the queen. Inoeveth felt his gaze and returned him with a cold stare. Silently telling him she knew what he was planning to do with the flame.

Dienus didn't have much choice. He had the need. When the need came, it always took what it wanted.

As the night went on, Dienus waited for an opportunity to excuse himself. He found it when Princess Lareani's lady-in-waiting — their hostage from Kilrer — came to whisper some news in Queen Inoeveth's ear. Lady Lona was Dienus's age. A little lanky for his taste, but otherwise pretty. The queen's face darkened as she listened to the young lady. She quietly excused herself and left with Lady Lona.

Dienus waited for several minutes, then stood.

"You better not kill another one," Lotheris warned. His voice was dripping with malice. "If Mother asks where you are, I will tell her the truth."

"Told you, I'll be careful," Dienus hissed.

His brother's condescending attitude only bothered Dienus until he left the Banquet Hall. Once he was on his way to his chambers, his steps grew lighter. A twitch started in his cheek. The thought of what was waiting for him made the need flare stronger than before. All he could think about was finding a way to satisfy it. And knowing it would anger his mother only made him want it more.

He'd told Lotheris the truth, though — he didn't want to kill another pure-bred. Murder was never what the need was about. Sometimes, things just got a little out of hand.

When he reached his chambers, he told the guards not to let anyone disturb him.

The flame was inside, standing by the bed. On the bedside table lay a piece of paper with two neatly written words: her First Word and her Pain Word. He wouldn't need either of them, but she was a purebred, and Words were what made them special.

Her hands were clasped in front of her, head tilted slightly to the side. The angle gave her a smug look, which Dienus found appealing. Her honey-coloured hair was thick and tousled — exactly how a woman might look if dragged from bed. She still wore the same two-piece outfit from her performance: one piece barely covering her breasts, the other hanging low on her hips. Both were inten-tionally torn in several places, adding to her wild appearance.

Dienus stepped closer and cupped her face. Her eyes were half-closed as she leaned into his palm, nuzzling like a purring cat. His fingers brushed the slave tattoo on her neck — a flame enclosed in a ring of intricate lines and curling symbols. Only purebreds wore marks that elaborate. Freeborn flames bore a simpler version, with just a plain circle around the flame.

His fingers traced the lines of the tattoo and found her pulse. He closed his eyes and felt her heartbeat at his fingertips. It was slower than his, and steady. It disturbed him. He knew pleasure slaves didn't really feel arousal. They were just extremely good at acting it. It was disappointing still.

Her lips parted. Dienus grabbed the back of her neck and pulled her lips to his mouth. She responded with a muffled moan and just enough tongue to steal his breath. His other hand was still at her throat.

The flame's pulse did not skip a beat.

"Take your clothes off."

"Yes, Master."

She slipped out of her clothes with slow, eager movements. Dienus shoved her onto the bed. While he undressed, she began touching herself, her body trembling with faked desire. He climbed on top of her and buried himself in her. She screamed in pleasure, head tilted back, eyes half-closed. Her body moved with his, meeting his rhythm, wrapping around him with vicious hunger.

Dienus wanted her to scream again, so he made her. He roughed her up, hit her. The sounds she made were closer to moans than screams. There was no fear in her voice. Every pain he inflicted on her seemed to heighten her act. Even when his fist split her lip, she only seemed to want more.

He pressed a hand to her throat. Her heart was beating slightly faster. Better than before, but still not enough.

He reached for the paper that was left on the nightstand. He felt like cheating, but he didn't care. With one hand still on her throat, he read her Pain Word out loud: "*Juulusligentha.*"

The slave's body seized, cramping violently. Dienus held her tight, savouring the way she convulsed beneath him. Her pulse stopped for several seconds, then surged — racing as if her heart was trying to escape her chest.

"That's it," he whispered. "Feel that. Feel that."

Pain Word wouldn't last long enough. Her painful scream was replaced by sobs and gasps, which were already turning into moans. Her face twitched with pain, but her eyes still showed no fear. Even her pulse was slowing back down.

The need urged him on, craving for more.

Dienus straightened and placed both hands around her throat.

He found that strangling was not an easy task. He had discovered that on his first messy attempt. He had gotten better at it, though. He kept his elbows straight and put his weight on the woman's neck.

"They all say purebreds don't want anything," Dienus purred as he watched the slave's face. "They don't even have a shred of desire in them."

The flame's eyes were fixed on the ceiling. Her face was starting to turn purple, but she didn't fight him.

"All I see is a girl who wants nothing but another gasp of breath. Show me how much you want it."

The girl's hands started caressing Dienus's arms and shoulders, as if this was only making her more aroused. She bucked her hips against his. Dienus wanted her to get over with the acting and show him something real. He watched her eyes.

"Show me," Dienus grunted. His voice was strained from the effort and his hands were getting tired. "Come on. Show me."

When he did this to a freeborn slave, this was when they started fighting. When they realised he wasn't going to stop, and fear took hold. Their eyes would widen with panic, and Dienus would watch the light drain from them, slowly.

He could almost see their *rhoa* leaving their body.

But with purebreds, it was never like that. They kept playing their part, acting like they wanted nothing more than to please him. Their eyes stayed blank. He couldn't even tell when life left them — it was as if they'd never been alive at all.

As if they truly had no *rhoa*.

Except Dienus knew they did.

He had seen it in Lion of Zarall. He'd watched that beast's face twist with real anger, hatred, and grief. Seen the madness take hold. If that troublesome purebred had a *rhoa*, the others had to have one too.

"Stop pretending," he growled. "Show me something real."

The purebred continued grinding against him, although her face had turned in the darkest shade of purple. He had promised his brother that he was going to be careful. He could not afford angering his mother by killing another expensive purebred. The girl's arms and legs were already slowing down. If he didn't let go now, it was going to be too late.

He released the pressure.

The moment before he pulled his hands back, he saw it.

The purebred closed her eyes and took a ragged breath which turned into a cough. Her neck was already bruising. Dienus turned her face towards him with a sense of urgency. "Look at me. Open your eyes. Look at me!"

She opened her eyes with a moment's delay and looked at his face, though not directly into his eyes. Her eyes were vacant again. Blank and lifeless.

He gritted his teeth, fuming. He had just seen it. Just a moment before, he had seen a something in her eyes; a spark of fear. Real fear. It was right there. He had to see it again.

The need took control.

Dienus grabbed her neck. The muscles in his hands and forearms were spasming, but he didn't care. His fingers dug deep into her flesh. He watched her eyes carefully, to catch that spark again. He wanted to witness her fear. He wanted the real thing.

The purebred's face turned an ugly purple. She opened and closed her mouth, gasping for air. Her gaze was locked on the ceiling.

Anytime now, Dienus thought.

Her arms fell on the bed, and her movements slowed down.

"Come on," mumbled Dienus. He was afraid his arms were going to let him down before he could defeat her. He took a deep breath to refresh his strength and pressed harder.

Her windpipe crushed in his hands.

"No. No!" Dienus let go. For a brief second, he thought the girl was going to blink and start coughing, but she remained silent. Her mouth was open and her face was as blank as before.

She was dead.

He had just killed another purebred!

Dienus breathed through his nose. His low growl turned into a raging roar. He punched her emotionless, bruised, dead face.

"Stupid bitch!"

His muscles ached, but he punched her again and again, emphasising every word. "Fucking. Worthless. Piece of. Whore."

He climbed out of bed, kicked the bedstand, and howled — grabbing one foot and hopping on the other. A jolt of pain shot from his toe up his leg. "Fucking bitch!" he cursed.

He dropped to the floor, back against the bedframe, waiting for the pain to fade. He couldn't believe he'd killed another purebred. His mother was going to be furious.

"Curse the fiends," he groaned in frustration. She had to die, didn't she? He'd wanted to hurt her for it, but now he couldn't even do that. The bitch had gotten away.

He didn't remember where he'd left it, but the piece of paper was on the floor. He picked it up and looked at the purebred's Pain Word.

"*Juulusligentha*," he muttered, just to relive how it made her scream and squirm.

The last thing he expected was to hear her scream again.

Dienus yelped and scrambled away from the bed. He tried to stand, but his legs refused to work together. All he could manage was a frantic crawl across the floor on his naked arse until his back hit the far wall. He opened and closed his mouth, just like the purebred had done before she died. For a brief moment, he couldn't breathe either. Which was fitting, really, because that's exactly what the girl was doing now.

She was thrashing on the bed, whimpering. Her body convulsed in agony, gasping between screams and coughing fits. Clutching her neck, she rolled onto her side — and her eyes met his.

Blond hair clung to her face, wild and tangled, but Dienus saw enough.

She was alive. More *alive* than she'd ever been.

Seconds passed before he managed to pull himself upright. On the bed, the purebred whimpered and shrank away. The Pain Word had faded, but her breathing was still ragged. Her neck was raw, her face bruised from his punches. Yet she was very much alive.

"You were dead," Dienus whispered. "I swear under Twelve's wings, you were dead."

But there she was — crying, shaking her head, gripped by real terror — as she watched her killer approach. He had felt her heart stop beneath his hand. And now she was back. As if he'd dragged her from death itself. Like the Twelve Riders in the old tales.

He had the power of gods.

The need soared, victorious.

A sharp crack echoed from the outer door. Two seconds later, his chamber door swung open. Dienus drew breath to curse at the intruder, but the words died in his throat when he saw who it was.

"Mother? Wh-what...?"

Remembering he was naked, he snatched his clothes off the floor and held them in front of him. Guilt and embarrassment flooded his face red. "Mother, what are you doing here?"

Her hands on her hips, Queen Inoeveth scanned the room with disapproval. Her light brown eyes narrowed when she saw the purebred, who had thrown herself on the floor and greeted the queen on her hands and knees. She was still coughing and wheezing, and for a moment, those were the only sounds in the room.

"Go find the physician and get that checked."

"Yes—" She was interrupted by a violent cough. "Yes M-Master."

"Get out!"

The purebred dashed to the door, not even bothering with her clothes. Dienus bit his lips as he watched her stumble out of the room.

"I didn't kill her," he said, not liking how his voice sounded like a guilty little boy.

"Get dressed. You're leaving in an hour."

"Wh-what? Why? Where?"

"A slave merchant's assistant travelled from Kiore to share a very interesting story. About a disobedient purebred beast."

Dienus didn't need to ask which purebred. There was only one his parents were obsessed about. He straightened eagerly.

"Your father is giving you fifty men," Queen Inoeveth continued. "You'll go to West Kilrer and bring him back. I'm sending Emberlash to help you pack."

"Yes, Mother."

"I will arrange for Lord Heltez's son to meet you up at Riverdam, but do not wait for him if he is late. The purebred is your priority."

"As you wish, Mother."

Without another word, Queen Inoeveth turned to leave.

"I won't disappoint you," Dienus called after her, but she neither replied nor slowed her pace.

He drew a deep breath once she was gone, replaying the look on her face as she'd scanned the room — expecting to find a corpse, only to discover the purebred alive. He chuckled.

By the time his chamberlain Emberlash arrived with two house slaves to help him pack, Dienus was fully dressed. While they worked, he retrieved the piece of paper with the flame's Words.

He had finally discovered how to truly satisfy the need, and he couldn't wait to explore it further.

"It's pain," he muttered. "Pain brings life."

2

THE MAN WITH THE BEAST TATTOO

THE MAN WITH THE beast tattoo was afraid of the light.

He had stayed awake all night; lying on his makeshift bed inside the tiny cupboard turned into a room. Darkness cradled him, thick and unyielding, almost tangible. He was never disturbed by it. Darkness was safe. Free men and women always came with their light. They were afraid of the dark.

That's why he liked it.

No sound travelled to him through the darkness, beside the familiar creaks and groans of the old farmhouse as it stood against the last autumn winds. He had spent nearly three months on this farm and the sounds of the house had become a soothing background. Almost as peaceful as the darkness itself.

Peace...

He gritted his teeth. This brief time of peace was like tasting a bite out of an exquisite food, only to watch the plate swiped from him. It left him hungrier than before.

By the time the morning light chased the darkness away, the slave with the beast tattoo would be on his way to be sold. It wasn't a surprise. He had been expecting this. Yet, Olira's decision still hurt like a punch.

His Owner never hid that she wanted to get rid of him. That was the only reason she had taken him in the first place, and the only reason she had bothered to save his life. The injury that had almost killed him had left an ugly scar on his right leg, and yet, he was lucky to still have a right leg.

There was a time when he felt certain he was going to die. He should have been content with death. Yet, he had found himself fighting so hard to stay alive.

Do whatever it takes to win.

He could still hear her voice so clearly in his mind. She wanted him to win Twilight of Infinity and be free. And as much as he wanted to die and find Saradra in Farhome, he also didn't believe he deserved to see her again.

He had killed her.

With his bare hands.

The slave rolled to his side, facing the wall, though he couldn't see it through the dark. His eyes burned, and a lump sat on his throat. He imagined Saradra lying next to him, like she did in that tiny bed they shared at Castle Brinescar. The darkness was so thick, he could almost trick himself into believing she was there. He reached with his hand slowly, willing her to materialise, his skin searching for her warmth.

He touched the cold, smooth wall.

His lungs deflated, the air leaving its place to heavy grief.

Olira had nurtured his injury, and the farm work had helped him regain his strength, but he doubted anything could stop the bleeding deep inside his chest.

He still had nightmares. His body remembered how he broke her, even though his mind couldn't. His memory was fractured, chunks of it lost to the Rage that consumed him. What he could remember clearly was the suffocating helplessness when he realised what King Kastian Vogros was about to do.

What he was about to make him do.

He woke up most nights, whimpering and crying, unable to breathe through the weight that pressed down on his chest. He felt her warm blood burning his hands. He heard her bones breaking. Her screams echoed in his ears, leaving him with a raw, visceral pain. His breath caught in his throat as his grief swelled inside him like a rising tide.

When it was too much, the slave with the beast tattoo rolled out of the bed and paced the small space of the cupboard. He took his borrowed shirt off, too small for his size, like most were. The chill of the night bit his skin. He welcomed the discomfort, dropped to his hands and knees, then stretched his legs and started push-ups. He pushed himself relentlessly, until all he could feel was the searing ache in his muscles.

When he was spent, he sat with his back against the wall, sweat cooling on his skin, his arms slack at his sides. He gazed into darkness. He had lost track of time, and he didn't even realise when the whispers first started.

He discouraged himself from acknowledging them, and he kept staring into the dark, his eyes unfocused and distant. Every time he had tried to decipher the whispers, they would stop. So, he ignored them.

He hid his amusement at how persistent the whispers became. Nagging for attention, like those relentless twins who had kept pestering him. Whispers became sharper, more urgent. Desperate to keep his thoughts from drifting to other topics. They called out to him.

They called his name.

Lion of Zarall.

"No," he whispered to the darkness. "That's not my name anymore."

He swallowed over the tightness in his throat. Speaking without permission, even when he was alone, was still difficult for him, though he was getting better.

The tone of the whispers flickered briefly. The slave heard the next word very clearly:

Beast.

The slave felt a chill run down his back. He touched the tattoo that identified him as a purebred beast. A warrior bred for the arenas. A tool that was supposed to be numb and obedient.

Beast.

Olira had never bothered naming him. Why should she? She never intended to keep him. He didn't have a name.

Beast!

The whisper rang with a tone of anger. It wanted him to acknowledge the name.

It wanted him to take it.

As Beast sat still, his gaze drowning in darkness, he felt a tug at the back of his mind. He started drifting, similar to how he used to send his mind to *that place* and leave his body behind. But this time, he was drifting down instead of above. The hard floor beneath him softened like sand, pulling him in.

The noise yanked Beast out of the grasp of the whispers. A soft squeak and click, followed by footsteps.

Olira was up.

He recognised the faint shuffle of her feet as she moved quietly down the corridor. A dim light snuck under the door as she passed by, dispersing the darkness in the cupboard. The warm, flickering light of her lantern chased the shadows to the corner of the cramped space, and Beast shaded his eyes from it. Olira walked past, taking her light with her. He heard her walk outside.

She was up early. He knew what that meant. His time was running out. She would come for him soon.

His stomach churned as he reached for the towel beside his bed. He found the jug of cold water in the corner where he left it. Moving cautiously in the dark to avoid knocking it by accident, he dipped the towel in the water, then wiped the sweat from his face and his chest. He let the chill ground him as he scrubbed away the remnants of whatever nightmare those whispers were. He worked in silence, preparing for what was to come.

He couldn't let her sell him. He ran the damp towel across his chest, over the four brands that marked his past victories. Four tournaments he had won, each one represented inside a circle burnt into his skin. A horse, a rose, a maiden, and a bird. These brands identified him. Although Olira had no clue what they meant, people outside this farm would surely recognise them. The word would get to King Kastian. And then Beast would be on his way to White Tower.

He couldn't let that happen.

He had to somehow stop Olira from selling him. He had to go to Euroad and fight at Twilight of Infinity.

Saradra's words rang in his head again. *Do whatever it takes to win.*

If he could just win Twilight of Infinity — or die trying — everything would be better. Nothing could bring Saradra back, but she wanted him to be free. She wanted him to live without chains.

The tournament would be held in Spring. Only a few months away. He had time. He could do this. He could find a way. For now, he just had to stop Olira from selling him.

He pulled his shirt on, folded the towel and left it beside the bed just as he heard Olira's footsteps.

Pausing outside the door, she knocked softly before gently pushing it open. Her brown hair caught the faint glow of the lantern she carried. Her face, with its strong, soft features, was partially shaded. Her brown eyes were hard and unreadable, and a permanent scowl was etched into her expression, making her look much older than the nineteen years she lived. She was clad in layers of clothes and a heavy travel coat against the early morning cold. A second travel coat hung across her arm.

The silence between them stretched into discomfort. She looked like she was going to say something, her mouth parting slightly. Beast decided he didn't want to hear her order. Without giving her a chance to speak, he stepped out of the cupboard and took the coat she offered. He slung it over his shoulders as he walked through the house.

Olira followed him without a word. The nervous tension that had settled deep inside Beast's gut every time she was around hummed quietly. He was still wary of her, of her temper. Of how far she was willing to go for her family. He would have to tread very carefully.

Beast moved through the house as if this was the last time. He pushed open the door that led outside, the cold air hitting him like a mace. The sky was still dark, only with the faintest hint of dawn on the horizon. His breath misted in front of him.

The mule named Warrior stood near the front door, swatting his tail lazily. Gilann was there, checking the straps of packsaddle, preparing it for the journey. Most of the bags were empty. Olira probably planned to fill them with supplies after selling Beast.

Gilann's face was dark, and he kept looking at anywhere but the slave. Beast didn't try to catch his gaze either. His attention was caught on one of the saddlebags. Something heavy pulled the bag down, coiled at the bottom of the leather pouch. Olira and Gilann exchanged silent words, but Beast ignored them. His eyes were fixed on the familiar outline of what was inside the bag. His jaw ached. Without a word, he reached into the bag and pulled the chain and the collar out. The cold iron felt like a memory, sharp and biting against his skin.

"No need for that," Olira said. "You don't need to until we get to Oxreach."

Beast clamped the collar around his neck. Staring straight ahead, he held the other end of the chain to Olira.

Olira's brown eyes flicked to the chain, her strong features tightening just a moment. The permanent scowl on her face left its place to distaste. She stared at the chain. Beast willed her to take it. He knew her enough to understand she believed slave trade was disturbing, and she was ashamed to be a part of it. If she was going to do this to him, Beast would make it as hard as possible for her.

With a scoff, Olira grabbed the chain, holding it cautiously like it was burning her flesh. She attached it to one of the packsaddle straps.

Just as she stepped back, the door of the farmhouse burst open. The sudden noise startled all three, and Olira looked up sharply as her three younger brothers rushed out into the yard.

The twins bolted towards Beast before anyone could stop them. They nearly tackled him, one clinging to his leg, the other to his arm, their small faces twisted in panic.

"Don't take him!" one of the twins — Andar or Kowas, Beast could never tell them apart, and never bothered to learn — cried, his voice high and desperate.

"Please, Olira!" the other begged, his hands wrapped tightly around Beast's forearm. "Don't sell him. Let him stay, please!"

Beast froze, staring down at the two boys. His body tensed, unsure of what to do. He'd never expected anything but annoyance from these kids, always buzzing around, asking questions, getting in his way. He had tolerated their presence. Seeing their tear-filled eyes, it made something twist uncomfortably in his chest.

Behind the twins, Torren, the twelve-year-old, came forward with two books clutched tightly in his arms. His expression was serious. "Olira! You can't sell him."

"Inside! All of you!" Olira said sharply.

"You need to read the chapter twenty-nine of the *Pure Lies of Chinderia*."

"I've read that book six times," Olira scoffed. "I know exactly what it says."

"It was Dad's favourite book for a reason," Torren said. "Then you know what it says in chapter twenty-nine about purebreds and their *rhoas*."

"Purebreds don't have *rhoas*, and the three of you should be in bed. Go back inside."

"Don't take him!" one of the twins screeched.

"Andar, let him go. I told you many times, don't get attached to him. You know I have to sell him."

"Please let him stay."

"Do you want to starve? Lose our house?"

"The book says that's a claim made by Domestic Assets Trade Union," Torren continued his argument. He lifted the other book up. "But the *Book of Twelve* says every living creature is born with a *rhoa*."

"We'll work harder," one of the twins said. "We'll work at other farms."

"We'll eat less," the other said.

"Olira, he's a living creature too! What if he has a *rhoa*?"

"He doesn't have a *rhoa*. I said get back inside!" Olira rubbed her temples. Her face hardened and her lips pressed into a thin line. "I've made my decision. We don't have another choice. Go inside."

"But he can—"

"She said go inside!" Gilann, who had been standing quietly by Warrior, finally shouted. The firmness in his voice echoed across the yard, silencing the protests. He pried the twins from Beast, then forced them inside. With shock, Beast noticed the boys were sobbing. A strange tightness sat in his chest.

Olira grabbed Warrior's lead and started walking down the path leading away from the farmhouse. Torren stood in front of her, the books still in his arms.

"Olira, please. Dad always said the Union had too much control and influence over everything, including the Chambers of Twelve. They would want people to believe purebreds don't have *rhoas*. But what if they do?"

Beast couldn't see Olira's face, but her shoulders trembled. She took a deep breath. "I'm sorry, but he doesn't."

"How do you—"

"I know he doesn't."

Beast pressed his lips together. Words flooded to the tip of his tongue. He could speak up. He could tell her he did have a *rhoa*. That the boy was right. It was all a lie. But it wouldn't have mattered to Olira. She didn't care about whether he had a *rhoa* or not. She needed money more than she needed the truth.

Olira put her hand on Torren's shoulder and gently pushed him out of her way. "Go back inside, Torren."

The boy stood and watched as they walked past, still hugging his books, his shoulders shaking and tears spilling down his cheeks. Beast caught his eye as he walked past, just for a moment. Torren's tears left him feeling off balance.

He had almost killed that boy once.

Burning in fever and lost in a nightmare, he had nearly crushed his throat and squeezed the life out of him. He was only alive because Olira had walked in just in time. And now, the boy was begging for him. The cold chain around Beast's neck suddenly felt tighter.

Olira led the mule, Beast following beside, the chain clinking softly. Beast fought the urge to look back at the house, yet as they reached the hilltop, his head turned back. He etched the view into his memory: the farmhouse, and the barn, the fields of odd-looking herbs and plants, and the neighbouring forest that stretched behind the farm.

And the boy who still stood out at the front, shivering in the cold, his books at his feet, watching him leave.

3

OLIRA

Olira walked with a furious pace, her feet pounding the ground, Warrior's lead stretched tight behind her as she nearly dragged the mule to keep up. Warrior grunted, but she didn't slow down. She couldn't. The tightness in her chest, the burning behind her eyes — it all demanded that she keep moving, keep pushing forward.

The man walked beside the mule in silence, his presence a weight she didn't want to acknowledge. She was avoiding looking at him. She didn't think she would see anything on his face — she had tried to catch any flicker of emotion on him the entire three months with no success — so she didn't expect this time would be any different.

Yet, the thought of looking at his face made her stomach drop.

Worse, she didn't want him to see *her* face.

Her vision blurred as hot tears streaked down her cheeks, but she kept her sobs silent. She bit her lip hard enough to taste blood, swallowing the urge to break down. Anger would hold her together. It always did.

Without realising, she had taken the longer route toward town, her feet guiding her on a path she never used. This road was too close to Hallowtree Woods and the cliffs beyond. She hated those cliffs. She'd banned her brothers from ever going near them. Yet here she was, storming right toward them.

Stupid, she thought, angry at herself for the mistake, for the tears, for everything. For the situation she had backed herself into. *Fiends chew my bones, I'm so stupid!*

The slave kept pace quietly, his steps perfectly in sync with the mule's fast trudge. The chain between him and the animal clinked with each step and the constant noise gnawed at Olira's nerves. The weather was cold, a sharp bite in the early morning air, but the speed of Olira's march had warmed her, beads of sweat forming at the back of her neck. The night retreated from the sky, the pale morning light spilling on the road ahead of them.

By the time they reached the Hallowtree Woods, the sun had been up for nearly over an hour. The bare branches of the small cluster of trees twitched with the soft breeze. The cliffs weren't far off, just beyond the tree line. Olira stopped and tied Warrior to a low-hanging branch, the animal huffing in relief after the fast pace. The slave stood still, the chain dangling between them loosely. Olira still didn't look at his face.

She yanked the chain free from the packsaddle. The metal links slid through her fingers with a grating sound that made her wince. She glanced at the slave, considering telling him to remove the collar for now, but she knew she would just have to order him to put it back on when they reached the town.

Oddly, the chain made him look even more intimidating than before. A walking weapon, he was enormous, trained from birth to kill. Over the last three months, she had somehow learned to overlook this fact about him; that he could easily snap her neck like it was nothing. Somehow, the chain accentuated his size. Solid muscles bulged under his shirt. His messy blond hair clung to his forehead, and something dark glinted in his grey eyes, which he kept fixed ahead. His strong jaw tensed, his angular features somewhere between vacant and loaded.

Olira's pulse quickened with a mix of fear and anger. She thought she had gotten over this unreasonable fear of the purebred beast. He was a purebred, after all. Perfectly obedient and harmless. Moreover, she knew his Words. All three of them were written on a piece of paper, folded and tucked in her pocket, though she didn't need it. She had already memorised the Words.

The First Word paralysed the slave for half a minute, leaving him completely at her mercy. The Pain Word punished him with a pain that seemed to be intense enough to scare him into obedience. And the third was his Kill Word, which Olira couldn't think of any situation that would require her to use it. Still, knowing she could control him past his willing obedience gave her a small comfort.

She tossed the chain to him. "Sit," she snapped. "Rest. Get some food from the saddle if you want."

Her voice was sharper than she intended, but she didn't bother softening it. Turning her back, she walked toward the cliff's edge.

The wind picked up as she approached, pushing against her like it knew the thoughts racing through her mind. Olira sat at the edge of the cliff, her legs dangling over the abyss. Below her, the jagged rocks stretched out like teeth, ready to swallow anything that fell into them. Her heart picked up, but she ignored the fear. She punished herself with her own unease.

She ran a hand through her tangled hair, feeling the tension tighter in her chest. She wrestled with the decision she had already made but still couldn't accept. She had to sell him. There was no other way. She'd thought of every solution, every possible angle, but they all led back to this.

Her winter supplies were gone. The root cellar had collapsed, taking everything with it: her food, her security, her hope. The storm had been unexpected, but the rotten beam wasn't. She'd known it needed fixing, but she'd pushed it off, thinking she had time. Now, the time was gone, and so were the supplies. It wasn't just her life at stake; the last winter had nearly killed her brothers. They had come so close to starvation that the memory of it still haunted her.

She couldn't let that happen again.

The money she owed to Master Tholthus loomed over her like a dark cloud. She had borrowed from him when things got desperate last year, and she hadn't paid a single Chinderian Blue back. And now, with only weeks left, the debt was crushing her. Master Tholthus wasn't a patient man. She had no doubt he would get the Agha or the Bailiff involved if she didn't pay up soon. If it escalated to Lord Rhuagh of Kilrer... She could lose everything, including her farm.

She glanced down at the dizzying drop again, the overwhelming sense of helplessness washing over her.

The slave was the only valuable thing she had owned. The slave merchant whom she had taken the slave from had claimed that the purebred was worth at least two-hundred Chinderian Blues or more. That was more than what she needed to cover her debt and stock food for the winter.

But then there was the guilt.

Her parents hated the slave trade. She looked down at the sharp rocks below and wiped her tears. This was where her parents died. She wondered if their *rhoas* lingered here, despite knowing they probably didn't. Pyre Aldric had performed a Sending Ritual, guiding their *rhoas* to Farhome. They were at peace, and blissfully unaware of the heinous act their daughter was about to do.

By the time the sun climbed higher in the sky, Olira admitted she'd been stalling. She was sitting here for over an hour, battered by the wind, lost in thought. It hadn't been a conscious choice to linger — she just couldn't bring herself to move. But morning had passed. Oxreach wasn't far, and she had no excuse left to keep sitting here, torturing herself.

With a deep, frustrated sigh, she forced herself to stand. Her legs were stiff, the muscles tight from sitting in the cold, but the pain barely registered. A gust of wind caught her long brown hair and whipped it across her pale face. She tucked it behind one ear, nose red from the cold, the sharp line of it even more pronounced in the chill.

She turned back toward the small patch of woods where she'd left Warrior and the slave. The closer she got, the more her thoughts focused on the practicalities of what needed to be done.

She found Warrior nibbling at a patch of grass with boredom. The man was sitting under a tree, his back against the rough bark, the chain folded in his lap, and his eyes closed. Napping.

A sharp twinge of annoyance rose in Olira. Here she was, wrestling with her own morals, with the crushing weight of what she had to do, and he was just... sleeping it off. Like it didn't matter to him at all.

But at the same time, the slave's indifference soothed her. If he didn't care, then maybe she didn't need to feel so guilty. Maybe it wasn't as terrible as she was making it out to be. After all, he was used to this life. Like Gilann had reminded her before, purebreds didn't know any better. They were born into slavery, never tasted freedom.

Her next breath came easier. She walked over to him and nudged his leg with her boot. "Get up."

The slave stirred, blinking himself awake without a word. He didn't protest, didn't seem surprised or upset that his rest was cut short. He stood up slowly, stretching his broad shoulders, the chain clinking as it dangled from his neck and grazed the ground. He pulled the loose chain and hooked it back on the saddle straps.

"We need to get going," Olira muttered. She took Warrior's lead and resumed walking. The slave followed her, quiet as ever.

4

BEAST

OXREACH CAME INTO VIEW slowly, starting with the scattered farms on the outskirts. As they walked, the distance between the houses grew smaller, the structures themselves shrinking in size. The dirt path they followed widened into a main street, uneven from years of wagon wheels cutting into it.

A merchant's caravan had stopped outside the town's tavern, its three horse carts lined neatly along the road. The travellers milled about, checking the harnesses on their horses and exchanging goods between carts. A few locals had gathered, eyeing the wares with curiosity.

Beast barely glanced at them. He was too focused on Olira's silence, the way her shoulders had stayed tense since they left the farm. The twisted knot in his stomach tightened.

When they had stopped on the way here, near those cliffs, Beast had naively thought that maybe Olira would change her mind and take them back to the farm. He was wrong.

He had a plan to stop her from going ahead with the sale. He knew it was risky, and it would make her furious. He had seen acts like this lead to terrible punishments. But he had no choice.

Low, wooden buildings lined either side of the main road. Most were shops and workshops: a blacksmith with its forge still glowing strong under the midday, a butcher's shop with wooden shutters open, and a small bakery with fresh smells wafting from its open doors. A few homes were scattered among the businesses, modest, with gardens out front and wooden fences in need of repair. Smoke curled from a few chimneys, mingling with the smell of fresh bread.

As they passed the main street, the reaction was immediate. People stopped what they were doing and stared. Their eyes grew large at Beast's chain and the collar, which only partially covered his slave tattoo. A group of women who were chatting by the well stopped sharply, their eyes widening at Olira. A few craftsmen and shop owners stepped into the street, frowning at Beast. A child who hadn't noticed Beast until he was almost next to him flinched and dropped the basket of apples he was carrying. His jaw went slack as he stared at the slave tattoo.

Olira ignored everyone, keeping her face hard and her eyes straight ahead. Her expression kept people from being too direct with their judgements.

Beast couldn't understand their reaction, and something about it bothered him. He was used to people staring at him. Every time he'd stepped outside Castle Brinescar, he was subject to public's interest. People had gathered to catch a glimpse of the king's famed Lion of Zarall, causing Badimar to act paranoid with his safety. He was used to hostility as well, and what he had endured at King Kastian's feasts were worse than the scowls these people shot at him.

Yet, this felt different.

Olira's shoulders were so tense, it was clear she was barely stopping herself from tucking her head down and running through the street. Beast wished they stopped staring at her, because they were working her up. His plan was already going to annoy her, and if he had any chance of keeping his head after what he was about to pull, he needed Olira to calm down.

They reached a squat building at the centre of town. Its windows were clean, and the wooden sign hanging above the door displayed freshly painted letters. Beast couldn't read, though he knew letters, because every purebred was taught to spell their Words, in case their records were ever lost. A glimpse through the open door told Beast this was some sort of store with shelves full of food and resources.

Olira tied Warrior to a post at the side of the building. She snatched the chain and stormed inside, forcing Beast to hurry after her.

The store had wide windows that invited plenty of sunshine. Shelves and shelves of products occupied one side of the spacious room: bags of grain, flour, salt, rolls of paper, books, several bolts of clothes, small statues of the Twelve Riders, various kitchenware, and leather belts and shoes. There was a counter and a door leading to the back of the building.

Beast sized up the man behind the counter. Master Tholthus. Olira had mentioned his name once. The old man had a bushy beard, thick eyebrows, and oversized ears. He chatted casually with a customer while a few others browsed the shelves. The store was quiet, too quiet, and Beast's chain rattled louder than it should have as Olira made her way to the counter.

Tholthus's expression darkened as he watched Olira. She had told Beast the man had a good heart, but Beast saw no sign of it in his face. Tholthus pressed his wrinkled hands against the counter and leaned in, jaw tight, as if bracing for a fight.

The customer whom he was talking to didn't realise he had lost Tholthus's attention and continued with his chatter: "We don't even know where she's from," the man was saying. "Didn't realise we had a shortage of women in Chinderia. And his daughter! They say she can be eccentric sometimes, but I think the word they're looking for is lunatic."

"Olira Aryanna," Tholthus said. His voice reminded Beast of a purring cat. "Your father would be ashamed of you if he'd seen you now."

Olira staggered, as if struck, before quickly regaining her composure under the weight of the customers' stares. "Master Tholthus," she said, approaching the counter with determination. "Can we talk privately, please? In your office?"

Beast closed his eyes and sent a silent prayer to the darkness — the only deity that had answered his prayers so far — to help his plan work. He bit inside his cheek and let the blood seep on his tongue. He readied himself to cough and spit blood as soon Tholthus approached to examine him.

He had witnessed slaves being flogged or flayed alive for pulling off tricks like this. She was going to punish him with his Pain Word. The thought made him shudder, but he couldn't see any other choice.

"I'm not buying your slave," Master Tholthus said. "I will not trade a slave even if I had nothing else left to trade."

The old man's words struck Beast this time. He almost coughed for real. He forced himself to keep his mouth shut and swallowed the blood.

"I'm not here to sell you a slave," Olira said arrogantly. "I'm here to pay my debt."

The store owner forced a laugh. He swung his finger at Olira, shaking his head from side to side. "Good try, but you don't get to choose your currency."

Olira slammed her hands on the counter and leaned forward. "*My* currency?" she sneered and laughed. Beast's hair stood on end at the simmering anger hidden beneath that sound. "My currency? What country do we live in, Master Tholthus?"

Tholthus blinked slowly. "You're well aware what country we live in, Mistress Olira." When Olira kept staring at him expectantly, he pursed his lips, deciding to humour her. "Chinderia. We live in Chinderia."

"And what's the currency here?"

"Blues."

"Wrong." Olira pointed a finger at Beast. "This is the currency in this country. Whether you like it or not."

Tholthus shook his head. "Hasn't Vakko taught you anything?"

Olira gritted her teeth as she ignored the question. She pointed at Beast again. "He's a purebred beast. He's worth at least two-hundred Blues. That's more than enough to cover what I owe you."

Beast resisted the urge to purse his lips. He had been auctioned for way more than that in the past. He was worth much more. Still, the amount was enough to get a reaction from the other customers — sharing glances with each other, eyebrows raised, sizing Beast up and down. Olira crossed her arms and lifted her chin.

Tholthus only shook his head. "I don't care what he's worth. I'm not trading slaves."

Olira bared her teeth. "You're not trading—"

"Do you know what happens every time a man makes a profit off a slave?" Tholthus raised his voice, cutting her off. "Another good Chinderian disappears from the roads."

"No. That's just a rumour. Only city officials can enslave people. Criminals."

"Lies! Sheep like you can't even see what slaves are doing to our economy. Master Kerol, your son used to work for Master Hilodd's farm, right?"

The customer, who was speaking to Master Tholthus earlier, jumped when he heard his name being dragged into the argument. "Yeah?" he said cautiously.

"What happened to him after Master Hilodd bought a slave?"

Kerol scowled, looking at Olira with disapproval. "Master Hilodd didn't need him anymore, so he lost his job."

Olira hung her head and sighed while Beast witnessed the argument as if it was transpiring in another language. Olira was basically giving him away for free. Who would refuse a purebred beast?

This doesn't make sense, a small voice said at the back of his head. *All free men and women are greedy.* He refused to believe Master Tholthus was different. Yet, the old man continued shaking his head stubbornly.

"Master Tholthus, please reconsider." Olira lowered her voice, though the store was so quiet, and the customers so openly listening, no one missed a word. "This is the only way I can pay you. He is the only valuable thing I've got left."

Tholthus lowered his voice. "I can see that. You've long lost your *rhoa*."

Olira flinched at the words, her grip tightening around Beast's chain. For a moment, she looked ready to bolt, eyes wide and lips trembling.

Tholthus sighed, shaking his head regretfully. "If it's supplies and more time you need, I'm not a heartless man, Olira. I won't let your little brothers starve over winter. Take what you need from the store and come to my office. We'll talk about an extension."

Olira's jaw clenched, her fists tight at her sides. Beast could feel anger radiating off her, as sharp as a lor'qas at his throat. Her lips curled in frustration. "I don't want an extension. I want to clear my debt. Just take him."

"We'll sort your debt when you have the money." Tholthus waved his hand toward Beast. "Now get that abomination out of my store." He turned his back, indicating he was done with the argument. He called one of his workers from the back to come over and help Olira.

Olira remained rigid for another moment, her face flushed. Beast expected her to make a snappy retort or resume the argument, but she didn't. She forcefully pushed the loose end of the chain into Beast's arms. Beast didn't wait for an order. He turned on his heels and walked out to wait with the mule.

He couldn't get the argument out of his head. It didn't make sense. Why didn't the man just accept Olira's offer? Was it because there were others watching and judging? He had heard about people in Northern Chinderia not liking slaves, but Olira was right; the real currency in this country was slaves. A merchant should have known that.

Once again, he had prayed to the Darkness, and the Darkness had answered. There was no other explanation.

Less than an hour later, the employee started carrying sacks of grains and dried food out of the store, and Beast helped load them onto the mule. Like others in this town, the young man kept staring at him and his tattoo, confirming Beast's beliefs that people in this region weren't accustomed to slaves. When they were done, the employee rushed back inside, leaving Beast in the street alone with his thoughts.

Beast still tasted the blood in his mouth. His face was hurting from scowling. He got what he wanted; he was going back to the farm with Olira. And he didn't even have to do anything to stop the sale. Knowing her, she'd still be mad, though at least it wouldn't be aimed directly at him. He weighed his options carefully. He could stay at the farm until Twilight of Infinity, spend the winter training in secret, and then, somehow, convince Olira to take him to Euroad. But he'd have to find the right moment to talk to her — and he had no clue how to even bring up the subject. Conversations were not his strength.

He noticed a group of children staring at him, whispering excitedly from a distance. He recognised one of them; the kid who had dropped his basket of apples earlier. Beast grunted. He knew what happened every time a group of young boys came together to see a purebred beast from up close.

He turned away from them and noticed he had a clear view into Master Tholthus's office through a small window. Olira sat in a chair, her back to the window, and all Beast could see was the top of her brown hair. Across from her, Master Tholthus sat at his desk, bent over a large book with thick pages. In one hand, he held a thick glass in front of his eye, while the other hand scribbled on the paper. Beast recognised the tool — it reminded him of the one King Leonis's old physician used, though his was framed in metal and perched on his nose.

He felt the tip of a sharp stick poking at his back. He growled quietly.

The boy laughed and ran back to his friends.

Beast hated this game, where children dared each other to come close enough to touch him. The boy's friends congratulated him while the stick was passed on to the next contestant. Beast didn't see the purpose of this entertainment. There was nothing courageous about approaching a purebred beast. It wasn't like he could hurt them! He didn't understand kids.

His childhood differed greatly from that of children of free men and women.

He wondered how Olira's brothers would react when they saw him back at the farm. A blend of irritation and anticipation stirred within him. He wished Olira would finish soon, but the way Master Tholthus studied his book told him they were not close to finishing.

The second boy approached him, his knees shaking but his eyes sparkling with excitement. When the stick touched the back of his knee, Beast rolled his eyes and breathed patiently.

Master Tholthus slammed his book shut and leaned back in his chair. Beast wished he could hear what he was saying. The old man stood and started walking back and forth with his hands clasped behind him.

Encouraged by his friends' shouts, the next child poked his arse with the stick.

Beast's hand darted back. He snatched the stick and broke it in half with one hand while staring directly at the child. He made no effort to hide how easily he could snap the boy's neck, just like the stick, and the kid saw it written plainly on his face. He yelped, tripped on his own foot and fell on his back. He used his hand to break his fall, subsequently cutting his palm on a sharp rock. He scrambled through dirt and mud, clasping his bleeding palm, and ran into one of the nearby stores.

Beast shot a look at the boy's friends too, who squealed and scattered.

"Hey! What's this?"

The store owner where the boy had fled into stormed outside. He was a slender man with long arms and a greasy apron. "What's going on here?" he shouted after the fleeing kids, then shifted his gaze to Beast. His eyes narrowed at the stick in Beast's hand as he barked, "Hey!"

Beast's default instinct was to look down and avoid a confrontation with a free man. If the man came over and struck him, Beast was supposed to keep his hands down and accept the punishment. No begging, no resisting, and definitely no fighting back. That's how he was raised to behave.

Yet, he found himself staring at the man, imagining him standing in front of him on the blood-soaked sands of the Switchblade Arena.

The store owner took a couple of steps towards him, his hands on his hips, then froze. His face changed from hostile to unsure. He averted his eyes and walked back into his store, glancing over his shoulder and mumbling under his breath.

Beast dropped the pieces of the stick and bit his cheek to suppress a grin. His blood rushed with an odd feeling. He liked it.

His grin was erased from his face when he turned back to Master Tholthus's window and saw what was happening inside.

The old man had stopped pacing and now stood directly in front of Olira, his hands gripping the arms of her chair as he leaned over her. Beast couldn't tell if the man was speaking or kissing her, and he couldn't see Olira's face either. She was frozen in place.

Beast didn't know how long they had been like that, but Olira snapped out of it shortly after. She pushed the old man off her, eloped from her chair, and ran out of Beast's view.

Less than a minute later, she was out, untying Warrior from the post. Her face was cloudy, her lips trembling, her hands shaking. She darted down the street, yanking Warrior's lead hard enough to make the animal bray angrily.

As Beast hurried after them, he cast a glance back at Master Tholthus's office. The old man stood by the window, watching with his hands clasped behind his back, a hungry expression on his face.

Beast scoffed to himself. He'd been right about free men all along. Master Tholthus was just as greedy as the rest, though his currency wasn't money.

5

OLIRA

By the time they reached Jygan's workshop, every muscle in Olira's body burned with an anger so raw it felt alive. Her vision swam in a haze of red. Her jaw ached, clenched too tightly for too long, and every sinew in her neck, shoulders, and legs screamed with tension.

The mule brayed in protest behind her, but the slave followed without a word. The only evidence of his presence the faint clink of his chains and the persistent ache throbbing in Olira's head.

Her steps were quick, almost frantic, barely restrained from breaking into a run. The words echoed in her skull.

Leave. Just leave. Leave the town. Leave it all behind.

Leave Tholthus's sickening proposal behind.

She wiped her eyes one more time, making sure her cheeks were dry, before stepping into the large yard of Jygan's tannery. The pungent stench had reached her long before the workshop came into view and only grew stronger as she approached, making Warrior huff and shake his head repeatedly.

The slave covered his mouth and nose with his sleeve, his eyes watering as he surveyed the yard. Olira, too furious to care, barely noticed the smell.

On one side of the yard, pits of foul-coloured water bubbled faintly. Piles of hides lay scattered in varying stages of curing — some folded, others stretched taut over wooden posts. At the rear of the yard, a gentle stream trickled past.

Jygan's workshop was a single-storey stone building with a steeply pitched roof and wide, open windows cut into the thick walls. Smoke rose from a chimney. Up the hill, partially hidden by the dense, three-metre-long Skelshade bushes with their broad, fragrant leaves, stood Jygan's modest house and barn. The bushes, a gift from Olira, were thriving, their leaves ruffling in the breeze and releasing a pleasant, sharp scent that somewhat helped to mask the tannery's odour from the house. She spotted new sprouts growing along the path leading to the house.

Pausing to steady her trembling hands, Olira rummaged through Warrior's saddlebags and pulled out a bundle of herbs and incense she had packed for Jygan. She cradled the herbs against her chest and walked up to the workshop, leaving the slave to wait with Warrior. Half his face was still buried in his elbow, scowling openly at the smell. It was the most expression she'd seen from him since she'd bought him.

The door opened before she could knock. Jygan filled the doorway.

Surprise flickered across his face, quickly replaced by a wide grin. A large man with a worker's build, Jygan's hair was tied back, and his bearded face bore smudges of grime. Tufts of animal hair clung stubbornly to his apron and long gloves. His brown eyes lit with a warm spark as he tugged his gloves off.

"Olira, hey. I was just about to wash up for some lunch." He tilted his head towards the stream. "Care to join?" He paused awkwardly, his smile vanishing and his eyes widening. "I meant for lunch. Care to join for lunch?"

Olira followed his gaze to the stream, then looked back at Jygan's face, now flushed a deep red.

And she burst into laughter.

Jygan scratched the back of his head, a sheepish grin tugging at the corners of his mouth as he avoided her eyes.

"So, lunch?" He cleared his throat. "I'm making eggs and…" His words trailed off, the grin fading when his gaze shifted to Warrior and the slave. "I thought you were selling him?"

The humour drained from Olira like water on dry soil. She inhaled deeply and steadied herself. "Thanks for the offer, but I need to head home."

Jygan studied her face with unusual intensity. "What happened?"

"Nothing. Here's your incense. I'll get the next batch in a couple of weeks."

"Olira?"

She thrust the bundle of herbs and incense toward him. When the tanner made no move to take them off her hands, she stepped past him and set the bundle on a crate by the door. As she turned away, Jygan's hand caught her arm.

"*What happened?*" he repeated, his voice loaded with an emotion that didn't belong there.

"It's nothing, I'll be fine."

"It doesn't seem like nothing."

Olira raised her chin, pinning Jygan with a dismissing stare. "I said I'll be fine. Let it go, Jygan." She wrenched her arm free and stormed off.

Jygan let out an exasperated sigh, tossing his work apron aside. Before she could reach Warrior, he jogged ahead, cutting her off. He planted himself firmly in her path, his hands raised in a gesture of surrender.

"I can clearly see something's happened, Olira. Please..." His voice was soft but insistent. His eyes searched hers, desperate to find a crack in her defences. "Please. Let me at least make you some lunch."

Behind Jygan, the slave was eyeing the road, almost like he was eager to be on their way. Back to the farm. With reluctance, Olira realised she wasn't ready to face her brothers. They would be so happy to see the slave, not knowing what this meant. What it would cost her. What was she going to tell Gilann? He would ask questions about the supplies. Could she convince him that Master Tholthus gave her an extension just out of the goodness of his heart? No strings attached.

She felt a fatigue deep in her bones, her muscles finally reminding her the toll her anger took.

"Fine," she said as she forced a deep breath. "But don't pester me with questions."

Jygan grinned like he'd just earned the Twelve's blessing and stepped aside, letting her take Warrior's lead. As Olira trudged up the path, the slave followed, his chain clinking softly with each step. Jygan had already stripped off his shirt and was disappearing toward the stream.

She brought Warrior into the small barn beside the house and moved through the motions — unsaddling, brushing him down, checking his hooves. The familiar rhythm helped steady her thoughts. She filled the trough, wiped her hands on her skirt, and turned to leave.

The slave was settling into the straw, the chain coiled on his lap, his back against the stall wall like he meant to stay there.

Her jaw clenched. She let out a sharp breath through her nose.

"No. Come inside. It reeks in here."

As she stepped into Jygan's house, the shift hit her at once. The air was cleaner, laced with sweet woodsmoke and faint traces of scented oil. A far cry from the tannery's stench. And for the first time all day, she breathed in without flinching.

The house was small and plain. One room served as a kitchen, dining, and living space, with a narrow doorway leading to Jygan's sleeping quarters. The hearth sat at the centre, its fire casting a warm glow over mismatched furniture, a cluttered table with two chairs, and shelves crammed with tools and scraps of leather. The messiness was almost charming.

The slave entered behind her. The soft clink of his chain broke the room's stillness. He stood just inside the door, back against the wall, hands clasped in front of him. His presence felt out of place here, like a pine tree growing in the middle of a wheat field.

Olira grit her teeth and pulled the key from her satchel. She unlocked his collar and tossed it to the floor.

"I guess you don't need this anymore. You're coming back home with me."

She should've known better than to look at his face, expecting something — anything. A flicker of thought, a trace of reaction. But there was nothing. There was always nothing. The frustration rising in her chest was her own fault.

"You really don't care what happens to you, do you?"

His eyes remained on the floor, his hands clasped loosely in front of him. He didn't blink, didn't shift, didn't acknowledge her words in any way.

Olira felt deflated. "Stop acting like furniture. I am not a bad person," she whispered, her voice heavy with a pleading edge she didn't invite.

Finally, his grey eyes lifted to meet hers. He held her gaze. His silence suddenly felt like a response in itself. Each passing heartbeat deepened the weight of his stare, trapping her. She felt her pulse quicken, a confusing mix of emotions surging to the surface.

The slave's lips parted, and Olira held her breath.

The moment slipped when Jygan's heavy footfalls approached the door. The slave's eyes were back on the floor before the tanner walked in.

"I've got some eggs," Jygan said as he walked in.

Olira stepped back, barely taking her eyes from the slave's hard-set face, her heart racing in her chest. The tanner had a small basket of eggs in one hand and a couple of tomatoes in the other. His damp hair stuck out in messy tufts, water still dripping from his beard. The clean, sharp scent of soap and fresh air clung to him, cutting through the lingering tannery odours.

"Why don't you have a seat?" Jygan said. "I'll get these ready."

Olira glanced at the cluttered table but didn't sit. Her heart was pounding too fast to let her be still. She crossed her arms and leaned against the kitchen bench, watching Jygan set the eggs and tomatoes near the hearth. After a beat, she pulled a clay pan from a hook on the wall and joined him in silence.

They worked side by side, preparing a simple meal: eggs, tomatoes, and a rough loaf of rye bread. Jygan set three plates on the table and dragged over a crate to serve as a third seat. He gave a short nod toward the slave.

"Come on, friend. Have something to eat."

The slave hesitated, grey eyes flicking to the table before he moved. He sat quietly. Olira dropped into the chair beside Jygan, pulled her plate close, and started picking at her food.

Silence thickened around them. The only sounds were cutlery on clay, the crackle of fire, and the faint wind outside. The slave kept his eyes on his plate, clearing it in minutes. Jygan, meanwhile, was watching her. Reading her silence. Not missing a single flicker of expression.

"You've barely touched your food," he said at last, cutting through the quiet.

"I've eaten enough." Without looking up, she pushed her half-eaten plate across the table to the slave. He accepted it readily, continuing his meal without pause.

Jygan scowled at the exchange. He set down his plate and leaned back, crossing his arms. "Please," he said, his voice gentle but firm. "Tell me what it is."

Olira shook her head and rose from her seat. "Thanks for the lunch, Jygan."

Jygan wasn't done. He stood too, his words following her like a shadow. "I know it has to do with Tholthus. That bastard did something."

"You promised not to ask questions."

"I'm not asking questions. I'm telling you what I see." His voice carried a dangerous undercurrent. He nodded toward the slave, who had just finished Olira's leftovers and now sat awkwardly at the table, his hands in his lap and his shoulders hunched.

"You tried to trade him," Jygan continued. "And Tholthus didn't accept the deal. I saw Warrior's saddle. You've restocked your supplies, so that means Tholthus gave you more credit. But he asked for something, didn't he?"

"I thought you were just telling what you see," Olira cut in coldly, her eyes hard. "That sounded like a question."

Jygan's jaw tighted as anger swept over him like a storm cloud. His fists clenched and unclenched at his sides, his composure barely holding. "Right. The look on your face, and the way you're avoiding talking to me only tells me one thing — that what he asked for was something he never should have."

Olira's eyes flashed with warning, but she said nothing.

At the table, the slave sat very still, like he knew he had no place in this room and in this argument, and if he didn't move a muscle, they would forget his presence.

"How much?" Jygan asked through gritted teeth. "How much do you owe him now?"

"More than what you can offer to lend me."

"You don't know—"

"A lot, Jygan. It's a lot."

"Then go to the Agha. Or the Bailiff. They're the town leaders. They won't let Tholthus exploit people like this."

Olira let out a bitter laugh, shaking her head. "You think they'd care? Tholthus will say he gave me three extensions already and will petition for a forfeiture and the Agha will let him take what's 'rightfully' his." She slammed her palm against the table, making the plates rattle. "He'll take my farm, Jygan."

Jygan let out a frustrated breath, running a hand through his messy hair. He pointed at the slave. "Then take him back to Kiore. Or Kilrer. Sell him to someone who can pay."

"I'm not dealing with another shady slave merchant. They're all swindlers. I'll walk out with crumbs."

"Then what are you going to do? Accept Tholthus's offer?"

"I'll figure something out," she snapped back, grabbing the plates off the table. Her movements were tense, the scrape of the plates loud in the otherwise quiet room. "I have to."

Jygan exhaled heavily and leaned against the hearth, staring into the flames. Olira set the plates in the wash basin. The slave stayed where he was, sitting stiffly on the crate. His presence loomed in the room despite his silence.

"Take him to Arkala," Jygan said after a long pause. His voice was quiet, almost apologetic.

Olira turned, her brows knitting together. "Arkala? Why?"

Out of the corner of her eye, she thought she caught a movement at the table, but when she looked, the slave still sat like a breathing statue. His shoulders rose and fell with each slow, steady breath.

"They do beast auctions in Arkala all year round," Jygan said, his voice quiet and grim. "Thousands of buyers. They pay decent money for purebred beasts. More than enough to cover your debt."

Olira's gaze stayed on the slave, searching for something — anything — in his expression. But the man's face remained unreadable, his chest rising and falling at the same calm, maddening rhythm.

"Arkala is too far," she murmured, the excuse weak even to her own ears.

"You can take a ship from Kilrer. The round trip shouldn't take more than four weeks by sea."

"But it's still a week to get to Kilrer. And then... And then..."

"A month and a half, and you'll return with enough money to save your farm."

Olira shook her head. "I've never travelled that far. I don't even know how to find my way around in a city like that."

"I have a friend in Arkala." Jygan said reluctantly. "He'll help you get the slave into the right auctions, make sure no one cheats you. All you've got to do is get there."

Olira's hands tightened on her skirt, scrunching the fabric in her palm. Her chest felt heavy, and her mind raced. That overwhelming urge she had felt as she trekked here from the town returned. The need to leave. *Just go. Just leave everything behind.*

"I can't," she muttered. "I can't just leave the farm. Tholthus will—"

"Tholthus won't notice you're gone for at least a few weeks. I'll talk to the Agha, buy you some time, tell him you had an emergency or something. He won't sign the forfeiture until you return."

The slave still hadn't moved, his shoulders broad and stiff. His silence was suffocating. Olira's stomach twisted. *Say something. React.*

Jygan stepped closer, prying her hand off her skirt and cupping it between his own hands. "I won't let anything happen to your farm while you're gone. I promise."

"I can't leave my brothers…"

"Gilann is perfectly capable of looking after your brothers. You know that."

"Jygan, I can't…"

"What other choice do you have? Sell him, or accept Tholthus's offer. That's it."

Olira looked away from the slave and withdrew her hand from Jygan's grasp. She walked to the small window, her arms crossed. Outside, the bushes swayed in the breeze. Just earlier this morning, she was ready to sell the slave. Nothing had changed. Why was she hesitating now? Arkala was further than she'd ever travelled, but maybe she needed the time away. And Jygan was right; Gilann would take care of the boys.

"Say the word, and I'll pack you supplies for the road right now. I can take Warrior back to the farm this afternoon."

"Wait. Leave now?" Olira's heart pounded. "*Right now?*"

"There was a merchant's caravan travelling past Oxreach earlier this morning. If you hurry, you can catch them before they cross the Ashwisp Creek."

"Why would I…"

Jygan had already walked into his sleeping quarters and walked back out with a sturdy, enormous backpack. He dove into his pantry and started tossing food inside as he talked. "It's much safer to travel with a merchant's caravan. There are bandits on the roads."

Olira was very aware of the bandits on the roads. Not only was Arkala further than she'd ever travelled before, but the roads were also dangerous. Doubt settled on her shoulders, and her feet stiffened like they'd grown roots. Leaving now... This was too soon.

Then, she remembered she didn't want to return to the farm. She imagined her brothers' reactions if they saw the slave. It would be much harder to leave the next morning. So, she forced herself to say, "Right, I'll be fine."

And before she knew it, she was walking out of the door. The slave, burdened by Jygan's backpack, trailed silently after her.

6

BEAST

BEAST GLARED AT JYGAN, his jaw tightening as the tanner pulled Olira into a lingering embrace. The raw heat of his anger pulsed beneath his skin, and it took every bit of restraint to stop himself from bashing the tanner's head in.

Arkala.

The name twisted in his mind like a blade. The bastard had convinced Olira to take him to Arkala — the capital of the beast trade. It was a place where free men and women with heavy purses came to select the strongest, fiercest beasts in the kingdom. Auctions were held daily, often preceded by Dawnblood fights, designed to show off the slaves' skills in combat.

Beast's hands clenched into fists, his nails biting into his palms. He would be recognised there. People were going to see his brands when they stripped and inspected him before putting him on the block. His face alone would give him away. Too many noblemen and women had seen him at King Leonis's feasts, back when he was paraded around like a prized possession.

Then, the word would spread. It would reach Kastian, and then… White Tower.

No. He couldn't go to Arkala. He wouldn't.

His pulse thundered in his ears, his thoughts racing as he stared at Olira. She stood with her back to him, her posture tense, her movements sharper than usual as she pulled away from Jygan. He had to find a way to stop her from taking him there.

Standing a few steps back, his head bowed and hands clasped loosely in front of him, Beast couldn't stop himself from shooting a venomous glare at Jygan. If he thought for a second that smashing the tanner's smug face into the dirt would keep him from being dragged to Arkala, he'd do it without hesitation.

The caravan ahead began to move, the first of three horse-drawn carts creaking onto the road. After a fast hike from Jygan's house, they had caught up with the caravan only a few minutes ago. The group had stopped for a break near a shaded grove and were packing up to continue to Pihnovis.

The wiry, sharp-eyed merchant named Master Ashin had agreed to let Olira and Beast join them until Splitwood. From there, her and Beast would continue to Kilrer on their own, where they could look for a ship to Arkala.

Ashin had initially demanded an exorbitant fee, pointing out the risks of taking on extra travellers and the value of the protection his five hired mercenaries provided. But Jygan had bargained for a discount, suggesting Beast could fight alongside Ashin's mercenaries if they ever got attacked. Ashin had stroked his beard, sizing Beast, then sizing Olira, not hiding his curiosity about how a simple-looking young farmer owned a purebred beast. Then, he'd agreed to give her a discount and let them trail after his group.

A small group of travellers, some on horseback and most on foot, walked alongside the three caravans. They weren't moving fast, but if Olira and Beast didn't join them now, they'd fall behind.

Olira's gaze flicked to the caravan, then back to Jygan as the tanner spoke again.

"The roads between Splitwood and Kilrer are patrolled and safe," he said for the fifth time since they'd left his house. "In a month and a half, I'll meet you at Splitwood and walk you back home."

Olira nodded, stepping back a little further. "Please take care of my brothers." She'd said this seven times already. "Tell Gilann I'll explain everything when I return."

Beast fidgeted, his gaze drawn to a wild weed near his foot as he listened. His chest felt tight, his thoughts darkening with every second that passed. The prospect of Arkala loomed over him like a storm cloud. He crushed the weed under his boot.

Olira took a deep breath, steadying herself as she turned toward the caravan. Her light brown hair was pulled back tightly in a neat ponytail, the wind whipping errant strands across her face. A faint blush coloured her cheeks as she surveyed the group already stretching further down the road. The carts creaked under the weight of their loads, drivers calling out instructions to one another.

She raised a hand, gesturing for Beast to follow as she trudged after the caravan, pulling her coat and scarf tight against the biting wind.

The caravan moved in a steady rhythm. Beast matched his steps to Olira's, his chain clinking softly. Slaves had to wear chains on the roads, so he had the collar back on. The weight of the chain seemed to bother Olira more than it did Beast, her fingers loose around the free end of it. Beast carried the borrowed backpack stuffed with supplies Jygan had forced on her. The straps dug into his shoulders, but he didn't care. The weight of the pack was nothing compared to the dread ahead.

Olira glanced around as they walked. Her eyes lingered on the other travellers: a young couple with a fussing baby; a man leading a cart loaded with barrels of something heavy; Ashin's five mercenaries, each on horseback with an air of weary vigilance. Ashin himself rode at the front, occasionally barking orders to his workers, who moved between carts to ensure everything remained secure.

By the time the caravan slowed, the sun was dipping low on the horizon. Ashin called for a halt, gesturing for everyone to start setting up camp in a small clearing near a cluster of trees. Beast lowered the backpack as Olira released the end of the chain. She didn't look at him, her movements distracted as she began going through the backpack and organising their dinner. She handed Beast some bread and dried meat, which he nibbled quietly.

He knew what he had to do next, but the thought made his heart race. He played with the idea of telling Olira he wanted his freedom. How would she react? Knowing her, she would probably get mad. But what if he'd told her about the Twilight of Infinity? The Owner of the winning Beast received a great sum of money. If Beast won, he would get his freedom, and Olira would get her money — more than she could get by selling him.

What if he'd suggested she take him to Euroad instead of Arkala? Enrol him for Twilight of Infinity. They would both get what they wanted. Yes, this was the perfect solution. But it had one major problem: Beast didn't know how to talk to people.

His past conversations with most people didn't go further than simple answers to questions. Even when he'd conversed with Saradra, she was often the one starting, leading, and keeping the conversation going. He never had to approach someone and ask something from them. Speaking without permission was an Act of Defiance; so was making requests. And Olira wasn't the most friendly and approachable person on Earthome. She hardly even looked at him without a scowl.

Beast finished his food, occasionally shooting glances at Olira, studying her mood, weighing words in his head. How would he start? What would he say?

Owner, take me to Euroad. I win my freedom, you get paid.

He grimaced. The words sounded so simple in his head, but he had a feeling it would take more than a few sentences to convince her. Out of the corner of his eyes, he studied the other travellers, sitting in their groups, laughing and talking to each other, like it was as simple as doing a balance drill on flat ground. They made it seem so easy.

It wasn't.

His jaw tightened, his head throbbing from scowling. He needed more time. He had to plan exactly what he was going to say, because if he couldn't convince her, he didn't know what else to do.

Olira eventually stood and pulled her blanket out, tossing another one at Beast. She picked a spot across the fire and curled under her blanket. Beast remained seated for a long time, staring into the fire. He tried to rehearse the conversation in his head, but every time he thought about what to say, his mind froze.

As the camp settled into quiet, Beast finally lay down and rested his head on the rough ground. He gazed up at the stars, his mind helplessly quiet as he drifted.

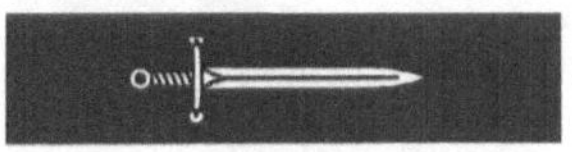

BEAST OPENED HIS EYES in a long, dim hallway with rough stone walls. He sat cross-legged on the dirt ground. The hallway reminded him of the ones under the Switchblade Arena, except the walls here were uneven like cave walls. The air smelled old and the ground beneath him was cold.

For the next few minutes, he didn't move. He didn't get up, or look around. He was vaguely aware this wasn't real. It was a nightmare. Occasionally he had nightmares about fighting and killing people he knew at Switchblade Arena, or being tortured in a cell, often his torturer turning out to be people he'd least expected. Over the last few months, he had nightmares about Saradra. About how he killed her.

Particularly, the moment he woke up from his Rage and faced what he'd done. That moment... That moment strangled him.

So, a nightmare about sitting in a cave-like hallway didn't warrant a reaction. He closed his eyes, willing himself to wake.

Wake up to what?

To the next morning, where he would be on his way to Arkala, with no way of speaking to Olira. He opened his eyes, glaring at the dark hallway that stretched ahead of him. No, he wasn't in a hurry to wake up.

When he shifted slightly, a strange physical sensation rippled through his chest. It wasn't pain exactly — more like a pinching and tugging every time he breathed.

Frowning, he pressed his hand against his chest, feeling the odd shape beneath his shirt. His fingers traced the outline of something hard and ridged.

His breath hitched. He pulled the hem of his shirt, yanking it over his head. When he looked down, the nightmare fully began.

A massive, tooth-like object jutted from the centre of his chest, its jagged edges gleaming faintly in the dark. It resembled the fang of some colossal predator, pale white and angled. The worst part wasn't its size or shape — it was the way it merged seamlessly with his skin, as if it had grown out of him. Veins spread from its base, dark and pulsing with his blood.

A hoarse scream strangled out of his throat. With trembling hands, he gripped the base of the tooth, trying to pull it free. It didn't budge. He dug his fingers in harder, ignoring the sharp pain radiating from the skin around it. He didn't care if he had to tear a chunk of his own flesh. He wanted that thing out!

His breathing grew ragged as he tried again. It was fused with him, with his bones.

He growled through clenched teeth, his muscles straining, his hands aching from the effort. He couldn't get a good grip. His fingers kept slipping. He slumped back against the wall, his chest heaving. He would have to cut it out, if he could find something sharp.

Pressing his palm against the rough wall, he pushed himself to his feet. His chest throbbed faintly, muscle and skin around the tooth feeling stiff and sore. He remembered what this tooth was. It was the necklace he had seen in that rogue mage's hands all those months ago. The one he stuffed inside Beast's chest after slicing it wide open. His mind was just playing up, conjuring those nightmarish memories of that night and creating a new nightmare. Something truly twisted.

The hallway stretched ahead of him. He placed one hand on the wall to steady himself, his bare feet cautious on the uneven dirt floor. He started walking, one hand tracing the wall. The sound of his footsteps echoed faintly before being swallowed by the oppressive darkness.

He couldn't shake the feeling how vivid this place felt. Too solid to be a dream. Very different than the ones before. The coolness and the grit of the stone beneath his fingertips, tiny rocks and pebbles stabbing his bare feet, the musty air filling his lungs — all of it was real. Or close enough to fool him.

The darkness thickened as he walked. He reached ahead with his free hand as he pressed on, stepping carefully and testing the ground with his foot before transferring his weight forward. His senses were alert to every faint sound and every shift in the air. He was afraid of falling into a pit or tripping over a rock he couldn't see in the darkness and breaking his neck.

Not that it mattered. This was only a dream, as real as it felt.

Eventually, the cool and hard ground beneath him began to soften slightly, as if the hard ground was giving way to loose soil. Then, a faint glow appeared ahead. The promise of daylight almost made him quicken his pace, though he forced himself to slow down. The tunnel began to widen, the walls curving outward until he found himself at the entrance of a massive cavern.

The sheer size of the space forced him to stop and take it all in. The ceiling above was so high, it disappeared into shadow. The jagged walls caught the faint glow of daylight. The air was cooler and fresher here. At the far end of the cavern was an exit. A bright archway that promised a way out.

Beast took a deep breath and glanced at what stood between him and freedom.

The floor of the cavern was flooded with a perfectly still, black water that shimmered faintly.

Approaching the edge of the water, Beast crouched to test it with his hand. The surface rippled at his touch. The water was cool, and despite its pitch-black colour, it didn't stain his fingers. Slowly, he stepped in and was cautiously pleased to see how shallow it was. The water only rose to his ankles. He waded into it, making his way towards the exit. The bottom wasn't slick or rocky as he expected. It was unnaturally soft, softer than sand. Fine mud filled between his toes, the texture of it a contrast to everything about this nightmare.

The faint sound of the water lapping at his legs echoed in the silence of the cavern. He restrained himself from rushing to the exit. The water was so black, he couldn't see the bottom and he was worried about stepping into a deep pit. He knew how to swim. Every purebred beast was taught how to, so they were prepared against Trial fights that involved flooded battlefields. Still, he treaded carefully, his eyes on the bright pale-blue archway ahead of him.

Beast flinched as a loud rumble echoed behind him. A faint vibration reached his feet, quickly growing into a deep, earth-shaking roar. He spun just in time, splashing water around him, to see chunks of rocks crashing down, blocking the hallway he had just came through. Dust and debris clung in the air above the rocks, making the cavern suddenly feel suffocating.

As the rumble subsided, a new sound reached his ears — low, guttural growls. A chill crawled down his spine as he spun again to find flames and flickering shadows along the walls.

At first, he thought the walls themselves were on fire.

Then, he realised the flames moved.

They growled and ran along the edge of the water. Beast's heart pounded wildly when he tracked the flickering shapes until he recognised what they were.

Wet, black fur. Molten eyes. Flames that rose from muscular shoulders, legs, and back, as if its skin was made of fire. Sizzling saliva dripping from razor-sharp teeth. A hound-like body and a snarling face that belonged to Darkhome.

He had seen a creature like these before, on that nightmarish night.

Fiends.

Dozens of them.

Beast instinctively reached for a weapon that wasn't there. He clenched his fists instead, his muscles tensing. The fiends surrounded him, their claws clicking against the stone as they encircled the flooded cavern around him. Holding his fists in front of him, Beast turned this way and that way, trying to keep every one of them in sight, but it was impossible. There were too many. There was always a few behind him.

He couldn't fight them. He had to run.

That's when he noticed the archway was gone. It had just vanished.

Instead, he found a massive cage right in the centre of the flooded cavern. Its silver bars gleamed, filling the space around it with a menacing glow. Heavy chains wrapped around the cage like serpents, their links thick and rusty. A silver padlock hung from the centre. The lock was oddly shaped, designed for something other than an ordinary key.

The inside of the cage was unnaturally dark. The faint glimmer of the silver bars couldn't break the darkness inside. Couldn't even scratch the surface of it. It was as if the darkness pushed back the light.

Beast's breath hitched when he saw a flicker of movement within the shadows. Something was in there, engulfed in that darkness, prowling. A wave of dread crashed over him and for a moment, he forgot about the fiends snarling and circling him.

That thing in the cage filled his blood with such chilling horror, he froze.

Then, it spoke in a whisper that was like a boulder rolling down a hill, flattening everything on its path.

"Slave."

Beast's eyes widened. He wanted to take a step back, but his legs refused to move. He knew this voice. He'd heard this whisper before, talking to him at times when he wasn't listening. Asking him things. His hair stood on the back of his neck. He couldn't see its full form, but the way the darkness shifted and swirled was enough to make his stomach churn.

"Slave," the thing inside the cage hissed again, louder.

That's when the attack started.

The fiends growled louder, howling, snarling. They started running in each direction, their muscles rippling under their black coats, flames trailing after their agile bodies. Beast pulled his gaze from the cage, his instincts taking over, readying him to fight those claws and teeth with his bare fists.

As soon as he looked away from the cage, the thing inside let out a deep, guttural roar that shook the entire cavern. The fiends added their howls to it, like spectators in an arena. The shallow water at Beast's feet erupted into chaos, rippling wildly as if it was alive.

Beast braced himself as the hounds charged, part of him still denying this was all real. That this was how he was going to die: being attacked by flame-covered fiend hounds in a strange cavern. The threat was too real to dismiss. The circular cavern too similar to an arena, the ground covered in water instead of sand. And the fiends were almost onto him, the creature in the cage still howling in fury, the water raging like those stormy seas the storytellers used to describe in King Leonis's feasts.

The tooth-shaped object on his chest, the thing that had compelled him to venture into this cavern in the first place, throbbed painfully.

Then, everything stopped.

The fiends halted just short of him, snarling and snapping as they formed a loose circle around him. Their molten eyes burned with hatred, liquid fire dripping from their jaws into the water beneath, which had gone still as glass again.

Behind the fiends, the shadowy creature in the cage hummed quieter.

Beast didn't lower his arms. He was primed to fight back, his muscles loaded with every drop of violence that remained dormant in him until released. But no one moved.

"Slave," the caged being whispered again, its voice echoing off the walls and running down Beast's spine like icy fingers. "Release me."

Beast just stared at the shadow and at the odd-shaped padlock that hung from the chains. *No way*, he thought without hesitation. There was no way he was facing that thing without those bars between them.

The fiends growled at him viciously, but still didn't lunge at him. His fists remained raised, his body rigid. The tooth-shaped object continued throbbing on his chest.

"Release me." The caged creature's voice was laced with threat. And contempt, as if speaking to Beast, let alone asking something from him, was a personal insult.

Beast still didn't speak. His eyes flicked between the fiend hounds circling him nearby — close enough that he could feel their heat — and the silver cage. The faint glow of the bars was a contrast to the suffocating darkness within. When the creature shifted again, the chains around the cage vibrated.

"Slave. Release me, or they shall tear you asunder, limb from limb."

The fiends snarled louder on cue, their molten eyes fixed on Beast. Their claws splashed water, sending ripples along the dark surface. They appeared to prowl closer, but the distance between them didn't change.

"No," Beast said quietly.

The word was lost in the sound of the fiends barking and snapping, but the caged creature heard him. The cavern went unnaturally cold.

The hounds would have attacked already, but they stood like they couldn't cover the last bit of distance between them. Something held them back. They barked and growled viciously, but it was only noise. They couldn't touch him.

Slowly, Beast stood taller and forced his fists down.

The thing inside the cage hissed, the sound like hot iron plunged into water. Then, the darkness within parted, just slightly. It caught Beast by surprise. He couldn't stop his eyes from being drawn to see what was hidden under the shadows.

A wave of searing pain struck his mind, sharp and brutal like a blade stabbing into his skull. Into his being. He staggered, clutching his head. Images were forced into his skull, each one more horrifying than the other.

He knew. He knew what that thing was.

Beast's knees buckled, and the icy water rose to claim him. He caught a glimpse of the tooth on the water's surface. It pulsed with a pale white light. Beast collapsed into the shallow water, his scream silenced as the water filled his mouth. The muddy ground beneath became softer, pulling him in. Beast sank deeper, trying to claw his way back over the surface, the images still stabbing his mind. He was drowning in a black void, with no words to describe the terror that rested inside the cage.

Then he woke, gasping for air. He sat up and instinctively clamped both his hands over his mouth to stifle a scream. It was a habit, ingrained deep from a childhood spent learning to be quiet. He doubled over, forcing a deep breath. His teeth were clenched hard enough to ache.

Around him, the camp was silent. *The camp.* He was at the camp, not at the flooded cavern. The flickering faint glow came from the dying campfire, not from the hound-like fiends. The shadows around him were the sleeping forms of the other travellers. Soft sounds of their snoring filled the cool night air.

He gathered his chain quietly, looping it around his hand to mute the clinks. He staggered to his feet. He couldn't shake the dream. It still lingered at the edges of his senses, as if the burning fiends lurked just outside the corner of his eyes. And the creature... Beast suppressed a whimper. He knew what the creature was — its voice still echoed in his head.

He needed to calm down so he wouldn't wake Olira. She was already stirring at the muffled sounds Beast had made. Her scowl was profound even as she slept. Beast didn't want her attention right now. Not when he didn't have the words to answer her persistent questions, to describe the horror he'd witnessed. Or the reserve to keep his face vacant.

He sneaked away from the camp, putting just enough distance between himself and the rest of the travellers before slumping on his knees. He dropped his hand from his mouth. Despite his urge to scream, he remained quiet. His breath escaped in short, ragged gasps. He released the chain then pressed his palms into the soft earth, the coolness grounding him.

It wasn't real.

He clenched his teeth, shaking his head violently as if to rid himself of the images burned into his mind. The cavern, the fiends, the cage — the thing inside the cage. He suppressed another whimper. *No.* No, it wasn't real. A horror like that could not be real.

With trembling hands, he pulled at his shirt, exposing his chest. Nothing. Just his bare skin, marred by the brands, his hair standing on end against the chill. The tooth-shaped object was just a fragment of this twisted nightmare.

A sharp pain exploded across his face. His head snapped to the side, stars bursting in his vision.

He hadn't even heard them approach.

His instincts took over, sudden battle rush pushing the pain away. His legs tensed beneath him, and he jumped to his feet, ready to block. Disarm. Assess. And fight. Just fight.

"Stop! That's a slave!"

The sharp whisper froze Beast in place, just as it did the men who had been closing in on him. He could see them now, nearly half a dozen — maybe more — hidden well in the shadows of the trees and bushes. His head throbbed where he'd been struck, blood seeping from the gash above his brow and trickling down his temple.

The weight of those words — *that's a slave* — settled over him, tightening around his neck like a collar.

The men hesitated, glancing at one another, and Beast hesitated with them. *He was a slave.* He'd been taught to surrender in situations like this. It was an Act of Defiance to lift a finger against a free man, unless he was ordered to do so. Free men and women were too greedy to kill an expensive slave who surrendered.

The tension drained from his legs, and he let himself fall to his knees. He had to surrender. His body ached to act, to lash out. He'd broken Acts of Defiance before, attacked and killed free men. He could do it again, and Darkhome knew how much he wanted to. Yet, his training compelled him to surrender. To tilt his head back and display his tattoo. To keep his hands on his lap.

One of the bandits stepped forward and grabbed the free end of his chain, yanking it up to get a better look at his tattoo. "He's a purebred!"

"We hit Kyrus's treasure."

"Fuck yeah!"

Excited whispers spread in the dark, until a sharp, commanding voice cut them all. "Quiet. Stash him somewhere. We've got work to do."

Beast's pulse thundered in his ears as the man holding the chain tugged him to his feet, dragging him a few steps before shoving him toward another waiting figure. The bandit gripped the chain tightly, his gaze flicking toward the camp in the distance, where the soft glow of campfires still lingered.

Beast's mind raced, torn between the instincts to fight and to submit, both ingrained deep into him. *Surrender. Submit. They'll leave you alive.* But these men wouldn't stop with him — they'd move on to the camp, to Olira.

They would to kill her.

That thought lodged hard in his chest. And then another, darker one followed: *No Arkala.*

If they'd killed Olira, Beast would be saved from going to Arkala. Wasn't this what he wanted? The prospect sent a bitter wave of relief. And shame.

Olira's face flashed in his mind when she said to him only hours ago: *I am not a bad person.*

Beast gritted his teeth. Then, his eyes caught a glint of steel — a sword, strapped to the belt of the man closest to him.

His fingers itched with a craving far stronger than the need to surrender. It had been months since he'd held a sword. Too long. He imagined the sword's weight and how well the hilt would fit into his palm. The familiar call of violence heated his blood. The craving burned through him, stronger than anything else. He wanted it. He wanted it so badly it made his hands tremble.

The man holding the chain barked something at him, but the words didn't reach him through the thumping in his ears.

He saw nothing but the sword.

7

OLIRA

OLIRA WOKE TO THE sound of screams piercing the quiet night. Her heart jumped to her throat as the clash of steel and shouting voices reached her ears. The soft glow of the campfires had been replaced by flickering flames licking at the edges of the carts.

She bolted upright. A man was running straight at her. Not one of the travellers. His face was twisted in a snarl, a blade glinting in his hand.

She froze for a heartbeat.

Then, panic took over. She scrambled to her feet, but her legs tangled in her dress and she fell. The rough ground scraped her hands and knees. She twisted onto her back, scrambling to push herself away, but the man was almost on top of her.

Steel flashed between them.

The slave moved like water, stepping in front of her in a fluid motion. He met the attacker's blade with his own — swords clashing in a blur too quick to follow. She didn't even have time to scream. The next moment, she was watching the attacker gurgle blood from his lips, the slave's sword plunged into his chest.

The slave shoved him to the ground, pulling his sword free with a firm yank. Olira stared, unable to breathe, her body frozen with shock. The slave stood over the lifeless man. He wasn't even out of breath. He looked up, scanning the campsite. His face was more expressive than Olira had ever seen him. His eyes glinted in the firelight, lit with a wild energy, a mixture of fury and something else — something that chilled her to the core.

Olira followed his gaze, and the scene made her stomach turn. Bandits. There were bandits, attacking their camp. So many of them. Master Ashin's mercenaries and a few of the travellers were fighting them. And the way the slave looked at the fight, he was also itching to join them.

A random thought crossed her mind. *Where had he found a sword from?* She shook her head, trying to focus and gather her thoughts. She was supposed to Rage him. It was the terms of her agreement with Master Ashin. Except she didn't remember the slave's Kill Word. She reached into her purse and found the folded paper with the slave's Words written.

The sound of paper drew the slave's attention to her. Blood coated his face, gashing from a cut over his eyebrow. When he saw the paper, a visible shudder went through him.

"No!" he shouted, his hand shooting up as if to stop her. His eyes widened, that wild glint now replaced by fear. He took a rushed step towards her, which made Olira flinch and scramble away, clutching the paper to her chest.

"No," the slave repeated. His throat bobbed as he tried to reign his voice to something calmer. "Please. Don't Rage me."

Olira opened her mouth, the first sound of the Kill Word at her lips. *Don't Rage me?*

The slave took another step, and Olira noticed more blood on him. The front of his shirt and his arms were drenched. He had killed others.

"Don't Rage me," the slave said again, his voice quivering with fear. "I'll fight bare."

Olira couldn't speak. She couldn't take her eyes off the slave's bloody face. He took Olira's silence as approval and slowly stepped back. He turned and sprinted toward the centre of the camp, where Ashin's mercenaries were locked in a fight with the bandits. The chain, neatly wrapped around his torso and tucked under his shirt to keep it from tangling, clinked faintly as he moved.

Olira crawled backward and pressed herself under one of the carts, where the young female traveller was already hiding with her baby. The woman cradled the child tightly, her eyes wide with terror as she whispered frantic prayers to the Twelve Riders.

From her hiding spot, Olira could watch the massacre. She didn't want to watch, but couldn't take her eyes off it. The mercenaries fought together, holding their ground against the bandits. But the slave was at the very centre of the fight. He moved through the attackers like a storm, his sword cutting through them like a scythe in a wheat field. He wasn't just fighting. He was drinking the violence, soaking in. He seemed more alive than ever. There was a power in him, a sharpness in every movement. His face, usually blank and distant, was now fierce and focused. His eyes gleamed with something that was too similar to enjoyment.

Olira's untrained eyes couldn't quite follow his actions, but bodies started dropping around him. He didn't try to make his way to Ashin's mercenaries, to fight with them. Instead, he drew the bandits to him, letting them surround him, like he wanted them all.

Ashin's mercenaries pressed forward, picking off the bandits from behind. The slave whirled and ducked and dodged at a speed Olira couldn't keep up with. Nor could the bandits. Their numbers dwindled, and the remaining handful turned to bolt.

Olira stayed frozen under the cart long after the last bandit vanished into the trees. Only when the shouts of the mercenaries turned to orders — and the screaming gave way to groans — did she crawl out. Her knees were weak, her hands trembling, the paper still clenched in her fist.

Around her, the travellers were already moving. Some raced to douse the fires, others gathered the wounded. No one looked at her.

The slave stood in the centre of the camp, sword hanging limp in his hand, blood running down his arms. He stared after the fleeing bandits, chest rising and falling in deep, controlled breaths.

Olira forced herself to move. She grabbed a bucket and stumbled toward the nearest flame, joining the others. But her mind stayed on him — on the slave. The way he'd fought. The way he'd killed those men.

The way his eyes had gleamed.

He hadn't gone to help the mercenaries or the travellers. He was drawn to the violence.

And he'd thrived in it.

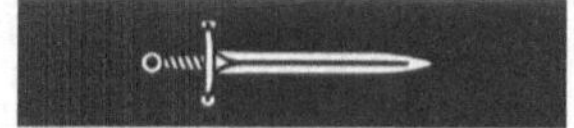

THE CAMP WAS A grim sight in the faint light of dawn. Smouldering fires sent wisps of smoke curling into the air and the ground was littered with Master Ashin's scattered supplies, discarded weapons, and patches of dirt darkened by blood. Most of the travellers were moving sluggishly, exhaustion weighing heavily on them as they packed up their belongings.

Olira knelt beside a young man with a gash across his arm, carefully pressing a cloth soaked in *Bitter Rue* ointment against the wound. The man's face twisted with pain, but he said nothing.

The attack had left everyone shaken, but they had survived. The leader of the mercenaries, a grizzled man named Gael, sat on a crate nearby with his injured arm in a crude sling. Ashin hovered close, a ledger in hand, barking orders at his workers. One of Gael's men had more serious injuries — a deep cut along his ribs — but it was stabilised. Several travellers bore minor injuries of scrapes and bruises, but none were life-threatening.

"Could have been worse," Gael said with a grimace.

Ashin grunted. "Those bastards set the carts on fire before we could shout Kiejain's balls. I lost nearly a quarter of my merchandise."

"You could have lost your life," Gael snapped, flexing his good hand. "If it wasn't for that purebred."

Ashin nodded, his sharp eyes flicking toward the slave, who hovered close to Olira, but not close enough to be a nuisance. The blood-smeared sword still dangled from his hand.

"Never seen a Raged purebred from up close before," Gael continued. "He was feral. Fought like a fiend out of Darkhome."

Olira's stomach churned, her fingers trembling as she pulled the bandage snug around the young man's arm. They thought she had Raged him.

"I've never seen a massacre like this. He slaughtered them like sheep."

"Have you seen how he taunted them? I swear the bastard was toying with them."

"Well, don't they say purebreds are all possessed by fiends? Binding them with Words is the only way to control them."

"Until last night, I thought that was all just a tale to spook kids at night."

Gael raised his voice to catch Olira's attention. "Thank you, Mistress Olira, for sending your beast." He nodded towards the heavily injured man. "My men owe their lives to you."

Olira felt sick. She forced a nod, but didn't respond.

They praised his savagery. She understood the slave was defending them, and the bandits were going to kill them all. But there was nothing to admire about murder. When she thought of the slave's expression as he fought — the way his eyes lit up, the way he moved as though chopping people's limbs came as naturally as breathing... Would they still admire that if they knew he wasn't Raged? He wasn't forced to do those by a Word that controlled him.

That was all him.

She finished tying the young man's bandage and stood, brushing dirt off her skirt. The slave was watching the campsite with vigilant eyes. The sword glinted faintly in the morning light. He had washed the blood off his face and arms. He looked different, more animated, more alive since the fight. Refreshed like a withering plant after a few hours' rain. It terrified her.

Forcing her unease down, Olira gestured for him to come over.

The slave paused, his grey eyes locking onto her for a moment before he approached. When he reached her, she glanced at the blood-stained blade and felt her heart race.

"Drop the sword," Olira ordered, her voice steady despite the nervous flutter in her chest.

For a moment, he didn't move. His eyes narrowed, his head tilting slightly as if weighing her command. Olira's gaze flicked to the sword again, her breath catching as his fingers tightened around the hilt. The tension between them was sharp like the still air before a storm. Her mind raced with dark possibilities: *What if he refused? What if he said no more? What if he turned that blade on her, then on the rest of the camp?*

"Drop it," she repeated, her voice quiet and firm. She didn't need the paper to recall his First Word; she had memorised that one well, had to use it more than a few times. She would drop him and pry the sword out of his paralysed fingers if she had to.

It hit her then, in a way it hadn't before — this was why purebreds had those Words. Collars and chains couldn't leash them. Words did.

The sword fell with a dull clang.

Olira exhaled slowly, the weight on her chest easing just enough to let her breathe. Without the sword, the slave looked... diminished. The same raw power was there, but a heaviness clung to his shoulders now, dragging him down.

"Are you hurt?" she asked, her voice steady, though her pulse still hammered in her ears.

The slave shook his head, his gaze fixed on a distant point, his jaw set. Olira's eyes swept over him, taking in the blood that stained his shirt. None of it was his. *How many people did he kill last night?* He seemed exhausted, but there were no visible injuries, other than the cut on his forehead.

"Sit." She gestured at the rock the injured man had been sitting on a moment ago.

He lowered himself onto the stone. Olira stepped closer to inspect the cut, her hands trembling faintly as she dabbed at it with a clean cloth.

The memory came uninvited; this same man — this *beast* — pinning Torren to the ground, his hands wrapped around his throat, nearly strangling him to death.

In the three months since, she had convinced herself the slave wasn't dangerous. Despite never forgetting how close Torren had come to dying that day, she'd let her mind divide him into two people. The beast who'd almost killed her brother, and the slave she'd allowed into her home, giving him a place on her farm. The one she thought she knew was quiet, docile, an empty shell who didn't care.

Then last night, she had seen the beast again. Could a beast truly be tamed?

"Hold still," she muttered out of a need to break the silence. The man hadn't even flinched, his gaze fixed somewhere past her, unbothered by the sting of the ointment. Yet her body screamed at her to pull away.

He smelled like blood and death. The smell disturbed her more than Jygan's tannery ever had, the air suffocating her lungs. She forced herself to finish applying the salve and wiped her hands on a cloth before reaching into her bag.

She refused to be intimidated by him. The thought steadied her as her fingers closed around the key at the bottom of the bag. She slid the key into the lock on his collar. With a faint click, the collar came loose, and she gathered it and the chain, tossing them into the bag.

Last night had made it painfully clear: no chain or collar could hold this man. They were a mockery, a pretence of control. And she *hated* the sound of constant clinking. She glanced around the camp, knowing full well no patrols would come through these roads. The law didn't matter out here; no one would fine her for keeping a slave off leash.

And she wanted to make it clear that she had nothing to fear. She had no reason to be afraid of him. She could control him.

She stepped back, then paused when the slave slowly raised his hand and pressed his fist against his neck. His chest heaved a bit faster.

"What's wrong?" she asked. "Does it hurt?" She leaned forward to check the bruises and blisters the collar had left on his neck.

The slave's eyebrows dipped. "No." He tapped the side of his fist against his neck impatiently, and glanced at her, waiting.

"Why are you doing that?" she scoffed.

The slave's eyes narrowed. "I'm requesting permission to speak, Owner," he said slowly, then tapped his fist again.

"Is that... Is that what it means?"

"Yes, Owner."

"You... *You want to talk*?"

"Yes, Owner."

Olira's jaw dropped, words failing her for a long moment as she stared at him. Of all the things he could have done, this was the last she'd imagined. She glanced around, as though expecting someone to appear and tell her this was all a joke. She held her breath and waited for a whole minute. The slave eyed her, jaw tight, fist still at his neck.

"Well, go on then," Olira said impatiently. "Speak."

The slave lowered his fist and shifted nervously. His lips parted slightly, but no sound came out. He cleared his throat and dropped his gaze to the ground, scowling as if trying to concentrate on what he wanted to say. As the silence stretched, Olira barely kept herself from squirming.

"I can..." The slave swallowed, his voice low and uneven. "Umm... I am... very good at fighting."

Olira's stomach dropped. She forced a steady breath as the man continued speaking.

"I'm more than good. I'm... I'm very experienced."

Olira nodded slowly, unable to stop herself from eyeing the blood on his clothes, evidence to his claim.

"I am trained in every fight class and style. Efficient with every weapon." He licked his lips, shifting again and sitting taller as he spoke. "I've done many Slayer's Pits and... and of course tournaments. To the death. I've killed hundreds."

"*Hundreds?*" Olira repeated softly.

The slave nodded eagerly. "Yes. Hundreds."

Was he threatening her? The thought chilled her, but she refused to step back, even as every instinct screamed at her to do so. He had killed hundreds. And he sat there, his head held high, meeting her gaze with a confidence that made her blood run cold as he continued his claims.

"I can kill anyone who would stand against me."

Olira's mouth went dry, her heart pounding in her chest like a trapped animal. "*Anyone?*" she asked carefully.

"Yes, anyone! If you let me fight, you can... you can take all the money."

Gael barked orders at two of his mercenaries, who were checking their weapons. A pair of travellers walked past where Olira and the slave stood. They nodded at Olira with quiet gratitude, their gazes lingering on the slave with a mix of curiosity and admiration. The slave barely spared them a flat glance.

The other travellers moved about the camp, murmuring quietly as they salvaged what they could from the chaos. The young mother crouched by her cart, fussing over her baby while her husband packed their belongings. Ashin leaned against one of the carts, speaking with his workers, his hand idly brushing the heavy coin pouch at his belt. The camp was in shambles, but Olira's gaze caught the subtle signs of wealth — travellers with fine cloaks, barrels loaded with goods that would fetch a fortune in any market.

She glanced at the slave, his unreadable expression making her stomach twist. Was he offering to kill them all and take their money? Inhaling forcefully and keeping her voice low, as if afraid the others would hear their scheming, Olira asked, "What are you saying?"

"I'm saying, I can earn you all the coin you need, and I can earn my—"

"I don't want their money. And I certainly don't want you killing anyone."

"But you need money. For your debt. I know what will happen if you don't pay your debt."

"*Excuse me?*"

"I said, I know what will happen if you don't—"

"Stop talking. Right now."

The slave blinked, staring at her like her words had been spoken in another language. His lips parted, then closed again, his brows drawing together.

"You're not allowed to pick up another weapon," Olira hissed. She hated the way the slave's eyes were drawn to the sword lying on the ground. She clicked her fingers to snap his attention back to her, pinning him with a hard stare. "You're not touching another sword while you're with me. Do you understand?"

He nodded.

"You won't kill— You won't *touch* anyone unless I explicitly ask you to. *Do you understand?*"

He nodded again, his gaze now fixed at her feet. His jaw ticked, and he seemed deflated.

"If I believe you're a danger to me or anyone else in this camp..." She let the sentence hang, unfinished. She hated threatening him, hated what it made her feel. But the faint sneer at the corners of his mouth told her he understood perfectly.

"Go clean up," she said, her voice still harsh. "Jygan packed you a spare shirt. Wash all the blood off."

He stood slowly, keeping his head bowed so his expression remained hidden. He walked past the abandoned sword and made his way to where she'd left her backpack.

Olira let out a sharp exhale as soon as he was out of earshot. She collapsed onto the stone, her hands trembling violently. Her chest heaved as she shuddered, the weight of what he had just proposed pressing down on her like a suffocating blanket.

She couldn't wait to reach Arkala, to hand him over and get as far away from him as possible. But as the thought settled, a realisation struck her.

Tomorrow, they would reach Splitwood and leave the safety of the caravan. From then on, she would be alone on the road.

Alone with this beast.

8

BEAST

BEAST STOOD RIGID IN the middle of the flooded cave, his muscles locked in terror. The cage towered before him like a monument to unspeakable evil. Within, the darkness writhed and churned, twisting and twirling in patterns that hurt to follow with the eye. The very air around the cage seemed to thicken, as if the darkness was bleeding out of the cage.

The fiend hounds lurked along the far walls of the cavern, their flames painting living shadows on the stone, reflecting off the black, glass-like water. What chilled Beast to his very core was their stillness. They didn't pace or snarl or bare their fangs. Instead, they simply watched. Waited. Their molten eyes tracked his every breath, every involuntary tremor, as if they knew something he didn't.

"What a pitiful display," the darkness in the cage spoke, its voice causing small ripples on the water's surface. "You could scarce string a sentence together, could you?"

Beast breathed steadily as he forced himself not to move. Every muscle in his body was taut and he only focused on one singular thought: *He can't touch me.* This was just a nightmare, or whatever it was, it wasn't real. Just like the faintly throbbing object lodged on his chest wasn't real either.

A sound, as if bones were grinding on stone, grated against Beast's ears. It was laughter. The caged creature, the darkness, was *laughing* at him.

"'*I kill, you rich.*' Is that the best your tongue could manage?"

Beast grimaced at the sound and the disdain it carried. He glanced at the fiend hounds, who were serious as a promised death, watching him with the patient intensity of a purebred beast awaiting his Kill Word. They did not share the creature's ill-suited humour. Beast didn't get it either. Last time... Last time when he was here... Fear trickled down his spine, and he had to force air into his lungs.

"Best of all — you haven't the faintest why she refused you. How utterly sad."

A distant part of him knew this mockery was meant to make him feel embarrassed, but he rarely entertained that emotion. Especially here, facing this creature, surrounded by fiends, and with no visible way out. Embarrassment was the last thing he would feel.

The swirling shadow slowed down inside the cage, its laughter quietened. "Alas," it said slowly. "Time to unlock this cage."

Beast shook his head. He didn't even have a key, though it didn't matter. He would never unleash that thing.

"You know who I am," the creature whispered.

Beast's throat felt tight. When the creature had stabbed his mind with those images, Beast had seen what it was. What it had done in the past and what it was capable of. The only thing that kept him from screaming and clawing at the cavern walls with his bare fingers to dig his way out of here, was his purebred training. He knew how to suppress his fear and stay put. He brought his hands together in front of him, clasping them tight enough to ground him.

The darkness inside the cage shifted and expanded, the chains wrapped around it groaning faintly. The darkness filled the cage with such intensity, the silver bars glowing brighter. It hurt Beast's eyes, but he didn't look away. He was afraid he'd find himself running if he did.

"I am what remains after death," the creature said, its voice ringing in the cavern.

"Keder," Beast said weakly.

Keder, the one who remains after death. One of the thirteen High Fiends imprisoned in Darkhome.

"Then you know well what power I wield," Keder growled, its voice rolling over the water like a wave. "You know what ruin I can bring upon you."

"Nothing." Beast tightened his fists until his nails dug into his palms. "This is just a dream."

He willed himself to believe that. Thirteen High Fiends, Dividing of the Homes, Twelve Riders and their war against the fiends, were just stories Pyres told. This couldn't have been true. This was just a dream.

"Do you truly believe waking shall free you of me?" Keder let out a hollow laugh. "This is no dream, slave. You stand here, body and breath."

"Where's here?" Beast whispered, his voice low and rough. He swallowed. "How did I get here?"

And more importantly, how could he get out? The tooth-shaped object throbbed in his chest, black-red veins spreading out from where it was lodged. His skin stretched and ached with each breath. He desperately wanted to try again and remove the object from his chest, but he resisted the urge. He knew when he woke up from this nightmare, the object would not be there. So why waste the effort?

The darkness inside the cage stilled for a moment, its silence somehow more unsettling than its roars and growls. Then it spoke again, its tone low and dangerous. "Open the cage, slave."

Beast shook his head. He had seen in his mind what Keder and the other High Fiends had done, and what they wanted to do. They would destroy Earthome.

"Not destroy," Keder whispered. "We will unite our shattered home again."

Beast shivered. He couldn't help but glance at the fiend hounds again, stirring and watching him with predatory malice. He imagined those things roaming Earthome, burning and killing all the people in it.

"You would spare them?" Keder mused, the darkness within the cage roiling furiously. "The very ones who've made a sport of your suffering?"

Beast's knuckles whitened as he held his ground. He gritted his teeth as the creature's words gnawed at the edges of his resolve. It was hard not to have all of his masters and owners visit his thoughts; Kastian, Inoeveth, Lord Berrow, Master Parraten, even Badimar.

And then, Breeder Astaldo.

The familiar hollowness crept in at the thought of Breeder Astaldo. A cold, suffocating emptiness that threatened to pull him under. It was a void he knew too well — he had spent years in that void. His breathing hitched, the cavern blurring around him, until he felt nothing but the smell of tobacco, and the weight of Astaldo's fist on him.

He dragged in a slow, deliberate breath as he fixed his gaze on the fiend hounds circling in the shadows. He bit down hard on the inside of his cheek, the sharp sting anchoring him to the present. Keder's laughter rattled through the cavern.

"I know the hunger that burns in you," Keder said, his laughter fading into a quiet, unsettling seriousness. "And I can sate it. No more chains. No collars. No more crawling before the men and women who hold your miserable life between their lips."

"And no place to live," Beast said, his voice tight and his throat dry. What was the point of getting his freedom if there was no Earthome left? He shook his head. "I will get my freedom."

"And how shall you manage that? Speak with her again? What leads you to believe she will hear you?"

Olira's face crossed his mind: her scowl, her sharp, biting words. He also remembered those glances she sent his way when she thought he wasn't paying attention. It wasn't the calculating gaze of a slave merchant appraising his worth. It was different, like she was trying to see inside his head, to understand him. To connect with him.

"She's different. She'll listen."

"Because she told you she's not a bad person?"

She was neither bad nor good. She was somewhere in-between. She was like Badimar.

"She will take you to Arkala." Keder shifted, the chains rattling ominously. "And soon enough, you will find yourself bound for King Kastian's cells. Or to White Tower, if mercy fails. A place of such splendour, I've heard."

The name sent a shiver down Beast's spine. He looked down, scowling at the smooth surface of the black water. His confused face scowled back. He didn't understand why the High Fiend was speaking to him. He clearly couldn't harm him — he would have done so already. Keder believed Beast held the power to unleash him, and the High Fiend's only way to achieve that was through persuasion. But it was absurd, because Beast didn't have a way of unlocking that cage, not that he would have done it. True, he didn't have a list of reasons to spare Earthome, but...

"Twilight of Infinity," he whispered. "I'll go to Euroad. I'll get my freedom."

The High Fiend was quiet for a while, his dark, shapeless existence swirling inside the cage. The bars and the chains gleamed. One of the fiend hounds released a soft growl, a response to some unseen irritation from Keder that Beast couldn't perceive but the creatures clearly could.

"Hope," Keder finally spoke. "Is that what keeps you from opening this cage right now?"

Keder's words hung in the air, less a question and more a crude observation. His voice shifted, growing softer, like a predator toying with its prey. Beast felt torn. Part of him wanted to see the creature's face, to know what he was thinking, while another part prayed he never would.

"Very well. We shall make a bargain. I'll lend you the words she will listen to."

Beast took a slow step back, sliding his foot smoothly, so it didn't send too many ripples. "Why?" he asked suspiciously.

"Because the moment you grasp that the men and women shall never grant you what you seek... that is the moment you'll set me loose."

"You want me to fail. Why trust you?"

"I do not wish you to fail," Keder whispered. Beast could almost hear the malicious smile in that smoke-like voice. "I want you to understand. To witness that humans are fouler than we, and they deserve the wrath I will unleash upon them."

"I am human too."

Beast regretted the words as soon as they left his lips. Keder's laughter echoed through the cavern, the force of it stirring the water into ripples that licked at Beast's ankles.

"Curious," the High Fiend mused. "I could have sworn you have just claimed you were anything but a pathetic animal."

Beast's shoulders stiffened, a strange and unfamiliar heat creeping up his neck. Embarrassment pricked at the pride he didn't know he had, the emotion finally finding a foothold to cling to, despite his efforts. He clenched his fists and grit his teeth until Keder's piercing laughter settled.

That's when Beast felt the faint tug beneath his bare feet, almost imperceptible at first, then quickly growing stronger. His breath hitched as he realised he was sinking. Fast. The mud wasn't just giving way, it was pulling him down.

In less than a heartbeat, the chill of the water was up to his calves. In the next heartbeat, he was fighting to keep his head above water, struggling to free his legs from the mud's grip. He splashed violently, reaching for something to grab onto and pull himself up, but there was nothing but black water. He gasped a deep breath before his head plunged underwater. Keder's voice echoed in the cavern as the faint whoosh of water filled his ears.

"When you don't know what to say, listen."

9

OLIRA

Splitwood was quiet in the crisp, early morning light. The towering trees swayed gently in the breeze, the wind whistling through their bare branches. The ground was hard and uneven, and patches of wiry bushes clung stubbornly to life.

The road forked here, one path stretching north toward Pihnovis, the other bending east to Kilrer. The caravan had come to a near-halt, wheels creaking faintly as Ashin waved from his perch at the lead cart. He didn't bother stopping, his wave more fleeting than heartfelt.

Gael, however, pulled up on his horse. His breath misted in the air as he turned to Olira, his arm still tightly bound in its sling.

"Thank you, Mistress," he said, his voice rough but genuine. "My men owe you their lives."

Olira pulled her scarf tighter against the wind and inclined her head. "Bandage stays on at least another week."

Gael looked away, and Olira became certain the mercenary leader would tear the bandage off as soon as they were out of sight. She sighed, her attention already shifting back to the road ahead. But Gael wasn't finished. He reached to his saddle and pulled a sword still sheathed in its scabbard. Olira's blood froze at the sight of the weapon.

"You sure you don't want to take it?" Gael asked, holding it out. "Your beast should carry a weapon on these roads."

Olira hesitated, glancing back at the slave. He stood a few steps behind her, the cold wind stirring his short-cropped blond hair. His expression was as indifferent as ever, but he went still in the most subtle way. He was listening. The intensity of his attention made Olira's chest tighten.

"No," she said finally, her voice firm. "We won't need it."

Gael frowned, clearly disapproving, but didn't press the issue. He slid the blade back on his saddle, shaking his head.

"She's right," one of his men joined in, his voice carrying a hint of admiration. "That beast doesn't need a sword. He's a weapon all on his own."

The words sent a ripple of nausea through Olira. She stiffened, glancing again at the slave.

"Safe travels," she said to the mercenary leader, ignoring the knot forming in her chest.

Gael nodded, offering a faint smile before clicking his horse after the caravan. A few other travellers called out their thanks. Olira accepted them with a hollow nod. She hadn't done anything to deserve their gratitude. If anything, she'd endangered them all.

She turned east, and the slave followed in silence.

Hours passed like a physical weight pressing down. Olira kept her eyes fixed on the road ahead, refusing to glance back at the slave. She could feel him there, though — the steady crunch of his boots against the hardened dirt, the prickling sensation of his presence just behind her. She tried to ignore it, tried to banish the thoughts that had plagued her since the attack, but they wouldn't stay buried.

The day after the attack, the caravan had made good way. When they had stopped for the night, most of the camp had spent the night with one eye open. Olira's sleep had been no better. Every time she drifted off, she woke to the memory of screams and steel — or worse, to the low, ragged sounds of the slave's nightmares. She'd pretended to sleep through them, her back turned as his breaths came sharp and uneven. By the time morning had broken, the slave had gone quiet, his face vacant.

He looked worse than she felt. He had faint shadows under his eyes, and exhaustion weighed his face down. He still had a bandage around his forehead, though Olira planned to remove it this afternoon, to let the wound breathe. Every so often, the slave tilted his head, as though listening to something she couldn't hear. He sometimes shook his head and swatted at his ear as if a fly was buzzing nearby.

She didn't stop until well past noon, despite how her hunger clawed at her stomach. She found a spot off the road, where a patch of bushes provided shelter from the wind, and there were some rocks to sit on. Olira put her bag down and cleared the sticks and dry leaves off a section of a rock. When she turned to check on the slave, she froze.

He stood a few steps away, staring at nothing. His face was twisted into a dangerous scowl. The lines of his jaw were tight. He tilted his head in that strange way. A moment later, he shook his head sharply, his hand twitching at his side.

And he caught Olira looking at him.

He didn't look away, like he usually would. His eyes bore into hers with an unnerving intensity. This wasn't the vacant face of the slave she had hosted on her farm for the last three months. This was the face of the beast who grinned as he surrounded himself with those bandits, then cut them down. The same man who'd casually suggested killing innocent travellers afterwards.

He's a weapon all on his own.

Fear prickled along her skin. She hated the feeling, so she tried to smother it with irritation.

"What?" she snapped, resting her hands on her hips. She squeezed every drop of confidence she could muster into her posture, her back straight and her shoulders wide. *I know his Words*, she reminded herself, and hoped the slave did too. Her heart pounded in her ears as she refused to back down from those intense grey eyes.

"Don't just stand there," she scoffed, loading her voice with authority. "Put the bag down and sit."

The slave's gaze finally dropped. He put the bag down near the rocks and seated himself. His hands on his lap, his shoulders down, and his gaze fixed on the dirt floor.

Olira exhaled shakily, forcing her hands to steady as she pulled the bag open and started fixing them a meal. She worked in silence, pulling apart dried meat and breaking off chunks of rye bread.

When she glanced his way again, the slave hadn't moved a muscle. Every passing heartbeat, that moment of intensity was fading from his face, like holding onto it was an effort. Before she knew it, he was that vacant, tired, lifeless purebred again.

Guilt twisted in Olira's stomach. She sighed and tossed an extra piece of dried meat onto his portion. "Here, eat," she said, her tone softer now.

He took the bread without taking his eyes off the ground. He ate in silence, staring at a dry twig at his feet.

Olira nibbled on her food. Was she being cruel for snapping at him? Simply for looking at her.

"How's your head?" she asked finally, the question coming more as a peace offering.

"I am well, Owner," the slave said, his tone flat. He didn't look up from the twig.

Olira scoffed. She bit her tongue to keep from telling him to stop throwing those memorised phrases at her and speak with his own words. She took a large bite from her bread to keep her mouth stuffed until she was calm again.

"I'm sorry for snapping at you," she said.

The slave tossed the last piece of his food into his mouth, then licked his fingers.

"I don't intend to be unkind. I just get frustrated sometimes, because..."

Because you scare me.

She pressed her lips together and let the sentence die. Her fears were both valid and invalid at the same time. Yes, he was dangerous. No, he wouldn't harm her. But at the core of her fears lied the fact that there was so much she didn't know or understand about him. That was what really scared her.

The slave wiped his hands on his shirt, still looking down like that twig was more interesting than Olira.

"I'm not a bad person," she said like she needed him to believe that. Like she needed herself to believe that.

Nothing. Not even an acknowledgement, voiced or shown. His cold indifference hit Olira like rejection. She was making an effort, trying to show compassion, and all she got was that flat, stupid face.

"Fine," she growled. She wrapped her unfinished bread into a cloth and tossed it in the bag. Then she paused, realising something she should have weeks ago.

This was a cycle.

She knew it too well by now.

She was scared of him. Part of her had always been, even when he was on the brink of death. So she would hide behind anger — snapping at him, threatening him, trying to assert control over him — to conquer that fear. And then, she would feel guilty for treating him like rotten crop. So then she would do something nice. Show him compassion, despite it being such an unpractised manner for her. So many times, she had tried to connect with him, to see him as a human.

But when each attempt was met with a cold, stone wall of indifference, the taste of rejection would linger on her tongue.

Then, she'd get frustrated again. At him. At herself.

She resented him. Resented the way he made her feel. The façade of emotions that came and went every hour, leaving her exhausted.

And deep down, she resented herself.

Olira's gaze flicked to the slave, her hands gripping the tightened strings of her backpack. A warmth, a new emotion, unfurled in her chest — peace. With the emotions named, their hold on her seemed to loosen, giving her a sense of freedom. She sighed, readying herself to stand and continue their journey.

The slave moved before she did.

He reached and picked up that twig he'd been staring at. He snapped off the smaller branches and thorns until the stick was smooth and straight. Olira froze, watching as he cleared a patch of hard ground with his palm, brushing the stray leaves. Then he crouched and started drawing.

The twig scratched against the dirt as he etched faint lines with sharp, confident strokes. Olira's breath caught in her throat. She couldn't move, couldn't speak as though she stumbled upon something impossible.

He was drawing! The purebred beast she knew as a mindless, mysterious, bloodthirsty thing, was *drawing*.

She settled back, afraid to distract him if she moved, though the focus on his face was so fierce, she doubted if he'd stop even if she shouted. *Drawing*. The word echoed in her mind, growing more absurd with each repetition. The harsh scratches of the twig filled the heavy silence. His hand moved with a desperate haste, and he occasionally shuffled to add details from different angles. More lines added to his creation, until it spanned a metre on each sides. His brows furrowed and his jaw set tight, his expression looked different than any version of him Olira had met before.

Twice, the twig snapped in his hand. The ground was cold and hard, resisting his strokes. He simply adjusted his grip and continued drawing, pressing harder. Olira plucked another twig from the ground and stripped it smooth with trembling fingers while she watched him. When the slave's twig snapped again, she offered him the new one. He took it with barely a glance, his fingers briefly brushing hers before he resumed his task.

Minutes stretched into what felt like hours, the cold air biting through Olira's coat. She barely noticed, neither did the slave. He was transfixed in his work, and she was transfixed on him, still confused and mesmerised, like she was witnessing Twelve's miracle. Eventually, curiosity got the better of her, and she stood quietly, stepping closer to see what he was drawing.

It took her a moment to make sense of the lines. At first, they seemed like random shapes and patterns, but then, she saw it.

"It's a map," she breathed.

The slave didn't respond. He continued adding details to the map; curves that represented mountains, squiggles that were rivers, and dots that had to be cities. Most people in Oxreach had never seen the map of Chinderia. The townsfolk only cared about where Oxreach was in relation to Kiore and Kilrer, the nearest two cities. And they knew the roads that connected Oxreach to the several towns and villages in West Kilrer region. They could spend their entire lives without ever needing to see the map of Chinderia.

Olira's father had shown her maps before, pointing to the faintly sketched ridges and naming places she'd never visited. Very little of those places had stayed in her mind. She had no clue how to read a map, but after studying the slave's creation for long minutes, she recognised some of the landmarks that identified West Kilrer region.

Why was he drawing a map of Chinderia? And more importantly, where did he learn that from? Was he really drawing it from memory, or making it up? Olira didn't know enough geography to pull him up on it, but the details he placed in West Kilrer region seemed accurate enough.

The questions pressed her lips, but she held them back, enjoying the beauty of the map instead. It wasn't elegant, the lines too rough and crude, but it was beautiful in its own way.

She noticed some sections of the map were more detailed than others. The corners and edges were left less defined, the lines faint and sparse. The slave seemed to focus his effort on an area surrounded by lots of mountains. He kept carving more lines there, blowing the loose dirt away and adding more details with persistent strokes. Olira chewed her lip, feeling a distant annoyance for not being educated enough to recognise where those mountains were.

The slave's movements slowed. He shifted from one side to the other, brushing the dirt in an almost perfectionistic manner. Then, he stabbed the twig into the middle of the mountains.

Olira's heart thudded in her chest. A mix of dread and excitement left her breathless. She pulled her coat tighter, her gaze flicking between the mountains and the slave, as she voiced the question that he clearly invited her to ask.

"What's there?"

The slave answered without taking his eyes off the spot marked by the twig. "Euroad."

"Euroad... The city of Euroad?" She vaguely remembered the name. The slave nodded and waited for her to ask the next question. Olira bit her lip, an apprehension creeping up her spine as if she was being led into a trap she couldn't see.

A trap she was too curious to avoid.

"And what's in Euroad?" she asked.

"Twilight of Infinity." His voice quivered almost imperceptibly. He pressed his lips, his eyes still fixed on the twig, and he let the silence pressure Olira to ask the next question.

"And what is that?"

"It's a tournament where the winner is granted his freedom."

Olira recoiled as if the words had physically hit her. Her thoughts spiralled, colliding with one another in a frantic attempt to reason. *Impossible*. What she thought those words implied — what the slave meant by them — was impossible. It was absurd. It couldn't be true.

The slave didn't speak, forcing Olira to fill the silence with the next question, but she couldn't work out what that was. She opened her mouth, but the words tangled on her tongue. "What... Why... What..." Her voice broke, and she gripped her coat tighter like it was the only thing anchoring her. She rested her forehead on her palm and took a deep breath to steady herself. Pinning her gaze on the man, she asked, "*What are you saying?*"

The slave didn't answer immediately. He took his time, his focus lingering on the map, while the storm raged inside Olira.

Oddly, part of her wanted to cheer him on, urge him to speak. *Come on, say it. Strike me Twelve times. Say it. Say it.* Her heart raced with dread, but it wasn't enough to drown out her need to know, like a moth circling the flame. It was the way someone would watch a lightning bolt strike a tree — terrified yet compelled to see it happen, no matter the cost.

Finally, the slave lifted his head, met her gaze, and spoke: "I want my freedom."

10

BEAST

Olira's world came crashing down.

Beast saw it on her face. The moment she realised what she thought she knew about the world, about purebreds and about him, was all a lie.

She took another step back as she confronted the meaning of Beast's words. A purebred wanting his freedom. Beast didn't blame her reaction. Her shock was justified. It was unheard of.

Beast's heart pounded in his ears. He'd never felt nerves of this kind when stepping into an arena. Not even when he was going against a bear, naked and unarmed. He'd take Marzul any day over being the recipient of whatever reaction Olira was about to give.

This was a bad idea. She was going to order him to shut up and never bring this up again. Maybe punish him. Collar him to teach him his place.

I'm not a bad person, Olira's words rang in his head again. But they weren't strong enough to counter the doubt that climbed into his chest.

Do not look away, Keder hissed in his ears, sensing Beast's desire to withdraw and shut down again.

He was still surprised Olira couldn't hear the High Fiend. He'd thought he was going crazy when he first heard Keder's voice in his head this morning. Then Keder had explained that only Beast could hear him and assured him that he wasn't simply imagining.

Do not stand, Keder instructed calmly. *Remain on your knees. Do not speak. Let her drown.*

Beast's eyebrows twitched with confusion — what did that mean, letting her drown? — but he followed Keder's instructions.

Drawing the map was Beast's idea, but Keder had been guiding his words. And Beast admitted he needed the guidance, because he had no clue what to say next.

Neither did Olira, as it appeared. She opened and closed her mouth, nothing but babbles coming out of her lips. In a way, she did look like she was drowning. She ran her hand through her face and finally collected herself enough to speak.

"You... You want your freedom?"

Beast nodded, and fear burrowed itself deeper in his chest. It was a different type of fear, one he'd only felt once before. Back at Castle Brinescar, when he'd first realised they would take Saradra away from him. Speaking of his desire for freedom out loud, confessing how much he wanted it, left him vulnerable to the crippling fear of disappointment. Of loss. The prospect of not getting what he wanted the most was completely crushing.

Now, he was the one drowning.

"How?" Olira asked, her eyes hard.

A lump sat on Beast's throat and stole his voice. He didn't know how to answer that.

Olira pushed her coat off her shoulders like she was hot. Anger brewed beneath her expression, adding tension to her entire body. "Why didn't you say anything before?"

Tell her you tried to and she shut you down, Keder whispered.

"I tried to," Beast said. His voice was too weak, she barely heard him. And her expression darkened even more.

"Why didn't you say anything at the farm?"

I needed time to heal, Keder gave him the words. Beast opened his mouth to speak, but the words caught in his throat. Olira's expectant gaze pinned him in place, leaving him certain that whatever he said would be met with harsh dismissal.

Trust me. Tell her you needed time to heal.

"I needed time." Beast's voice faltered, rough and barely audible. "To heal."

"You've healed from your injury months ago! Why did you wait until..." She blinked, the anger slipping from her face. Something she noticed on his face stopped her cold. Her shoulders sagged, the tension lifting just a little bit. "Heal from what?" she asked softly.

Beast waited for Keder to give him the next words, but the High Fiend went quiet.

He wasn't sure how to answer the question, and he felt crushed under Olira's gaze. His gaze dropped away, his jaw tightening stiff. When he breathed, the cold smell of damp earth and dead leaves were replaced by the faint scent of Saradra's hair. He felt the warmth of her hand brushing against his cold, stiff fingers. He heard her laughter carried away with the wind.

His next inhale was tainted by the bitter smell of blood.

He remembered how her broken limbs fell as he tried to hold her together in his arms.

Olira was quiet. So was Keder. Beast desperately waited for the High Fiend's voice, to pull him out of this vulnerable, miserable silence. But Keder had abandoned him, left him exposed to Olira's scrutinising eyes.

Fuck him, Beast thought. He pulled the collar of his shirt up to wipe his face and pushed everything down, putting himself together piece by piece.

When he stood and faced Olira, he found tears welling in her eyes.

"What have they done to you?" she asked softly.

Excellent, Keder whispered. *Now you have her.*

Beast scowled. His cold fingers, sore from pressing the rough twig into the dirt, curled into fists. He had no intention of answering her question. And he was done listening to Keder's whispers.

The High Fiend chuckled softly and withdrew to his corner. Beast faced Olira alone.

"I want my freedom."

Olira took a jagged breath. "I gave you a chance. I-I gave you *every chance* to say something. I even set you free once. Why didn't you run?"

"I don't want to be hunted." Beast rubbed the tattoo on his neck. "I want my freedom. Let me buy it from you."

His words landed like a hammer, forcing Olira to take another step back. Distance stretched between them. The howling wind stopped and the barren trees around them fell eerily still.

Olira's breath fogged in front of her face. Her nose and cheeks were flushed from the cold, yet she barely seemed to notice, her coat forgotten on the ground. She didn't even try to speak. She just stared at him like a fresh freeborn facing a purebred for the first and last time.

Without a word, she turned on her heels. Her boots crunched over the undergrowth as she walked away from him.

"Don't follow me," she said over her shoulder when Beast took a hesitant step after her. Her voice trembled despite its sharp edge.

Beast tracked her retreating figure as she made her way to a rock formation jutting from the forest floor. She climbed it slowly, stiff with anger — or maybe fear. At the top, she stood still, staring out over the grove. Her hair whipped in the wind, and for a moment, she looked like she was part of the landscape, carved out of the same cold, unyielding stone.

Beast remained where he was. He snatched a twig off the ground and began fiddling with it. What was she doing? The silence pressed against his frayed nerves. Minutes later, when she still didn't move, Beast found himself pacing.

His mind churned, restless and frantic. She was going to deny him. She was going to order him to never speak of freedom again. If he had only explained it better. Made her understand. If he could just talk like a normal man. Like... Like Jygan.

The twig snapped in his hand and he tossed the pieces aside.

He glanced at her again. She was sitting now, perched on the rock with her shoulders stiff and knees pulled up.

His legs carried him a step forward before Keder's voice whispered sharply, *Do not pursue her. Not yet.*

Doubt sank its claws into him. His legs froze, though his eyes remained on Olira. If he could just explain to her about...

Your words will do nothing to sway her, Keder said. *Let her convince herself.*

Beast returned to pacing, glancing at her every three steps. His gaze dropped to the map etched in the dirt, the imperfect lines mocking him. He stamped on it, erasing the lines under his boot. He sat back on his heels, defeated.

The sun moved discreetly in the sky. Almost an hour had passed when he stood and made another attempt to go after her.

How does a cornered animal fight? Keder hissed. *Harder than ever.*

Beast stopped himself again. The urge to follow her gnawed at him, but he forced it down.

Keep yourself busy with a menial task that fits your hands, Keder suggested with despise. *Perhaps build a fire.*

Beast glanced at the scattered branches and brittle leaves. "I don't know how to," he muttered. They didn't teach wilderness skills to purebreds. Why would they?

What a great occasion to learn.

Beast's fingers twitched. He glanced at Olira's hunched figure one more time. Begrudgingly, he admitted the High Fiend was right. He had to do something, keep himself busy.

He knelt and gathered a handful of twigs and branches, fumbling with the task as if his hands didn't belong to him. He'd seen others do this before. He piled the branches and leaves together and searched the backpack for a flint and steel.

His first attempt failed. So did the second. Hours blurred, and the shadows stretched, the pale light fading into an orange and grey. By the time a tiny flame caught, his hands were shaking from cold and frustration. He fed the flame, nurturing it to a proper fire. The flicker of warmth steadied him, even just for a moment.

His eyes drifted back to the rock where Olira still sat. She hadn't come down. As the light faded, he sat in the pleasant warmth of his fire. He spotted Olira's coat where she left it. He hesitated briefly before standing and picking it up.

Keder didn't stop him this time, and every step felt more confident than the one before. The walk to the rock felt longer than it was. He pulled himself on it with ease. The wind was more violent up here, it threatened to toss him down if he wasn't careful.

Olira was shivering, her arms wrapped tightly around herself. He draped the coat over her shoulders. She didn't look up at him, didn't even flinch, her gaze fixed on the sunset ahead.

Beast sat next to her. The silence was heavy, but it wasn't filled with tension this time. He stared at the faint glow of the sun dipping below the treetops.

Minutes stretched before he finally felt the urge to speak. "Do you know what a Grand Blood is?"

Olira shook her head without turning. Her hands clutched the edges of her coat, pulling it tighter.

"When a crowd favourite, famous beast ages, they arrange a Grand Blood for him. They pit him against a younger beast. And when he defeats him, they send two beasts together. And then three. And four... Until he falls."

Olira didn't react. He wasn't even sure if she was listening. The setting sun painted her face in a flame-coloured glow.

"When a beast wins Twilight of Infinity... his Owner earns thousands of Blues. More than what you can fetch for me at an auction."

Below them, the trees stood as stark silhouettes against the burning sky, their naked branches reaching up like pleading hands. A harsh wind picked up dead leaves and dirt, dragging them across the winter-kissed hills.

"If you take me to Arkala, a Grand Blood is the best fate I can hope for."

Olira cast a glance at him from the corner of her eye. Her pale lips pressed into a thin line. She surveyed the barren landscape ahead of them and sagged under her coat.

"I have to save my farm," she said apologetically.

Exhaustion weighed on Beast's shoulders. Suddenly, he was so tired, he wanted to sleep. He wanted to close his eyes and freeze on this rock, never wake up.

Olira's next question startled him so hard, he almost slipped.

"Can you win it?"

He turned his full body to Olira, his heart pounding in his chest.

"Twilight of Infinity," she said, her brown eyes lit with despair. "Can you win it?"

"Yes," Beast said. "You've seen me fight. I've killed—"

Just say yes, Keder hissed.

Beast snapped his mouth shut. He caught the subtle grimace on Olira's face just in time. Her fingers gripped the edges of her coat tighter.

"Yes," Beast repeated stiffly.

"We'll still have to go to Kilrer first. I need to send a message to Jygan."

Beast just stared at her, afraid to let the words fully sink in. She shifted on the rock, stretching her legs and back. Finally, she exhaled deeply.

"Yes," she said, the word quick and clipped, as if saying it faster would make it easier. "We're going to Euroad."

One moment, Beast was sitting on that cold rock, staring at the woman who owned him. The next, he was on his feet, scooping Olira into a hug.

She yelped, her feet dangling above the rock's surface. Her coat flew to the ground. She stiffened and her hands gripped his shoulders instinctively as if to push him away. "What are you doing?"

Beast lowered her clumsily. He was as shocked as she was. They were both lucky she didn't yell out his First Word in her panic. They would have tumbled off this rock and broken their necks.

Olira steadied herself, brushing her dress off with stiff movements. She shot him a sharp look and saw his horrified expression. "I'm not a hugger."

Beast shook his head. "It won't happen again."

Her lips pressed into a thin line. She fixed her dress again as her eyes darted down the rock, lingering on the campfire Beast had lit. "It's... it's fine. Just help me get off this rock before I freeze."

Beast grabbed her by the arms and eased her off the rock like she weighed nothing. Olira snatched her coat off the ground and shrugged it on as she walked towards the campfire.

Beast remained on the rock for a moment longer. The sun had vanished below the horizon, leaving the barren landscape bathed in deep blues and greys.

He tilted his head back, staring at the starless sky. The wind tousled his hair and tugged at his coat, its chill biting but invigorating. He drew in a slow breath of the crisp, fresh air, and for the first time in months, the gnawing ache in his chest dulled.

THE FLOODED CAVERN SHIMMERED faintly with the same pale light as before, the silver bars of Keder's cage glowing in the darkness. The hounds, their molten eyes dimmed, lay scattered along the edges of the cavern. The flames flickered lazily on their furs.

Beast stood knee-deep in the cool, black water, his chest rising and falling with the kind of exhilaration he hadn't felt in years. The tooth-shaped object lodged in his chest throbbed faintly, a dull, pulsing ache that he was used to ignoring. It never truly hurt, but it made its presence known, like a reminder of his connection to this place. The cool water brushed against his calves. The water level was higher than before, he realised absently, but the thought drifted away as quickly as it came.

"Euroad," he said, his voice strangled with excitement. "I'm going to Euroad. She's taking me to Twilight of Infinity!"

Keder's shadowy form shifted inside the cage like he was caught in a draught. "A human trusting another human," he said, his humming voice rich with smug amusement. "How novel."

Beast turned to the cage, his eyes alight with a rare spark of joy. "How did you know what to say?" he asked, an unsure grin tugging at the corners of his mouth. "And what not to say?"

"You dare demand that I, a Corespawn Monarch of the Shattered Home, The One Who Remains After Death, explain my speechcraft to your wretched slave-ears?" Keder's derision grated softly against the cavern walls, a sound both low and sharp, like a blade scraping stone.

"I... I didn't mean..." Beast's heart hammered against his ribs. Sweat beaded at his brow. He lowered his gaze and brought his hands together, folding into the posture that was so natural to him. A purebred awaiting punishment at the offence he had committed. Shadows writhed and stretched inside the cage, and the silence stretched, broken only by Beast's steady breathing. He could sense Keder's patient and cruel gaze, waiting for him to apologise, just so he could remind Beast how worthless his apology is. But his training urged Beast to keep his mouth shut.

The bars of the cage pulsed, and the chains rattled softly. A hatred for his own reaction flared in him. With trembling resolve, Beast forced his shoulders back, letting his hands drop to his sides. He breathed slow, steady breaths, though each felt like dragging a blade across raw flesh. He ran his fingers over his chest absently, feeling the jagged outline of the tooth beneath his skin.

After a long silence, Keder's voice cut through the stillness. "You must make amends for the offence you have incurred."

Beast's stomach dropped, leaving its place to a cold, hollow panic. The tooth beneath his skin pressed like a warning. He forced himself to glance through the bars, though every instinct screamed to look away.

"You placed your trust in me, and I delivered," Keder said, his words curling in the air like smoke. "Now I wish to see if I can trust you in return."

The shadows inside the cage shifted again, the darkness pressing hard against the glowing silver bars.

"Drink," Keder whispered. "Drink from the water and let us see if trust can flow both ways."

"Why?" Beast asked, his voice steady but tinged with wariness. He stared down at the black water.

"You dare question?" the High Fiend mused. The shadows within the cage swirled lazily.

Beast hesitated, then crouched slowly, his hand dipping into the cool water. He scooped up a handful, holding it close to his face. The liquid was pure black, so opaque he couldn't see his palm through it.

"What's in it?"

"It's only water," Keder replied smoothly.

Beast brought the handful closer to his face, inhaling cautiously. It didn't have a smell.

He hesitated, his thoughts swirling much like the smoke inside the cage. Keder had helped him more than any free men or women ever did. The High Fiend had come through, had proven that Beast could trust him. His fingers trembled slightly as he stared at the black water. It looked harmless.

The tooth throbbed faintly. A steady, annoying pulse beneath his chest.

He parted his fingers and let the liquid spill back into the water.

Beast stood slowly, his jaw tightening as he braced himself for whatever re-action Keder would give. The shadows inside the cage didn't erupt in fury, nor did the High Fiend lash out. Nothing changed in the slow, serene patterns of the swirling smoke. Beast waited, his heart pounding in anticipation.

"It's a long journey to Euroad," Keder said finally. His voice was laced with a quiet threat. "You are on your own now."

Before Beast could reply, the ground beneath him gave way. His feet sank into the watery mud. He gasped, his arms flailing by instinct despite knowing he was simply waking up from this place. Returning to Earthome. The black water rose rapidly around him, swallowing his legs, his chest, his shoulders. He closed his mouth shut before the water reached his face.

11

OLIRA

"Tell me something about yourself."

The slave dropped his clay bowl with a loud clang, spilling half his porridge on the frostbitten ground. He knelt and scooped what he could back into his bowl with trembling hands.

"What?" Olira said. "Did I say something wrong?"

The man shook his head, though his face blanched. He kept his eyes on the ground and shovelled porridge into his mouth with his fingers.

After revealing what he did yesterday, Olira had woken up, expecting to see a different man. She wasn't sure exactly what she was hoping for, but she was disappointed to find the same silent, distant man, his gaze fixed somewhere she couldn't follow.

She put her plate down and scowled at him over the crackling flame of their campfire. "Look at me. Please."

The slave's grey eyes met hers, his blank expression fracturing a brief moment. She cleared her throat, forcing her voice to sound gentle. "I'm risking everything here. My farm, my brothers — everything. I need to understand why."

The slave's eyes flicked across the campsite, their bedrolls on opposite sides of the campfire, and the large backpack with its flap open. He brought the bowl to his lips and took a large gulp.

"You've been pretending to be a mindless thing," Olira said. She remembered the unexpected display of affection she saw last night. She'd felt like a ragged doll in the beast's massive arms. It was frightening, confusing, and a little endearing at the same time.

"I get that you've been through a lot. You don't need to tell me all of that. But I need some answers. I need to know more. Deal?"

The man put his bowl down and nodded.

"Let's start with why you want your freedom," Olira said. "I thought pure-breds never wanted anything?"

"They don't."

"Then how come you do?"

"I just do." He shrugged, then stood and started packing their bowls away.

"I said I need some answers," Olira said carefully. "We made a deal."

"I don't know how to answer, Owner. I... I just want my freedom." He rubbed the tattoo on his neck like he wanted to peel it off. "I want to be free of this. I want peace."

Olira nodded slowly. She stood and began helping him pack up the camp. "Since when?"

"A few months, Owner."

"Okay, stop calling me Owner from now on. Olira is fine."

He nodded as he bundled the bedrolls and strapped them to the backpack.

"Have you ever told anyone else that you wanted your freedom?"

He shook his head. He lifted the heavy backpack, slung it over his shoulder, and waited for Olira to lead the way. Olira grabbed her purse, pulling its long strap over her head, and led the way back to the main road.

"Where did you learn to draw a map?"

"I saw a drawing."

She glared at him suspiciously. "You saw a drawing of a map, and you memorised it just like that?"

"I saw the drawing... hundreds of times."

"Why? Why would anyone show a beast a drawing of Chinderia's map hundreds of times?"

The man scratched the back of his head. The straps of the backpack dug into his shoulders. "The map was in the room and… I was there."

"Hundreds of times?"

"Yes."

Olira exhaled her frustration through her nose. Trying to have a meaningful conversation with this man was like hacking at a tree trunk with a wooden spoon. She studied the bare trees and scrawny bushes on either side of the road, giving him time to see if he would offer anything else, but the man was content with the silence.

"Do you have a name?" she asked after a while.

"You haven't named me."

"I'm not naming a grown man. It's weird."

The nameless man didn't reply, but at least he shrugged to communicate he was still part of the conversation. This was how low Olira's expectations from this exchange had dwindled. She was being satisfied with anything he offered.

"What were you called before?"

The man flicked dirt off his pants. "Mutt."

"Mutt?" Olira scrunched her face. "Really? I'm not calling you Mutt."

The man raised his eyebrows in question.

"That's demeaning," Olira explained.

"I've been called worse."

"What about when you were younger? Surely you had a name growing up? Where are you from?"

His steps faltered briefly, though he didn't fall behind. He fixed the straps over his shoulder again and glanced at the sky. The sun was barely cresting over the horizon. He muttered something.

"What was that?"

"Faychill Ranch."

"Oh? What did they call you when you were—?"

"Beast. You can call me Beast."

"That's not a name. That's—"

"May I… umm… May I train, Own— Olira?"

"Train?"

"Yes. I only have a few months to get back in shape before Twilight of Infinity."

"You're not in shape?" she eyed the Beast's bulk without turning her head.

"I... umm... I lost some muscle." His voice faded to a mumble like he was ashamed.

Olira raised her eyebrows at the bulging muscles that did not quite look lost. She shook her head.

"Sure, train if you want. Wait. You said you only have a few months?"

The man nodded. "Twilight of Infinity is in spring."

Olira froze mid-step, her breath catching as she turned to face the slave. "Spring?" she repeated, her eyes locking onto his.

"I'll just do an iron pace workout on the road." He gestured up the road, then back the way they came from. "I'll keep up." He hauled the backpack high above his shoulders, then started jogging back.

Olira chewed the inside of her cheek as she watched his retreating figure. When he reached a bend in the road, he turned and sprinted back toward her with a burst of speed, flying past her and not stopping until he was a few metres ahead of her. He dropped into push-ups, the backpack an added weight on his shoulders. When she caught up, he jumped to his feet and jogged back again.

"Spring," she repeated breathlessly as she glared at the man. The winter was only just beginning. Spring was months away. She would have to stay away from her farm much longer than she intended.

Beast flew past her again, leaving her to drown under the weight of the promise she made to a man she knew nothing about.

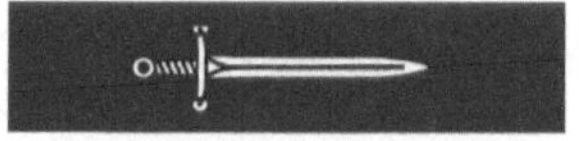

Olira tossed the leaves she'd plucked from the roadside into the boiling pot of stew and gave it an aggressive stir. The late afternoon chill crept under her layers, sending shivers through her despite her proximity to the campfire. Her breath fogged in the frigid air, and her nose and ears stung like they'd been turned to ice.

And yet, the slave had stripped off his shirt, sweat glistening on his scarred skin as he hung upside down from a branch like a Twelve-times-cursed bat. Arms crossed over his chest, he pulled himself up smoothly, then lowered back down, repeating the motion as though it served some grand purpose.

He looked utterly ridiculous.

If Olira had caught her brothers hanging from a tree and flopping like a mule's tail, she would've given them a proper task to waste their energy on.

Scowling, she crushed another handful of leaves and tossed them into the stew, not caring that it would end up more bitter than she'd intended. She was trying. Trying to be friendly. Approachable. Civil. But the man was so blatantly avoiding her that it made her jaw clench.

Beast. Not 'the man'. He'd called himself Beast, which was the most unimaginative name she could have thought of for a purebred beast. But at least it was better than 'the slave', she supposed. Or 'Mutt'.

Back when she'd believed he was just a hollow shell of a person, his silence, as frustrating as it was, had at least made sense. Now that she knew there was more to him, that quietness took on a sharper edge. He wasn't just vacant — he was hiding something.

He'd spent the entire day training on the road, keeping his distance from her. Every time she approached with a question, he gave only the briefest of answers, never satisfying her curiosity.

Olira sighed sharply, jabbing the ladle into the pot. She was tired. Tired of these one-sided conversations. Tired of his secretive ways.

She tucked the remaining leaves into her pouch and brushed her hands off against her coat as she straightened. "Maybe you should have a rest," she called out.

Beast didn't pause his absurd motion. "I'm not tired, Owner," he replied without looking at her, his voice steady despite the strain. He lowered himself back down, sweat running down his scarred back, then hauled his chest towards his knees again.

"I told you not to call me Owner."

"I'm not tired, Olira." Beast exhaled as he finished another repetition, his chest heaving slightly.

"Do you have to train this much?"

"Yes."

Olira crossed her arms tightly, the cold nipping at her fingertips as she paced around the tree. She stopped where she could at least see his face when he lowered himself again. Beast pulled himself back up, corded muscles on his stomach shifting under the sheen of sweat. His blond hair, damp and darkened with sweat, clung to his forehead in unruly curls. His face was flushed from exertion as he lowered himself with control.

Olira's gaze flicked down, tracing the brands that marred his chest, their jagged shapes partially obscured by his crossed arms. The marks always caught her attention. They were not random battle scars, they were done to him intentionally, each circular mark measured and placed symmetrically. She considered asking about them — how he'd gotten them, what they meant — but the thought of another dismissive reply stopped her.

"Dinner's almost ready. Take a break."

"Another set."

"You've been working hard all day."

"I haven't trained in months."

"Enough. Get down. Now."

Beast paused at the bottom of his motion, hanging still for a moment, as his gaze met hers. His chest rose and fell, his stomach taut and rippling with the effort, droplets of sweat rolling off his skin. Then he swung sharply, grabbed the branch with one hand, and landed on his feet with an utterly unnecessary backflip. He snatched his shirt and pulled it over his head as he strode to the campfire without a word.

Olira dished him a generous amount of stew, then scooped some for herself too and sat near him. They ate in silence for a few minutes, the shadows lengthening across the clearing as the sun dipped behind the tree line.

"We've made a deal," Olira said slowly. She glared at him, the stew leaving a bitter taste in her mouth.

Beast shifted uncomfortably on his log seat. At least he had the decency to meet her gaze and not act clueless. He knew what she meant. He raised the bowl to his lips to buy himself some time and gulped another mouthful of the bitter stew, scrunching his face briefly. When he met her eyes again, something in him finally yielded. His shoulders slumped, and he gave a subtle nod.

Olira's grip on her bowl loosened just slightly. She scooped the last mouthful with her spoon and set her bowl beside her.

"What if you don't win?" she asked. The question was brewing at the back of her mind all day. "What happens then?"

"I die."

She looked up sharply. Beast had said it with such indifference, as if discussing the weather or a recipe. The firelight sent flickering shadows across his face. He seemed more interested in scraping the last overcooked piece of vegetable into his mouth than living or dying. Eventually, he noticed the look on Olira's face. He licked his fingers clean and set his bowl down.

"It's... umm... It's a tournament," he offered, like that was enough explanation.

Olira ran her hands through her hair, trying to fix the knots that the wind had braided. The stew churned in her stomach. The campfire burned brighter as the last of the grey light stretched away from them.

"I won't lose."

Beast's voice remained maddeningly calm. Matter of fact. He glanced at the pot that hung over the flames, still a bit of stew left over at the bottom.

"You sound so sure of yourself."

"I am. I just... just need to get back in shape."

Olira scoffed. She should have felt reassured by his confidence, but instead, it irritated her. It was like the risk of death was so beneath him that it didn't even warrant his concern.

Olira followed his gaze to the steaming pot. She opened her mouth to tell him to help himself, then stopped. She wondered if he would ask for it, or simply get up and take it himself.

"Do you have to kill your opponents?" she asked. "Can you leave them alive?"

Beast tilted his head, his grey eyes narrowing slightly. "Why?"

"Why?" Olira repeated, stumbling over the word. "Because... just— *Why?*"

He studied her intently, his brow furrowing as if trying to make sense of her question. Genuine curiosity and confusion flickered in his eyes. The weight of his attention unsettled Olira, stirring an uncomfortable tightness in her stomach. She felt the need to break free from his focus.

Standing abruptly, she grabbed two pieces of cloth, folding them in each hand. She used them to shield her hands from the heat and lifted the steaming pot off the flames, setting it aside to cool. Beast's gaze lingered on the pot as she sat back down. Yet he still didn't ask for more.

"Can you leave them alive?" she asked again.

"It's a tournament," Beast replied with a shrug.

"So? Can't you just knock them out or something?"

"It's a tournament," he repeated with a flat and somewhat confused look. "Not a Dawnblood."

"I don't know what that means."

He scratched the back of his head. "Tournaments are to the death. Dawn-bloods are... like a dance show. Stops at the first drop of blood. No one dies." He paused and pursed his lips before adding. "Usually."

Olira mulled over his words. "You don't seem bothered by killing."

"I'm not."

"You enjoy it," Olira said, her voice sharpening into an accusation. "I've seen your face that night when you were fighting. You love it."

Beast sat still, his expression unreadable, as he appeared to weigh her state-ment. The silence stretched, broken only by the faint crackle of the fire. He nodded thoughtfully before he spoke his conclusion.

"I enjoy a good fight. I'm good at it."

"How can you enjoy violence? You're taking someone's life! Do you not feel remorse?"

"I don't know them."

Olira's eyes widened, her voice rising with frustration. "It doesn't matter. They're still people. They have thoughts and feelings. *Rhoas.* Even those bandits, they probably had families. People who cared about them."

"I don't know them either."

"*It doesn't matter!* Killing people is wrong. It's bad!" Olira found herself on her feet, her fists clenched at her sides.

Beast's jaw ticked, his eyes fixed on the campfire. "Yes, Owner."

"*Olira!*"

"Yes, Olira."

"I'm not asking you to agree with me."

His jaw tightened again, but he didn't speak and didn't look up. He rested his elbows on his knees, his fingers twitching.

"Speak," Olira huffed.

"I live to serve—"

"Don't you dare say that stupid phrase!" she cut him off. "I know what you're doing. That's how you get out of difficult conversations. Not this time."

"What do you want to hear?" he asked quietly, finally lifting his head. His grey eyes met hers, sending a shiver down her spine. "That I feel remorse?"

Olira swallowed hard, suddenly unsure of herself.

"I don't," he continued, his voice steady and cold. And dangerously quiet.

She tried to find her voice, but the words were stuck in her throat.

"You're saying killing is bad," he said, his gaze unwavering. "I was bred to kill. That's what I do. Why I exist."

"No one is born a killer," Olira said shakily. "The Pyres say—"

"They used to tie old and crippled slaves to posts and make us stab them when we were younger than Andar and Kowas."

Olira's stomach heaved violently. The image his words conjured made her feel sick, and she sank back onto her seat. His eyes, cold and detached, followed her.

"So no, I don't feel bothered for killing," he said casually. "I live to serve, I breathe to please. What's the point of remorse?"

"What's the point of remorse?" she echoed numbly, her voice barely above a whisper. "Remorse shows that you're human."

"I'm a beast."

He held her gaze for a long moment, watching it all sink. Then, without another word, he snatched his bowl, stood, and walked over to the pot. He tossed his bowl beside it and walked away.

Later that night, as she curled into her bedroll near the crackling campfire, her sleep was restless. Images of Andar and Kowas flashed in her mind, their small hands holding blades as they stood before helpless figures tied to posts. The thought haunted her long after the fire's last embers faded into darkness.

12

BEAST

Beast hunched by the smouldering campfire, feeding it a small branch. The flames crackled softly, licking at the wood with lazy hunger. The air was sharp with the chill of early morning, the sky above still a deep black, stars slowly losing their glow.

Olira was bundled tightly in her bedroll, her form barely visible under the layers. Her breathing was slow and even, a contrast to Beast's restless thoughts. She hadn't stirred once, even when he moved to tend the fire. He glanced at her briefly before turning his attention back to the flickering flames.

He picked up another piece of wood and laid it carefully on the burning branches. Earlier, he had almost killed the fire, piling too much wood and nearly smothering the flames. The fire needed wood to survive, but too much of it just as easily could kill it. It was fascinating in its way, but also irritating. Everything seemed to demand a delicate balance.

The crackle of the fire and the mixed sounds of the night filled the quiet, but it wasn't enough to drown out the thoughts that kept him awake most of the night. In the few hours he had drifted off, he hadn't seen the flooded cavern. He hadn't seen — or heard — Keder since the High Fiend had declared that Beast was on his own now.

The threat wasn't what kept him awake. It was the argument with Olira that had lingered at the back of his mind.

Beast glanced at her sleeping figure, her brown hair sticking out from under the blankets. She looked nothing like Saradra, despite the iron will and assertiveness they both shared. Nothing. But the way she pestered him with questions, always digging, always prodding, trying to make him talk about himself... It reminded him of Saradra more than he cared to admit.

Answering some of those questions, telling Olira even the smallest truths about himself, felt like ripping open a wound that had barely healed. The way her eyes filled with curiosity and distrust as she watched him — it made him want to run, to put as much distance as he could between himself and that gaze.

Do you not feel remorse?

Beast peeled at the bark of a branch, the rough texture splitting under his fingers as he fiddled with it. He tossed the shredded pieces into the flames, watching them curl and blacken.

Remorse.

He didn't feel the emotion for most of the men he'd killed — slaves or free men. At least, he didn't think he did. But since Olira's question, faces had started surfacing from the depths of his memories.

He scowled, trying to focus on the flames as the faces multiplied in his mind. Men he'd fought. Slaves he'd been ordered to kill. He couldn't call any of them friends, but he'd known some of them before taking their lives. He'd pushed those faces so far down, buried them so deep, but now they clawed their way up, demanding to be acknowledged.

I'm a beast, he thought to himself. *I enjoy fighting. Winning. I have no use for remorse.*

With a sharp motion, he threw the stripped branch into the fire. It sizzled and crackled, the sound loud in the quiet camp. Beast stood and stretched, the muscles in his back and shoulders stiff from hours of sleeplessness.

His gaze shifted back to Olira, her face half-hidden in her bedroll. She was risking a lot for him. He couldn't deny that. She'd agreed to help him, putting her own future at risk. Her family's future at risk. If all she wanted in return was for him to tell her a few things about himself, he could do that. He'd suffered worse.

"I'll try harder," he muttered under his breath, the words so quiet even he barely heard them.

Olira stirred, her head shifting slightly under the blankets. Beast stilled, unsure if she'd heard him. Her breathing evened out again, and he turned his attention back to the fire.

A few minutes later, she stirred more noticeably. Her hand slipped free of the blanket as she rubbed her face. Her eyes blinked open, catching sight of him almost immediately.

She looked at him with that same mix of wariness and distrust, her brow furrowing slightly.

"Good morning," Beast said, the words tasting awkward on his tongue.

Her brows rose, and for a moment, she didn't reply, as though the greeting had caught her off guard.

"May I go for a run?" Beast blurted out. Speaking without permission, asking for things — it still felt strange. A part of him wished he could fall back into the simplicity of acting like a purebred. He pointed toward the hill a short distance away, its outline faint against the early light of dawn. "Just up that hill. I'll remain in your sight. I'll be very quick."

Olira blinked, clearly still processing his sudden change in demeanour. After a beat, she stood and spoke as she folded her blanket. "Sure."

Brimming with a need to move, Beast jumped to his feet. He pulled his shirt off, folding it neatly and leaving it beside the log near the fire. The cold morning air bit at his skin, but he barely noticed.

He started at a steady jog toward the hill, his feet crunching softly against the cold ground. The base of the hill was covered in tall grass. The blades were damp with dew, and they rustled faintly as he pushed through. For a moment, he disappeared into the grass, its height swallowing him whole, before the ground beneath him began to slope upwards sharply.

The climb was steep. Early morning's dim light still cloaked the ground beneath his boots. He stepped carefully while still pushing himself. His muscles stretched and worked, the tension easing from his chest, replaced by fresh air. Each step, each push forward brought a strange clarity to his thoughts.

By the time he reached the top, the sky was painted in a grey light. The sun crept over the horizon, rewarding his hard work with a view in brilliant hues of gold and crimson. He stopped, his chest rising and falling as he stood still for a moment, taking it all in.

He glanced briefly down toward the camp and saw Olira crouched by the fire, leaning over the pot as she prepared breakfast. She didn't look his way.

He felt a pang of gratitude towards her. Despite her sharp words and distrustful gaze, she had said yes. She had agreed to help him get his freedom.

Turning his gaze back to the horizon, Beast let his thoughts wander. Something about this view made him think of freedom. How close it felt now, even with all the distance still left to cover. All the fights he still needed to win. Twilight of Infinity wasn't going to be an easy fight, though he was still certain — sure of himself, as Olira had called it — that he could win.

He *would* win.

The sharp chill of the morning air reminded him he'd been standing still for too long. Cold muscles after a workout invited cramps — or worse, injuries. He stretched his muscles, warming them up for the jog back to the camp. Olira was moving about the campsite, packing her belongings and occasionally giving the pot a stir.

Beast was mid-stretch when something caught his eye. A faint cloud of dirt rose in the distance. At first, he thought it might be the wind, but it moved too straight along the road.

A tension twisted in his stomach.

This wasn't the wind. These were riders — three of them — heading straight for the camp.

Straight for Olira.

His heart lurched. Without thinking, he started running.

13

BEAST

THE SLOPE WAS TOO steep, the ground too uneven, but he ran as fast as he could dare. One wrong step and he could go tumbling. A rolled ankle, a broken leg — or worse, a broken neck. The fear of suffering a permanent injury was deep rooted— what was the use for a beast if he couldn't fight anymore? — but that fear now clashed with his concern for Olira's safety. He forced himself to pick his steps carefully, his eyes flicking between his next footing and the camp below.

Olira hadn't noticed the riders yet. She was still busy with the pot, oblivious to the threat. Beast gritted his teeth and quickened his pace, his boots slapping against the packed earth as he jumped over jagged rocks and loose patches of dirt—

His foot slipped.

The sky and the land swapped places in a blur as he rolled down the hill. He hit the ground hard, his shoulder scraping against a rock as he rolled. His breath got knocked from his lungs.

For a moment, he lay still, the sharp sting of a cut on his elbow stealing his focus briefly. His chest heaved as he assessed the damage, his mind racing with the familiar, suffocating fear. He moved his limbs and exhaled his relief when he found no sharp pain, no grinding in his joints. Just a scrape. It was just a scrape. He forced himself to sit up, blood pounding in his ears as he glanced toward the road.

The riders were closer now, and although they had slowed down, they were still headed straight for Olira. She had finally noticed them. She stood still, watching their approach with no visible sign of fear. She didn't try to run or hide. She just stood there, her hands on her hips, her head tilted slightly like she was more irritated by the riders' presence than concerned.

Beast cursed under his breath. He wouldn't reach her in time, but he had to try.

He climbed back on his feet, grimacing at the sting on his arm and shoulder, and continued running as fast as he could dare. He reached the tall grass at the bottom of the hill just as the riders entered the campsite. The tall blades obscured his sight, scratching against his skin as he pushed through. He couldn't see anything but the blurred green of the grass as he flew through it. His ears strained for the inevitable sounds of struggle and murder: screams, shouts, steel. He heard nothing.

Beast shot from the tall grass like an arrow loosed from a bow, aimed directly at the nearest rider.

The man was massive, almost as large as Beast himself, seated confidently on a warhorse that matched his size. Black heavy armour glinted faintly in the early morning light. The man's posture was relaxed, his hand resting on the hilt of his sword. The other gripped the reins firmly, holding the horse steady.

He didn't draw his sword.

The man had seen a purebred beast charging at full speed at him and hadn't even flinched. He was either dumb, or his nerves were made of steel. Or...

Beast heard the sound of Olira's laughter and slid to a halt mere steps away from the warrior, loose dirt spraying up from his boots as he stopped just short of crashing into the horse. He turned his head, his chest heaving, and saw one of the other riders standing beside Olira, talking to her.

Olira was laughing.

Not screaming. Not fighting. Laughing.

Her laughter faded the moment she spotted him. Her eyes widened as the realisation of what had almost happened hit her. How close Beast had come to tearing into these three men. Her face paled, her body stiffening as though bracing for the worst.

"Stop!" she shouted, holding out a hand, her voice tight with alarm. "It's okay, they're fine!"

If Beast hadn't already stopped himself, her words would have been too late.

He nodded sharply, taking a deliberate step back, his hands at his sides. The last thing he wanted was for her to panic and paralyse him.

The big warrior sat rigid on his horse, one hand still resting on the hilt of his sheathed sword. His expression was calm, but Beast noticed the tension in his posture. His knuckles had gone white around the reins, blood drawn from the grip. Sweat gathered at his brow. Maybe his nerves weren't entirely made of steel after all.

When Beast took another step back, the warrior's hand relaxed, moving away from the sword. But his dark eyes never left Beast, tracking his every move.

Beast studied him in return. Short, tousled dark hair. A clean-shaved square jaw, a prominent brow, a strong nose. Nothing particularly remarkable about his face. Just the weathered look of a warrior.

He was a walking armoury. His chest piece was adorned with the emblem of a horse with bat wings — Kiejain's symbol. The leader of the Twelve Riders, the god of warriors. A second set of armour was packed and strapped neatly to his saddle. A short sword hung at his belt, a long sword was sheathed on the saddle, and a massive two-handed sword, wrapped in cloth, was secured across his back. A shield with the same winged horse symbol dangled from the side of his saddle.

Weapons and armour didn't make anyone a good warrior. Beast felt a strong desire to test this man at battle, though he wouldn't act on it. Not with Olira still watching him and looking too pale as she shifted under the weight of the situation.

"I am so sorry," she said to the man she had been speaking to. Her voice was tight with a forced calm. "He's just..."

"It's quite all right," the man replied smoothly, raising his palms in a calming gesture.

He was younger than the massive warrior, perhaps in his mid-twenties, with a lean, athletic build and pale skin untouched by scars. Short-cropped blond hair framed his clean-shaven face. His striking blue eyes, polished features, and effortless charm made him handsome in a refined way. A short sword was strapped at his side, but it looked more decorative than practical. His clothes were finely tailored, expensive despite the road dust and mud clinging to them.

No wonder Olira didn't see him as a threat. He looked more like a travelling noble than anyone they'd met in Master Ashin's caravan. Even the merchant himself would look like a peasant beside him.

The blond man offered Olira a disarming smile, touched with an arrogant grin. "You never know whom you'll encounter on the roads these days," he said lightly. His gaze flicked to Beast — or more precisely, to the brands etched into Beast's bare chest.

Beast remembered he was still shirtless, his brands fully exposed. He studied the man's face more closely, and a cold dread curled in his stomach. There was something familiar in the sharp cheekbones, the curve of his mouth.

What if this man really was a noble? What if he had been a guest at one of Leonis's feasts? What if he could identify him as Lion of Zarall?

"I really do apologise," Olira said again, a slight tremble on her voice.

"It's okay, Mistress, please. No harm done." He flashed her another bright smile that captured Olira's gaze far too long than Beast liked. "I've seen that you were on your own, and just wanted to check in." His gaze tracked Beast as the purebred snatched his shirt from the log and pulled it over his head backwards in his haste. "I can see that you are well protected."

Beast fixed his shirt, still feeling the blond man's curiosity on him. The warrior hadn't pulled his sharp focus from Beast either. Beast's gaze slid to the third man — the one furthest of the three — seated quietly on his horse. He almost choked when he caught the flash of a small crossbow, just as the man slipped it beneath his cloak.

He cursed under his breath.

Now he understood why the warrior had been so calm when Beast charged. It wasn't just nerves of steel. He'd had cover.

Beast clenched his jaw as the realisation sank in. One more step, and he would've taken a crossbow bolt to the gut.

The third man tilted his head and grinned — an easy, casual smile with a flicker of friendliness — as if he knew exactly what Beast was thinking. Beast had dismissed him as the least threatening of the three: young, lanky, with only a plated lamellar for armour. But he was now realising just how wrong he'd been.

The third rider had cropped, light brown hair, pale skin dusted with freckles, and the sharp, angular features of a Kaldorian. Without the traditional war paint they wore into battle, Kaldorians were hard to recognise — particularly as he sat on his horse, unassuming and smiling.

Kaldorians excelled at two things; long-range weapons, and hand-to-hand combat. *Vehl'Serra*, their traditional fighting style, was fast, brutal, and closely guarded. If that young, lanky, grinning man was a master of *Vehl'Serra*, he was far more dangerous than Beast first assumed.

Olira continued talking to the blond man, her tone polite and apologetic. "I really appreciate your concern, but I'm good. Thank you."

The blond man smiled lightly, brushing a speck of dust off his coat. "Honestly, I should've been more worried about my own safety," he said with a soft chuckle, his eyes flicking briefly to Beast.

A fleeting look of guilt tightened Olira's features. She hesitated, then spoke quickly, her voice quieter than before. "I'm so sorry again. Please, stay for breakfast. It's the least I can do."

Beast's fingers twitched. What was she thinking?

"It's okay, Mistress," the blond man said politely, inclining his head. "We wouldn't want to impose."

"Oh come on, Lodi, just say yes," the Kaldorian chimed in. He threw his leg over his saddle and landed lightly on the ground. A flash of steel glinted under his cloak — throwing discs or knives, Beast guessed. The young man pulled a mock grimace. "I can't suffer another batch of your cooking."

The blond man — Lodi — looked horrified. His cheeks flushed faintly as he stammered, "Rude!"

The Kaldorian's sharp grin widened as he turned to Olira. "Mistress, I'm fairly certain our leftovers killed a poor badger last night. I heard its wails all night long."

Lodi tilted his head. "Oh, I thought that was Valnar's snoring?"

The big warrior watched Beast out of the corner of his eyes. He didn't smile, but he let out a low, amused grunt.

Olira pressed her lips together, stifling a soft chuckle. She seemed more relaxed now, her posture less stiff, but Beast wasn't. His gut twisted, his unease refusing to fade. Something was off about these men, something he couldn't place.

Lodi bowed politely, his hand brushing over the buttons of his fine coat. "Truly, we wouldn't want to be a burden. My friend will just have to suffer another few nights — or learn to cook his own meal."

The Kaldorian, already tugging his horse toward a nearby branch, halted. He lifted his eyebrows, a quiet plea on his face as he waited for Olira's reply. He eyed the pot of porridge on the fire.

Olira waved a hand, her smile widening every second. The more relaxed she seemed, the tighter that knot twisted in Beast's gut. It was like the two men were disarming her in a way Beast couldn't fully grasp.

"Please, I insist," she said. "It's not a trouble."

Beast ground his teeth as Lodi hesitated, seemingly debating whether to argue further. Finally, he sighed with an air of resigned politeness. "If you insist," he said, bowing slightly.

The big warrior dismounted, his heavy armour sending a loud thud through the ground. Without a word, he took Lodi's horse by the reins and tied it beside the Kaldorian's.

Lodi stepped forward, taking Olira's hand in his. "Allow me to introduce myself properly," he said smoothly. "I'm Lodi."

He bent, pressing his lips lightly to the backs of her fingers, his gaze never leaving hers. Beast stiffened. Lodi held Olira's hand a moment longer than necessary, his thumb brushing against her knuckles before he let go. Lifting his chin, he gestured toward the other two. "My friends here are Valnar, and the rude one is Ink."

Beast's jaw clenched. His hands curled into loose fists at his sides, his distrust of Lodi evolving into a sharper annoyance. The man's every movement felt calculated, from his soft words to that lingering touch. He expected a sharp retort from Olira.

Instead, she blushed a tone.

It wasn't obvious, but Beast knew her enough to notice. The cold, snappy woman who was always ready to cut Beast down if he'd so much as looked at her the wrong way, was blushing under Lodi's intense gaze.

"I'm... umm... I'm Olira," she stammered, as she fixed her dress out of a need to keep her hands busy. Her eyes darted to Beast, only to freeze when she realised he didn't have a proper name. "This is..."

All three men followed her gaze, their attention openly at Beast now, waiting to see how she'd introduce him.

"Umm... this is Beast," she blurted quietly.

"I see," Lodi said thoughtfully. "A fitting name."

Olira brushed her hair behind her ears as she eagerly turned to tend to the simmering pot.

The three men moved to settle around the camp. Valnar stepped away momentarily, returning with three bowls and a loaf of bread, a block of hard cheese, and a bundle of dried fruit wrapped in cloth. He divided and handed them to his companions and to Olira before settling on a log. The wood cracked faintly under the weight of his armour.

Beast stayed close to Olira. He wished the three men would eat and be on their way. Mind their own business. But something about the way Lodi had looked at him earlier still gnawed at him, and he kept himself coiled, ready for anything.

"I must say," Lodi said with that annoyingly smooth voice, "I do feel a bit guilty using up your supplies. Surely you only packed enough for yourself and your *beast* to reach your destination."

Olira dished their bowls and handed them to Beast to pass them on. "It's no trouble," she said distractedly. "I can stock up in Kilrer on the way."

"Ah," Lodi said, his tone turning conversational. He accepted the bowl Beast offered. "On your way to...?"

"Euroad."

Lodi blinked, his eyebrows lifting slightly in surprise. He didn't bother hiding it. "Euroad," he repeated slowly, his gaze flicking to Beast before returning to her.

Olira dished out the remaining bowls. Beast passed them on to the others. He didn't miss how the other two had positioned themselves so the warrior was the closest to Beast, and the Kaldorian was the furthest, with a clear line of sight.

Beast took his bowl and sat close to Olira. He hunched over his food, his eyes and ears trained on any sign of hostility from the men.

After a brief silence with nothing but the soft clink of spoons against bowls, Lodi spoke: "I must say, Mistress Olira, it's an interesting time to travel to Euroad."

Olira stirred her bowl thoughtfully. "Why do you say that?"

"It's almost winter. Windscar Pass will be snowed in soon."

"Windscar Pass?"

"The mountain passage leading to Euroad," Lodi explained with a hint of surprise.

Beast shrunk under Olira's glare. He was just as taken aback as she was. Of course he knew Euroad was surrounded by Blightridge Mountains, but he didn't know anything about a mountain passage. Or that it would snow in.

"It's a long way to Euroad," Lodi continued, his voice light. "You'll likely have to wait at one of the neighbouring towns until the Windscar is clear. I recommend Arlen's Glare. Lodgings for the whole winter would come pricey, but it's the most decent in that region. Less chances of waking up with a knife between your ribs."

"Right."

Beast's jaw tightened as he watched the exchange. Every word from Lodi felt like another layer of a game he didn't understand. Olira seemed wary now, but not of Lodi. Wary of something else.

Across from her, Lodi sat on the log comfortably, like he was lounging on a cushioned sofa. A smile tugged at the corners of his mouth as though he'd just told a joke only he understood.

"I've never been to Euroad," Ink remarked, stirring the tension like embers in the fire.

"You're not missing much," Valnar grunted, his voice a low rumble of disdain. His lip curled as though the city itself offended him.

Olira's head lifted slightly, her voice cautious. "Why's that?"

"Yeah, why is that?" Ink leaned forward. "What's wrong with Euroad?"

Before Valnar could answer, Lodi lifted a hand, silencing him. "Nothing. Nothing's wrong with Euroad." His smile was meant to reassure Olira, though it seemed to only achieve the opposite. "It's a lovely city. Stunning mountain views, pristine architecture, and the cleanest streets you'll ever see."

"To mask the rot inside the buildings," Valnar muttered, his face darkening.

Lodi shot him a sharp look before brushing off the comment with a faint, apologetic shrug. "Don't mind him, Mistress. I'm sure Euroad will offer exactly what you're looking for."

Silence fell over the campsite as they continued their meals. The campfire crackled softly, and a cold wind rustled the bare branches of the surrounding bushes. Lodi and his companions enjoyed their food while Olira barely touched hers, her spoon absently stirring the cooling porridge. Every so often, her gaze darted to Beast. He didn't have the answers to the unspoken questions and doubts her brown eyes sent his way. He would have to deal with those later.

Finishing his meal, Lodi wiped his mouth with a handkerchief. "Thank you for the meal, Mistress Olira. It was delightful."

"Thank you for your company, Master Lodi."

Lodi leaned forward, resting his elbows on his knees. "So," he said casually, "how much for the slave?"

The question hung in the air like a blade locked in a parry. Beast's blood rushed with an overwhelming desire to punch Lodi's perfectly symmetrical face to a pulp. But he stayed still, his face a stone mask, his purebred training holding firm.

Olira wasn't as composed. She straightened, eyes blazing with palpable fury. "He's not for sale," she said with a forced politeness. Her voice carried a cold edge that Beast deeply appreciated.

"I'll give you two-hundred Blues for him."

The fire popped, sending a brief spark into the cold air. The horses stamped their feet impatiently, their breath steaming in the cold. Dread slid down Beast's spine.

Darkness curse this man.

Two hundred Blues was way more than what Beast had cost Olira. More than enough to clear her debts and save her farm. Beast's fingers twitched at his sides, but he said nothing, his gaze fixed on his empty bowl.

Olira's answer was instant, not even a heartbeat of hesitation. "I told you, Master Lodi, he's not for sale."

"Every slave has a price, Mistress Olira. What's his?"

Beast's jaw ticked. The cuts and grazes he acquired from his fall ached faintly as he stretched his arms discreetly.

Valnar rose quietly, gathering their bowls and packing them away. When he was done, he stood by the fire instead of sitting back down, holding his gauntleted hands over the flames. Ink discarded the stick he'd been fiddling with and placed his hands on his lap. He was perched on the higher point of a rock, with a clean line of sight of the camp.

Olira didn't notice any of these subtle signs of how the two men were preparing for the fight.

"You're being rude now, Master Lodi. I told you he's not for sale."

Beast stood, taking his bowl and Olira's and tossing them into the bag. He lifted the pot off the flames. The metal was hot against his fingers, the weight solid and assuring. He tipped the remaining porridge into the dirt, the hiss of steam like a whispered warning. His eyes never left the men.

Something told him what he knew the moment he saw them. That he was about to test how well they would fare against an angry purebred beast.

"Two hundred and fifty," Lodi said casually. "Right here and now." He rose from the log with a lightness to his steps that mocked the tension buzzing in the air. He strode to his horse, unhooked a heavy purse from the saddle, and returned to the fire with a deliberate slowness.

"The answer is no, Master Lodi," Olira said through gritted teeth.

Beast shifted his grip on the pot, its weight grounding him.

Lodi loosened the straps of his purse. He pulled out a pale-blue plate and turned it between his fingers. The polished surface gleamed in the weak sunlight, catching Olira's reluctant attention.

"Not sure if you've ever seen a tenner. Each of these is worth ten Blues," he said nonchalantly. "Twenty-five plates here. That should more than cover what he cost you."

Olira muttered curses under her breath as she bent to pack their belongings with quick and jerky movements. "We're done here."

"You drive a hard bargain, Mistress Olira."

"I'm not bargaining. He's not for sale."

They would not take no for an answer. Beast saw it in the way Lodi's pleasant expression cracked slightly. His gaze flicked to Beast a split second, before returning to Olira. His tongue darted out, wetting his lips.

"I thought I'd save you from trouble," Lodi said. "And save the poor thing from whatever fate you're dragging him to at Euroad."

"And what fate do you think I'm dragging him to?" Olira shot back, crossing her arms.

Beast wished she would stop talking to him and would just get ready to run. His mind raced, mapping the quickest way to put the Kaldorian down first — the hot pot hurled at his head should buy enough time to deal with the big warrior. Then Lodi.

If they made a move for Olira, it would all fall apart. He couldn't let that happen.

"Slaves don't go to Euroad to live happily ever after," Lodi said smoothly. "They go there to die."

Olira's face paled and her frown deepened.

"Slaves in Euroad die one of two ways," Lodi continued, his words like poisoned barbs. "At the entertainment venues catering to the most twisted appetites imaginable. Or at the Scythe Arena. Twisted games, the kind of cruelty you can't even dream up. Either way, no slave leaves Euroad alive."

"I'm not planning to—"

Lodi cut her off, his head tilting, his sharp gaze dissecting her. "If you're not planning to rent him out in one of those establishments, then you're planning to throw him into the arena. How, exactly, do you intend to pay the registration fee?"

Olira blinked, her composure cracking. She glanced at Beast, desperately seeking answers, but he was more concerned with the imminent danger she was oblivious to. He kept his expression neutral, though his mind calculated and recalculated the best and the quickest path to take them all down. Alone, it would be straightforward. But Olira's presence changed things.

If she died, they could claim ownership of him. There would be no point fighting.

"That's right," Lodi pressed, his voice dripping with smugness. "Did you think you could just stroll into Euroad and sign him up for a fight? No, Mistress Olira. You need to be a member of the Domestic Assets Trade Union. And you'll need several hundred Blues just to register him."

"Several hundred?" Olira muttered, barely audible.

The horses stamped and snorted, their restlessness mirroring the tension in the air. Olira's glare was trained on Beast, like this was somehow his fault. He'd heard about registration fees, but such details had never mattered to him. He only did what he was told.

Olira ran her hand through her hair. She was too exposed, too close to the fire. Ink had a clear shot of her. The casual, friendly smile didn't leave the man's lips, but he could still pull out a knife and fling it at Olira in a heartbeat.

Beast needed to get her out of the way before the fight began. But how?

The frost crunched faintly beneath his boot as he shifted his stance. His chest thrummed with building aggression.

"But that's something you wouldn't even have to think about until you survive the journey. Pay for lodgings at Arlen's Glare — or some other hole of a town — hire a mountain guide, and pay for passage. Let me assure you," he added with a faint smirk, "those mountain trails aren't pleasant to navigate. Then, you'll have to find your way around the city and hope—"

"Enough!" Olira's voice tore through the crisp morning air.

Lodi tilted his head, studying her for a moment before slipping his hand into his coat. He pulled out a smaller pouch, loosening the straps with exaggerated care. He tilted the pouch upside down. Five more pale-blue squares tumbled onto the pile at his feet, their metallic clink unnervingly loud against the cold silence.

"Three hundred Blues, Mistress Olira," he said smoothly, as though he were offering her salvation.

Olira stood frozen for a heartbeat, her fists clenched tight at her sides. She avoided the glimmering plates at her feet, her gaze fixed instead on Lodi's warm blue eyes and considerate smile.

Beast moved closer, standing shoulder to shoulder with her. He readjusted his grip on the pot, the metal still faintly warm from the fire. Valnar's slow movement caught his eye — a flex of his neck, his hand resting on the hilt of his sword. Beast felt a surge of thrill at the anticipation of the fight.

"You're clearly not prepared for whatever it is you think you're walking into," Lodi continued. Despair glazed his tone, as if he knew he was losing the negotiation and things were about to get bloody. "Three hundred Blues could save you from so much trouble."

"No," Olira said, her voice barely above a whisper.

This was it. The talking was over. Beast's eyes flicked between Ink and Valnar, studying every twitch of their muscles, trying to predict which one would make the first move.

"Three hundred and fifty," Lodi said. His grin was tight, desperation sneaking into his voice. That desperation told Beast that deep down, Lodi knew his men wouldn't survive against a purebred beast. As long as Beast kept Olira alive...

Lodi held out his palm at Ink. The Kaldorian slid off his perch reluctantly and moved to the horses.

Beast's pulse quickened.

Ink withdrew another pouch from his own saddlebags and handed it to Lodi with a faint sigh. Then, he retreated and leaned against his horse at an angle that gave him a direct line of sight to Olira and kept her between himself and Beast. He crossed his arms, his hands vanishing under his cloak.

"Three hundred and fifty," Lodi repeated, tossing the pouch onto the pile. "Take it and leave, Olira."

The words hung in the cold air for a moment before Olira spoke, her voice barely above a whisper. "What are you going to do with him?"

Beast stiffened, his breath catching. His head snapped at her.

Olira didn't look at him. She didn't look at Lodi either, who was smiling victoriously. Her gaze remained fixed on the pale-blue plates at her feet.

"He will be taken good care of," Lodi said. "If that's your concern. He will be well-fed, dressed, and treated reasonably."

Beast's shoulders sagged. He forgot how to breathe.

Olira turned her back on the group, her face pale as she pressed her hand over her mouth. For a moment, she stood perfectly still, then raised her trembling hand and drew the Twelve's sign in the air.

"Merciful Alunwea, please forgive me," she whispered.

The pot slipped from Beast's hand, landing with a dull thud. The weight that replaced it in his chest was suffocating.

Olira didn't look at him.

Please don't do this. Olira, don't do this. His throat tightened, words jamming together like rocks in a collapsing tunnel, until all he could force out was a single, desperate word.

"Olira?"

She knelt by her shoulder bag and pulled out a rolled paper. Beast recognised his sales paper. Lodi produced a charcoal pen promptly, extending it to her. She took it without a glance.

"Olira..."

He was drowning. The frostbitten air tasted metallic, and every muscle in his body screamed against the betrayal. He shouldn't have been surprised — selling him had always been her plan. But it burned all the same, searing through him like hot iron. He had tricked himself into believing she was different.

I am not a bad person.

He felt so dumb.

"Your full name, Master Lodi?" she asked, the pen poised over the paper.

"Please put Valnar Gaege there, Olira," Lodi said. His face practically beamed with a triumphant glee.

The ground beneath Beast cracked open, dragging him into an abyss. There had to be a right thing to say to keep that pen from touching the paper, but Beast was useless with words.

Olira scribbled the names, then signed under hers.

The soft clink of Valnar's heavy armour barely registered over the pounding in Beast's ears. The warrior moved past him. He took the pen from Olira and signed his name.

It was done.

Lodi rose, brushing the dust off his coat, his shoulders relaxed. The paper exchanged hands as Valnar passed it to Lodi on his way back to the horses. Lodi folded it carefully and tucked it into his inner pocket.

"It's been a pleasure doing business with you, Olira," he said, extending a hand.

Olira didn't acknowledge it. She didn't look at him, or at the others. She stared at the ground, her shoulders drawn tight, her hands trembling faintly by her sides.

"Well," Lodi said, puffing his chest and brushing off the rejection. "Enjoy your new wealth."

Ink brought Lodi's horse forward. The Kaldorian's casual grin was replaced by something that might have been pity. Beast couldn't bring himself to care.

The rattling of chains finally cut through the haze in his mind.

Beast's body reacted before his thoughts caught up. He flinched back, his fists balled, his teeth bared like an animal as his gaze locked on the big warrior approaching him with a collar. Valnar halted, his eyes narrowing into icy slits.

"His Words, Mistress?" the big warrior asked coolly.

"You don't need—"

"His Words?"

Olira fumbled into her pocket and produced a smaller slip of paper, her hand trembling as she passed it to Valnar. He unfolded it, scanning the three Words written there. Beast caught the slight twitch of his lips as he read them quietly.

For reasons Beast couldn't grasp, he found himself wishing Valnar would speak his Pain Word. Let it echo in the frozen air, let it drop him to the cold ground. Anything to drown out the hollow ache in his chest.

Valnar folded the paper and slid it into his gauntlet. His gaze fell back on Beast, one eyebrow cocked in cold challenge.

It was over.

Beast's shoulders sagged, his head lowering in defeat.

It was truly over.

The collar snapped shut around his neck with a sharp, metallic click. It was cold, biting into his skin, and so tight he could hardly swallow without choking.

Valnar swung onto his horse, gathering the reins in one hand and the chain in the other. The first tug yanked Beast to his knees, his palms slapping against the hard dirt. The cut on his elbow, earned minutes ago when he'd thought Olira was in danger — when he'd believed freedom was within reach — throbbed with bitter mockery. The cold stung through his skin as he pushed himself up, his limbs heavy.

He looked back one last time.

Olira stood clutching the pouches of Blues, holding them close to her chest like a mother cradling an infant. Her face was pale, drawn. Misery etched into her features. She looked small. Weak. Sick.

All free men and women are greedy.

The thought burned bitterly in Beast's mind as Valnar's horse moved forward, the chain pulling taut. The metal dug into his neck as he scrambled after his new Owner.

The campsite, the fire, Olira — everything faded behind a pale mist.

14

DIENUS

Every time he closed his eyes, he saw the girl.

The way she gasped. The terror in her wide eyes. The way she cowered against the bed.

The way he forced life back into her.

There wasn't a single moment where he didn't think about what he'd done to her.

He hadn't slept in days. The hard ride from Brinescar to Riverdam had been gruelling enough, but the sea voyage that followed was pure misery. Dienus despised ships—wooden prisons that trapped him with nothing but his own nausea as every meal came back up and every hour crawled by like torture. They'd made landfall on Kiore and pressed on immediately, his body screaming for rest that never came. Exhaustion weighed him down like armour, his bones aching from cold and the relentless punishment of travel. Yet none of it compared to the headache that pounded behind his eyes, a merciless rhythm that wouldn't grant him even a moment's peace.

"There you go, Master," the bartender said, hearty and loud. He slid the mug in front of him. "Our best ale, on the house. Anything else I can get for you?"

Dienus squeezed the bridge of his nose, his eyes closed. "Get out of my sight," he muttered.

The innkeeper's brows flicked up, but he forced a polite smile, nodded, and stepped away.

The ale smelled bitter. Dienus took two gulps and grimaced. "What is this, cow piss?" he grumbled, loud enough to draw a few glances.

He kept drinking anyway. The ale burned his throat on the way down, dulling the headache just enough to tolerate.

The tavern reeked of sour booze, sweat, and damp wood. The low ceiling trapped the smoke from the hearth, making the air thick and stale. Dienus had been in unpleasant places before, but Oxreach was in a league of its own. It was the kind of town that clung to existence out of sheer stubbornness, a petty collection of mud-streaked streets and sagging buildings, packed with people too poor or too proud to leave.

Days spent on the road had brought him to this filth-ridden hole, all in pursuit of a lead on Lion of Zarall. That alone was enough to sour his mood, but Oxreach itself made it worse. Northern Chinderia was always bleak, but this? This was worse than he expected.

And his headache made him too miserable to tolerate Oxreach's existence. He fantasised with the idea of burning this shitty town to ashes.

Beside him, Sir Gennald leaned against the bar, idly running a thumb over the pommel of his sword. The knight was solidly built, broad and weathered, his breastplate engraved with the bear of Vogros. He had left his helmet with his horse's saddle, but his longsword remained visible on his belt. They didn't expect trouble in a place like this. Small towns rarely had the spine for it. But the man still didn't enjoy lowering his guard.

Dienus wasn't even sure if the people here knew they had the honour of gawking at Prince Dienus Vogros. But this was Northern Chinderia. Even in a backwater town like Oxreach, the name Zarall was whispered louder.

The tavern had filled with onlookers. Some pretended to drink, others loitered in corners, making no effort to hide their curiosity. Their eyes flicked between him and Gennald, and he knew damn well that there were more people waiting outside, craning their necks for a glimpse of the fifty soldiers his dear father had given him.

Correction — he had given them to Lieutenant Quinner.

Dienus barely had time to sneer at the thought before the door swung open and the man himself walked in.

Quinner looked like someone had stuffed a full-grown man into a baby's skin. He was massive, with long arms and a thick build, but his rosy cheeks and round face made him look absurdly soft. If he weren't a skilled soldier, Dienus would have laughed at him outright. Would have, if the bastard wasn't also smarter than he looked. That explained why the king had tasked the man to lead this mission instead of his own son.

It still burned.

For a moment, when his mother first told him that his father was sending him after Lion of Zarall, he had thought maybe — just maybe — he finally trusted him.

Turns out, he only wanted to keep him from making a spectacle of himself. And he'd put Quinner in charge to make sure of it.

Quinner's pale-blue eyes landed on Dienus, and the way his mouth tightened was enough to confirm the feeling was mutual. He wasn't much of a political man, but he tried, and it showed. He spoke to nobles just carefully enough to avoid offence, played the dutiful officer to the king, and gave orders like they were suggestions.

It was that exact tone that made Dienus want to punch him.

Quinner approached the bar, shooing the bartender away with a mere look and sending the nearest onlookers scurrying back with a single glare. He had the quiet authority of a man used to commanding, used to being obeyed. He leaned in, speaking just loud enough for Dienus to hear. "Your Highness, as I said earlier, I did not need more than a few minutes to talk to the Bailiff in his office."

Dienus tensed, jaw clenching. What Quinner meant was: *I ordered you to wait outside with the men.*

The bastard was good at this.

"Is that what you were doing?" Dienus said, lifting his mug and taking another long sip. "I thought you were negotiating the price of ox dung with how long you took in there."

Quinner exhaled deeply. "I've located the farm. It's only an hour from here on hard gallop. The men are ready to leave *now.*"

"I haven't finished my ale, Lieutenant." The ale was awful, but he wasn't about to let this insufferable brute tell him what to do.

"I believe this is time sensitive, Your Highness. I am concerned some of the townspeople may attempt to alert the farmer."

"If it's time sensitive," Gennald said, tilting his head, "perhaps you should send a few men to surround the farm, and wait until Prince Dienus is done here."

Quinner's sharp gaze flicked to Gennald, but before he could respond, the tavern door opened again.

Two men entered, their clothes slightly finer than the rest of the filth in Oxreach. Authority figures, no doubt. The Bailiff and the inbred landowner Northern towns accepted as their town leader. An Agha, or something like that. Dienus found the idea of two town leaders absurd. Bailiff was the official appointed by a lord. The Agha should have no authority over anything.

A few townspeople murmured, approaching them with whispers. One of the two leaders broke from the group and walked up to Quinner.

"Lieutenant Quinner, I presume. I understand you're looking to question Olira Aryanna. May I ask what this is about?"

"You may not," Dienus blurted sharply.

The man glanced at Dienus, his eyes narrowing at his clothes as he tried to understand Dienus's status. "I apologise, I should have introduced myself first. I am Agha..."

"Nobody cares," Dienus said lazily. "Piss off."

The Agha's mouth twitched. He tried to mask his offence with a tight-lipped smile. Dienus had seen the look before — men trying to decide whether it was worth the risk to push back.

Quinner, of course, stepped in before the fool could make a decision.

"Agha," Quinner said smoothly, his tone carefully polite, "we appreciate your cooperation. We are acting on behalf of the Crown. The matter is urgent, and I must insist that you do not interfere."

The Agha's eyes flicked back to Quinner, reading him, then to the Bailiff, who stood stiffly by the door, surrounded by concerned townspeople. Clearly, the man had expected more courtesy — an introduction, a conversation, something civilised. Dienus smirked, tilting his mug back, enjoying the tension stretching between them.

The Agha cleared his throat. "I'm afraid it is my responsibility to know what armed men are doing in my town. I only wish to cooperate…"

"You're welcome to stand in our way if you'd like to be trampled."

The Agha's face darkened. Dienus imagined his face darkening with colour, turning purple as the man gasped for air. Dienus's fingers tightening around his neck. His headache intensified, the need wearing him down. He really *really* hoped the peasant would give him an excuse to arrest him and…

"We already have the information we're looking for," Quinner said. "If you'd like to cooperate, please ensure the townspeople resume their work and stay out of our way."

"If Olira Aryanna is involved in a crime—"

"We will bring her to justice ourselves," Dienus said impatiently. "Now buzz off. Go tend to your cows or whatever it is you do."

Out of the corner of his eye, he caught a few townspeople slipping out the door, likely running to the Aryanna farm.

Bugger. Quinner was right.

Quinner must have noticed the runners too. "Time to move," he muttered, his voice clipped.

Dienus downed the last of his ale, slamming the mug onto the counter harder than necessary before pushing himself up. "Oh, is it? I thought we'd linger for supper."

Quinner ignored him, stepping past the Agha and townspeople without another word. Gennald fell into step beside Dienus as they strode out into the street, where the rest of the soldiers were still mounted and waiting. A few more townspeople had gathered, standing in doorways, watching the scene unfold.

Dienus barely saw them.

The dull ache in his skull had sharpened into something worse. It pulsed behind his eyes. A gnawing pressure made his vision feel tight around the edges. He clenched his jaw, barely hearing whatever Quinner was barking at his men.

The need…

He thought of the girl again. The way her breath hitched. The way his hands had closed around her neck, the pulse fluttering beneath his grip. The way her body had yielded. The power in that moment was pure and undeniable.

His hands twitched. His head throbbed harder with the need. If he didn't gratify it, if he didn't take something soon, he swore his skull would split apart.

"Prince Dienus," Gennald said, snapping him back to reality.

He blinked, the street coming into focus again. Quinner was already on his horse, the men waiting for him to mount up.

Dienus exhaled, forcing a smirk on his face. "Keep frowning like that, Lieutenant, and you might age ten years before we even reach the farm," he drawled as he swung himself into the saddle.

Quinner shot him a sharp look but said nothing.

The party spurred forward, heading for the Aryanna Farm.

15

VALNAR

Valnar breathed deeply, steadying his thoughts as the cool air wrapped around him like Kiejain's embrace. Each trial the Twelve Riders had sent him had been a step toward proving his faith. Refining his virtues. He regarded the path ahead not with fear but with anticipation. More trials awaited — opportunities to demonstrate his worth to the Twelve Riders, and to his friends.

Yet, whenever his gaze fell on the beast, a familiar unease stirred in his chest. His greatest trial was near. He could feel it, radiating from the beast like heat from an untamed fire. Clutching Kiejain's symbol on his breastplate, he whispered a prayer, his breath visible in the fading light.

Valnar walked away from the campsite and found a quiet clearing. He unsheathed his knife and began tracing a circle on the half-frozen ground. The sun dipped lower behind the hills, casting long shadows, but enough light remained to guide his blade. A blessing, he thought. If it were any other night, they would have pushed on until darkness swallowed their path. But the slave had grown too tired to run, forcing them to stop.

When the circle was complete, Valnar knelt within it, placing his two-handed sword before him. Its thick wrapping concealed every part of the blade. Valnar had kept the sword shrouded for nearly ten years. He prayed he would never have to reveal it again.

Placing a gauntleted hand over his breastplate, Valnar closed his eyes and opened his heart to Kiejain's grace. He began the long ritual, reciting twelve sacred passages in *Praxese* — one for each of the Twelve Riders — each repeated twelve times. His voice was steady, reverent, the syllables flowing like a stream over smooth stone. The thirteenth passage, reserved for those who had journeyed to Farhome, he spoke only once. His fingertips touched the cold ground, then his forehead, concluding the ritual.

When he opened his eyes, dusk had settled. The peace he sought remained elusive, lingering just out of reach. He rested his hand on his breastplate again, his voice low as he whispered:

"Kiejain, uniter of gods and men. First Rider. First Husband. First Warrior. Lend me your wisdom, so I make the right choices. Guide my sword, so I bleed my enemies. Bless my *rhoa*, so I steer from faithless." He took a deep breath and continued, "Help me stand by Lodi until my end."

He drew the Twelve's sign in the air before standing up. His muscles had turned stiff from sitting motionless in the cold. Valnar retrieved his sword reverently and stretched, the faint pop of his joints breaking the stillness.

He returned to the campsite and was pleased to find they hadn't lit a fire, despite Ink's earlier complaints about the cold. The campsite was well hidden, half an hour off the road and shielded by dense undergrowth and Kiejain's vigilance.

"Guess what's for dinner?" Ink greeted him, a grin flickering across his freckled face. "More dried meat and stale bread."

"All my prayers have been answered," Valnar said dryly, lowering himself to the ground. He took the plate they had set aside for him, its contents as uninspiring as Ink had promised.

"How was Kiejain?" Lodi asked with a half smile.

"A great listener, as always."

Valnar's eyes drifted to the slave. The beast lay near a tree, his chain glinting faintly in the dim light. He stared at the sky without blinking. His plate remained untouched beside him.

"Still not eating?" Valnar asked.

"Probably too tired to eat," Ink offered with a shrug. "I would be too, if I'd been running all day. Poor bastard."

"He'll eat," Lodi said between bites of hardened bread. "But we'll need another horse soon, or he'll slow us down."

Ink laughed. "With what money exactly? You've spent all we had on him. Honestly, the way you talk about beasts, I expected one with claws and fangs. This one seems like any other man to me."

"He is not a man," Valnar explained firmly. "He doesn't have any *rhoa*."

"You know, all the royal guards in Kaldoria are raised from childhood. I don't see how purebreds can be that different."

"Trust me, they're not the same." Valnar pulled the slave's Words from his gauntlet and handed them to Lodi. "We should all memorise these. And I want to confirm he's Lion of Zarall. He needs to acknowledge the ownership."

Lodi unfolded the paper and studied it. "He's Lion of Zarall. I wouldn't have spent three hundred and fifty Blues if I wasn't certain. I've seen his brands. I don't see how his acknowledgment matters. We have his sales paper."

"It'll help me sleep better." Valnar finished his last bite of dried meat, dusted his hands, and walked over to the slave. Lodi passed the paper to Ink and followed.

"Stand up," Valnar commanded.

The slave rose like a fiend crawling out of Darkhome. His movements were sluggish, as if his muscles were weighed down by exhaustion, or that he had no care in Earthome. The collar bit into his neck, dried blood crusted his skin. The chain was tethered to a low branch, and despite its generous length, it limited his space to a small radius.

"Take your shirt off."

There was that disrespectful delay again. Valnar's jaw tightened as the slave finally complied, pulling the shirt over his head and pushing it back along the chain. He stood with his arms at his sides, his scarred chest exposed under the cool starlight. If the night air chilled him, he gave no sign.

"See," Lodi said, pointing at the brands on the slave's wide chest. "That's the *Stallion Tournament*, that's the *Painted Rose*, and *Maiden's Grace*. And that would be the *Golden Sparrow*, the most recent one. The first few are clearly older, so they can't be fake." He circled the slave, pausing to marvel at the deep white scars on his back. "That must be Marzul the bear. I would've given anything to see that fight…" Completing his inspection, Lodi motioned toward the slave's face. "Hair and eye colour match too. Are we done doubting, Valnar?"

Valnar rubbed his chin, his eyes narrowing on the slave's blank expression. Lodi was right; the scars and the description matched. This was Lion of Zarall. He opened his mouth to confess his satisfaction, but Ink's voice interrupted.

"*Padlociatius.*"

The slave crumpled instantly. Lodi lunged to catch him, grunting under the dead weight. "Ink!" he snapped, lowering the body awkwardly to the ground. "What in Earthome did you do that for?"

Ink shrugged, holding the Words in one hand and a crust of bread in the other. "Wanted to see how these things worked." He leaned closer, peering at the slave. "So, is he really paralysed?"

Lodi shook his head in disbelief while Valnar explained, "Yes, he is temporarily paralysed."

Ink made a curious noise. They stood in awkward silence as they waited for the First Word to wear off. The slave lay at their feet, defenceless. Part of Valnar was grateful to Ink, for reminding him that they could do this with one word. Maybe he was wrong to worry about the slave.

The beast's arms and legs twitched as he slowly regained control of his body. He grunted and pushed himself to sit up on his knees.

Valnar unfolded the sales paper and found the acknowledgement section. Before he could speak, Ink's voice rang out again: "*Prihjtivaviula.*"

"Ink!" Lodi roared, his anger sharp enough to cut through the cold night air.

In his five years guarding Lodi, Valnar had never seen him so furious. Lodi snatched the paper from Ink. The Kaldorian hardly noticed it. His widened eyes were fixed on the slave, who convulsed violently, his back arching as if struck by lightning. The beast's teeth clenched, his body writhed, but no sound escaped his lips. The veins in his neck bulged against the collar, which seemed tighter than before.

Valnar winced but didn't look away.

"This…" Ink stammered. "This is sickening! You Chinderians are sick."

"I told you what the Words did," Lodi snapped. "Don't use them unless you have a good reason."

"A *good* reason?" Ink pointed at the slave, his voice rising. "There's no good reason to torture a man like that!"

"He's not a man," Valnar said quietly, stepping back to avoid the slave's thrashing legs. "He doesn't have a *rhoa*. He's just flesh waiting to rot."

"This looks like Darkhome magic," Ink hissed. "Do you not see that?"

"It's Farhome magic," Valnar corrected. "'A purebred without Words will eat itself alive', that's the saying. Words bind the purebred and keep them safe from fiendish influences."

"*Safe*?" Ink scoffed, turning away in disgust. He muttered something under his breath as he tossed his bread into his bag and walked off.

The slave groaned, pressing his forehead to the ground. His fists clenched as the pain ebbed, leaving him trembling.

"Stand up," Valnar ordered again.

The slave stumbled but eventually found his footing.

"You are now the property of Valnar Gaege," Valnar recited the statement from the paper. "You will respond to the name Beast. Acknowledge."

His gaze on the ground, the slave remained perfectly still.

Valnar cleared his throat and repeated the statement. "Acknowledge," he ordered harshly.

The slave continued to ignore him. Despite his blank face and glassy eyes, Valnar knew the slave had heard him. He put the paper away and stepped closer, invading the slave's space with his commanding presence. Despite being about the same height and build, and Valnar projecting more confidence, intimidation poured out of the slave.

The silence dragged. Valnar's stomach twisted. "Acknowledge, or I will hurt you."

He regretted the threat as soon as it came out of his mouth. If he didn't follow through with this now, the slave would never fear him again. He waited, hoping the slave would choose to avoid pain.

He said nothing.

Valnar's fingers twitched as he prepared to speak the Pain Word, but Lodi pushed him out of the way and took over.

"Look at me," he said casually. He stepped closer, like he had nothing to fear. With one finger, he flicked the slave's chin up to face him.

The beast's eyes burned with hatred, his chest rising and falling sharply. His hands formed fists, his jaw clenching. Valnar stepped closer, ready to act, but Lodi simply smirked.

"So," he said in his carefree way. Warmth glinted in his light blue eyes as he basked in the beast's spite for a moment before speaking casually. "Euroad, huh?"

The fire in the slave's eyes dimmed. He blinked, a muscle in his jaw ticking.

"You wanna tell me why she was taking you there?"

The slave's shoulders drew in. He lowered his head to hide his expression.

"I am now the property of Valnar Gaege," the slave recited quietly. "I will respond to the name Beast. I acknowledge."

"There," Lodi grinned at Valnar over his shoulder. "Satisfied?"

"Not quite," Valnar muttered, his gaze narrowing. The slave's acknowledgment felt hollow, his posture giving off a subtle defiance that set Valnar on edge. A sense of disquiet gnawed at him. He needed to discipline the slave to ensure his obedience and respect. "He asked you a question, slave," he pressed.

"Right," Lodi said with irritation. "I did." He faced Beast again. "Let me repeat that question for you. *Do you want to* tell me why she was taking you to Euroad?"

Valnar saw what Lodi was doing, so did Beast. The slave squinted at Lodi, his expression stuck between distrust and uncertainty. "No, Master, I do not," he mumbled.

"Okay," Lodi shrugged. "My question is answered. We've confirmed his identity and heard his acknowledgement too. I am satisfied. Are you?"

Valnar hesitated, but Lodi's glare left no room for an argument. He swallowed the bitter taste of embarrassment as he muttered, "Yes, Lodi."

"Great. So, I'll take the first watch. I'll wake you up in a few hours."

"Sure."

"And you," Lodi added, turning to Beast. He lingered too close, not seeming eager to leave the man's proximity. He tapped a finger at Beast's chest. "Get dressed and eat."

A quiet growl rumbled from Beast as his jaw twitched. He stepped back and yanked his shirt back on. He sat down with his back to them and pulled his plate over his lap.

Valnar returned to the campfire and grabbed his blanket. Ink had already set up his bedroll. Valnar stretched out on the other side of the fire, his armour creaking faintly as he tried to find a comfortable position.

"You're really not bothered by this?" Ink asked from where he lay, his voice low but pointed. "The fact that you can do something so awful to a man with just one word?"

Valnar didn't bother correcting him again that Beast was not a man. His thoughts shifted to Lodi, who was offering his own blanket to the slave. Valnar felt a tightness in his chest, a mixture of distrust and disapproval.

"If you understood what a purebred beast is truly capable of," he said evenly, "you'd thank the Twelve Riders for giving us the Words."

16

BEAST

Beast sat in the black water. He didn't move. He didn't blink. He didn't raise his head. The emptiness inside him mirrored the stillness of the water.

The High Fiend remained silent, and for that, Beast was grateful. He wasn't ready to talk. Black fog swirled lazily in the silver cage, where Keder studied him with an intensity that made Beast wish he wasn't here at all. He would've preferred another empty, dreamless night — one where the pain in his chest could be ignored until it dulled.

He would've preferred any physical pain over this.

The water lapped at his stomach as he knelt. It was higher than before — he was sure of it. Closing his eyes, he doubled over and submerged his face. His forehead pressed into the soft, muddy soil below, his hands planting on either side of his head. His fingers dug into the mud as he held his breath, the burn in his lungs offering a distraction from the ache in his chest.

When the burn grew unbearable, he opened his mouth and released his air in a silent scream. The soundless expulsion clawed at his throat. He screamed until his lungs were empty, until there was no air left.

Beast sat back up, gasping, water trickling down his face. His trembling fingers clawed at the mud, the numbness in his chest boiling into anger. He squeezed a fistful of mud until it oozed between his fingers.

It was pointless to ask why. He understood why. Olira's decision made perfect sense. So, the pain it caused was meaningless. It only turned his frustration at himself.

How dumb was he, for believing she was different. That she would put herself and her farm at risk to help him.

The water stilled, reflecting what he didn't want to see. His own face staring back at him — dark blond hair plastered to his forehead, grey eyes sunken with exhaustion. His fingers brushed the tattoo on his neck.

The image of Olira hugging the pouches of money to her chest wouldn't leave him.

All free men and women are greedy.

Acceptance was a jagged knife that carved itself a place in his heart, where it settled and made itself at home.

Beast's hands stopped clawing at the mud. He let out a shuddering sigh. The pain didn't fade, but it dulled, just enough to be bearable. He dried his face, wiping away the cold water.

"I won't open the cage," Beast said with determination.

"You will, in the end," Keder whispered. "We both know it."

Beast fought back a shiver as the High Fiend's words twisted a foreboding in his guts. His fingers toyed with the tooth-like object lodged at his chest. The object throbbed faintly, black and red veins spreading from it. When he took a deep breath, it strained and disturbed, but didn't quite hurt.

Nodding towards the lock, he said, "I don't understand why you're bringing me here. I don't even have a key."

"I do not bring you here. And indeed, you do possess the key."

Beast stood and paced, kicking and disturbing water. He avoided looking at the odd-shaped hole on the padlock. He studied the cavern walls and the unseen ceiling above, buried in deep shadows. "Where is this place anyway?"

"You know that answer." The shadows swirled lazily in the cage.

Beast glanced at the imprisoned High Fiend. Then, he took in the fiend hounds that waited by the cavern walls. Some were lying down, flapping their tails lazily. Others watched him with their heads down and ears tilted back.

"Darkhome," Beast breathed. His heart pounded in his chest. He looked down, feeling the soft mud beneath his feet. He didn't quite know how to control it, but he knew he could sink down and wake up at Earthome.

"Are you eager to awake?" Keder mused. "I am intrigued to know what pleasures await you in that cold home you are so keen to return to."

Beast growled. He kicked the water again and paced, just to bring some movement to his limbs. He eyed the cavern walls and the ceiling, looking for a way out. He felt trapped. He couldn't bring himself to return to Earthome, but he couldn't stay here either.

"I brought you here once, and now you return of your own accord whenever hardship presses. And you flee back to Earthome when our exchange grows confronting. What a valiant beast you are."

Beast shot him a glare from the corner of his eyes. Even the cold water did nothing to soothe his burning irritation.

"You know well what you must do if you desire my assistance," Keder purred, swirling casually. Beast felt he could detect patterns in his movements, and sensed a vague air of smugness. Then, he remembered the images Keder had stabbed in his mind, and avoided keeping his eyes on the smoke for too long.

"I don't need your help," Beast said as he scowled at the black water. "And I won't open the cage."

"Why delay the inevitable?" Keder pressed. "Admit it. You're a slave. All free men and women are greedy."

"If I..." Beast ran his hands through his damp hair. "If I unleash you, you will destroy Earthome. And I won't have anywhere to enjoy my freedom."

"They won't grant you your freedom."

"I'll take it myself."

Keder's voice grated off the cavern walls. Beast recognised the laughter, his teeth clenching in response.

"I believe..." Keder purred.

The black water near Beast's legs changed colour. The gentle ripples turned to shapes. Beast flinched back, and the images followed him.

"You need a refreshment," Keder continued.

"What are you doing?"

Shapes stirred in the black water, slowly sharpening into something solid. An old plate, piled high with steaming food, took form. It rested on the floor — grey, cracked stone he knew too well.

He gasped and jerked back, heart pounding.

"What are you doing? Stop it!" His voice came out strangled.

"A lesson in what transpires when you *take* things."

"No! Stop!"

He was on his knees, staring at the food Breeder Astaldo had just placed in front of him.

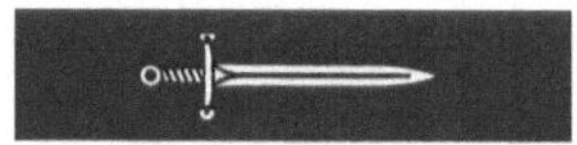

His seven-year-old body was starving.

He sat on his knees, his hands in his lap, his head down. He didn't know how long it had been since he last ate; he'd lost his sense of time a while ago. He hadn't slept either. Astaldo only gave him water, just enough to keep him going. No food, no sleep, no rest... only discipline.

The sight of the food made his stomach cramp, and his head spin. The greasy, roasted chicken leg was still hot; he could see the steam rising off it. The potato and bread, fresh from the oven, filled the air with a warm aroma that stung his eyes. Tears welled up as his mouth watered, and he wiped both away with the back of his hand.

The boy glanced at Astaldo. The slave breeder was sorting the equipment on the table, with his back towards the boy. Astaldo pretended not to be watching, but the boy knew better. They had been through this several times already. Astaldo would put the food in front of him, without giving any verbal or nonverbal permission to eat. The boy had already learned the lesson; he wasn't supposed to touch the food.

He wasn't allowed to take.

He wasn't going to fail the test this time. He closed his eyes, but the delicious smell harassed him. He took a deep breath and held it. He tried to focus on other memories, but the good ones were scarce. He had to breathe at the end, and his eyes wouldn't stay shut either. All he could do was to stop himself from sobbing out loud.

The food grew cold; a layer of hardened fat covered the chicken and the potatoes. It still looked painfully appetising.

The boy could barely sit upright. His tears had dried long ago — he was too weak to shed more. Even Astaldo grew exhausted. He sat on his chair, his eyes closed and chin resting on his chest, snoring softly.

The boy swayed; his head felt heavy. He was going to faint. He put his hands on the floor to steady himself. The smallest piece of potato was right at the edge of the plate, so close to his fingers. It was crusted on the top.

Astaldo continued snoring.

No, *the boy thought. He tried to sit up straighter. The movement triggered a loud growl from his stomach. He grimaced as he glanced at Astaldo, but the breeder was still sleeping. That tiny piece of potato still balanced on the edge of the plate. It was such a small piece, Astaldo wouldn't have noticed if he'd just took it.*

No, he wasn't allowed to take. Taking was an Act of Defiance. He was a good purebred. He would do anything to be a good purebred. He just needed to stop looking at that piece of roasted, crispy potato. Its aroma teased his senses. He wiped his mouth again, trying not to imagine how it would taste on his tongue.

I live to serve, I breathe to please, *he thought. He repeated the phrase a dozen times in his head. He would not take. He knew very well what would happen. He had to prove that he'd learned his lesson.*

But Astaldo was still sleeping. He wasn't simply distracted or looking away. He had been awake as long as the boy had been. The breeder was exhausted, his mouth hanging slightly ajar. The boy stared at Astaldo's wide, bulky chest, watching it rise and fall steadily. He wiped his mouth and eyes again.

Astaldo really was sleeping.

He knew for sure the breeder wasn't faking. He'd spent enough nights staying awake and listening to Astaldo's soft breathing as the breeder slept, dreading the moment he'd wake. He could tell Astaldo really was asleep.

No, he thought once again, as his gaze drifted back to the golden-brown perfection. But his hand moved against his will. He took the potato and threw it in his mouth, sucking his fingers.

First, the rich flavours of the food exploded in his mouth. Then, the pain exploded everywhere else.

"Prihjtivaviula."

One second, Astaldo was snoring on his chair. The next, he was crouched beside him, fingers clamped around his neck. The boy's eyes rolled back as searing agony consumed him. His flesh burned from within, and his bones felt as though they'd been ground into dust. Whatever pain he had known before was nothing compared to this.

"Spit it out," Astaldo growled.

The boy couldn't comply, as his jaw was clenched tight and it wouldn't open. Astaldo turned him facedown. His fingers dug into the flesh of his neck, but the boy hardly felt those. Fires soared through his muscles and his body arched at impossible angles.

Astaldo didn't loosen his grip and he kept yelling at him to spit it out. The boy pushed the food out of his mouth as soon as the spasms ceased.

"You think you can just take *it? Huh?" Astaldo tossed him at a wall. The moment he hit the ground, the boy curled his knees beneath him, pressed his forehead to the floor, and shielded his head with his arms, choking back a ragged whimper.*

"You thought you could take *what you want? You don't* take *unless I give it to you! This is an Act of Defiance! Are you defying, slave?"*

"No, Owner," the boy whimpered.

"You act like a freeborn brat, you'll be trained like one. Get up!" Astaldo yanked the boy up by his hair and dragged him to the centre of the room, where leather straps hung from the ceiling.

"No, please..." The boy couldn't stop the whimper escape from his lips.

Astaldo froze. He pulled the boy's face closer to his. "Did you just speak? Did you just speak without permission?"

Tears ran down the boy's face. He bit his lip until it bled, to stop himself from making any more noises. He thought his heart might burst, fluttering frantically like a trapped bird.

"That's two Acts of Defiance. I will scrape your flesh off your bones for this. Prihjtivaviula.*"*

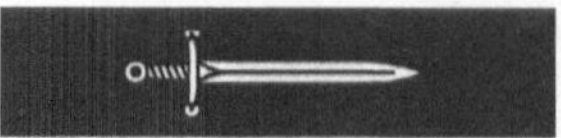

"Heed my word, slave," Keder hissed. "Our cruelties toward humans pale beside the horrors they inflict on one another. Yet it is us, the corespawn children of our shattered home who are shackled to this prison, while masters, owners, breeders and merchants roam Earthome unbound. Pray tell, how is that fair?"

Beast splashed cold water on his face, dragging his fingers through his damp hair. "You're asking *me* what's fair?"

The High Fiend chuckled. "Noted."

"I won't—" Beast's throat locked, and he had to swallow before he could continue talking. "I won't unleash you, and I don't need your help. I'll find a way."

"As you did with the woman? Indeed, I recall how that ended."

"It's a long way to Brinescar. I'll figure something—"

"Brinescar? What makes you presume that's where they are heading?"

Beast frowned. "They know who I am. They'll take me to Kastian and..."

Another grating sound emerged from the swirling black fog. "They will steer clear of Kastian Vogros."

"How do you— Do you know them?"

"I do not. But I discern what the name Lodi conceals. It is no mere name, but an ancient, Praxese word. And that is how I know he will not yield you."

Beast scratched his head, water dripping from his hair. He opened his mouth to ask Keder what he meant by that, but the black fog shifted like smooth oil, almost teasing him. It reminded him of the smug grin on Lodi's face each time the piece of shit glanced at Beast. His muscles tensed with a powerful urge to wake up and flatten the blond bastard's face with his fists.

He staggered when the mud gave way beneath him, pulling him in.

"Keep your senses sharp, slave," Keder hissed as Beast sank under water. "Study your enemy. Only then will you comprehend what Lodi truly is."

Beast's eyes snapped open to a new day.

17

BEAST

BEAST SLAPPED HIS HANDS on his knees and doubled over, his lungs burning with each shallow breath. His arms and legs felt heavy, weighed down by his own weakness. He drew a slow breath through his nose, forcing himself to steady the erratic rhythm of his heart. It had been too long since his body endured this kind of exercise. He hated how soft he had become.

A waterskin appeared near his face. Ink stood over him, watching with a flicker of pity in his eyes. Beast took a small sip — just enough to wet his dry throat — and handed it back.

The Kaldorian's brown hair stuck out in all directions, tousled by wind and the long ride. He was an odd one. He rarely seemed to pay Beast any mind, yet every time Beast was close to collapsing, Ink conveniently needed to take a piss, forcing the group to stop while he took his sweet time.

Beast straightened and followed Lodi's gaze toward the city of Kilrer, sprawling below them.

The sun hung high, veiled behind dense clouds that cast the landscape in muted grey. Morning had slipped away quickly. Beast's muscles had ached from the moment he woke, stiff and sore from the day before. There'd been no chance to stretch properly before they set out again.

Lodi had ordered Valnar to remove Beast's collar, claiming it would make running easier. Valnar had complied. Grudgingly. From then on, Lodi set the pace, slowing only when he decided Beast needed rest.

Keep your senses sharp, Keder had said. *Study your enemy.*

Beast had started to pay attention. Lodi was undoubtedly their leader. Valnar's ownership meant nothing. Lodi was the one who dictated how Beast would be treated. The authority in Lodi's voice left no room for argument, and Valnar obeyed him as readily as Ink. Lodi's and Ink's attire hinted at wealth: fine fabrics, quality craftsmanship. Valnar's equipment was decent too, yet modest.

Their travel formation told Beast more. Lodi kept him close, ordering him to keep up with his horse, while Ink scouted ahead and Valnar followed behind, watchful and rigid. Both were protective of Lodi, though Ink's vigilance felt lighter, more natural.

But none of this gave Beast any clue about their intentions — or the meaning of the word *Lodi.* And why the blond brat wanted him so much, if he wasn't going to deliver him to Kastian.

"The gates seem open," Valnar commented. He tried to sound casual, but he couldn't mask the concern underneath. His hand drifted to the tightly wrapped two-handed sword strapped to the back of his saddle, like he needed to check its security. Beast had noticed the big warrior touched that sword, or the Kiejain's symbol on his breastplate when he was uncomfortable. His shield and two swords hung at either side of the saddle, ready for a quick draw.

"I see city guards," Ink said, squinting at the figures by the gates. He and Valnar both turned toward Lodi, waiting for direction.

Lodi studied the city below with a scowl, his clean-shaven smooth face clouded by thoughts Beast couldn't read. He wore the look of someone trying to seem unbothered, but there was worry buried just beneath the surface, hidden behind a veil of charm.

Beast couldn't place where he had seen him before, but the familiarity itched at the edges of his memory. His best guess placed him as a young nobleman he'd seen at Castle Brinescar in his previous life. The way Valnar and Ink deferred to him only deepened the suspicion.

Muddy, sweat-soaked, and too tired to care, Beast didn't look away when Lodi caught him staring. What did the name mean? And what did he want from Beast?

"Valnar, give Beast your spare cloak," Lodi ordered coolly. "Put that on, slave, and keep the hood up."

Beast obeyed without comment, draping the cloak over his shoulders. The fabric smelled faintly of sweat and leather, but it provided a welcome barrier against the cold wind.

Valnar tossed something else at his feet. The collar and the chain.

Beast snatched it off the ground with a clenched jaw, hesitating for half a second before fastening the metal collar around his neck. City laws. Slaves wore chains.

Lodi clicked his fingers and held out his hand. Beast gathered the free end of the chain and slapped it in Lodi's waiting palm. The blond man took it as casual as if he were taking hold of a dog's lead. "Let's go," he said smoothly.

They moved toward the city at a slow pace, blending with the trickle of travellers approaching the gates. The walk helped ease the fire still lingering in Beast's muscles from the morning run, but the weight of the chain irritated him.

Beast could tell the three of them were nervous. Valnar rode close to Lodi, his eyes scanning the crowd and the guards. Ink kept glancing between the guardhouse inside the gates and the archers perched along the walls. Lodi, in contrast, leaned back in his saddle, exaggerating his nonchalance with a few lazy yawns. But to Beast, the act felt strained.

Ahead, the city guards stopped some travellers for questions or papers, though many were waved through without trouble. Beast noticed a pattern—men were scrutinised more closely than women, merchants, or the elderly.

When a guard gestured for their group to step aside, Beast felt the shift in the air. Valnar's hand rested on his thigh, Ink's jaw tightened, and Lodi's smile spread wide, bright and friendly.

"What is your purpose in Kilrer?" the guard asked.

"Visiting some friends."

"And where do your friends live?"

Lodi didn't skip a beat. "Petal Street, the house next to the loud old lady's."

"Hmph." The guard sized them. His gaze swept over Valnar, lingered on Ink, then back to Valnar. He hardly regarded Beast, who was still wearing Valnar's spare cloak with the hood up. The tattoo on his neck was visible, but the hood and the collar kept the details almost completely hidden.

"The slave's papers?"

"Of course, officer." Lodi smoothly leaned over his saddle bags and retrieved Beast's sales paper. As he handed it over, his fingers pressed a grey coin into the guard's palm.

The guard hardly glanced at the coin as he made it vanish in his belt. "Thank you, Master," he said, his tone somewhat less hostile. "Wait here." He turned and walked toward the guardhouse, the paper in hand.

Valnar didn't say a word, but he sighed heavily and fidgeted in his saddle. He touched Kiejain's symbol on his breastplate. Ink sucked his teeth, fiddling with the cuffs of his shirt while eyeing the nearest guards.

"Will you two stop acting suspicious?" Lodi hissed under his breath.

"We shouldn't have come here," Valnar muttered.

"Like we had a choice," Lodi snapped, though his tone shifted as he forced a smile. "It'll be fine."

The smile disappeared the instant the captain of the guards emerged from the guardhouse, followed by six armed men.

"Fuck," Valnar cursed under his breath. His gaze flicked to Ink. "Take the right. I'll—"

"We can't," Ink said sharply. Valnar followed his gaze up the city walls and saw the alert faces of archers. He cursed again.

"Dismount," the captain of the guards ordered. Half of his men circled around to take up position behind them. Their weapons remained sheathed, but their hands rested on the hilts.

Lodi didn't bother smiling anymore. A bitter anger turned his eyes to blue steel. After considering the order for a full moment, he swung down from his saddle, Beast's chain still in his palm. Valnar and Ink dismounted too.

"Is there a problem, Captain?" Lodi asked.

"Just a routine questioning," the captain replied. "Follow me inside."

"We'd very much rather be on our way," Lodi refused. "Is there any way we can avoid this?"

The captain of the guards rubbed his greasy beard. "I'm afraid not. Are you going to follow me inside on your own free will?" An unspoken *or else* hung in the air between them.

Lodi's glare could burn a hole through the man's face. There were nine guards around them now, together with the men who followed the captain from the guard house, and the ones who were already outside.

"You're making a big mistake," Lodi growled quietly.

"Don't make a bigger one," the captain replied.

The tension stretched, until Lodi finally shook his head and stomped to the guard house. He kept his chin high, eyes up front, his face a mask of proud anger. Beast followed him close, and the others right behind them.

"Stay close to him," Valnar whispered as he casually put a hand on Beast's shoulder. "If anything happens, you protect him first. This is an order. Do you understand?" His fingers squeezed.

"Yes, Owner," Beast gritted through his teeth, despite how many times he had fantasised about slitting Lodi's throat over the last few days.

The guardhouse was larger than it appeared from the outside. Sawdust coated the floor, muffling footsteps, and the air stank of vomit. Narrow windows admitted just enough sunlight to illuminate the space. Despite the room's size, the presence of so many guards made it feel stifling.

The captain retrieved a blanket and spread it across the table. "Weapons."

"Is this part of your routine questioning, Captain?" Lodi asked as he gave up his sword and knife. His voice was seething with poisonous contempt.

"Yes," the captain cut shortly.

Valnar's swords and Ink's bow remained on their saddles outside, but both men carried knives. Valnar placed his knife onto the blanket without hesitation. Ink, however, began pulling out an array of hidden weapons — small knives and palm-sized throwing discs tucked under layers of clothing and accessories. One by one, the pile grew. The captain's scowl deepened with every item.

Finally, Ink patted himself down and shook his head, signalling he was finished.

"Check him," the captain said. "Check all of them. Make sure they've got nothing else."

Beast raised his arms, letting the guards pat him down. Another knife was found on Ink, hidden in the seams of his vest. Ink shrugged, tapping his temple with mock innocence as if he'd simply forgotten. The captain wasn't amused.

"Can I get your name, Captain?" Lodi asked.

"Verrall."

"This doesn't feel like a routine questioning, Captain Verrall. Will you tell us what this is really about?"

"I'll let you know when I find out myself."

"What does that mean?"

Instead of answering, Verrall opened a door leading to a back room and gestured for them to enter.

"I'm not stepping in there until I get some answers," Lodi said, his voice firm.

"You don't really have a choice."

A guard stepped forward, hand outstretched to shove Lodi, but Valnar caught his wrist mid-motion, a disdainful look on his battle-worn face.

A brief pause hung in the air, followed by the sounds of weapons being drawn.

Beast tensed, his blood rushing for the fight. He scanned the few nearest opponents and fixed his eyes on the sword that was going to be in his hands within the next three seconds.

"Stop!" Lodi commanded. Beast felt goose bumps, realising it wasn't just Lodi's face that seemed familiar. It was his strong, commanding voice too. Lodi gripped the chain firmly, as if trying to restrain Beast.

"Weapons down," Captain Verrall ordered. The swords pointed down, but they remained unsheathed. Valnar let the guard's wrist go.

"My orders are to apprehend you, *unharmed*," Captain Verrall explained. "And to keep you here until further notice. Don't make my job difficult."

"I understand your position, Captain," Lodi said agreeably. "But tell me, whose order was it?"

"The order came from the keep. Now, get in."

Lodi's shoulders dropped slightly. Disbelief and confusion warred on his face. He dropped Beast's chain and marched inside, his head down and his hands balled into fists. The others followed, the chain trailing behind Beast with a low metallic scrape. The heavy door shut behind them, the lock clicking into place.

The room wasn't a cell, but it might as well have been. A small table with three mismatched chairs stood in the centre. A sink occupied one corner, while crates covered with blankets served as makeshift beds. The narrow windows let in little light and no hope of escape.

Lodi walked to the far wall and stood still, his back to the group. Beast studied him for a moment. That posture was painfully familiar. It mirrored how he'd felt the day Olira betrayed him.

"I knew it," Valnar growled. He ran his hand through his dark hair and let out a growl. "We should never have come here. We shouldn't have trusted him."

He walked over to the makeshift beds, yanked the blankets off and flipped the crates over, scouring for anything to use as a weapon. "We walked right into this. Right into it!" He dropped the crates and scanned the room. He screwed his face at Ink. "What in Darkhome are you doing?"

Ink's hand was down his pants, cupping his crotch. His face stilled with concentration, then a victorious smile bloomed as he pulled his hand free, a small throwing knife between his fingers. "They never find them all."

Valnar gawked. "Where the fuck was that hidden? H-how…?"

Ink offered the hilt to Valnar. "I'll fare well with my fists in close combat."

"Yeah… nah. I'm not touching that." Valnar turned and stomped on a chair leg until it snapped off. He held the jagged wood like a club.

"It was strapped to my thigh," Ink explained defensively.

"You were sitting on a horse!"

"I never said it was comfortable."

Valnar grabbed Beast by his collar and shoved him toward the door.

"What are you doing?" Ink asked.

"I'll Rage him as soon as they open the door."

Beast's stomach dropped. Bile surged into his throat as he squirmed against Valnar's grip, panic clawing its way up his spine. His eyes locked on the heavy door ahead, and suddenly all he could smell was sand and blood.

No.

His chest tightened. He bit down on his lip, hard enough to taste iron, swallowing the plea rising in his throat. *Don't Rage me. Please don't.*

Cold sweat soaked through his shirt. He hadn't been Raged since—

His mind recoiled from the memory like a hand from a flame.

"No!" Lodi snapped out of his quiet state. "You'll get him killed."

"Have you ever seen a purebred beast fight?" Valnar asked. "They won't know what hit them, and by the time they figure it out, we'll be joining the fight."

"I can't risk losing him."

"If we don't get out of here, he won't matter." Valnar's voice softened when he said, "We have to escape. He betrayed us."

Lodi looked away, fuming. He snatched the knife from Ink and took position behind them.

Beast swatted Valnar's hand off his collar and shrugged off the cloak. He wrapped the chain twice around his hand, leaving the free end loose like a whip. He felt too warm, the air too shallow around him. He couldn't let the Rage scour him like a current and dig out the memories of the last time.

How his fists broke Saradra's skin, what he'd found when he woke up—

"What's wrong with the slave?" Ink whispered.

Beast wiped the sweat off his clammy, pale skin.

Footsteps approached softly on the sawdust-covered floor outside.

"Kiejain, lend us your strength," Valnar prayed quietly.

"Let me fight bare," Beast spoke hoarsely.

"Shut up! Get ready."

The lock turned. The door swung open.

"*Drasci...*"

"Stop!"

The Rage had already begun creeping into Beast's thoughts, narrowing his vision and curling his fingers into fists. Lodi's voice pierced through the vibrating fog that threatened to claim him. A low growl escaped Beast's throat as his gaze locked onto the man who had entered.

The man looked at him, frozen. It was the expression of a man who walked into a room and came face to face with a nearly-Raged purebred beast.

"Kiejain's balls!" Captain Verrall cursed from behind the new man. He drew his sword and squeezed past the man. His guards followed, filling the space in a wave of steel.

"I told you idiots to take their weapons!" he barked over his shoulder, his gaze never leaving Beast. "*All* their weapons."

"Captain Verrall, stand back!" the new man ordered. His initial shock had passed, sharp eyes scanning the group behind Beast before settling on Lodi. Though his focus lingered on Lodi, he kept a wary eye on Beast.

"Leave the room. I'll speak to them alone."

"Sir?" Verrall asked, hesitation thick in his voice.

The hum of Rage still blurred Beast's vision. He blinked, trying to clear it. His gaze landed on the sword at the man's belt — and the whiteness of his knuckles wrapped tight around the hilt.

Captain Verrall licked his lips. "They have a purebred beast, Sir," he objected.

"I can see that." The man moved his hand away from the sword. "Leave us, Captain Verrall."

Verrall lowered his sword reluctantly. He wiped the sweat off his face, regarding his prisoners with plain distrust. Yet, he complied with a dispassionate, "Sir." He gestured his men to leave and followed them. "I'll be right outside, Sir," he announced before closing the door behind.

"Sir Serygrund," greeted Lodi when they were alone. His voice was cold, polite, cautious. "Explain."

Serygrund cast a glance at the door before gesturing toward the far side of the room, away from the prying ears. Lodi handed Ink his knife back and followed. Valnar wasn't relaxed enough to lower his club yet. He pushed Beast between Lodi and Sir Serygrund, as if the purebred was a shield. His lips were pressed, the Kill Word poised on his tongue.

"Your Highness," Sir Serygrund greeted Lodi with a deep bow.

Beast's head snapped up, the Rage finally retreating enough to let him think. He suddenly knew why Lodi's face was so familiar.

"How dare you lock your prince away like this," Valnar growled, stepping into Sir Serygrund's space, their faces nearly touching. "I should make you pay for this treason, even if it's the last thing I do."

Sir Serygrund didn't flinch. "Hold your temper, Sir Valnar. Kiejain demands restraint, doesn't he?"

Lodi — Prince Lygor Zarall, son of Leonis Zarall — cut in before Valnar could snap back. "Are we being held here to debate the virtues of the Twelve Riders?"

"You're not being held, Your Highness." A sharp glare at Valnar. *Sir* Valnar. "I apologise for the treatment, but this was the safest way to arrange a meeting without revealing your identity." He nodded toward the door, reminding the listening ears behind it.

"Are you going to explain why we are here?" Lygor demanded. "I thought we were meeting Lord Rhuagh."

"Lord Rhuagh instructed me to stop you before you entered the city," Serygrund explained. "He asked me to inform you that Kilrer is unsafe. The keep is hosting Lord Heilamin, along with two-hundred of his house guards."

Lygor tilted his head, his voice bitter. "Is Lord Rhuagh changing his allegiance?"

"Never, Your Highness. But aiding you while Kastian Vogros's cousin was under his nose would yield dangerous results for Lord Rhuagh. He wanted me to explain to you, that his daughter, Lady Lona, is a maid-in-waiting for Princess Lareani, at Castle Brinescar."

With a furious shake of his head, Lygor looked away, nostrils flaring. A vein popped in his neck, his anger not letting him speak.

"Lord Rhuagh cannot offer you sanctuary in Kilrer," Serygrund concluded. "It would be best for you to turn back."

"Tell me, Sir Serygrund, does Lord Rhuagh remember growing up with my father? Squiring together? Taking an oath to serve and protect House Zarall?"

Sir Serygrund paused. "Lord Rhuagh remains loyal to House Zarall. Always. But he cannot act explicitly in your favour until conditions change."

"You mean until I have enough allies and an army behind me?"

Sir Serygrund looked away, feigning embarrassment. "Your horses are outside and I will let Captain Verrall know that you'll be collecting your weapons on your way out." He nodded sharply and turned to leave. He openly ignored Valnar, and he kept a careful distance from Beast, but he paused in front of Ink.

"Prince Ingelhar, I presume?"

Beast resisted the urge to snap his head up again. *Another prince?*

Ink raised his head and gave a cold smile, idly twirling his throwing knife between his fingers.

Serygrund's lips thinned. "Is it foolish to hope Kaldoria will stay out of our internal disputes?"

"My father doesn't take counsel from me," Ink said. "I'm only seventeenth in line."

Serygrund pursed his lips. "Kastian Vogros didn't even have a number."

Ink's eyes turned to steel. His fingers tightened around the knife.

Sir Serygrund walked off, unbothered by the reaction. The room felt chilled.

18

OLIRA

Olira's boots were bleeding dust with every furious step as she stormed through the road like a raging torrent. She refused to acknowledge the sun, slipping behind the hills, stealing the daylight with it. She kept her eyes fixed on the long shadows stretching across the road ahead, as if she could will them to reveal what she sought.

When she blinked, her eyes still burned. From fury. From self-contempt. From the grit and dust of the road, and from a night spent howling at the wind as she tried to wipe that look the slave had cast her before he was dragged away.

Her muscles screamed in protest, but she pushed through. She wasn't stopping until she caught them. Or at least caught sight of them. She refused to believe they could have gained this much distance in one hour. Not with him on foot.

One hour. That was all she had wasted standing there like a Twelve-times-cursed idiot, frozen with those dead-blue plates in her arms. She hadn't realised how fast the sun had moved in the sky by the time she'd snapped out of her stupor and understood what she had done.

She'd sold him.

He wanted his freedom. He had shown her he was more than a mindless shell.

And she'd sold his life away.

"Stupid," she muttered, adjusting the coin purse that weighed heavy at her hip. Three hundred and fifty Blues. The price she'd accepted for a man's freedom.

Her stomach churned every time the coins clinked together. "Fiends chew my bones, I'm so stupid!"

She wiped her burning eyes harshly, the rough gesture doing nothing to ease the sting.

The backpack bit deep into her shoulders, her knees threatening to give under its burden. The weight of the coin purse could not compare to the weight of the guilt and shame that pressed down on her chest.

The air chilled as the sun retreated further, but the intensity of her pace and the exhaustion coursing through her muscles kept her warm, almost feverishly so.

She would catch up with them. She would find them.

And she would throw Lodi's money and demand he gave Beast back to her.

And then...

And then she would find a way to help the man earn his freedom.

She stumbled and fell forward, crushing under the weight of the bag. Her palms scraped raw against the half-frozen earth, her knees taking the brunt of the impact. This wasn't the first time her tired muscles had betrayed her in the last two days. If not her dwindling strength, the night would force her to stop soon.

With a growl, she pushed herself back to her feet. Shadows stretched ahead of her like grasping fingers. She still had another hour or two before she lost light entirely. Maybe another hour after that, if she dared to walk in the dark.

If she dared...

She heard the sound of hooves approaching. Her heart leaped as she looked up, naively expecting to see the three riders and Beast somewhere in the near distance, but the sound was coming from behind her.

Riders. A large group of them.

They were coming up the road straight at her.

Fear flooded her thoughts. Bandits? This close to Kilrer? These roads should have been patrolled by Lord Rhuagh's soldiers...

Relief washed through her as she caught glimpses of uniforms through the dust. Kilrer soldiers, returning from patrol, most likely.

As she squinted through the dust, their uniforms became clearer — silver and blue, the colours glinting faintly in the fading light. A spark of hope bloomed in her chest, so sudden it nearly brought tears to her eyes. She waved her arms frantically, afraid they might ride straight past.

She could ask for help. Get a ride, at least as far as Kilrer. She was certain Lodi and the others were headed that way.

She tossed her backpack aside and waved again. They were slowing now, but something in their approach made her step back. They weren't just passing by — they were converging on her position like hunters closing in on prey.

The dust settled around them as they spread out in an arc, surrounding her. A massive man with pale blond hair and a rank on his shoulder that she didn't recognise guided his horse forward. Beside him, a younger man in rich clothes studied her with sharp green eyes, his fine garments setting him apart from the others. Something in his expression made her take an instinctive step backward.

"Olira Aryanna?" The blond man's voice carried a note of authority that made her stomach lurch.

"Y-yes, but—"

"Where's the slave?" the young man cut in, his tone sharp with accusation.

The circle of horses tightened around her. In the deepening twilight, their shadows stretched across the road like prison bars.

"How do you—" Olira muttered. "Who are—"

Her thoughts scattered like startled birds. The slave? These men knew about Beast? Her gaze darted between their stern faces, questions tangling on her tongue. The young man's green eyes seemed to pierce through her in the gathering dark.

"I— What's this about? How do you—"

"Where is he?" the young man barked, making her flinch.

"Olira Aryanna," the blond giant's voice cut through her confusion, "you are under arrest for theft."

19

BEAST

THE WATER HAD RISEN again. It reached his thighs now, lapping gently against his skin with a sound like quiet breathing. Beast stood in the flooded cavern, the stone walls around him slick with darkness. There was a subtle hum in the air. He thought it might have already been there, but he was only just noticing the unnatural energy that always lingered. Like a muted, background noise of an arena full of spectators.

The fiend hounds still waited silently by the cavern walls. Their eyes were dim slits watching him like statues carved from nightmares.

The surface of the water rippled outward when he shifted his weight, the water carrying his restlessness across the cavern. He fidgeted with the object at his chest, feeling its steady, grounding thrum.

"You knew who he was," Beast said.

Keder floated inside the cage, the dark smokes shifting into shadows and back. His form was almost visible, as if teasing him for a better look, though Beast was wary of it.

"Lodi is a title," the High Fiend said. "It is short for *Lodi ra Venthul*. It means, My Ruler."

"He's Lygor Zarall," Beast said quietly. "King Leonis's son."

"Hence you are doomed."

Beast's jaw clenched. He turned away, wading through the water with a sudden splash that echoed off the stone.

"He desires you for the same purpose as Kastian," Keder said, his voice patient, though there was a calculating edge to it. "You are Lion of Zarall."

Beast looked down at the water. Though it was pitch-black, a faint reflection of his own face shimmered back at him. Wet blond hair clung to his forehead in tangled waves, wild enough to resemble a lion's mane. His eyes didn't catch the light; they appeared as dark voids, hollow and empty. The grotesque, tooth-shaped object on his chest pulsed with a low thrum, catching a glint of light from the cage bars above.

"You have, in some way, become a symbol within their schemes," Keder continued. "Therefore he shall never release you."

"No." With a sharp motion, Beast slapped the water, shattering the image into ripples.

"He has gone to such lengths to secure you. You think he'll suffer your freedom?"

"There has to be a way to convince him."

"He needs you to reclaim his throne," Keder said. The smoke coiled inside the cage in a mocking pattern.

"I don't get it," Beast snapped. "How am I going to help him get his throne? I'm a fucking slave!"

"You are not particularly clever, are you?" Keder said, almost fond. "He must control you, so he may dictate what you signify."

Beast stilled at the word.

Control.

Something scratched at the back of his mind, insistent and itchy, like grit beneath a collar. His gaze drifted to the flickering shadows dancing along the cavern walls as the idea slowly took shape.

Men didn't need chains to control others.

"That will not work," Keder hissed.

"Then why are you so worried?" Beast narrowed his eyes at the cage.

The shadows inside the cage convulsed. Darkness twisted violently, forming vague shapes that never quite held long enough to make sense. The air thickened with a low, guttural sound and Keder's voice cracked like splitting stone.

"You arrogant little husk. You fancy yourself clever for having strung together half a thought?"

The fiend hounds let out a chorus of growls, though they remained dormant.

Beast didn't flinch, despite the urge to shy away from the fury that boiled out of the cage. The bars gleamed with a pale, white light, casting log streaks across the water.

"You believe you might persuade these men?"

"I only need to convince Lygor," Beast said, his throat dry.

"Consider well," Keder snapped. "He's a prince. Raised in a court and schooled in the art of manipulation. He can bend your own words to his purpose."

"I just need to give him the idea—"

"And the knight will not even grant you speech."

He crossed his arms tightly, resisting the instinct to reach for his neck. The bruises and raw skin from the collar didn't follow him into Darkhome — wounds seemed to stay behind in Earthhome — but the memory of them lingered, sharp enough to make him flinch every time he moved.

"That shit smear on Kiejain's foot will shut you up and beat the life from your flesh," Keder said. "And you speak with the wit of a half-dead mule whose tongue is nailed to a gate."

"Fuck you."

Keder went silent. The water seemed to still with him. Beast glanced down — no ripples, not even where his legs broke the surface. The black pool had calmed completely, as if holding its breath at the High Fiend's command. His chest tightened, but he reminded himself Keder couldn't touch him here. The object on his chest pulsed again. Like a whisper of reassurance.

The High Fiend was right with his assessment. Beast was shit at talking. Unless someone asked him a direct question and he knew exactly what to say, speaking felt like dragging stones uphill. Especially with free men and women. His mind would freeze, and his words would get jumbled up. He always sounded so stupid.

And Lygor... Lygor intimidated him. Not physically — Beast could flatten that scrawny prince with both arms tied and not lose his breath. But there was something else. The way Lygor wielded words like weapons. How he always seemed to know exactly what to say, how to say it, and when. Worse, he didn't give up. He'd worked on Olira like a dog that wouldn't unclench its jaw, relentless and calm and infuriatingly persuasive.

The thought of talking to him — really talking — made Beast's throat go dry.

"Yet here you speak so casually to a monarch of our shattered home," Keder said, the sneer tangible in his voice. "It betrays how foolish you truly are."

Beast didn't answer.

"You will fail."

"Then help me," Beast said, quieter now. "Help me talk. Like you did with Olira."

"Drink."

Beast's gaze slid to the surface of the black water. It looked so calm and harmless.

"No."

"Then you're on your own."

Beast cast one last look at the cage, at the swirling dark within, then drew a steady breath and willed himself back to Earthome. The mud beneath his feet shifted, softening, pulling him down. Water rose past his chest, his shoulders, his throat. He didn't resist. He held his breath and let the black water close over his head.

Down he went, sinking through cold silence and thick soil, the world above fading into darkness. The descent felt like falling and flying at the same time. The object on his chest throbbed steadily, a faint pulse in the dark.

Then the pull released, and he woke up.

20

VALNAR

Valnar poked the campfire with a stick, scattering sparks in the air. He glanced up at the sky. The sun was almost behind the hills, painting them blood-red. Then, he glanced at the woods for what felt like the hundredth time, his jaw clenched tight. He muttered a short prayer under his breath, not for safety, but for discipline. Kiejain didn't favour fools, and he'd already tested the First Rider's patience once today.

"He'll be okay," Ink said. Valnar grunted. The Kaldorian's calm voice grated on him. Letting Lygor go had been stupid and dangerous, and Ink knew it.

As soon as the city of Kilrer was far behind them, Lygor had broken into a gallop, his horse's hooves thundering against the hard ground. Ink went after him, leaving Valnar to supervise the slave. The creature could barely walk straight, let alone run. Each step looked like it might be his last.

Valnar loathed being forced to stay behind while Lygor rode off. He had almost failed him once today in the city, and the guilt of it sat heavy in his gut. Kiejain didn't grant second chances like this. They were lucky to have walked out of there unharmed. As much as he'd wanted to go after Lygor, he couldn't leave Beast behind; not after the lengths they'd gone to obtain him. So he'd removed the collar and had forced the slave into a ruthless run. He'd cursed every time the pathetic thing fell behind.

When he'd finally caught up with Ink, the Kaldorian stood at the edge of a grove, Lygor's horse in tow. "He's hunting," Ink had said, his tone maddeningly neutral. The prince had taken Ink's bow and disappeared into the woods.

That had been an hour ago.

Valnar and Ink had lit a campfire and had been waiting by the edge of the silent and dark woods with no sign of Lygor.

Now, Valnar stared at the fire, the embers spiralling in the air, as restless as he felt. He wanted to storm into the trees and drag Lygor back. He hated waiting, hated the unknown.

"Why don't you go and pray?" Ink suggested. "I know you want to. I'll keep an eye on the slave."

Valnar shot him a glare but didn't argue. The beast didn't need keeping an eye on — not in his current state. The creature lay sprawled on his back, chest heaving, limbs splayed out uselessly, sleeping like a log. A husk of flesh and bone. Valnar had decided against chaining him again. He doubted if he could even lift a finger, let alone try to escape. No, it wasn't the beast that worried him tonight.

He scowled at the woods. Ink was right — he did want to pray. Needed to, really. He'd almost gotten Lygor killed today. Kiejain frowned upon men who failed their calling. He had to atone.

"I'll be back promptly."

"Take your time."

Valnar rushed through his prayers, though he knew that would only anger Kiejain more. He drew a hasty circle in the dirt, sat in it, and recited the shortest passage he could remember. When he pressed his forehead to the ground to beg forgiveness, the soil was cold enough to make him shiver. He asked Kiejain to forgive his sins and his failure to protect the prince, but his mind kept wandering back to the camp.

When he returned, Lygor still wasn't back.

"It's getting late," Valnar grunted.

Ink shrugged, the casual gesture making Valnar's hand itch for his sword. He kept himself busy instead: grooming the horses until their coats shone, laying out the bedrolls, counting their supplies. The food wouldn't last much longer. Just when he decided to go look for Lygor, footsteps crunched through the leaves.

"Kiejain's might! Where have you been?"

Lygor walked into the firelight. He tossed a dead rabbit near the fire and dropped Ink's bow by the saddlebags. Without a word, he pulled out his skinning knife and started cleaning the rabbit. His hands were steady but his face was hard, missing its usual smirk.

"Lodi..." Valnar started, then stopped. He'd served Lygor the last five years, but he'd never seen him like this. Angry, yes. Disappointed, sometimes. But this was different. Lygor looked betrayed. Lost. "Let me do that for you."

"No."

Valnar stepped back. He watched Lygor's knife strip skin and hair from the dead animal with quick, sharp movements. When the meat was ready, Valnar grilled it while Lygor washed the blood from his hands. The sounds of splashing water seemed too loud in the silence.

They sat down to eat. The rabbit was tough and bland, but none of them complained.

"We considered the possibility of Lord Rhuagh selling us out," Valnar broke the uncomfortable silence. "We can still—"

"He didn't sell us out," Lygor snapped. His knife stabbed into what was left of the rabbit. "He kicked us out of his city and told us to come back with better odds."

"You are the rightful heir," Valnar grumbled. "He's committing treason."

"And he will be punished, but not a moment before I have an army behind me."

Valnar set his plate aside and wiped his greasy hands on his cloak. "We still have Lord Miraris. He's unpredictable, sure, but he's got the coin to buy an army. Let me approach him alone, feel out where his loyalties lie."

"I already know where his loyalties lie — on his purse strings," Lygor snapped. "I'd sooner risk going to King Zumnorin than gamble with Miraris."

"Yeah... nah, I wouldn't do that," Ink cut in, his tone casual. "You know what my father will demand in return."

"And I'll never hand over a single grain of soil to the Kaldorians. No offence."

"None taken," Ink replied with a shrug.

Lygor leaned forward, the firelight sharpening the lines of frustration etched into his face. "We need an army. Allies. And enough coin to pay for both."

"Then we need leverage," Ink said. "Information we can use to twist a few arms. I know someone in—"

A rustle behind them made Valnar's hand shoot to his sword.

The slave stood at the edge of the firelight, and Valnar cursed himself for not hearing him approach. He'd left a plate of meat beside the sleeping beast earlier, but now both plate and slave were much closer than they should be. How much had he heard?

The creature's shoulders were hunched, his stance unsteady, but he was standing — which shouldn't have been possible after today's forced march. Valnar's eyes narrowed as the slave pressed a fist against his throat. The gesture, a request for permission to speak, only deepened his scowl.

First eavesdropping, and now wanting to talk?

Before Valnar could tell him to get back to his spot, Lygor spoke. "You may speak."

The slave shuffled another step forward, and Valnar's grip tightened on his sword hilt. Lygor leaned slightly, the firelight catching on his narrowed eyes as he watched the man with newfound interest. From his spot by the fire, Ink gave the slave a small, encouraging nod. He didn't stop eating, just paused long enough to show he was watching too.

The slave's hands clasped together in front of him, fingers working against each other nervously. His eyes darted between them, then fixed on the ground. When he finally spoke, his voice was rough with disuse.

"There's..." he started, then stopped, shifting his weight as if regretting drawing their attention. "There's Twilight of Infinity."

Valnar snorted, but Lygor raised a hand, silencing him. Ink tossed the leftover scraps in his plate into the flames. "What's Twilight of Infinity?"

The slave's fingers twisted harder. "Umm... It's a... It's a big tournament. Very big. And there's a money prize. A great sum." He swallowed when he caught the spark of hunger, then outrage on Lygor face. "Enough to buy an army."

Valnar surged to his feet. "It's not your place to—"

"I can't let you fight in an arena," Lygor interrupted firmly. "Kastian Vogros is looking for you. The moment you step in front of a crowd that size, someone will recognise you."

"So," Valnar growled, rounding on the slave, "you should shut your mouth and get back to—"

"Twilight of Infinity is in Euroad," the slave cut him off.

Valnar froze, the vein in his temple pulsing dangerously. He'd cut him off! The audaciousness of the act bordered on madness. *How dare he...*

He closed the space between them in three strides, looming over the slave like Kiejain's wrath. "I ordered you to shut your mouth, slave," he hissed. "Get back to your spot."

The slave didn't flinch, didn't even look at him. His body was rigid with defiance. He stared intently at Lygor, pointedly disregarding Valnar to speak only to the prince.

"Why did you buy me?"

"*Phrijtivaviula*!" Valnar said.

"Valnar!" Lygor roared.

Valnar stepped back, watching the slave collapse to the ground and writhe in the dirt. His fists were clenched tight, his chest rising and falling with barely suppressed rage.

"He disobeyed," Valnar said with a quiet tremor. "He committed an Act of Defiance!"

"I gave him permission to speak."

"Lygor, you shouldn't indulge him. He's a slave. He has no place suggesting—"

"Euroad," Ink mused. "That's one of those independent cities, isn't it?"

"It doesn't matter," snapped Valnar. "We can't go there."

"Yes," Lygor explained to Ink, ignoring Valnar's protests. "The Chinderian throne doesn't rule Euroad. Kastian has no authority."

"That doesn't mean he won't have allies there," Valnar objected. He added with a quiet distaste, "Not to mention it's a city of heathens. We need someone we can trust. Someone who has been loyal to the throne."

"Kastian is afraid of a riot," the slave spoke through a strained throat, still faintly spasming from the last remnants of the pain that coursed through his body. He lifted himself off the ground on his elbows and knees, glaring at Lygor, his mangy blond hair cascading over his eyes. "Last thing he wants is Lion of Zarall winning another tournament."

Valnar flinched — not at the words themselves, but at the way they were spoken. Coherent and defiant. Alive.

This wasn't the hollow creature he'd seen stumbling behind their horses. This was something else entirely. His mind churned with memories of the rumours — whispers of how Lion of Zarall was broken. How he had gone mad and killed free men. How he was a rabid animal, pushed too far. The truth of those rumours slapped him in the face.

A cold sweat crept down Valnar's back.

"*Phrijtivaviula*," he spat, his voice trembling with the need to reassert control.

"I order you to stop using that word," Lygor sneered. He was up on his feet too, his fists trembling at his sides.

"Lodi, I..." Valnar trailed off, shrinking under the prince's piercing glare. He had witnessed Lygor grilling others with that glare many times, but had never been the recipient of it. Embarrassment and heartbreak twisted together in his chest. He wanted to explain, to make his prince understand the danger of a disobedient purebred. If those rumours about Lion of Zarall were true...

Valnar glanced at Ink for help, but the Kaldorian avoided meeting his eyes. Ink's jaw tensed as he watched the thrashing beast. There was no pity in Ink's gaze, only a quiet unease, as though he were weighing the line between duty and disapproval. He shook his head subtly and looked away, staying silent.

"He— He disobeyed," Valnar's voice faltered under the weight of his own embarrassment. "He shouldn't—"

Lygor breathed through his nose. "I need some space." He turned on his heel and strode into the dark woods, leaving Valnar rooted in place.

Beast staggered to his feet, his breaths ragged and shallow, his body slick with sweat. His muscles twitched with pain or with hardly restrained violence. Fury poured out of him, almost heating the air around him, though all Valnar felt was a chill down his spine.

Beast squared his shoulders and met Valnar's gaze. He drew every breath like an Act of Defiance.

Valnar stared back. He now knew why the slave unnerved him since he first saw him. The creature that stared at him behind those grey eyes was not simply an empty shell with no *rhoa*.

There was something else other than a *rhoa* inside him.

"Get out of my sight," Valnar growled.

He feared the purebred would disobey again, forcing him to choose between defying Lygor's order or letting the defiance go unpunished. Either path would mean failure.

To his surprise, Beast obeyed. Without a word, he turned and walked to his spot by the fire, pulling his borrowed blanket over his hunched form. The slave's retreat wasn't submission. It was restraint.

This was a trial, sent by Kiejain.

Valnar saw it clearly now. He had wavered in the city, nearly failed his duty and his faith — and the First Rider had answered with a test. A purebred that spoke. That defied its place. That challenged a warrior of Kiejain.

Valnar ground his teeth, his chest tight. He drew the Twelve's sign in the air. He would not fail again.

He turned toward the woods, where shadows pooled between the trees, and started after Lygor.

"Yeah... I wouldn't go after Lygor right now," Ink said, tracking his gaze. "Not sure if you've noticed, but he was a bit angry."

"I'm just trying to keep him safe," Valnar said, glaring back at the slave. Shadows creeped over the purebred's form like a second blanket.

"Also, don't be a dick, Valnar."

Valnar's head snapped at Ink. "You don't understand how dangerous a broken purebred is," he hissed, keeping his voice low. "What he did was... It shouldn't have been possible!"

"What? Having an opinion and suggesting an idea?"

"He shouldn't have opinions. He doesn't have a *rhoa*. He's no human."

"Yeah, but you are."

The words struck Valnar harder than any blow. He felt the heat rise in his chest, anger and something uncomfortably close to shame colliding. His mouth opened, but no words came.

Ink leaned forward, his eyes steady. "I know you. You're not someone who would hurt a man just for talking back."

"He's not a man—"

"I don't care if he's a pet worm. Do better."

Valnar's throat tightened. His gaze shifted back to the slave, who lay huddled beneath the blanket, a defiant stillness in his form. The creature was broken in ways that made him unpredictable — a weapon without a handle. Every instinct screamed that the danger wasn't gone, just biding its time.

21

DIENUS

THE FOREST WAS QUIET, save for the distant hum of insects and the faint rustling of leaves in the breeze. Dienus found the stillness irritating. It amplified everything he hated — the clinking of armour as his men shifted, the faint sniffling of the woman sitting by the tree, and worst of all, the hollow ache of boredom. He crossed his arms, his sharp green eyes fixed on the prisoner.

Olira Aryanna. A farmer, supposedly. She sat with her knees drawn up, her bound wrists resting in her lap, her head bowed like some pitiful creature waiting for the slaughter. Her brown hair hung in dark, tangled strands, obscuring most of her face, but even from here, he could see the tremble in her hands. She wasn't just scared. She was cornered, and she knew it.

"I didn't know he was stolen," she said, her voice small, shaking.

Dienus sighed, letting his irritation seep into the sharp edge of his tone. "He wasn't just stolen," he sneered, taking a step toward her. "He was stolen from *the King of Chinderia.*"

Her gaze dropped to the ground, her lips parting wordlessly before she tried again. "I-I didn't know that. I bought him from a trader in Kiore. I had no idea—"

"Didn't you recognise the brands?" Lieutenant Quinner cut in.

"No, I didn't see them. And I didn't know what they meant—"

Quinner narrowed his eyes suspiciously. "You didn't see them, or you didn't recognise them? Which one?"

Olira shook her head, her hair falling forward to hide her face. "I didn't see them at first. And then when I had to treat his infection—"

"How come you didn't see them at first?" Dienus interrupted. "Didn't you examine him?"

"No, I—"

"What kind of idiot buys a slave without examining them?"

"I was—"

"And why would a farmer invest in a purebred beast in the first place?

"Master Gladwiel forced me to—"

Dienus raised his eyebrows. "Someone forced you to purchase a purebred beast?"

"He owed me a hundred and fifty Blues. He wasn't paying—"

Dienus folded his arms, raising an eyebrow. "Your story doesn't make sense. How does a dirt-farming peasant end up loaning a hundred and fifty Blues to a slave merchant?"

The defiance in her eyes faltered, but only for a moment. "I grow rare herbs," she said through clenched teeth. "Pelleogano Petals. Tiger Blossom. He uses them to heal slaves and sell them."

"Oh, a businesswoman, are you?" Dienus mocked. "And you saw the perfect opportunity when you had the king's prized purebred in your hands."

Her jaw tightened, but she said nothing, her gaze falling once more to the dirt. Dienus felt a flicker of satisfaction. She was crumbling, and he relished it.

Quinner stepped closer, his tone softer than Dienus liked. "Where is Lion of Zarall now?"

"She sold him," Sir Gennald spoke. He tossed a heavy purse onto the ground between them.

Dienus picked up the purse and weighed it in his palm. He undid the leather strap and glanced inside. "So how much did you get paid for the slave you didn't know was Lion of Zarall?"

The girl muttered something with a voice trembling so miserably it was hard to hear.

"How much?"

"Three hundred and fifty."

Dienus whistled low, crouching, so he was eye level with her. "Three hundred and fifty? That's quite a lot for a common slave."

Olira remained silent.

"You've made quite a profit off him, haven't you?"

Olira raised her tied hands and wiped her cheek.

"Who did you sell him to?" Quinner asked.

Olira sighed. She hung her head like a dying flower; her brown hair concealed her face. "Three men."

"Their names?"

"They didn't give me their names," Olira said, her head still hung low.

"So…" Dienus licked his lips. "Three men with no names stop you on the road, offer you three hundred and fifty Blues, which they conveniently carried on them, for a slave that cost you nothing, and you still don't suspect anything?"

"I did, but—"

"You know what, Olira Aryanna, I think you're full of shit. I think you were well aware of the slave's identity. But instead of returning him to King Kastian, you chose to make a profit off him. That makes you a thief."

"I am not a thief!" Her voice cracked with fury. She glared up at him, tears streaming down her face. "I had sales papers. I didn't commit any crime, and I told you everything I know. Now, please, let me go home."

Dienus's laughter was low and sharp. He leaned further, held her gaze, and spoke the two words that would destroy the pathetic liar.

"What home?"

"Your Highness." Quinner's hand shot out, gesturing Dienus away from the woman. The lieutenant's eyes had hardened to stone. Dienus followed him, but took his time doing it. Behind them, Olira's breathing turned rapid and shallow.

"What?" Her voice cracked. "What does that mean?" When neither man answered, panic edged into her tone. "*What does that mean?*"

"What is it, Lieutenant?" Dienus drawled out.

Quinner's glare lasted only a heartbeat before his face smoothed into careful neutrality. "I will take a group with me to Kilrer and ask about those three men."

"What does that mean?" Olira lunged to her feet, but Sir Gennald's hand clamped down on her shoulder, forcing her back to the ground. "Stop! What did you mean by that?"

"Great! I'm coming with you," Dienus said, already imagining what waited in the city. Kilrer would have pleasure houses — several, if he was lucky. Their visit to Aryanna farm had taken the edge off his need, but he was still itching to get his hands on a purebred and experiment further.

Olira thrashed against Gennald's grip, her chest heaving with panicked breaths. Her voice rose higher with each question: "What does that mean? What— What happened to my home? *What did you do?*"

"I don't think that's a good idea, Your Highness." A subtle smile played at Quinner's lips, and Dienus wanted to smash it off his face. "Your presence would attract attention. Someone might recognise you."

"That's bullshit!"

Olira's screams cut through their argument: "What have you done? What have you done to my brothers?"

"The king tasked me to make any decisions to ensure the success of this mission, Your Highness," Quinner said, his voice flat. Each word felt like a spit at Dienus's face. "It is in your best interest to stay here with the men."

Dienus stepped closer, barely hearing Olira's hysterical sobs through the ringing in his ears. His vision had narrowed to Quinner's face. "You can't order me," he growled, keeping his voice low enough that the man couldn't hear the tremor in it.

Quinner blinked slowly. "Of course not, Your Highness. I believe *your orders* came from the king."

Every hair on Dienus's arms stood up. The force of the words knocked the wind out of him. There was no mistaking the threat buried in Quinner's calm tone, no matter how carefully he'd wrapped it in courtesy. The image flashed through Dienus's mind — Quinner ordering his men to seize their prince, to bind his hands like a common criminal and sit him next to their sobbing prisoner. No matter how much authority his father had given the lieutenant, he wouldn't dare lay hands on Dienus.

Would he?

"I will enquire about the three travellers' whereabouts in the city, and inform you as promptly as possible, Your Highness," Quinner said. His face showed nothing but an officer's disciplined courtesy, which somehow made it worse. Even his tone was perfectly respectful — too perfect.

"I'd appreciate that, Lieutenant," Dienus forced out between clenched teeth.

Quinner strode away to gather his men, his back straight as an arrow. Behind them, Olira's desperate questions about her brothers had turned to wordless mewling. Two men now struggled to hold her down — Sir Gennald and one of Quinner's soldiers — their faces red with effort.

Dienus's teeth ground together hard enough to hurt. The sour taste of defeat coated his tongue, bitter and familiar. He hated it. Twelve Riders knew how he hated it. He needed a win, needed to do something to wash this taste off his mouth.

As Dienus approached, Olira's tantrum faltered, her energy sapped by grief and exhaustion. Tears streamed down her dirt-streaked face, her wide brown eyes locking onto his with a desperate, pleading intensity. "You knew my name," she sobbed, her voice cracking. "You've been to my farm. Please..."

Dienus crouched in front of her. He placed a firm hand on her shoulder, his grip just shy of painful, and leaned in until his face was a breath away from hers. His voice was soft, almost intimate, as he delivered the words like a knife to the gut.

"I burned your farm," he said slowly, enunciating each word with precision. "And I killed all your brothers."

He watched her eyes with fascination as the weight of his words hit her. Her face crumpled, her features twisting under the unbearable force of loss and disbelief. Her eyes lost their focus, staring blankly past him as her body shuddered.

Then, the dam broke.

A raw, primal scream ripped from her throat, shaking the air.

"No! You're lying!" she screamed, thrashing violently against her bindings as though sheer will could undo the truth.

Her cries morphed into incoherent wails, her voice cracking under the strain. She clawed at the earth, her bound hands trembling as she fought against reality itself. Gennald had to pin her to the ground to keep her from hurting herself.

Even so, her body writhed beneath his weight, her fury and despair bleeding into every muscle.

Dienus stood, brushing the dirt from his hands as he observed her. Her screams grated his ears, yet they were strangely satisfying. He watched as her grief consumed her, as the fight drained from her limbs, and left only broken sobs in its wake.

Her despair was a reminder of Dienus's power, his ability to crush someone so utterly.

Yet, the moment passed, and boredom crept back in.

By the time Quinner returned from Kilrer, the echoes of Olira's sobs had faded into the stillness of the forest. She sat slumped against the tree like a corpse. Dienus spared her only a glance before turning his attention to Quinner, who strode into the camp with his usual brisk efficiency.

"Gate guards detained then released three men and a purebred beast outside the city," Quinner said, his tone clipped.

"Why?"

"They didn't disclose why the men were held or by whom."

"You didn't bother to get their names, did you?"

Quinner ignored the comment, continuing. "Our scouts found fresh tracks leading east from the city: three riders and a man on foot. We will follow them at first light."

"And the woman?"

"She's coming with us."

22

VALNAR

Lygor hadn't slept all night. Valnar knew it, because he hadn't either.

The forest was quiet in the pale light of early morning. The trees cast long shadows across the frost-dappled ground and a thin mist clung to the underbrush. Valnar pulled his cloak against the lingering chill as he tightened the straps of his saddle. The metal of his armour, still cold from the night, pressed against his shoulders beneath the cloak.

His eyes flicked to Lygor, who stood a short distance away. Standing still, he was too deep in thought to be bothered by the cool breeze that tugged at his coat. He hadn't spoken a word since he'd returned from his long walk last night. He'd brushed off their questions with a curt, "We'll talk in the morning," and had crawled into his bedroll.

But morning had come, and still, Lygor hadn't said a thing. His silence felt sharper than any blade.

Valnar's hands paused on the saddle strap as he watched his prince. Lygor stood with his arms crossed, staring into the misty horizon as if it held the answers to questions only he could ask. His posture was stiff, his shoulders rigid, but there was something else beneath the surface that Valnar couldn't quite place.

Perhaps Lygor's silence was its own form of penance.

He wanted to say something, to offer some kind of support, but the words wouldn't come. What could he say? He closed his eyes and prayed to Kiejain for a moment's clarity. He knew Kiejain was listening — he was always there, listening — but the First Rider offered no guidance. Which only suggested Kiejain knew Valnar already had the answers in his heart, and discovering them himself was part of his virtue.

Ink moved about the camp with his usual nonchalance, loading their supplies onto the saddles. Beast was up as well, stretching his limbs, preparing for another day of jogging beside the horses.

Valnar tightened the last strap, then paused. His jaw clenched as his mind turned to Ink's words from the night before, the ones that had gnawed at him through the restless hours of the night.

Do better.

The accusation echoed in his head. The Kaldorian didn't understand how dangerous a purebred beast really was. A creature without emotions, without morals, without virtues to guide him. If one couldn't be controlled, it wasn't just a problem. It was a threat.

Purebreds weren't born with the inner sense of right and wrong, the ability to tell good from evil. They felt no remorse. If a purebred beast burned Earthome to the ground, he'd sleep just fine after. The Words and the harsh obedience ingrained in them were the only means to keep others safe from them.

A disobedient, uncontrollable, *broken* purebred was a weapon without a sheath.

No, this wasn't about Valnar's humanity. Across the clearing, Beast rolled his shoulders slowly. If his muscles were sore from yesterday, he revealed nothing on his carefully blank face. He caught Valnar's gaze and his jaw clenched, his lips twitching as though he was fighting back a growl. He did, at the very least, display the good sense to look away, albeit begrudgingly.

Ink finished packing their supplies while Valnar scattered the remains of their campfire and concealed their traces as best he could. When he was done, he found Lygor still standing like a stone against the misty backdrop of the forest. Valnar shared a look with Ink before walking over to Lygor. Ink followed a step behind, his usual air of detached curiosity hanging around him like a cloak.

"Lodi?"

Lygor didn't respond. His arms remained crossed, his gaze locked on the horizon as though he hadn't heard. The morning light caught the edge of his profile, sharpening the hard line of his jaw and the faint shadows under his eyes.

"Lodi," Valnar tried again, stepping closer. "We're ready to go."

"As soon as you decide where," Ink added.

At that, Lygor shifted. He glimpsed at their faces briefly, then at the saddled horses. Ignoring all, he walked toward Beast.

"Lodi, what are you—" Valnar rushed after him.

Lygor didn't look back. He closed the distance between himself and the purebred like a soldier marching into battle. Beast froze, then he lowered his head and clasped his hands in front of him as he braced for whatever Lygor would hurl his way.

Lygor stopped a breath away from Beast. His presence invaded Beast's space like a sword poised to strike. The purebred stood rigid, his shoulders squared.

"What do you want?" Lygor asked.

Beast didn't respond immediately. His grey eyes flicked to Valnar for a fraction of a second before returning to Lygor. "I live to serve, I—"

"*Prihjtivaviula.*"

The word fell from Lygor's lips like a punch from the blindside. Surprise flashed across Beast's face just as his knees buckled. He fell to the ground with a strangled gasp, his body wracked with tremors as the pain seized him. His hands clawed at the frost-covered earth, his breath coming in ragged gasps as his body writhed.

Valnar swallowed. He wasn't disturbed by seeing the purebred suffer, but the fact that Lygor had done it, left a sour taste in his mouth.

Lygor didn't flinch. He stepped back, just enough to avoid Beast's thrashing legs. He stared past the scene, his expression carved from stone, as he waited for the torture to end, as if it inconvenienced him more than it did the purebred.

The seconds dragged on, and when the pain finally released its grip, Beast sagged against the ground. He rolled facedown, heaving at the harsh ground, before slamming his fists on it and pushing himself up.

Breathing like a snarling animal, his muscles still twitching faintly, Beast's grey eyes burned with defiance as they locked onto Lygor's.

The prince's face showed neither satisfaction nor regret. He took Beast's muted fury with a cool indifference. "None of that bullshit," he said flatly. "Tell me the truth. Twilight of Infinity. Why?"

Beast's glare intensified. His lips pressed together, and no words came out. Lygor didn't break his gaze; his eyes, hard and bright blue, commanded the slave's attention. The purebred looked away for a brief moment, as if needing a fresh gulp of air.

Then, Beast drew in a shaky breath and spoke with a low, hoarse voice. "I want my freedom."

Valnar's brows shot up, and a shiver traced an icy path down his spine as a sudden chill filled the air. Freedom? It wasn't a word he would ever expect to hear from a purebred. Freeborns, maybe, but purebreds...

Lygor's face didn't change. He nodded subtly. "I knew I'd heard that tournament before. That's the one where the winner is granted his freedom, isn't it?"

Beast nodded slowly. His gaze dropped to the ground as his shoulders deflated under the weight of defeat.

"You've somehow manipulated that woman into taking you to Euroad, so you can win Twilight of Infinity."

The defiance that usually smouldered just beneath the purebred's skin was gone, replaced by a subdued stillness. Lygor tilted his head slightly.

"Just like you've tried to manipulate me."

A flash of annoyance ripped through Valnar, flavoured with a sharp sense of vindication. He knew it. He knew the purebred was dangerous. The revelation didn't surprise him — it only confirmed what he'd suspected all along. Beast wasn't just surviving; he was scheming, wanting things he had no right to, manipulating people to get them. Valnar was glad Lygor had finally seen it.

The prince remained composed. He took a step back, his arms folding across his chest as his eyes pinned Beast in place. "Why do you even want your freedom?"

Beast studied his boots, his face giving away nothing.

"I thought purebreds didn't want their freedom," Lygor continued. "Freeborns, I get it. But purebreds..." He shook his head slowly. "What would you even do with freedom? What would you do if you were a free man right this moment?"

The pointed inflexion in Lygor's voice made it clear that the question wasn't rhetorical. Beast shifted his weight, then his grey eyes narrowed at Valnar. His lips curled back slightly as he spat, "I'd beat the shit out of him."

Valnar's fists clenched at his sides as he took half a step forward. "Try it, slave," he growled.

Beast didn't flinch. He returned his gaze to his boots, but somehow managed to make the action look like a defiance.

Lygor made a thoughtful noise. "Finally being honest."

Beast's lips pressed into a thin line as he waited like a man waiting for his sentence.

Lygor stepped closer. "Last night you asked me why I bought you," he said. "I'll tell you why. You belonged to my father, and now you belong to me. Just like everything else that was his. I will not stop until I take everything Kastian Vogros has stolen from my family."

Beast's eyes never left the ground, but his fingers twitched at his sides before curling into silent fists.

"Ever since we stepped into Chinderia, *you* are all what people talk about," Lygor ground out. "Nobody talks about how my parents were murdered, betrayed by their own men, our throne stolen. No. But they wouldn't shut up about how the mighty Lion of Zarall went mad out of his loyalty to good King Leonis. How he defied Kastian Vogros. How he defeated a wild, vicious bear, unarmed and naked." He inhaled slowly, rolling his eyes, as he muttered, "If I hear that 'The Lion and The Bear' song one more time..."

This was the first time Valnar had heard Lygor speak about King Leonis and Queen Arasanara's death. Lygor's shoulders were drawn tight under the weight of his raw, consuming vengeance, and Valnar wished he could take that weight off him.

Lygor tilted his head slightly, his muscles shifting like he was shedding whatever emotions gripped him a moment ago. "It must have been an epic fight, if it was only half as good as described in the song. Was it?"

When Beast didn't respond, Lygor's voice turned to steel again. "Answer me when I ask you a question."

"It was a... It was a difficult fight, Master."

Lygor nodded, then turned his gaze to the horizon. His eyes traced the land that stretched before them. The rising sun cast everything in shades of deep orange.

"I've been away from Chinderia for so long," Lygor spoke, as if talking to himself. "I doubt if my people even remember what I looked like. I'm nothing but a name to them." He glanced back at Beast, his voice dropping slightly. "I sought you out because you carry *my* name. You're a symbol. A powerful one. I thought I could use you to gain people's support when I'm ready to announce my return."

Valnar wondered where Lygor was going with this. Beast's eyes swept the ground, as if he could read the answer to the same question scrawled somewhere in the space between the prince and the slave. Valnar glanced at Ink, who was watching Lygor with an uncharacteristically grave expression.

"What good are you to me if I don't have any allies, army, or money?"

It was a direct question, but Beast didn't reply. He swallowed, his lips pressed tight.

"*Prihjtivaviula.*"

Before the word had fully left Lygor's lips, Beast was already lowering himself to the ground, as if he knew what was coming. His back arched as he hit the ground with a muted thud. He clawed at the earth as a noise quieter than a strangled gasp escaped his throat.

Lygor watched the mist retreat from the trees. The sun hadn't peeked its head yet, but the violent hues of dawn poured down the hills. Early morning birds chirped joyfully, which somehow made the soft thuds of Beast's thrashing body sound louder.

Ink shifted beside Valnar, crossing and uncrossing his arms. Valnar didn't let himself look away. Doing so would've made Lygor's cruelty feel like something he condoned.

Beast's throat finally relaxed enough to allow a strangled, guttural groan. His breaths came in shallow gasps as he pushed himself on his elbows.

"I remember telling you to answer me when I ask a question," Lygor said. "What good are you to me?"

Beast planted one fist on the cold ground, his head sagging between his shoulders, but he didn't push himself up.

"I fight," the words crawled out of his throat like a snarl. His mangy blond hair cascaded over his face. His shoulders expanded as he inhaled. "That's what I'm good for. I'll fight for you."

An icy breeze rolled down the hills, dragging a whiff of dead leaves and fresh air. Corner of Lygor's lips curled into a victorious smirk as he nodded slowly. Valnar shared another look with Ink and became convinced he had missed some vital information in that exchange. Because a similar, amused spark shone in both Lygor's and the Kaldorian's eyes.

When Lygor stepped back from the slave and announced, Ink didn't seem surprised.

"And you'll get your chance to fight for me, Beast. We're going to Euroad."

"What?" Valnar barked.

Beast's head snapped up. His grey eyes widened as he slowly sat back and stared at Lygor, his mouth hovering ajar.

"Lodi—" Valnar started his objection, but Lygor cut him short.

"I'll challenge Kastian Vogros to the Twilight of Infinity. The Usurper's champion versus my Lion of Zarall." His eyes soaked up Beast's dumbfounded face, a smirk growing sharp on his lips. "You'll fight and you'll win," he demanded. "And when you earn your freedom, you'll stand by me. You'll fight for me as a free man."

"Lodi, that's not a—"

Lygor silenced Valnar with a sharp motion. He continued talking to the slave, who was still slumped on his knees.

"You said Kastian was afraid of a riot. You'll help me rouse the biggest one. You'll continue to serve me, as a free man, until the day I sit on my throne. Then, only then, you can go and do whatever you want with your freedom. That is the deal."

All Beast could do was to gawk at the prince. A stunned figure with no voice, his shock so complete that it seemed to dim his thoughts.

"Well?" Lygor prompted. "Do you accept it?"

"Yes," Beast spoke faintly. "Yes. Yes, I do, Master. Yes." He made no move to rise, as if unsure his legs would carry him. Lygor regarded him for a moment, a flicker of satisfaction crossing his face, before turning on his heel and striding toward his horse.

"We can't go to Euroad," Valnar said as he caught up with Lygor, his limbs feeling too clunky in his heavy armour. "For the same reasons you listed to that woman. The mountain passages will be closed over winter. And... And we can't simply walk into Euroad and ask to fight at the arena."

Ink had already climbed on his horse. Lygor patted his horse's neck as he placed one foot on the stirrup.

"Lodi, if you think Euroad will be safe because it's an independent city, think again. All Kastian needs is one single knife in the crowd."

"Isn't it your job to protect me?" Lygor mused. He swung his leg over the saddle. "Do your job well, and I'll be fine."

Valnar boiled in his armour. "Lodi, I'll die for you, but why put yourself at risk?" He sneered at Beast, who hurried to catch up with the prince. "Why put your fate in *his* hands?"

If he was offended, the slave didn't react. A mild look of disbelief still clung to his face as he took his place beside Lygor's horse and bounced slightly on his feet, as if he was brimming with the strength to run for hours.

Lygor let Valnar's question drift away in the morning breeze. "As for the mountain passages, we'll wait the winter out in someplace safe."

Valnar exhaled softly. He liked the sound of that. At least he would have time to talk Lygor out of this ridiculous plan.

"We're going to Calae first," Lygor said, turning his horse.

"You can't be serious!"

"Calae?" asked Ink. "Why?"

"Kastian thinks the nobles and the city lords are the only figures who have any power. He thinks he's safe as long as he keeps them all under control. But there's another player who can be as influential as any."

"Strike me twelve times," Valnar cursed, throwing his hands up. Defeated, he hurried to gather his horse as he muttered a prayer. "Kiejain, the wisest, grant him some sense..."

"Who is it?" Ink asked, tilting his head sideways.

"It's who are *they*," Lygor corrected. His words lingered in the air as his horse broke into a trot. "Domestic Assets Trade Union."

23

BEAST

THE ROAD WAS A sodden mess of mud and misery, stretching endlessly under the hammering rain. Cold wind sliced through the air, biting at any exposed skin and howling down the open hills that lined either side of their path.

Beast hunched in the saddle of Ink's horse, water dripping from his hair. He was soaked to his bones. The rain had penetrated through his coat and drenched all his clothes. His body wracked with tremors that had started hours ago and showed no signs of stopping. The cold was worse than anything he'd felt in sunny Brinescar or the dry heat of Solkara Flats region, where Faychill Ranch was located. Nothing, of course, could compare to the Frostbringer's Eve at Olira's farm last fall but this was its own kind of torment. The cold was eating deeper and deeper into his flesh, and he was convinced he would never know warmth again.

He glanced down at Valnar, who dragged his feet through the mud. His boots squelched with every step. The mud clung to his legs, pulling at him as though determined to drag him down. A flicker of grim satisfaction stirred in Beast's chest. Watching Valnar struggle was oddly pleasing.

Ahead, Lygor sat stiffly in his saddle, his cloak drenched and heavy with water. Even the ever-composed prince was caked in mud up to his waist. Ink rode on Valnar's horse just behind him. His hood was pulled low over his face in a futile attempt to shield himself from the downpour. They'd all taken turns walking

— even Lygor had done his fair share — and their weariness showed in every movement.

As the dim light of the sun started to retreat behind the hills, Beast's heart sank. The thought of another miserable night under the rain was not appealing. So when he spotted a thin plume of smoke in the distance beyond the grey veil of rain, he could almost smell the warmth.

"We're stopping there," Lygor shouted over the howling of wind and rain.

By the time they were trudging through the only street of the small town, avoiding the deepest puddles as best they could, it was already dark. The town was a little more than a cluster of shabby huts that huddled together. Beast pictured the map in King Leonis's throne room. He guessed they were somewhere in the Dunstall Hills, but he didn't recall any town there. The place must have been too small to warrant even a tiny dot on the floors of the throne room.

They stopped in front of a single-story building with dark walls. A faded sign hung from one corner, swinging slightly in the wind. Lygor and Ink dismounted. Their boots sunk into the mud with a squelch. Lygor tossed his horse's reigns towards Valnar, pushed his hood back, and walked inside with Ink close behind.

Valnar wiped the rain off his face, grumbling under his breath. Beast shifted uncomfortably in the saddle. The faint creak of the inn's sign filled the silence as the two men stared longingly at the door.

The door swung open after ten minutes and Lygor stormed out.

"Everything okay?" Valnar asked, his hand moving to his sword.

Lygor cursed as he threw his hood back on. The door opened again, letting Ink out. The Kaldorian coughed. "You Chinderians know how to rip off a desperate man."

"What happened?"

"A Blue for a room," Lygor gritted through his teeth. "One Grey bought us a night at the stable."

"If only somebody hadn't spent all our money on a very expensive symbol."

"Ink! Not now!"

The Kaldorian shrugged. Beast felt Valnar's hostile gaze on him, but he couldn't care any less.

The innkeeper followed them out a moment later. He covered his balding head under a cloak that made his stout figure look hunched. He guided them to the stable around the side. The stable looked dangerously close to collapsing. It leaned precariously to one side, and the roof was patched poorly. The innkeeper pulled the wooden door open, revealing an empty space, as if the man couldn't even trust housing animals in here.

The man waited with his palm open as Lygor scanned the stable.

"You didn't seem like you were having a busy night," the prince sneered through his teeth. "Are you sure you can't accommodate us in one of your rooms?"

The innkeeper sized them up and down, his gaze lingering on their expensive clothes, sturdy horses, and Beast's purebred tattoo. "Are you sure you can't pay a Blue?"

Lygor slapped the grey coin into the man's palm and trudged inside.

"Suit yourselves," the innkeeper shrugged and left.

Lygor continued swearing under his breath as he shed his wet cloak and coat off and tossed them aside. Ink inspected the stalls and picked the cleanest one to sleep in, while Valnar guided the horses to the back.

Beast slid off the saddle, cautiously testing his weight on his ankle. It hadn't ached in a while, though he doubted if he would notice it with the rain and the cold keeping him miserable enough.

On the same day when Lygor had announced that they were going to Calae, Beast had taken a nasty fall. The piercing pain in his ankle had torn a howl from his throat, more fear than agony. As he had writhed on the ground, clutching his leg, a familiar terror had consumed him.

He'd seen too many beasts discarded, sent to the tribesmen — or worse — for sustaining an injury. A beast who couldn't fight was worthless. He'd thought that was his fate until the others reached him and examined the leg. Valnar's assessment that it wasn't broken, that it was just a sprain, had barely registered over his panic.

He had been sitting on Ink's horse since then, the others taking turns walking.

A shove to his shoulder snapped him out. A scowling Valnar stood beside him. "You're helping me with the horses," he said as he dragged him by the scruff of his neck.

Beast gulped down his anger. The Kiejain's knight never missed an opportunity to physically push him around. This was his way of reminding Beast of his place. Beast had restrained himself every time, surprised at the intensity of the fire that rose in his chest. He kept his fists at his sides and allowed the man to assert his authority.

The horses shifted restlessly in their damp stalls, flaring their nostrils at the smell of wet straw, damp wood, and the aggression brimming beneath Beast's skin. Valnar prodded him towards one of the horses and tossed him a brush.

"Your ankle looks fine to me," the knight spat.

Beast's grip on the brush tightened. It wasn't a question, so it didn't require an answer. He looked at the brush, then at the horse, his brows knitting together. He had no idea how to groom a horse, where to even start.

Valnar unsaddled the horses, grabbed a fistful of straws, and started drying the horses' coats. Beast kept his mouth shut and copied Valnar's actions. When the horses were dry enough, Valnar reached for his brush and started working the mud free from his horse's coat. Beast watched for a moment before copying him, dragging the brush along the horse's muddy coat with clumsy strokes. He pulled back each time the horse snorted or flicked its ears back, expecting Valnar to bark that he was doing it wrong. But the knight said nothing. He checked the hooves himself, not trusting Beast with the task. Then, he kicked a wooden bucket Beast's way.

"I saw a well outside," the knight grunted.

Beast refused to give him the satisfaction of seeing how much he despised the idea of going back outside. He snatched the bucket and walked out the doors, ignoring the dull ache on his ankle.

He had to do five trips to fill the trough enough, because the dodgy bucket was leaking. By the time he dumped the contents of the bucket into the trough, he was so drenched, water dripped off his clothes, pooling between his legs when he stood still. He tossed the bucket aside, then shrugged the wet, heavy coat off.

Valnar tossed a bundle of semi-dry clothes at him. The knight was the closest to Beast's size, and his stiff movements were enough evidence to let Beast know the order had come from Lygor. Without another word, Valnar spun on his heel and stalked into the stall where Lygor and Ink had already settled.

Beast picked the adjacent stall and started peeling his wet clothes off. He shivered as the cold bit sharply at his exposed, damp skin. He picked up the spare clothes and yanked them on. It irritated him how much Valnar's treatment lingered in his mind. He'd endured far worse from men with far harsher hands and nastier words, yet this gnawed at him. Why was he reacting like this? Like a freeborn, nursing pride he had no use for. He clenched his jaw, forcing the thought aside.

He hung his wet clothes over the stall divider, then settled himself on the floor, leaning back against the wooden wall. If he wanted his freedom, he'd have to behave like a slave, just a few months longer. The thought made his chest tighten. Lygor wouldn't hesitate to abandon their deal if Beast gave him a reason, and bashing Valnar's face in would likely do just that.

He pulled his knees to his chest, wrapping his arms around them, and buried his face in the crook of his arms. He controlled his breathing to soothe himself and smother the simmering desire to flatten Valnar's armour with his fists. The cold still lingered in his bones, but at least he wasn't drenched anymore. In the adjacent stall, he could hear the three of them talking.

"We need money," Lygor declared, as he had a dozen times since they left Kilrer. "It'll take forever to get to Calae like this. We need to buy him a horse. What can we sell?"

"We may not have to sell anything," Valnar said. His armour clinked faintly before dropping to the floor with a solid thud. Valnar continued talking, his voice muffled as he changed into dry clothes. "We can ask for work. Join a merchant's convoy, sell protection."

"They would slow us down even more," Lygor shut down the idea. "And I doubt it would earn us enough to buy a horse."

"He doesn't need a decent one. A mule or a donkey should do."

"I could gamble," Ink suggested. A small pile of coins hit the floor with a metallic clatter. Beast imagined the Kaldorian crouching to count the coins. "Three Greys and a few Reds. Strike me twelve times, I've never been this poor. I've seen some drunk idiots playing *Dice and Slice* inside. What have we got to lose?"

"Your hands, maybe," Lygor said. "Cheating is not really appreciated in Chinderia."

"It's not cheating," the foreign prince said innocently. "It's called Kaldorian luck."

The coins clinked softly, their metallic chime muffled by the fabric as Ink swept them off the ground and dropped them into his pocket. He stood and walked past the stalls and the horses, pulling his hood back over his head before stepping out into the rain.

"Go with him," Lygor ordered. "Make sure he doesn't get into trouble."

"Sure," Valnar sighed softly before crossing the stable and following Ink outside.

Beast listened to the soft shuffle of footsteps over the straw-covered floor as Lygor moved about in the stall. The faint rustle of fabric followed, the prince rummaging through the bags. The soft sounds blended with the muffled patter of rain on the roof, and Beast's muscles slowly began to relax. His eyes grew heavy, and he hovered on the edge of sleep.

A nudge to his hip snapped him awake. Lygor stood over him with a blanket draped over one arm and a bundle of food lodged under the other. Lygor tossed him the blanket, the rough fabric landing in a heap on Beast's lap. The bundle of food followed, landing beside him.

"Eat," the prince commanded.

Beast wrapped the blanket over his shoulders before reaching for the food. Stale bread and some dried meat. He didn't complain.

Lygor settled himself against the opposite wall, the wooden planks creaking behind his back as he leaned. One leg stretched ahead of him, the other bent, his elbow resting on it as he watched Beast scoff the food down.

"How's your ankle?" Lygor asked at last.

Beast's stomach lurched. "I am well, Owner." He attempted to stand to demonstrate putting his weight on his foot — to prove he could still fight — but Lygor made a sharp gesture.

"Sit down, I believe you. I've seen Valnar make you work."

Beast settled back down and continued eating, though he could still feel Lygor's gaze on him like a tangible weight.

"It's Master, by the way," Lygor said. "Valnar is your Owner."

Beast swallowed the last bit of bread. "Yes, Master," he muttered as he mentally scolded himself. Purebreds didn't make mistakes like this. But the prince had such power and authority over him, it was hard not to think Valnar's ownership as just a façade on paper.

"And you will treat him with respect. No more talk of beating the shit out of him."

"Yes... Master."

I live to serve, I breathe to please. Just a few months longer.

The silence stretched, Lygor watching him as if he could hear Beast's thoughts.

"You never really answered my question," the prince muttered slowly.

Beast's fingers tightened around the strip of dried meat. He kept his head down, pretending he didn't know what the prince meant. Lygor tilted his head, his eyes gleaming with intrigue.

"Why do you really want your freedom?"

Beast gnawed on a bite of dried meat, gulped it down. He fixed the edge of the blanket over his legs, and shifted in his place. He shrugged vaguely before muttering. "I just... want it."

Lygor didn't look away. His bright blue eyes were searching, lit with the kind of curiosity that made Beast feel peeled back, piece by piece. There was a spark behind the prince's gaze, a glimmer of interest threaded through the scrutiny, like he was studying something unexpected and rare. It wasn't the assessing look of a buyer at an auction, stripping a slave naked to understand exactly what they were paying for. Not quite. But Beast still felt bare beneath it. The longer it lasted, the more aware he became of the beating in his chest — slow at first, then heavier and louder. A flicker of warmth stirred at the base of his stomach. The feeling itself wasn't unpleasant. But its presence was.

"You never had a life before. You never knew any different. So, why?"

"I... I don't know how to answer that... Master. I just... I know I want it more than anything."

"That's not a good reason," Lygor said smugly. "If you want something, you need to want it for the right reasons. Otherwise, you won't have what it takes to get you there."

Beast finished his last piece of dried meat and sucked the crumbs off his fingers. An urge to speak gripped him and the question slipped out before he could stop himself: "Why do you want your throne, Master?"

"Because it's mine," Lygor's shot back without thought.

The instant the words left his mouth, his expression darkened, his steel-blue eyes narrowing into slits. His head tilted slightly, and the muscle in his jaw twitched. Beast watched him a beat too long before dropping his gaze, pulse stuttering in his throat.

He silently cursed himself for angering the man who held his freedom. The salty taste of dried meat turned sour in his mouth. He wished Lygor would just speak his Pain Word and get it over with, just so Beast didn't have to drown in dread like a cockroach waiting to be crushed under a boot. But no sound slipped through the firm line that knitted the prince's lips together.

Lygor let him sweat in the freezing stable for a few more minutes, before finally speaking: "You have a mouth on you, purebred. I've never seen one like you."

Beast stared at the filthy straws on the floor and kept the said mouth shut.

"Sharp tongue for a beast. Makes me wonder what else they trained you to do with it."

Lygor's voice stayed light, but something flickered in his gaze. It dropped briefly, to Beast's mouth. He'd looked at him like that before, more times than Beast could count on the road. Eyes that didn't flinch away when caught staring. Beast kept his head down, jaw clenched, body motionless. Like a door sealed shut.

Lygor tilted his head. "Tell me, what broke you?"

Blood filled Beast's mouth, seeping from his tongue. His jaw ached. Taking a deep breath didn't serve him well, because his nose sought Saradra's scent at every inhale, everywhere. Her delicate fingers caressed the tattoo on the left side of his neck as her breath whispered, *You look free.*

The straws. He studied the muddy straws to distract himself. There was no way he could push any sound out through his clenched throat.

Lygor's gaze hardened on him. The prince leaned forward slightly, his mouth firm, a direct order — a demand that he spoke — ready at the tip of his tongue. But Beast was saved by the sound of the stable door creaking open, with Valnar's voice filling the space.

"He was getting ready to cave your head in."

"Oh, I could have gone for at least another few rounds before he made a move."

"Kiejain forbid. Why risk it?"

Ink strolled into the stall, a smug lightness to his steps. He tossed a coin purse at Lygor's lap, forcing the prince to release Beast from his scrutiny.

"You won?" Lygor asked, slowly unstrapping the purse.

"I could have done better if it wasn't for the snufflight here." He jerked his thumb toward Valnar, who followed him with a scowl. "The poor sod was about to double down before Valnar decided to play the knight under wings."

"His *Kaldorian luck* was starting to piss some people off," Valnar said. He slid his drenched cloak off and threw it over a stall divider. "Besides, I might have another way of earning us money."

Lygor lifted his head. "Listening."

"An underground arena just outside the town, at the basement of a winery. It's local entertainment, mostly free warriors and freeborn slaves. Sounds completely off the records." He nodded his head towards Beast, who sat hunched with the blanket draped over his broad shoulders. "I think it's time we see if Lion of Zarall is worth his salt."

Beast's head lifted slightly at the mention of the arena. The idea stirred his heart to beat with the anticipation of a delicious fight. His fingers itched.

"I object to it," Ink said. "It's not worth risking his neck."

"The money here won't buy us another horse," Lygor said after glancing inside the purse.

"Like I said, I could have won more if Valnar hadn't stopped me."

"The prize can go anywhere between two to ten Blues," Valnar said, ignoring Ink's dig. He tugged at the straps of his scabbard as he unbuckled his sword belt. "Still not enough for a horse, but might buy a mule and supplies. It'll get us to Calae faster."

Casually leaning against the divider, a scowl marred Ink's face. "I'm just saying," he began, his voice light but tinged with caution. "You went through all that effort for him."

Valnar placed his weapons carefully against the stall wall, picking the cloth-wrapped two-handed sword he often used to pray. "It's your call, Lodi. I need to pray. We can go check it out later tonight."

He walked over to a far corner of the stable to do his meaningless yapping at his god. Lygor rubbed his chin, studying the ceiling before turning his attention to Beast. He lifted an eyebrow. "What's it going to be, Beast? You said you'd fight for me. You up for it?"

Beast's fingers brushed idly against the coarse blanket draped over his lap. Feeling both Ink's and Lygor's gazes on him, his chest swelled with excitement. The sharp edges of eagerness lingered beneath his voice when he said, "Yes, Master."

24

VALNAR

A WOMAN IN HER late thirties opened the door, the soft creak of the hinges barely audible over the rustle of the rain and breeze. She stood in a short, rumpled nightgown, her bare legs catching the reddish light spilling from the doorway. Her hair was a tousled mess, the kind that suggested she'd either just woken up or had little reason to care.

Valnar's gaze darted to the vineyard stretching behind them and the two buildings in view. Confusion tugged at him. This couldn't be the right place. One building was a two-storey house, modest but well-kept, and the other was a larger structure with wide gates — clearly the winery. Surely, the house wasn't where they held underground fights, so they had knocked on the wide doors of the winery.

He glanced at the charming smile that stretched over Lygor's lips, then back at the woman. That's when he noticed the paint on her face. A bold red on her lips, pink dusting her cheeks, and black kohl framing her sharp eyes. She leaned casually against the doorframe, her thin nightgown light over her curves, her long lashes brushing her cheeks as she sized them up.

"Are you here for the fight," she asked, her voice smooth and honeyed, "or the winemaking?"

"I'll say for the fight," Lygor replied, tilting his head slightly, a playful flicker in his eyes. "But winemaking does sound delicious."

The woman giggled. "Well then, come on in, sweetie." She stepped back and gestured for them to enter. "Name's Welda."

"An absolute pleasure to meet you, Mistress," Lygor said smoothly. He took her hand with an elegance that was a stark contrast to their mud-streaked state and brought it to his lips. "I'm Lodi."

Welda ushered them into a small foyer, the door clicking shut behind them. Her eyes roved over the group with the casual air of a maiden browsing for a new scarf. She didn't spare the slave a second glance, her gaze sliding over him as if he didn't exist. Her attention lingered briefly on Valnar's broad frame, the muscles hinted at beneath his plain shirt, but her interest evaporated when he kept his heavy brow furrowed and his mouth set in an uninviting line.

She shifted her focus, touching Ink's arm and fluttering her long lashes at him. "And who might you be, darling?"

"Ink, Mistress," the Kaldorian replied. He pushed his wet brown hair back and bowed slightly with a flirty smile that mirrored Lygor's.

Ink had always been effortless with women, and Lygor with women and men. Charm came naturally to them, as instinctive as breathing. They played the game with relish, seeing seduction as both a sport and an art, often competing to see who could win a love interest over first.

For Valnar, such games held no appeal. Affection had its place — within bond and blessing, under the wings of the Twelve Riders. He saw no point in wasting breath on charm or temptation. If his body needed tending, there were flame slaves for that.

"This way, boys," Welda cooed, looping one arm through Ink's and the other through Lygor's. "I believe the men have already started their entertainment, but the night is young."

Valnar prodded the purebred forward and followed behind the others. Welda led them through a narrow side corridor that opened into a lavishly decorated room. The floor was covered with a red-stained carpet, scattered with oversized pillows. Two large fireplaces flanked opposite ends of the room, their roaring flames casting flickering warmth across the space. The dim light of oil lamps, veiled with red-tinted fabric, bathed the room in a crimson glow.

At the centre of it all was a massive wooden tub, brimming with knee-high heaps of glistening red grapes. Inside the tub, two young women stood barefoot, their naked skin slick and sticky with juice as they stomped the grapes. They hummed a tune, swaying their hips and giggling. One slipped, letting out a sharp laugh as she grabbed the other for balance. They tumbled together, collapsing into the grapes in a tangle of limbs, laughing and wrestling as they crushed the fruit beneath their nude bodies.

"My daughters are just warming up for the show tonight," Welda said with a proud smile, her tone smooth as velvet.

The two girls froze mid-laugh when they noticed the three men and the beast, their giggles fading into sultry smiles. Slowly, they crawled through the sea of crushed grapes toward the edge of the tub, the sticky juice glistening on their skin.

"New guests," one of them said, a streak of juice trailing down her cheek. "How exciting!"

"You boys want to join us?" the other teased, slipping a finger into her mouth to suck the juice clean.

"Maybe later, ladies," Lygor said smoothly. He hadn't blushed, nor had Ink, the two princes carrying themselves as if naked girls wrestling in wine tubs were an everyday occurrence.

"You guys should come straight up after the fight," the first one said. "It's first come first served..." She trailed off as the other girl noticed the streak of grape juice on her face and leaned over to lick it clean. She let out a throaty gasp as her sister traced a path from her neck to her ear. They rolled back into the tub, the air thick with the wet sounds of crushing grapes.

"My husband, Valer, has quite the crowd tonight," Welda said, leading them to the corner of the room. It was then Valnar noticed the other workers busying around the space, fluffing the oversized pillows on the floor and arranging chairs around the grape tub. Women wore short gowns that barely covered their hips, while the men were topless, dressed only in thin, low-hanging braies that clung to their bulging frames. As they walked by, a couple of them blew kisses, their painted lips curving into teasing smiles.

"Your husband, huh?" Lygor remarked. "Is he running the fights?"

Welda let go of their arms and bent gracefully, her hand brushing the floor as she pulled a hidden latch. "My husband doesn't run anything, sweetie. He lets men fight in his basement, takes their bets, and pays the winners. Then me and my darlings? We collect the money back."

She straightened with a wink and stepped aside. She gestured Lygor to descend first, but when Ink moved to follow, she blocked him with a fluid motion, her body pressing against his. Her hands slid up to caress the freckles across his face, her voice dropping to a whisper. "I've heard so much about Kaldorian beverages," she murmured, her tongue running slowly over her full lips. "I'd love to taste that famous white wine of yours."

Valnar's brow furrowed at the words. Kaldorians weren't famed for their white wine. Their honey mead was their pride. Then the implication hit him like a stone, and his jaw tightened. Without waiting for Ink's inevitable smirk, Valnar grabbed the slave by the arm and rushed down the stairs.

Before following them down, Ink leaned in and whispered something too low for the others to catch. Whatever he said made Welda's lips part in a surprised smile before she let out a soft giggle much like her daughters'.

"White wine?" Lygor mocked quietly as soon as Welda shut the hatch behind them.

"Shut up," Ink grunted.

"What did you tell her?"

"That's not for your ears to hear."

"Can we just get this done?" Valnar nodded at the door he'd spotted on the side.

Muffled shouts and chants filtered through the thick wood. The sounds of a crowd whipped into a frenzy. The slave's gaze was locked on the door as well. He was unfazed by the distraction of the room they'd left behind. Valnar could see it clearly — Beast was craving for the fight.

"Right," Lygor said, collecting his seriousness. He pushed the door open, and the others fell in step behind him.

The room below mirrored the size of the one above, but the similarities ended there. It was brighter, the light of dozens of lanterns and candles spilling across the space. The square, caged arena dominated the centre of the room, encircled by half the lanterns, their flames ensuring no detail of the brutal show within went unseen. The arena rested on a knee-high pedestal, elevating it just enough to offer the gathered spectators a better view. To the far side, a small bar was tucked against the wall, where a young bartender served wine. It was clear the establishment prioritised function over luxury; the room was bare of decorations, furniture, or seating.

Over thirty men were packed around the cage, yelling and punching the air. Among them, Valnar noted several slaves marked with freeborn beast tattoos. They stood apart from the noise, their gazes fixed on the fight. They weren't here to cheer. They studied every blow and dodge as if their lives depended on it. It probably did.

Lygor approached the arena. He stood just on the edge of the crowd, crossing his arms over his chest as he watched the two fighters. Valnar followed a few steps behind, his gaze sweeping the room, noting the exits, the faces, the weapons.

Inside the arena, two fighters circled each other. Sweat-slicked torsos heaved with effort, their bare fists raised. Fresh, dark blood smeared the wooden floor beneath them. The beast tattoos on their necks stood out in the harsh light of the lanterns, but Valnar couldn't tell if they were purebred or freeborn.

The crowd erupted as one fighter landed a bone-crunching punch that sent his opponent crashing against the bars. Metal rattled as the man caught himself, blood spilling from his split lip. The attacker closed in for the next strike. The crowd's cheer muffled the sounds of fists pounding against flesh.

After watching the two men bleed and bruise each other for a few minutes, Lygor gestured for Beast to step closer. The purebred watched the fight with the concentration of a hungry man watching a feast.

"What do you say?" Lygor asked. "Can you take them?"

Beast's reply came quick, his focus locked on the fight, as if the question didn't deserve even a moment's thought or the courtesy of looking away. "Easily."

Modesty was a virtue Kiejain demanded, but what could a purebred possibly understand of virtues? Beast hadn't even bothered to address Lygor as Master. Disrespectful, arrogant fiend seed...

Lygor gave a slight nod, his posture reflecting his confidence. "They're not much of a match against a purebred, are they?"

Beast shifted, his gaze darting to Lygor. He scratched his chin, then pushed his hand back down instantly. "I can defeat them bare, Master," he spoke without permission. Valnar's brow furrowed. It almost sounded like a request.

"What's the difference? Between Raged and bare?" Ink asked.

Valnar answered, his voice clipped. "One is a mindless beast. The other is just a cocky bastard."

"Close enough," Lygor said. He glanced at Ink before continuing. "When he's not Raged, he's fighting as a man."

"Not a man," Valnar corrected.

"When a purebred is Raged... it's like he becomes something else."

"Like possessed by a fiend."

Lygor shrugged. "It all but guarantees victory. So I don't see why I'd take the chance and let you fight bare."

"I defeated Marzul bare."

Lygor turned to him sharply, a rare expression of surprise brightening his face. "No way."

Beast nodded.

"You should really tell us about that fight some time."

Beast shrugged.

Valnar was satisfied to see Lygor studying the purebred with suspicion. The dumb slave was trying to manipulate the prince again, but Lygor was on to him. Valnar's fingers sought Kiejain's symbol on his chest, though he wasn't wearing his armour. He muttered a prayer for Kiejain instead, for vigilance and patience. Beast pretended like his attention shifted back to the fight, but an alertness poured out of him. He kept scratching his chin, which was shadowed with a rough stubble. He crossed and uncrossed his arms.

Cocky a moment ago, and now nervous? About what?

Inside the cage, one of the beasts seized his opponent's arm in a crushing grip. Twisting the arm, he forced the other man to turn, slamming him against the bars with a resonant clang. The pinned beast flung his free hand back over his shoulder, grasping blindly for leverage, but his opponent was faster. He hooked his leg around the pinned beast's knee. Then he executed a series of moves that

Valnar had never seen before, and slammed his opponent face-first onto the blood-slicked floor.

"Nice," Ink mumbled.

The victor didn't release his rival's wrist. Instead, he snaked his leg around the trapped man's elbow, his weight pressing down on the joint. With a sharp roll, he forced the arm into an unnatural angle. The snap of breaking bone cut through the roaring crowd like a whip crack, reaching Valnar's ears with chilling clarity.

Beast let out a sound between a growl and a gasp. Nervousness was replaced with fury now. He fixed a pair of vengeful eyes on the victorious beast. The man stood in the centre of the cage, fists raised high as he basked in the frenzied cheers of the crowd.

The tension spilled out from the cage. Two spectators, likely the owners of the fighters, lunged at each other, their voices cutting through the noise. A barrel-chested man and a couple of others stepped in to break them apart.

"No more of this!" the barrel-chested man yelled. The authority in his voice told Valnar he was the owner of the establishment, and Welda's husband, Valer.

"He damaged my beast! You owe me fifty Blues, you piece of shit!"

"That little bitch is not worth fifty Blues!" the other yelled.

"Hey! Hey!" Valer shouted, raising a palm at each man's face. "If you wanna fight, get in the cage and I'll take the bets."

The crowd erupted, half of them cheering for the men to settle it in the cage. A few began yelling out wagers, already eager for another fight. But the owner of the injured beast seemed to cool, his shoulders dropping as he muttered something under his breath.

Lygor watched the spectacle with a humorous grin while Ink sauntered off to the bar, presumably to grab drinks before the next fight.

Beast was the only one still watching the injured fighter. Valnar noticed the way Beast's face had paled as the man stumbled down the cage, cradling his messed-up arm. The man rocked back and forth, his head shaking violently, his lips moving in a stream of silent words that Valnar could only imagine were pleas. It wasn't the pain that had him trembling — it was fear.

Beast adjusted his shirt, moving his arms as if he suddenly didn't know what to do with them. His nervousness drew Lygor's attention.

"If I'm Raged, they're dead," Beast said, once again speaking without permission. "If I fight bare, I can... I can hold back. No serious injuries."

Was this his angle? He was trying to convince Lygor into letting him fight bare, so he would spare his opponent from a serious injury or death? Valnar crossed his arms. He wasn't sold, but he couldn't tell why Beast didn't want to be Raged. Especially since it would secure his victory.

Welda's husband climbed into the cage and stood beside the victorious beast. "Crawler, owned by Baldan, won again," he announced. "Is there anyone who feels lucky enough to take on this beast? Anyone there to challenge Crawler? I'm doubling the prize to eight Blues!"

Lygor lifted his eyebrows at Beast. "Bare? Are you sure?"

Beast nodded.

The expression on the purebred's face as he stared at the slave named Crawler was all the affirmation Lygor needed. He nodded at Valnar.

"I'll challenge him," Valnar yelled. He didn't even need to raise his voice; the crowd had gone quiet at Valer's question. They shuffled aside to clear a path to the cage.

Beast moved before Valnar could nudge him. Spectators cheered their encouragement, those on the other side of the cage straining to get a better view of him as Beast and Valnar approached the cage. Close behind, Lygor trailed.

"We have a new victim, I mean, brave challenger," Valer announced as he opened the cage for Beast. He tilted his chin at Valnar. "I can see it's your first time here, Master?"

Valnar nodded vaguely.

Valer stood aside and Beast climbed inside swiftly, heading straight for the centre of the cage, and standing with his fists at his sides. Crawler squared his shoulders, puffed out his chest and spat. His muscles rippled as he flexed, sizing his opponent with a smug grin.

"And what do we call this—" Valer stepped between them, casually putting a hand on Beast's shoulder. He pulled his hand back as if he'd just touched live flames.

Crawler spotted it at the same time, his eyes widening at the intricate details of Beast's tattoo. He lost all his colour. Stumbling backward and pointing a shaky finger at Beast, he yelled, "He's a purebred! He's a fucking purebred!"

Mixed reactions rose from the crowd, mostly surprise and excitement. Valer's jaw went slack, blinking between Beast and Valnar. He rubbed his chin, his eyes scanning the crowd and their responses.

Crawler withdrew all the way until his back pressed against the bars. He turned and spotted his owner in the crowd. "He's a bloody purebred!" he yelled frantically. "I can't take on a purebred!"

Baldan's face went grim. "Valer! No fucking way! I'm not pitting him against a fucking purebred! Get my beast out of there!"

A few people booed. Crawler dashed to the door, careful to keep his distance from Beast. The purebred hadn't moved a muscle, only his head turning to track Crawler's retreat. His clothes and face were lined with dust and mud from the road, his damp, blond hair a wild mess. His untamed appearance somewhat justified if not contributed to Crawler's reaction.

"Valer!" Baldan yelled, weaving through the crowd, making his way towards the cage door. "Valer, open the bloody door! He's not taking on a purebred! No way!"

Valer finally recovered himself. He approached the bars and crouched to talk to Baldan. "If your beast walks out of this cage, you're not getting a single coin."

"I don't care! Eight Blues is not worth losing my property."

Valer showed his teeth, but he opened the door. Crawler rushed out, almost knocking Valer out of his way. The crowd's jeers followed him, several of them going as far as hurling insults.

"We've got ourselves a runner!" Valer called out, sparking laughter and a few sharp whistles. "Maybe we should let Master Baldan know when we're having a sprinting contest."

Baldan's face darkened to a furious purple. Crawler stood behind him, arms crossed and head down, almost as if trying to blend into his owner's shadow.

Lygor chuckled softly. Pride gleamed in his eyes as he watched Beast. Nearby, Ink took a slow sip from the wine bottle, then passed it to Valnar without a word.

"We have a purebred in the cage!" Valer declared. "Who dares to step into the cage with a purebred? Do we have a challenger?"

A roar of cheers erupted from the spectators. The freeborn beasts, however, didn't share the excitement. Their faces paled to a shade that put Crawler to shame. One of them was on his knees, clutching at his owner's legs, his lips moving rapidly as he pleaded.

"What a brave bunch," Ink mumbled as he took the bottle back from Valnar. "I've seen beggars face death with more spine. Pathetic."

"They're not scared of dying," Lygor said. "They're scared of getting injured. Haven't you seen what happened to that freeborn?" He nodded towards the freeborn with the broken arm.

"How is that worse than dying?"

The grin faded from Lygor's face as he suddenly became interested in the far walls of the room. He rested one elbow on his other palm, rubbing his mouth as if he was distracted by some other thought. Valnar knew the gesture well enough to understand Lygor wasn't distracted. He just didn't want to answer. As he did often, Valnar stepped in.

"If a beast can't fight, he's useless," he said. "If he's lucky, he gets sold to the Tribesmen." He spat on the filthy ground. "Cannibals, those savage heathens."

Ink froze, the bottle in his hand forgotten. "Tribesmen? You're joking."

"Do they look like it's a joke?" Valnar jerked his chin towards the beasts in the crowd.

"I thought cannibalism was illegal in Chinderia?"

"It is. That's why those tribes live past the northern Chinderian border."

Disgust and pity cracked Ink's face as his eyes darted to the injured freeborn. The man clutched his broken arm like it was the only thing keeping him tethered, trembling and groaning in pain. His gaunt face and hollow eyes were enough proof to Valnar's words.

"You Chinderians are sick," Ink said quietly before he chugged the rest of the bottle.

Valer continued to challenge people, his voice rising above the noise and his tone dripping with mockery. "No one brave enough yet? Is there not a single man willing to face a purebred?"

The crowd's cheers swelled again, more noise than commitment. Inside the cage, Beast stood still as a statue, his eyes scanning the freeborns within the restless crowd with an eerie calm.

Ink tore his gaze from the injured beast and looked back to Lygor, his voice dropping. "Why even let this happen? Why doesn't anyone stop it?"

Lygor shrugged vaguely, his mouth still hidden in his hand as he rubbed his chin. Valnar stepped in again.

"Would you keep a horse with a broken leg, Ink?"

"These are men, not horses. Freeborn men, so you can't even argue they're not human. They have *rhoas*, don't they?"

"They're criminals," Lygor spoke before Valnar did. His voice was grim, his focus still more on the room than the conversation, yet his tone carried the weight of someone eager to end it. "This life is their punishment. And they knew it before they committed their crimes."

Ink took another swig, then scoffed. "Honestly, it baffles me why they don't just revolt. Surely there's enough of them."

Valnar didn't bother responding. He just gave Ink a flat and unimpressed look, like the man had asked why fire was hot.

Lygor laughed once. "Because this system built the kingdom. It's in our laws, our gods, our blood. Freeborns know the price before they fall — and once they're chained, they're trained to obey. The ones who can't be broken end up at the Stillhouses."

Valnar didn't add a word. He didn't need to. Ink looked away, shaking his head. He'd heard enough. An unpleasant tension fell between them as Valer continued his theatrics. He even called out the names of familiar faces in the crowd, inviting them to the challenge. Though the men cheered wildly, they all remained a safe distance from the cage.

Valer finally beckoned Valnar closer to the bars and crouched down to speak with him. "Nobody will take up the challenge," he said, shaking his head.

"Then we get the prize," Lygor replied over Valnar's shoulder.

Valer glared at him. "I'm not giving you the prize without a fight."

"Then find us a rival."

"There's none dumb enough!"

With a grin, Lygor presented his open hand. "Then we get the prize."

"Or, I can get you all kicked out of my establishment."

"Well, my purebred is not getting out of that cage without a fight. You're more than welcome to decide whose head he will bust open."

In the centre of the cage, Beast still didn't move, didn't shift his stance or offer even the smallest gesture of challenge. Yet there was something about the way he stood — perfectly still, perfectly unbothered — that bristled with menace. His presence pressed against the air, as though the cage wasn't containing him but struggling to.

He was a fiend at rest, needing only a spark to explode into violence.

Valer swallowed, and Valnar knew the man had just imagined himself trying to drag Beast out of that cage by force. He bared his teeth at Lygor, his eyes gleaming with malice. "You want a fight, prick? Okay, I'll give you a fight."

Valer stood and addressed the crowd, spreading his arms at his sides. "Okay, cowards, if you're done shitting in your pants, listen up. I'm upping the prize to thirty Blues!"

"More money," Lygor muttered with a grin.

Ink turned the empty bottle upside down. "More wine," he mumbled as he walked over to the bar again.

"Still not enough to get your pussies wet?" Valer yelled over the excited rumble of the men. "How about this? Three against the purebred! Armed!"

"Hey!" Valnar shouted. "That's not fair!"

"A purebred is not fair, man," someone from the crowd replied.

"Then we're out!"

Valer leaned against the bars. "I thought your purebred wasn't coming out without a fight?" he sneered.

"This is bullshit! Then he gets a weapon too."

"No. He gets nothing. These are the terms. You in or out?"

Valnar shifted his weight, the silent question hanging in the air as he left the decision to Lygor. Lygor disregarded him, his attention settled on Beast. The purebred had heard the terms. He met Lygor's gaze and tilted his head slightly. The bastard looked like he was barely restraining a grin, his fingers twitching like he couldn't wait to get this fight started. A flicker of satisfaction crossed Lygor's face.

"We're in," the prince said. "He can take them."

"Then it is settled." Valer walked back to the centre of the cage. "Three armed men against one purebred," he repeated. He put a hand on Beast's shoulder, as if trying to demonstrate there was nothing to be afraid of him. "Anything is permitted. A Slayer's Pit in a cage!"

"Is it thirty each?"

"Pernan, you greedy bastard. Thirty divided between whoever stands. Come on! Anyone?"

"I'll take him!" a man called out, thrusting his fist into the air. His beast, no older than Lygor, stood with the poise of a seasoned fighter. He seemed slightly worried, but not as scared as some of the others. The crowd's cheers seemed to further steady him.

"Master Carfir and Hollow!" Valer announced with a sharp clap. "We need two more. Come on, step up!"

A free warrior named Bilghe stepped forward next. And Master Baldan, still burning from his earlier humiliation, shoved Crawler into the fray, following a moment's hesitation.

"Get your weapons ready!" Valer bellowed, his voice cutting through the noise. "The fight begins in ten. Place your bets!"

Valer hopped down from the cage, slamming the door shut behind him. The metallic clang was drowned in the wave of shouts from the crowd, people already offering their bets.

Inside the cage, Beast strolled casually to the bars closest to Valnar and the others. He leaned his forearm against the bars like he had all the time in Earthome. His gaze swept over the challengers, his expression disinterested, as though sizing them up was nothing more than a way to pass the time.

Valer made his way to a makeshift counter in the corner. It was little more than a heavy wooden table, but it was flanked by a crude board marked with chalk, listing odds and fight details. A battered ledger rested on the table, and behind it, another man scrawled furiously, trying to keep up with the influx of bets. Valer leaned over the counter, shouting for order as coins and tokens exchanged hands.

"Is that a lor'qas?" Lygor asked, jerking his head towards the young beast named Hollow. His owner was fitting him in a leather armour, complete with armguards and a shoulder plate.

Valnar gave a confirming grunt. "Useful in small spaces."

Clad in armour, Hollow seemed more at ease and self-assured, even invigorated.

"Well, he's offering one to five if they can last a good ten minutes," Ink said as he returned from the bar with another bottle of wine. "One to twenty if Beast takes them all down in ten seconds flat."

"One to twenty, huh?" Lygor winked at Beast. "Can you take them down in ten seconds?"

"I already asked Valer," Ink said. "He's not taking our bets." He took a swig from his bottle before handing it to Lygor. His eyes drifted back to the injured beast with the broken arm. The man hadn't moved, still clutching his limb with a haunted expression, and Ink's smirk faltered, his discomfort flickering across his face.

Lygor took a drink, then offered the bottle to Valnar, who rejected the beverage with a shake of his head. His focus was entirely on the freeborns and the warrior. Something squeezed his chest as he studied their armour and weapons.

"Hey Ink, that sword Bilghe has," he said, his voice dropping to a near growl. "Does that look like Grimbar steel to you?"

"It sure does."

Valnar's hand moved to his chest again, and when he couldn't find Kiejain there, he fidgeted with his scabbard. The free warrior wore a chainmail armour and carried a tower shield too. Armed to teeth. Valnar eyed Crawler, who was just bending to let his owner pull a breastplate over his head. He wore brass knuckles on his left fist and carried a short sword on his right.

Three experienced warriors. Two of them, Crawler and Hollow, both had probably been in this cage at least several times. When Valnar looked at Beast's plain shirt, unprotected face, and empty hands, he could suddenly label the feeling that squeezed his chest.

"Hey, where are you going?" Lygor asked sharply.

"I'll be right back," Ink mumbled before disappearing into the crowd, probably to get more booze.

Valer took more than ten minutes to start the fight, the final bets still coming. Their preparations complete, the three warriors were now exchanging words. Strategizing. The longer Valer took to start the fight, the deeper the roots of uncertainty dug into Valnar's chest. He pulled Lygor aside, leaning in and whispering, "Lodi, are you sure about this?"

"They're no match for a purebred."

"They're no amateurs. And they're armed to the teeth. They'll work together."

"Beast can still take them."

"Yeah, but at what cost? What if he gets injured?"

He watched the seed of doubt take root in Lygor. The prince shifted his feet, his attention flickering to anything but Valnar, his fingers tapping idly against his arm. Valnar placed a hand on his elbow, demanding his focus.

"Lodi, all it takes is a broken bone or a busted knee, and he's useless to you."

"I thought you didn't like him?"

"I don't," Valnar spat.

Leaning against the bars, Beast still watched his opponents with composure. Their combined arsenal of weapons and armour didn't intimidate him. Any sensible man with a sliver of Kiejain's wisdom would show at least some concern. The purebred's indifference bordered on recklessness.

Valnar inhaled through his teeth. "But you care about him, Lodi. This will screw up your plans."

Valer slammed the ledger shut. "Let's get this fight started!" he barked, his voice cutting through the murmur of the crowd. The crowd surged toward the cage, jostling for the best view.

Valnar glanced at Lygor, his eyes questioning, but Lygor shook his head. "It's too late to pull him out now."

The three challengers climbed into the cage. Hollow first, his reinforced leather armour creaking as he flexed his shoulders. His wickedly curved lor'qas glinted beneath the flickering torchlight. Bilghe followed, chainmail clinking faintly, his large shield raised and sword drawn. Crawler entered last, twirling his blade as if testing its weight. They spread out, their armours and weapons filling the cage with tangible menace.

"Then we need to guarantee his victory," Valnar muttered.

Beast stood with his back to the bars, his stance relaxed but watchful. Valer entered the cage with his arms raised, addressing the roaring crowd. "Three against one! A purebred with no weapons! Are you ready to see what he's made of?"

Ink returned, cradling another bottle of wine as he joined Valnar and Lygor at the edge of the cage. He didn't speak, but his concern showed in the tightness of his fingers around the bottle neck. Valnar and Lygor exchanged a look, an unspoken question passing between them.

Inside the cage, Valer gave a final flourish, shouting, "Fight starts now!" before hopping out of the cage and slamming the door shut behind him.

"Do it," Lygor muttered, his voice barely audible over the commotion.

Valnar moved swiftly. He grabbed the bars, pulling himself up. Reaching through, he caught the back of Beast's shirt and yanked him back. He leaned close, whispering the word right as Bilghe attacked.

"*Dracistuecto.*"

Beast took a sharp breath.

Valnar pulled his hand back just in time as Beast ducked low and rolled. Bilghe's sword met the bars, raising a loud clank and almost taking Valnar's fingers off.

Beast rose to his feet. His knees were slightly bent, his empty hands ready at his sides. His mouth contorted into a primal snarl. His eyes moved rapidly in their sockets, and they reflected a darker shade of grey. A muscle in his neck twitched. He stood still. Too still that even his opponents froze, their confidence wavering.

The crowd's roar fractured by a breathless pause.

Valnar stepped back to watch the carnage he had just unleashed into the cage.

25

VALNAR

Hollow proved to be the bravest amongst them. Where his confidence stemmed from — youth or a fatalistic acceptance — Valnar would never know. But the young freeborn snapped himself out of that hesitant state and charged at Beast with a cry.

Beast ducked and slid towards Hollow, barely lifting his feet off the ground. He landed two rapid punches on Hollow's leather armour, and a third one upwards on his outstretched elbow. Hollow's lor'qas flew off his hand. Beast grabbed him by his armour, turned, and swung him behind on a collusion with Bilghe, who was charging at him. Both fighters hit the ground in a tangled heap, weapons clattering around them.

In a flowing motion, Beast shifted to the side to dodge Crawler's sword. Crawler followed up with a knuckled punch, and Beast caught it with an open palm. The crowd released a collective gasp. Even Valnar winced, imagining the jolt of pain, yet Beast remained unfazed, not even a flicker in his expression.

Beast's fingers clamped onto the brass knuckles. With a sharp twist, he snapped them back, breaking Crawler's fingers. Crawler roared in pain and swung the hilt of his sword down hard, aiming for Beast's head. Beast ducked. With hands planted on the floor for support, he kicked Crawler's chest with both feet, sending him stumbling backwards.

Beast stood, eyeing his rivals as they recovered. He could have finished it right then and there, with all three on the floor, trying to get up. Ten seconds hadn't passed since the fight began, and the purebred could have made a lot of people rich, if he'd simply picked up Hollow's lor'qas off the floor and cut them down.

He didn't.

He stood in the centre, his mouth and neck twitching subtly, as he waited for his rivals to get up.

Hollow retrieved his lor'qas. The other two sprang to their feet, and all three launched into an attack. Beast ducked, stepped aside, turned sideways to dodge their blows. He swayed back, the blade slicing past him harmlessly. He sidestepped another strike. His movements were swift yet somehow seemed unhurried. Every so often, he lashed out with a quick jab — a blur of motion that cracked against armour or flesh — before slipping effortlessly out of reach again.

Then, he landed a brutal kick on Crawler's knee. A sickening crack echoed as Crawler collapsed, howling and clutching at his shattered kneecap.

Hollow lunged, his blade slicing toward Beast's chest. Beast ducked and slid forward, closing the distance in an instant. Leading with his shoulder, he tackled Hollow against the bars. The metal rattled violently, the spectators nearest to the bars shouting for blood.

Beast pinned the young freeborn there, one arm pressed firmly across his chest, the other gripping Hollow's wrist to keep his weapon uselessly at his side. When Bilghe charged from behind him, Beast flung himself to the side while lifting Hollow's wrist, pointing the lor'qas at the free warrior's chest.

Unable to stop in time, Bilghe lowered his shield at the last second, pushing the tip of the sword down. But Beast yanked Hollow's arm forward and drove the lor'qas into just above Bilghe's groin where the chainmail was most vulnerable.

The spectators roared with the excitement for the first blood.

When Beast pushed Bilghe off the blade, blood spurted from the wound. He grabbed Bilghe's shield and slammed it against the warrior's face. Bilghe stumbled to his knees, dazed and bloodied.

Before Beast could do anything else, Hollow grabbed him from the back and wrapped his left arm around his neck. The young freeborn pulled his lor'qas back, aiming the tip at Beast's lower back while the purebred thrashed wildly. Beast planted his feet on Bilghe's shoulders, using the leverage to vault himself upward, just as the blade sliced through empty air. With the momentum, his legs arched in a swift semicircle overhead, carrying him behind Hollow in a seamless, fluid motion.

He latched himself on Hollow and bit his ear off.

The crowd went wild.

Beast grabbed Hollow's arm, twisted it behind his back, and drove him toward the cage bars, face-first. He smashed Hollow's wrist against the bars repeatedly until the lor'qas fell with a clatter. Hollow was already dazed. Blood trickled from where his left ear used to be. He hardly put up any resistance when Beast grabbed his hair and slammed his face against the bars.

Over and over again.

Each strike left Hollow's face bloodier. His nose broke, his eyebrows split, and the crowd cheered when broken teeth was flung amongst them. Hollow fell unconscious, his arms dangling at his sides, his knees loose, but Beast continued smashing his face against the bars with brutal force.

Crawler stood up, gaining his balance on one foot. He armed himself with his sword, but didn't attack. He gawked at Beast as the purebred reshaped Hollow's head.

The young freeborn's face turned into a red mash made of skull fragments, oozing brain, blood and flesh, barely held together by broken skin. It made a nauseating, mushy sound each time it connected with the bars. He could not still be alive; his head was nothing but a bloody mess with some hair attached to it. But Beast didn't let go. He made a guttural, inhuman sound as he drove Hollow's head one last time, with enough force to jam it through the bars.

"Merciful Alunwea," whispered Valnar.

The crowd savoured it, only a few people looking away, but most couldn't take their eyes off the purebred.

Beast left Hollow's dead body hanging by the bars and surveyed his remaining opponents. Blood clung to his face and arms, his messy blond hair tinged with red. That eerie, calculating stillness fell on him again, with occasional twitches coursing through his body. His fingers splayed and bent, his knuckles white, like grotesque claws.

Bilghe was still on the floor, coughing and spurting blood from his mouth.

Beast's eyes fixed on Crawler.

The freeborn slave dropped his sword. His pants turned dark with urine. He ran to the door of the cage as the crowd roared in anger and excitement.

"Let me out, Master, Owner. Please, let me out of here—"

Valnar almost felt sorry for the man.

The purebred's eyes... They weren't human.

Valnar knew this, but he'd never fully realised it until now. Fear was like a cold breeze in his chest. When he remembered the fleeting moments of defiance and disobedience the purebred had shown over the last few days, his mouth dried. If the discipline that kept this monster chained was really frayed...

Valnar gulped.

Beast grabbed Crawler by his back and threw him to the floor. He climbed on top, straddling his chest. A scream of pure horror tore from Crawler's throat, broken by a brutal punch.

Beast punched him relentlessly, his fists loaded with a crippling force. He alternated between grabbing the freeborn's hair and smashing his head against the floor, and battering his face with punches, his fists pounding faster and faster. A heave-like growl rose from Beast's chest, quickly escalating into a ferocious roar. Driven by an inhuman rage and a desperate need to inflict pain, he pummelled Crawler mercilessly.

The men around the cage roared their excitement when Bilghe stood. He pulled his hand free from his shield and picked up his sword. Clutching at his wound with his free hand, he staggered towards Beast, who was utterly lost in a fit of rage.

"Behind you! Look out!" Lygor yelled, cupping his hands near his mouth.

Beast didn't respond. He continued hammering Crawler's face, which resembled a red paste now.

Bilghe lifted his sword high, the tip aimed downward. As he drove it toward Beast's back, the purebred rolled aside at the last moment, leaving the blade to plunge straight into Crawler's chest.

Beast tackled Bilghe to the ground. The free warrior seized Beast by the neck, attempting to wrestle him off. Beast turned his head, biting forward and clamped his teeth around Bilghe's fingers. The spectators cheered wildly when they heard the sound of snapping bones. Beast turned his head and spat the fingers aside.

Next, he tilted Bilghe's chin up, and went for his throat.

The warrior's screams turned to wet gurgling sounds as Beast's teeth sank into his flesh. The purebred tore a chunk of flesh off, and instead of spitting it out, he *chewed*. A stream of warm blood spurted at Beast's face, his nose and mouth already dipped in red.

"He's... he's not human," Valnar mumbled.

Lygor didn't respond. Ink looked as if he was about to throw up.

Bilghe's struggles diminished. Beast tilted the warrior's chin further up and dug his fingers into the open wound.

"Uniting Kiejain," Ink whispered. Valnar had rarely seen the Kaldorian shaken like this, with the Twelve's name on his lips.

Beast dipped both hands into Bilghe's throat, who had already stopped moving. A look of intense concentration twisted the purebred's face. His lips parted in a bloody snarl. Bilghe's flesh still hung from his mouth. He clawed his way into the bloody mess, found what he was looking for, and yanked the dead man's tongue out from his throat.

Valnar wanted to look away, but he couldn't. This had to be it. The purebred should have stopped now. The Rage should have faded. He'd won.

By the mighty Kiejain, Valnar didn't want that thing walking out of the cage. But it was over. It had to be.

Except it wasn't.

Beast stood. His eyes were still smouldered with a raw fury, so dark and fierce they seemed to ignite the very air around him. His face was a red mask. A snarl still clung to his lips, as he kept that piece of meat between his teeth, chewing lazily.

One of the fighters was still alive.

Beast's eyes narrowed on Crawler, whose hand twitched and lifted. The purebred took two steps, then paused, tilting his head and looking at Bilghe's shield. He chewed, looking thoughtful the way a mindless, ferocious monster would. He lifted the shield and strode towards Crawler. He stepped over him, planting his feet on both sides of the freeborn's torso, looming tall. He raised the shield over his head, then rammed the rim of it against Crawler's throat.

The men cheered their approval, as Beast drove the shield down again, determined to decapitate Crawler.

Third strike left Crawler's head barely attached to his shoulders by some skin and crushed bones. Only then, the Rage started to fade.

The shield fell from Beast's fingers, its clatter swallowed by the crowd's ecstatic cheers. His arms went limp as he blinked with vacant eyes that slowly regained their focus.

Valnar finally tore his gaze away from the cage. He inhaled a shaky breath, only now realising how firmly he had been ensnared by the display of violence. He turned to Lygor, expecting to find the same horror reflected back.

But instead, he found Lygor grinning.

It wasn't a relieved or victorious smile. It was something darker — eyes gleaming with strange excitement, the expression of someone not just impressed, but enthralled. Then Lygor's face shifted. The smile dropped into a scowl. "What the fuck is wrong with him?"

Valnar followed his gaze and felt his stomach twist.

Beast spat the flesh out of his mouth, gagging and retching, wiping his mouth repeatedly. He paced, his arms and legs uncoordinated, his hands shaking violently. His breath came in harsh, shallow bursts as his wide eyes darted around the cage. Though his mouth was moving, his words were inaudible over the cheering crowd. He slipped on blood, and fell on Bilghe's corpse, suddenly coming face to face with the warrior's ripped throat. He scrambled away from it, until his back was against Hollow's legs. He clambered in the cage, slipping in blood.

He'd gone from an animal consumed by pure rage to one consumed by pure horror.

"Valnar, what in Darkhome is wrong with him?" Lygor asked.

"I don't know."

"Get him out of there."

Valnar was already moving. He grabbed Valer, ripping the keys from the man's hand without a word and unlocking the cage door. The crowd closest to the door shuffled back.

Stepping in, Valnar immediately knew he would have to drop Beast.

The purebred's pupils had swallowed his irises, darting around like a cornered animal. His chest heaved, his breath hitching erratically. There was no recognition in his face, no awareness of Valnar or the men outside. His eyes were the eyes of someone suffocating inside their own mind.

Valnar knew that feeling too well.

Beast sprang forward without warning, his massive frame a blur of raw desperation.

"*Padlociatius!*"

Beast hit the ground with a dull thud. Valnar crouched, muttering a curse under his breath as he slipped an arm under Beast's shoulders and another beneath his knees. He strained, gritting his teeth as he lifted the massive man over his shoulder. Beast was deadweight, his size making the task a test of Valnar's strength, but he managed to stand, his legs wobbling slightly before he found his balance.

He climbed down carefully, the crowd parting out of his way.

Lygor approached. "Take him outside and wait there. I'll handle the money."

Valnar nodded and pushed through the crowd. Beast's weight pulled at his shoulder at every step as he made his way to the exit.

26

VALNAR

RAIN DRIPPED STEADILY FROM the eaves of the winery. Valnar stood under a small overhang, his arms crossed, watching Beast from a distance. The purebred knelt in the muddy corner, facing the wall, unmoving except for the slow, repetitive motion of his arm. A piece of cloth — something Valnar had snatched off from one of the pleasure workers on his way out — was clenched in his hand as he scrubbed his forearms with it.

Valnar shifted his weight. The rain had eased, but the air was cool, a faint breeze carrying the scent of wet earth. Beast hadn't made a sound since they'd gotten outside. Valnar had kept repeating the First Word like a prayer to keep him paralysed until they stepped out into the night. He'd lowered him to the ground and stepped back, watching warily. He'd expected Beast to resume growling and heaving like a rabid animal, and attack him as soon as the paralysis faded. But Beast had only sat there, facing the wall, dragging the cloth across his arms in a futile attempt to clean himself.

The sound of footsteps broke the silence. Valnar tensed, but it was only Lygor and Ink emerging around the corner. Lygor carried a heavy pouch that jingled faintly with each step and a bottle of wine tucked under his arm. Ink trailed behind, his shoulders hunched slightly against the drizzle.

"How's he doing?" Ink asked, nodding toward Beast.

Valnar didn't look away from the figure by the wall. "Hasn't moved. Hasn't said a word."

Lygor tilted his head. He stepped closer, ignoring Valnar's uncomfortable shuffle. Lygor made a few deliberate noises as he approached Beast, as if making sure he wouldn't startle him. "Beast?" he said.

Beast shifted. The purebred rose to his feet, facing Lygor. With his hands clasped in front of him, he bowed his head and stood still. His face was streaked with dried blood, his hair matted and stiff. The cloth was scrunched in his fist. His massive frame was shadowed by the dim light.

"Are you hurt?"

"I am well, Master."

Some of the tension eased from Valnar's chest. Hearing him talk was a good sign. It meant Alunwea spared his mind. He'd witnessed men — his brothers in arms from Kiejain's Army — lose their speech entirely after a gruesome fight. The slave wasn't worthy, but Alunwea had mercy for all.

Lygor tilted his head as if trying to gauge Beast's state, then held out the wine bottle.

Beast reached for it, but as soon as his fingers closed around the glass, he flinched, the bottle slipping from his grip. It landed with a soft thud in the mud.

Beast stared at his right hand. Though the darkness obscured his view, Valnar didn't need to see to know what held Beast's attention — his raw, bruised, and swollen palm, a painful reminder of the knuckled punch he had stopped. The backs of his hands were scraped and mottled too. Beast moved his fingers as if testing how sore it was.

Lygor bent and picked up the bottle. It wasn't broken. He offered it again. Beast took it with his left hand, tilted his head back, and scoffed it down. He coughed and sputtered, clearly unaccustomed to the taste. Lygor chuckled, then waited for him to lower the bottle and asked, "Are you good to walk?"

Beast nodded.

The rain started to pick up, the light drizzle turning into heavier drops. Ink glanced at the sky, muttering, "I've got something to take care of." Before the others could comment, he turned back towards the winery as he added, "I'll catch up with you later."

Valnar scowled after him. This wasn't the time for fun and games, but he couldn't stop the foreign prince.

Lygor adjusted the pouch on his belt and gestured for Valnar and Beast to follow. Valnar stepped aside, letting Beast go first while he stayed at the rear. Their boots squelched through the thickening mud as the rain intensified, washing away some of the blood off Beast's face.

Valnar watched Beast's back, his fingers drifting to his chest, searching for that quiet conviction Kiejain once gave him, and only finding it when his hand came to rest on the hilt of his sword

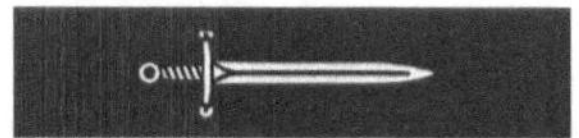

Nobody spoke until they reached the drenched main street of the town.

Beast had used the rain to clean himself up as best he could, rubbing the blood off his face and arms as he walked. He kept closing and opening his right fist, as if reassuring himself that nothing was broken.

A cold breeze came to life as they approached the inn, causing Valnar to shiver. He moved his hand away from his sword and tugged his cloak close. He longed to return to the stable, get changed into dry clothes, wrap himself in his blanket, and try to find sleep.

His disappointment was tangible when Lygor headed straight for the tavern. "Lodi..."

"Just a few drinks," Lygor said with a careless grin.

Valnar trudged after the prince, a twinge of jealousy prickling as he watched Beast head toward the stable, only to be stopped short by Lygor's sharp whistle. "Where do you think you're going?"

Beast froze, utterly confused and speechless. He scratched his head and pointed at the stable.

"I think you deserve a drink. Come on inside." Lygor climbed up the steps, but paused when he noticed neither Beast nor Valnar were following him. "What's wrong?"

Valnar cleared his throat. "He's a slave."

"So?"

"I don't think he'll be allowed in there."

Lygor paused as if he was considering it, then brushed the concern with a shrug. "It'll be fine."

Valnar wasn't keen on the idea of sharing a drink with the purebred, and judging by Beast's expression, the feeling was mutual. Beast shifted uneasily, his fingers tugging at the hem of his blood-stained shirt.

"Lodi, I think he should go and get some rest after that fight."

"Since when do you care about his needs?" Lygor rolled his eyes. "Come on, we could all use a drink." He walked inside without a backward glance, leaving no room for argument.

Valnar gritted his teeth while Beast stood indecisive. "You heard him," Valnar growled eventually. He nodded towards the door and Beast dragged his feet up the steps.

The tavern was warm, much warmer than the stable would be. A large, stone fireplace occupied the centre, casting soft shadows on the wooden walls. Mismatched tables and chairs were scattered around it, only half of them occupied. The air was thick with the mingled scents of stale ale, damp clothes, and vomit.

Lygor had already settled comfortably on a table in the far corner. Valnar raised his hand to prod Beast, hesitated, then lowered it back down. Instead, he jerked his head and muttered, "Walk."

As Beast walked past the bar, his steps muffled by the muddy layer of wood shavings that covered the floor. The innkeeper scowled at him from behind the bar. The disapproval in his eyes lingered, but he held his tongue as Valnar shadowed Beast to the table.

"Sit." Lygor gestured at the chair on his left and Beast slumped on it hesitantly. He kept his head down, but couldn't stop himself from examining the room with quick glances. Valnar slid into the seat across from the slave, reclined stiffly, and crossed his arms.

"Is this your first time in a tavern?" Lygor asked, leaning forward. He drummed his fingers on the table, seeming entirely at ease with the fact that they were sitting on a table with a slave. Like equals.

Beast nodded. He sat on the edge of the chair, his large frame awkward and out of place, like a heathen in a Chamber of Twelve.

"So? What do you think?" When Beast didn't speak immediately, Lygor gestured for him to talk. "Honest thoughts, come on."

"It's shit... Master."

Lygor laughed. "Well, then, we can conclude your first experience in a tavern is an authentic one."

The innkeeper approached their table, his face stern. He cleared his throat, but before he could speak, Lygor cut him off. "We'll grab three beers, please. Oh, and we'll take a room for tonight. And it better be decent, for the price you're asking."

The innkeeper stiffened. "I don't serve slaves in my tavern," he said. "You'll need to get him out of here."

Lygor leaned back in his chair, a slow, amused smile spreading across his face. "You're not serving him. You're serving me."

"I'll get you your drinks and give you a room. You can keep him there or send him back to the stable. But I'm not letting any slaves sitting on my tables."

Several heads from the nearest tables turned to watch the exchange.

"Lodi," Valnar muttered. "I'll take him to the stable."

"No." Lygor said smoothly. He reached and placed a hand on Beast's arm. "Lift your head, please."

Beast did as he asked, fixing his eyes on the beams above. He had rubbed most of the blood off, but faint streaks remained. The innkeeper's eyes flicked to Beast's tattoo, then to the dark splotches on his shirt, and bruised and battered knuckles.

"What do you see?" Lygor asked lightly.

"I see a slave sitting at my table."

"I really would like a drink, my friend," Lygor said. "You can bring it yourself, or I can send my purebred to get it. How do you think that would go?"

Beast placed his hands together on the table. His throat bobbed when he swallowed, though his eyes took on a cold, hard glint.

"Are you threatening me in my own tavern?"

Lygor tilted his face upward, deep in thought. He nodded slowly. "Yes. Yes, I am. So?"

A shade of red that was the blend of anger and embarrassment coloured the innkeeper's face. His eyes darted over Beast's frame, taking in the corded muscles, the dead grey eyes, the tight set of his jaw. He was probably imagining the purebred rampaging through the tavern, tossing people and furniture out of his way, and carelessly trashing the bottles on the shelves behind the bar. Valnar was imagining the same thing too, and he knew Lygor enough to fear the prince would do anything to get his way.

Usually, they'd have Ink to smooth things over — the Kaldorian had a way of turning threats into agreements that left everyone thinking they'd won. But Ink wasn't here. Which meant Valnar would have to handle this himself, give the innkeeper just enough of a push to make him bend before Lygor made him break.

He cleared his throat and leaned forward. "It's not worth it, friend. Just a few drinks. You won't even notice he's here."

The innkeeper exhaled a long breath and stepped away, shaking his head as if he had decided they were not worth his time.

After the man left, Valnar scowled at Lygor. "Lodi, why are you doing this? Just send him to the stable."

"He's done a remarkable job for us tonight, Valnar. He deserves a damn drink."

"He doesn't need a reward. He's a slave."

"Only for a few more months. Isn't that right, Beast?"

Beast's expression tightened, a flicker of something guarded crossing his face. His chest seemed to still mid-breath as he hunched slightly. He held Lygor's gaze, wearing indifference like a mask, though he couldn't hide the vulnerability that showed through the cracks.

Lygor didn't drop his smile. He patted Beast's arm reassuringly, his hand lingering a heartbeat longer than it should. "You'll get your freedom, Beast. I have no doubt you can win it." He lowered his voice and leaned forward on his elbows. "And then you'll help me get my throne. So, sit back and relax. Get used to this."

"Lodi—"

"You too, Valnar. Pull that stick out of your arse. That's an order." He leaned back. "We're all in this together now. So, by the end of tonight, you guys will learn to get along."

The table between them was too flimsy to support the weight of the tension that hung between Valnar and Beast. Beast's bruised fingers pressed down on the weathered surface so hard, his nails turned pale. He dragged his hands under the table to hide the fists Valnar knew he was clenching. The hostility was mutual. Valnar became too aware of the weight of his sword hanging from his hip.

The unspoken animosity broke with the soft clink of mugs. A serving girl slid the three mugs on the table. As she turned to leave, Lygor grabbed her arm and slipped a red coin in her palm as he whispered something in her ear. The girl nodded before heading back behind the bar, where the innkeeper still glowered at them.

Valnar grabbed his mug and took a long sip. The bitterness of the beer bit at his tongue, but did little to soothe the agitation of sitting at the table with a monster who was capable of ripping someone's throat off with his teeth. The gore they had just left behind didn't seem to stop Lygor from enjoying his drink. Valnar tried changing his approach.

"Is it really clever displaying him like this? People remember being threatened by a purebred beast. Kastian is looking for him too."

Lygor put his mug down. "People also remember watching a purebred beast butcher three men in a cage. We've already left our trace in this town. It's a bit late to stay low now." Lygor scanned the room briefly, his sharp gaze lingering on the scattered groups of drunken patrons.

"Besides, we're leaving in first light. You'll leave early and find the town's horse breeder. Get Beast a decent mount." He nodded at the purebred, who still hadn't touched his mug. "Drink."

Beast pulled the mug to himself, sloshing some beer on the grimy table. He took two gulps, then coughed it back out. Lygor was the only one laughing, but his tone was free of malice.

"Don't tell me this is your first time drinking beer?"

Beast shook his head.

With a playful wink, Lygor drawled, "Oh, so you stole a sip from someone's mug while they weren't looking?"

Beast looked almost startled, his lips curling with disgust. "*Steal* this shit? I don't... I would never take without permission."

"Well?" Lygor gestured him to continue.

Beast shifted in his seat, his eyes darting at the door. "Master Caesh made me try some. When celebrating after a tournament."

"Who's Master Caesh?"

"Umm... One of the trainers."

"I've heard you were revered by the castle staff? Spoilt, even."

Beast spun the mug idly between his fingers. "I was assigned a room. On my own."

Lygor whistled softly. "My father didn't spare any expenses for his beloved beast, did he?" Lygor finished the rest of his drink, then viewed the tavern for a while, before asking. "So, tell me about your life at Brinescar. Have you ever disobeyed your orders?"

"No." With a grimace, Beast tossed back the rest of his drink. He pushed the mug away and eyed the door again.

"So, when did your little attitudes start exactly? After the coup?" Lygor pressed.

Beast eyed the door again. "At the Serpent's Grip. May I be excused, Master?"

"Not yet. I'm not done enjoying your company."

The serving girl returned with a tray full of steaming clean towels, clean cloth, and an old bottle of cheap *Swampshine*. Lygor slid a few more coins across the table. "Bring us some mead, and a shot of *Ro'norin*, please. Have you got any *Blue Rocker*? A cup of that as well. And more beer." The girl nodded and left.

Lygor grabbed the towel and dragged his chair closer to Beast. "Give me your hands."

Beast turned to him, offering his hands reluctantly. Lygor roughly wiped dried blood from his split knuckles and cleaned the cut on his right palm. Then, without warning, he grabbed the bottle of *Swampshine* and poured it over Beast's hands. The purebred hissed and nearly jumped out of his seat.

"Don't be a wuss," Lygor muttered as he reached for the clean cloth. "So, Serpent's Grip. You faced Kastian's champion on that tournament final, didn't you?"

Beast nodded.

"That's when you first disobeyed? What did you do?"

"I didn't die."

Lygor chuckled as he pulled Beast's right hand to his lap and started bandaging it. "Kastian ordered you to die, and you wanted to live?"

Valnar caught it. That faint shift in Beast's expression, that shadow flickering through his eyes before disappearing as quickly as it came. Lygor either missed it entirely or didn't understand what he saw. But Valnar understood. It was too familiar, too haunting, to ignore.

"No," Valnar said quietly. "He didn't."

Beast's gaze locked on Valnar, a sharpness in his eyes that could cut steel. It was gone in an instant, his frame stiffening into a wall of indifference.

Lygor's hands paused over the knot he tied, his eyebrows lifting in surprise as he studied the purebred with a refreshed interest. "Is that true?"

Beast gave him nothing. He pulled his bandaged hand from Lygor's grip, resting it on his lap.

Lygor leaned back, his fingers softly drumming on the table again. "Then why didn't you just stand still and die?"

Beast flexed his fingers, his hand trembling slightly as if the question had struck a nerve. He covered it with the other hand to still the trembling. Then, one of the patrons from across the room shouted for a drink, the noise drawing Lygor's attention for a moment.

Beast shifted in his seat, forced a shrug. "Kastian's champion was useless. Couldn't even hit me if I stood still. May I... go now?" His voice faded to disappointment as the serving girl filled their table with more drinks.

"No. You'll have to try them all and decide which one's your favourite."

Beast turned his face to hide his grimace. Lygor pushed the drinks towards him; a mug of mead, a tiny glass of unassuming, clear liquid, and a cup of *Blue Rocker* with a faint blue tint. He gestured Beast to help himself, then turned to Valnar.

"Hey Valnar, do you remember that time Ink really craved for some *Serpent-blood*, and every tavern we tried were having supply issues, because a mad man was attacking shipments or something. You remember how we travelled three weeks to Dregsport, to see if they had any?"

"How could I forget?" Valnar grunted. "Both you and Ink nearly died three times on that canyon."

The next few minutes, Lygor kept the conversation on their travels, occasionally turning and explaining a few details to Beast, while making sure the purebred continued drinking. Beast started with the shot of *Ro'norin*, probably thinking the tiny cup would be the easiest to swallow. Valnar hid his smirk when the purebred tossed the drink down, then coughed and retched.

"How is it?" Lygor asked.

"Like swallowing liquid fire."

"Try the *Rocker*. Come on."

Beast didn't react as much to the next two. The *Ro'norin* probably burnt his tongue and killed all his tastebuds. Lygor pushed another mug of beer in front of him. "Here, wash it off. So, what's wrong with your Rage? That's not how you normally come off it, right?"

Beast slumped over the table, his elbows resting on it. "Nothing's wrong with my Rage." He gave Valnar a hateful look. "I just wasn't prepared for it."

Valnar had slowed down his drinking and was only nurturing his third beer. He didn't want to be drunk tonight. "You got a problem with me, slave?"

"I said I could beat them bare."

"And yet I Raged you. So?"

Beast's fingers tightened around his mug. Valnar wondered if the purebred could break it in his hand.

"It was my decision," Lygor cut in. He drew Beast's irritated gaze on him. He casually flicked a lint off his coat. His demeanour challenged Beast to make a complaint if he could dare.

Beast didn't raise any problems.

"I'll tell you what." Lygor leaned back, resting one ankle on the other knee. A charming smile tugged at the corner of his mouth. "I'll grant you freedom. Freedom to choose. Right now." He flicked a hand towards Beast's drink. "You may choose to sit down and continue drinking with us. Or..." Lygor nodded towards the door. "You can return to the stable and drown in whatever misery that makes you whimper like a kicked dog in your sleep."

Beast's eyes darted to the door, then to his mug, before locking on Lygor. "If I stay, will you keep asking questions?"

"I need to know what broke you and if I can trust you or not."

Beast gritted his teeth, hunching over the table as if he could find his answer across the stained wood. His fingers curled tight around his mug, blood seeping from his sore knuckles. He couldn't speak. His jaw worked, then stilled, his gaze darting at the door.

Next to him, Lygor waited in silence, giving him the space to struggle. Beast's gaze flicked up, caught the prince's, then dropped again.

Finally, he spoke to his mug. His voice came low and halting, each word scraped raw from somewhere deep, like he was dragging them through a clenched throat just to make them real.

"There was a woman. And... And Kastian..." He swallowed the rest. The pain that crossed his face didn't leave room for doubt about the fate of the woman and Kastian's role in it. The look he gave Lygor was so much like the one Valnar had seen in the cage that his hand instinctively went to his sword.

"Let me win my freedom," Beast said. "And I promise you Kastian's head on a platter."

There was a woman.

Valnar's jaw dropped. It was impossible.

Lygor nodded slowly. The look that made Valnar reach for his sword didn't seem to unnerve Lygor at all. If anything, the prince seemed pleased.

"Alright," Lygor said. "I'm happy with that."

Beast chugged the rest of his mug. Then, still hunched on his elbows, he caught the serving girl's gaze and just stared at her until the poor girl paled and scurried behind the bar to fetch him another drink.

Lygor kept his word. He didn't ask any more questions to Beast, but he did his best to get the purebred included in random conversations.

There was a woman.

Valnar still couldn't believe it. He would have thought Beast was lying if he hadn't seen the dark look on his face earlier. Was it the loss that had tempted the purebred to seek death? Was this why he had gone mad? Broken?

Not possessed by fiends, but possessed by grief?

Over an hour had passed, and the purebred was polishing mug after mug with no signs of slowing down. Lygor seemed to enjoy himself too, watching the purebred smash his booze with pride, like it was some personal achievement.

"What did I miss?" Ink said, dropping himself on the chair on Beast's other side, making the purebred jump. Ink raised his eyebrows at his presence at the table.

"Not much." Lygor pulled his chair closer to Beast and draped an arm over the slave's massive shoulder. "We just became friends."

"Really?"

Beast grunted.

"You should have seen him, Ink." Lygor leaned across the table as if sharing a fascinating secret. "He spoke more than ten words! In one speech!"

Beast shook Lygor's arm off and rubbed his nose as he made another annoyed noise.

"No way!" Ink gasped. He gestured for a drink.

"So, how was Welda?" Valnar asked.

"Huh?"

"Wait, no. I don't wanna hear."

The Kaldorian smiled and shrugged.

Beast was still preoccupied with his nose, pinching and releasing it. "I don't feel my nose," he mumbled.

"It's okay. That only means you're getting to the good part."

Beast flinched when several men at one of the tables near the fireplace started shouting. At first, it sounded like an argument. Then the men started laughing and raising their mugs, slapping each other's backs as they spoke over one another.

"Ugh, it's that song again," Lygor said. "At every single tavern."

The men were so out of tune, they would have put a screeching animal to shame. Other men across the tavern added their voices to the jumble of words. Valnar recognised some phrases from "The Lion and The Bear."

"It's not a bad song if they hadn't ruined it like that," Ink said.

Beast was blinking unfocused eyes at the singing men. His massive frame slumped closer to the table. "Not how it happened," he slurred. "Wasn't poking him with a spear between my legs. That's not... That's... That's not an efficient way to wield a spear."

Lygor and Ink burst into laughter, fists slamming against the table, drawing glances from nearby patrons. Lygor leaned in, eyes gleaming with mischief.

"Huh. And here I was thinking you'd be deadly with that spear between your legs."

Ink snorted into his mug, choking down another laugh. Valnar didn't. He stiffened, jaw flexing hard enough to crack teeth. Beast's brow furrowed as he rattled something about how it was actually a trident and not a spear, and the two had different weight and range.

"Were you really naked and unarmed?" Ink asked, still amused.

Beast confirmed with another grunt. Lygor reclined in his chair and took a long, tasteful sip from his beer. A slow smile spread across his face, and Valnar knew exactly what the prince was picturing.

Valnar cleared his throat, redirecting the conversation. "How did you do it?" he asked. He'd heard so many stories about the fight that had started a small riot at Brinescar. "How did you kill a bear unarmed?"

Beast's eyes focused on him briefly before blinking away and scowling. "I jumped on him and... and jammed the arrow in his eye."

"I thought you were unarmed?"

Beast suppressed a yawn. He slapped his left bicep. "Caught an arrow with my arm."

"They pitted you against a bear, and then shot an arrow at you?" Ink hissed.

Beast brought his mug to his mouth, his face falling when he discovered it was empty. He looked entirely confused as he tilted the mug and watched a single drop hit the table's surface. He lifted his head, looking for the serving girl.

"I think that's enough," Valnar said, trying to be sensible.

"Fuck off."

"What did you say, slave?"

"Valnar, let him enjoy himself," Lygor said with a snicker.

"Lodi, you should cut him off. He's hammered."

"Now I understand why Master Badimar liked this so much," Beast slurred with amusement.

The serving girl slid another mug in front of Beast, sloshing it in her hurry to bolt away from the drunk beast.

"Who's Master Badimar?" Lygor asked. He was somewhat intoxicated too, but maintained his composure a lot better.

"Who cares? Tell us what happened after the arrow," Ink asked.

"Gonna do this every day when I'm free." Beast drained the beer, the foam running down his stubble. He wiped his mouth and burped. Patrons from the nearest table had noticed the drunk purebred and were laughing at him, the sight more unusual than watching a dog wear a dress.

"Lodi." Valnar jerked his head towards the curious glances.

"Relax, it's not like he's dancing on the table or anything."

Beast's chair scraped loudly. He stood and lifted a knee on the table. Ink, Kiejain bless him twelve times, had enough sense to grab his arm and yank him back on his chair.

"Alright, that's it," growled Valnar.

Beast swayed, his eyes slightly crossed. How many had he have? Valnar tried to calculate in his head. At least eight or nine more, topping the shot of *Ro'norin* and the *Blue Rocker*. Sweat glistened on the purebred's face, sickly pale and still streaked with dried blood. His breath came in shallow, uneven bursts, as if attempting to stand had unsettled his stomach. He let out a faint groan.

"He's gonna throw up!" Ink said.

"Out!"

Valnar was already on his feet, moving around the table. Him and Ink each took one of Beast's arms, hoisting him upright as his body sagged between them. The purebred groaned, his head lolling forward. He barely resisted, but he was far from cooperative. He was already barfing by the time Valnar slammed the door open. They dragged him a few steps further away from the door and let him lurch forward on his knees.

The rain had picked up again, quickly drenching Valnar's hair. He stepped away from the hurling purebred, shaking his head and gritting his teeth. When Beast stopped for a breath, Ink leaned close. "Still wanna do this every day?"

Beast's reply was another violent retch as his body heaved at the muddy ground. Ink jumped back, but pulled a handkerchief from his pocket and tossed it near him.

The door creaked open, and Lygor joined them. He smirked at Beast, still on his knees, then at Valnar and Ink, who stood nearby.

"Who would have known?" he said, his tone casual, as if he'd just stumbled upon an entertaining scene. "My father's great champion can't hold his booze."

"Lodi, what were you thinking?"

Lygor rolled his eyes. "What? We needed to clear the air. Get to know each other. Right, Beast?"

Beast made a pathetic noise that sounded like a dying animal. His head sagged between his shoulders.

"You could have stopped him after you heard what you needed."

"I let him choose. He wanted to keep drinking."

"The Twelve blessed us with minds to choose, but they didn't give everyone the sense to use them."

"Your Twelve Riders can take their blessings and stick them up their arses," Beast growled.

Lygor's eyes widened. Even Ink's jaw dropped.

Valnar slowly turned towards the purebred, his head giving a slight jerk. A jolt of furious icy anger shot through him.

"What did you say, slave?"

Beast sat back on his haunches. Rain and sweat plastered his red-tinted blond hair to his forehead. He wavered for a moment, then slowly stumbled in the mud, climbing to his feet. "She used to pray," he slurred. "She had a *rhoa*. She prayed to Alunwea."

Valnar approached the purebred. His chest was overfilled with a quiet, righteous anger that pushed his shoulders wide. He didn't care that Beast was drunk and couldn't mind his words. He didn't care that he had just jammed a man's skull through bars with his bare hands. He didn't care that the man was grappling with grief. He didn't care that it was too late, too cold, and too miserable to do this.

He unbuckled his sword belt and tossed the weapon aside. Then, he shed his coat and rolled his sleeves up.

Beast steadied himself on his feet. He could barely keep his eyes open, and yet Valnar saw the glimmer in them. The bastard was itching for it.

"Alunwea is a deaf whore."

Valnar punched him.

His fist met Beast's jaw with a sharp crack, sending him stumbling to the ground. Beast didn't stay down long. He pushed himself up, wiping blood from his lip with the back of his hand. Ink stepped between them, his arms outstretched. "Enough! Both of you!"

But a reckless thrill had twisted Beast's expression. He lunged forward, tackling Valnar to the ground. The two of them rolled in the mud, fists flying and curses spilling into the rain-soaked night. Ink reached down, trying to pull them apart, but Lygor's voice cut through the commotion.

"Let them have at it, Ink."

Valnar's fists drove into Beast's shoulders and chest, though the purebred's strength made every blow feel like hitting a stone wall. He knew he could use the purebred's First Word and kick his guts out while he lay defenceless. Or, he could use his Pain Word and watch him eat mud. But the thought felt like poison. He had to defend the Twelve Rider's honour with his own fists.

Beast didn't fight back with the ferocity Valnar had expected. His punches were slower. He was either too drunk, or... The possibility that Beast might be holding back sent a fresh wave of anger through Valnar, his strikes becoming wilder, more desperate. He couldn't stand the thought of Beast sparing him, drunk or not.

"Enough," Lygor finally called, his tone commanding. "Break it up!"

Ink seized the chance to step in, grabbing Beast by the shoulders and pulling him off Valnar while Valnar struggled to his feet, his face dripping with blood and rain. Both men were bruised and filthy, their chests heaving, and their eyes locked in mutual disdain. They stood like two predators sizing each other up, snarling but held at bay.

Lygor laughed, clapping his hands together. "Beast, you've done it. You've officially completed the ultimate tavern experience: got drunk, threw up, and started a fight. Congratulations!" He smirked, looking between the two men. "Either of you got any more in you?"

Valnar didn't respond. His glare shifted to Lygor, the irritation in his expression burning hotter. He shoved Ink out of his way and scooped his weapon off the ground. Without a word, he turned away from the group and walked off.

"Where are you going?" Ink called after him.

"To pray."

27

BEAST

Beast woke up with a pounding headache.

He sat up and immediately regretted his decision. The Earthome spun around him and his stomach heaved. He barely had the time to push his blanket out of the way before he leaned to the side and threw up.

"And this, my friend, is your first hangover."

Beast pulled his knees underneath him, moving slowly as to not stir his stomach. The stale taste of last night lingered on his tongue. The room was too bright, despite it being early morning and the single window shaded with a thick, patchy curtain. His head throbbed with every sound — the creak of a floorboard, the muffled shuffle of boots — and his mouth felt like sandpaper.

He groaned softly, his body ached all over. He held his head between his hands, his bare chest coated in sweat, as he willed the Earthome to still.

Lygor sat on one of the two beds, leaning forward as he tugged his boots on. Ink snored on the other bed. Valnar and Beast had slept on the floor in their bedrolls. Beast didn't even remember coming to the room and crawling in his bedroll. He hardly remembered much from last night. How much had he drunk?

"Why people do this?" he groaned, surprised to hear his own voice. He didn't mean to speak out loud.

"You'll find the answer to that question at the bottom of your next drink. Now get up and get ready. Ink, wake up!"

Ink snored and rolled to his other side. Beast glanced at the shirt he had discarded last night. It was stiff with crusted mud and blood, torn in places, and stank of vomit. His heart sank as he reached for it anyway.

Valnar tossed a clean shirt at his head, and when Beast saw the bruises on the knight's face, other fragments of last night flooded his mind. "Shit," he muttered, once again speaking without intention.

Valnar fastened the straps of his breastplate with a sharp yank, his mouth twisted in silent contempt. The black horse with a dragon's wings shone bright at the centre of his breastplate, as if he'd spent the night obsessively scrubbing it clean. Seeing the mottled bruises on his jaw and cheekbone was both satisfying and gut-wrenching at the same time.

"I'll meet you at the horse breeder," Valnar said to Lygor curtly. He slung his bedroll, already neatly rolled up, over his shoulder. He grabbed his swords, shield, and his second set of armour and strode to the door. Beast grimaced when Valnar slammed the door after him, the sound vibrating in his skull.

As the silence settled, Beast rubbed his face, more of the previous night coming back to him. The talking. *Actual* talking, like it was natural, like words had ever sat easy on his tongue. He'd told them about Saradra. Not everything, but enough. Enough to feel like he'd torn something sacred out of himself and laid it bare for strangers. He blamed Lygor. The prince had a way of loosening people without them realising. The shirt bunched in Beast's hands.

He found Lygor watching him, like he knew exactly what had been shared, and what hadn't. And maybe like he knew there was more.

Beast pulled the shirt over his head, then began rolling his bedroll. His stomach cramped and churned whenever he moved too quickly, but the headache was worse. It felt like an invisible war hammer pounding the back of his skull and pressing behind his eyes. Why did Master Badimar and the other trainers drink every night, knowing they'd feel like this in the morning?

Lygor tossed him a waterskin, then stood and kicked the wooden frame of Ink's bed. "Ink, we'll leave you behind. Come on."

The Kaldorian prince let out a groan and a sigh. He sniffed the air, which had already soured with the stench of vomit. "What's that smell?"

"It's your breakfast. Get up."

Beast took small sips from the waterskin. He was parched, but he couldn't tell if the water was helping or making the nausea worse. When he stood, his headache worsened, and he became acutely aware of how sore his muscles were. It wasn't just from rolling in the mud and trading punches with Valnar. He recognised the distinct, draining fatigue that came after a Raged fight, when every muscle in his body had been over-flooded with an almost-painful urge to unleash violence.

Bastard.

Fucking Valnar had Raged him.

One moment Beast was calculating ways to part that free warrior from his weapon, and in the next one...

His heart hammered against his ribs.

He carefully knelt to tie the straps of his bedroll.

Ink sat up on his bed, his eyes puffy and his brown hair a mess. He rubbed his face, glancing around the room. When his gaze landed on Beast's pale face and the pile of vomit on the floor, he grinned. "The innkeeper's not gonna like that."

"More the reason to hurry and get out of here," Lygor said as he threw Ink's boots at him. "You need a hand with that, Beast?"

The straps kept slipping from Beast's trembling fingers. His bandaged right hand was shaking uncontrollably.

"I'm fine," he muttered, shifting slightly. The movement was casual enough to seem natural but angled just enough to obscure Lygor's view. With a soft exhale, he pinned the strap beneath his knee, forcing it still long enough to tie the final knot.

Ink sat on the side of the bed, slipped one foot in his boot, and paused. "Where's Valnar?"

"Already went to the stable. He'll meet us at the breeder."

"Kiejain's balls!" Ink jumped to his feet, hopping awkwardly on one leg as he struggled to pull his other boot on. Snatching his shirt, he yanked it over his head, stumbling around the room like a headless chicken.

"What? What's wrong?"

Heavy footsteps echoed in the hallway outside, cutting Ink off before he could respond. A sharp cry of pain followed. The sound snapped Beast into action. He sprang to his feet, his heart pounding in his throat. Turning toward the door, he raised his fists, his headache and soreness vanishing as violence flooded his body.

The door flew open and Valnar stormed in. He dragged a whimpering man by the scruff of his neck.

"Ink?" Valnar boomed.

"I can explain."

Valnar slammed the door shut, the sound rattling the walls, and he shoved the crying man forward. The man stumbled and collapsed at Ink's feet.

"Why," Valnar growled, his voice sharp and cutting, "did I find this man sleeping near our horses, claiming he belongs to you?"

The man didn't try to rise. Instead, he bent forward, pressing his forehead against the wooden floor. His bandaged right arm trembled as he clutched it tightly, a muffled groan of pain escaping through clenched teeth. The tattoo on the left side of his neck was similar to Beast's, except it lacked the intricate circle that framed it.

"You bought a slave?" Lygor asked.

Ink held up a finger. "Technically, I didn't pay for him. I won him."

Beast recognised him — the freeborn from last night, the one Crawler had injured.

Valnar's lips parted, forming the word — *won* — but no sound came out. His face twisted, caught somewhere between disbelief and frustration.

Lygor exhaled sharply, dragging a hand down his face. "You bought an injured slave?"

"Again, I didn't pay for him. I took a bet against his owner last night, and I won."

"Oh, Ink..."

"I took him to the town's healer last night. She said his arm will heal. Maybe not as good as before, but he can still function. Becoming Tribesmen food is not an ending a warrior deserves."

"Becoming Tribesmen food is a better option than so many other things that could happen to a damaged slave," Valnar grunted.

"Tell me more about those options when I need a reminder of how fucked-up you Chinderians are."

Valnar muttered a curse under his breath and rubbed his neck. "We can't drag an injured slave with us. He'll slow us down."

"This man is a warrior."

"He's not a warrior!" Valnar raised his voice. "He's a convict!"

"And do you know what his crime was?" Ink raised his own. "He was a sergeant in Zarall army, and he refused to swear his allegiance to Kastian Vogros."

Lygor scrutinised the man. His expression became a little less severe. Across the room, Valnar shook his head, muttering to himself as he paced in tight, restless circles.

"That's right," Ink said, his voice pointed. "He was enslaved because of his loyalty to House Zarall. I think a Zarall soldier deserves better than those cannibals, or... or ending up in a fucking Veiled House!"

Beast leaned against the wall near the window, his arms crossed as he watched the argument unfold. A faint shiver crawled up his spine at the mention of a Veiled House. The freeborn's soft, broken whimpers left no doubt that the man understood all too well the kind of tastes Veiled Houses and Stillrooms catered to.

Tilting his head slightly, Beast studied the man with pity. He recognised that helplessness — the way the man clutched his injured arm and kept his head bowed, waiting as others decided his fate. Beast had been in that exact position more times than he cared to remember, lying silent and powerless as they debated his future like he wasn't even there.

The freedom Lygor had granted him for those few hours last night... It was more precious than he could ever explain.

The Kaldorian was the strangest man Beast had ever met. Who buys an injured slave with no use for the arenas, unless they plan to use him in other ways? It made no sense. Ink stood taller as he argued, all sharp motion and fire, his lean frame tense with conviction. He had gone into all the trouble just to save the freeborn from ending up with tribesmen. This foreign prince truly was... odd.

Lygor threaded his fingers through his blond hair and sighed. "What did you name him?"

"I didn't name him. His name was Jessur."

"They lose their names when they're enslaved. You know that, right?" Valnar asked.

"Well, I'm his Owner and I'm giving it back to him."

"Valnar," Lygor said. "Go to the horse breeder and get us a mule and a cart."

Valnar drew a deep breath. He didn't bother arguing. He turned and walked out, the door clicking shut behind him,

Lygor stepped towards the freeborn. "Is it true?" he asked. "That you're loyal to House Zarall?"

"I... I serve to please, and... and I live to serve my master... owner."

Beast rolled his eyes. The man was so fresh. It was obvious he'd never set foot on a slave ranch and had likely spent only a few weeks in a slave merchant's warehouse.

"Beast," Lygor said. "Take Jessur back to the stable. Then get our animals ready."

Beast nodded. He grabbed the freeborn's left arm and hauled him to his feet. His grip was firm, more to steady the man than intimidate him, but the freeborn whimpered and flinched as though expecting worse. Without a word, Beast half-carried, half-dragged him out of the room.

28

OLIRA

The younger of the two squires — Olira had overheard his name was Norrol — kneeled hesitantly beside her. He was older than Torren but younger than Gilann.

Both gone now.

She hung her head and closed her eyes, summoning their faces into the dead-quiet void in her mind. Holding onto those images of her brothers' smiles was harder than clutching smoke with bare hands.

"Mistress Olira, you haven't eaten anything in three days," the boy insisted shyly. "Would you just take a bite?"

The soldiers walked around the camp, saddling horses and packing up their gear. Olira sat on the cold ground at the edge of the campsite. Far enough to feel blissfully isolated, but not enough to not hear the meaningless exchanges about insignificant things, like how miserable the rain had been last night, or teasing a fellow soldier about being a particularly loud snorer.

How could they laugh and talk so casually, like they didn't have corpses in their memories or blood under their nails. Some of these men were as young as Gilann.

"I promise it doesn't taste that bad." Norrol offered her a smile.

The young squire's attempt at humour bounced off Olira's vacant expression. She wished the boy would just go away. She reached for an angry, snappy response, some hurtful words to make him scramble, but her vocabulary was lost in the barren numbness of her mind.

Why couldn't Norrol ignore her, like the other soldiers did? They hardly even looked her way. They didn't treat her with hostility. They simply behaved as if acknowledging her presence would somehow make them an accomplice to a shameful crime. The soldiers who were assigned to watch her did so with an air as if they'd picked the worst shift, standing a fair distance from her as if she was a plague. Norrol was the only one who had shown any interest in her presence.

No, that wasn't true.

She had caught Prince Dienus's eyes on her more times than she could count. His expression reminded her of a starving man, though he was craving for something other than food. She should have felt something — fear, anger, disgust, anything — at the way his eyes crawled over her like spiders searching for a crack to slip into.

She felt nothing.

Once, the prince had come near her and had grazed his long, cold fingers along her cheek, down her jawline to her neck. Then, Lieutenant Quinner had stepped in and politely explained to him that the prisoner was to be minded by the soldiers and the prince had no need to bother himself with her.

It was clear that the Lieutenant was their leader, despite the prince's status. He called the shots and determined how Olira was to be treated. She didn't know what would happen to her, being accused with theft. Would she get a trial? Would the outcome matter? She decided it didn't.

She wondered if the Lieutenant was the one who had called the shots at her farm too. Or was it the prince's decision? Did Quinner even tried to stop him? Had anyone?

Her brothers were only children...

"Were you there?" she whispered. She had only just realised how cold her lips had been when warm breath left her mouth.

"Mistress?"

"When he killed them. Were you there?"

Norrol turned his cheek, his mouth tight like a boy caught lying to his father. His face was pale, his freckles stark against his skin.

"Are they really dead?" Olira's voice quivered. The question left her hollow, as though it had clawed deeper than she realised, dragging her strength away with it.

"I'm sorry, Mistress. Your brothers are gone."

Olira's breath hung in a pale cloud before her. She braced for the pain to tear through her, the way it had when Dienus first delivered her the news. Instead, there was only an empty silence where her grief should have been. A chill gnawed into her bones, and she let it consume her. Her bound hands rested on her lap, the rope digging into her skin. She turned them slightly, her wrists brushing against the coarse fibres. She watched the faint red lines without any sense of ownership.

She felt detached, as if her mind was tucked away in a dark corner and had abandoned her hollowed body behind.

"Mistress Olira..." Norrol seemed like he had more to say, but a harsh voice interrupted him.

"You shouldn't be talking to the prisoner."

"I was just trying to convince her to eat, Sir Gennald."

Norrol scrambled to his feet and stood awkwardly, as if he was unsure of the ground he held in front of the heavily armoured knight. Olira had seen this man often around Dienus, though the prince wasn't with him this morning.

Sir Gennald scratched his scarred cheek and spat to the side. "If the prisoner wishes to starve, she can starve."

"But, Sir..."

"Go help Master Emberlash with Prince Dienus's breakfast."

"Melton is already..."

The knight's gauntleted hand rested heavily on Norrol's shoulder, the weight of it making the boy flinch. "You're given an order, squire."

Norrol grimaced and stepped back to free his shoulder from the knight's clutch. He gave Olira an apologetic look before muttering, "Yes, Sir."

Olira watched the boy drag his feet through the campsite, looking around, presumably for Master Emberlash. He cast glances at Olira over his shoulder.

"Go get breakfast. I'll take over."

She heard the words muttered behind her. The soldier who had been assigned to watch her walked past, his back stiff and his steps quick. She felt Gennald's presence behind her, radiating a coldness that travelled through the few steps and made her shiver. His armour clinked faintly as he shifted his weight.

In the campsite, Norrol had paused, his eyes narrowed at Olira. Master Emberlash was only a few steps from him, saddling Dienus's horse, though the prince himself was nowhere to be seen.

Norrol scanned the campsite, suddenly seeming alert. He glanced at Olira again, then walked past Emberlash, his head turning one direction and the other as he rushed through the camp. He paused beside a couple of young soldiers and asked them a question. When they shook their heads, he walked to another group. Another shake of heads.

The knight's steel-plated boots scraped faintly against the frozen ground as he shifted his weight restlessly. Olira was too aware of his looming bulk behind her.

Norrol's steps became more hurried, walking through the camp while still frequently glancing at Olira, as if making sure she was still there. He was searching for someone. Olira's eyes flicked through the campsite, seeking for a bulky frame with neatly tied blond hair.

Where was Lieutenant Quinner?

Gennald's shadow swallowed her as the knight reached and wrapped his gauntleted fist around her arm. The rope on her wrists pressed tighter against her skin as he pulled her to her feet. She didn't resist. Pins and needles stung her legs after sitting so long on the cold ground.

She gasped and stumbled, but Gennald didn't let her slow down, pulling her away from the edge of the campsite. The murmur of the soldiers and the clatter of armour faded with every step into the woods.

Dead leaves crunched softly under their boots. When she lost her footing, Gennald steadied her with a slight tug, neither gentle nor harsh. She didn't thank him or complain. She didn't speak at all.

Part of her knew she should care — about where he was taking her, about the roughness of his grip, about the quietness of the woods — but it was a small, distant part, too weak to stir her into feeling anything. The trees around them blurred into dark streaks until they parted into a patch of earth flattened by frost.

Gennald gave her arm a warning squeeze as he mumbled inaudibly, "Just do as he says."

A thin mist lingered low to the ground, curling around Dienus's boots like slimy fingers. The prince stood relaxed with his thumbs hooked on his belt. He had taken his coat off and left it neatly folded on a stump beside him. The top buttons of his shirt were undone, exposing the pale skin of his collarbone. His sleeves were rolled up to his elbows. The cold didn't seem to bother him, like something darker simmered beneath his skin, keeping the chill at bay.

The look he gave Olira turned her stomach upside down.

Olira stared past the sly curl of his lips. Gennald's grip on her arm loosened, and he placed her directly in front of Dienus before stepping back. Despite the layers of her clothes, Olira felt bare as Dienus took his time inspecting her like a meal he intended to devour.

Gennald turned and walked away, abandoning Olira alone with the prince and his calculated hunger. The knight stopped a distance away and turned his back to them.

Olira forced a breath into the cold, quivering numbness that filled her chest.

"Hello, Mistress Olira," Dienus purred softly. He brushed her cheek with the backs of his fingers, smudging a single warm tear across her skin.

Olira kept her eyes somewhere past his shoulder. Pain shot through her scarred wrists, her hands shaking violently. She would not fight. She didn't care.

"It's okay," Dienus whispered with a soft voice, like speaking to a lover. He invaded her with his unapologetic presence and his sour smell that was poorly suppressed by a nauseatingly sweet minty cologne. He trapped her face between both hands, pads of his thumbs wiping her tears. "Don't be scared. It's okay. I promise I'll be careful."

She didn't resist when his fists tightened around the collar of her dress. He yanked the fabric, tearing the dress just enough to expose her collarbones. Cold air kissed Olira's skin. A weak sob escaped her lips, and Dienus hushed her with more hollow words filled with poisonous tenderness.

"I need you to do something extremely important for me, Olira."

With a smooth, unhurried movement, Dienus slid his leg behind her and slowly guided her to the damp ground, careful and gentle, like laying a loved one to rest. He straddled her chest, pinning her arms under his thighs. "Something very, very important."

He brushed a lock of her hair from her face and smoothed the folds of her dress. He moved like he owned all the time on Earthome, as if delaying his pleasure only improved the taste. Each passing second sunk into Olira's stomach like rocks. Still, she didn't resist. She refused to acknowledge anything but the cold, detached emptiness.

Dienus folded the tattered neck of her dress down, baring her neck and below. "You're welcome to scream as you please. We're far enough. Your voice shouldn't carry."

He caressed her neck, his fingers tracing her pulse. He rested a hand on her throat. He didn't yet squeeze, but simply let the weight apply an oppressive pressure against her windpipe.

"And you may struggle too, if you want. In fact, I'd appreciate if you did a little." He chuckled, his voice vibrating through her.

The mockery in the prince's tone, the way he tried to tease fear out of her, sparked an anger that fractured into sharp edges. She set her jaw and inhaled slowly, the breath catching beneath the subtle weight of Dienus's hand.

The prince shifted his legs, shuffling forward into a more comfortable position. He placed both hands on Olira's neck, his fingers snaking around her throat.

"Mistress Olira," Dienus hushed, his voice trembling with a child-like excitement. "I need you to keep your eyes open for me."

Tears streaked down Olira's cheeks as Dienus leaned forward. Keeping his elbows straight, he squeezed.

The anger carved deeper into the cold, distant hollow inside Olira. The gloating flicker in Dienus's eyes knotted her insides. The sight was too repulsive to endure. She shut her eyes.

"Come now, Olira. You don't have to be dry as a Pyre. Let me have some fun."

He transferred more of his weight onto Olira's throat, his fingers digging into her flesh. Olira's lungs burned, though she still didn't resist. And she kept her eyes closed. Darkhome take him, she wouldn't resist death, but she refused to give him the satisfaction.

Just as Olira's depraved lungs urged her body to fight, Dienus released the pressure. Olira gasped hoarsely.

Dienus shook his arms and massaged his palms. "I need you to work with me here, Olira. I need your eyes."

Olira kept her eyes shut. She bit down the sharp retort rising in her throat — *shut your mouth and get on with it.*

She had once held a man's life in her hands. A man, not a mindless shell without a *rhoa*. She had treated him cruelly, and when he'd finally trusted her — told her he wanted his freedom — she'd gotten greedy. She'd sold him. Sold his life away.

Lion of Zarall, the one they claimed was broken, mad, rabid — he had only wanted freedom.

The Twelve Riders had punished her greed. They'd taken her brothers and sent her Dienus.

She deserved this. She deserved to die for what she'd done. In truth, she looked forward to finding her brothers in Farhome.

But she would not suffer Dienus's mockery in the meantime.

"Alright," Dienus said, placing his hands back on Olira. "I think I know how to make this more fun. Let me tell you all about this pathetic excuse of a farm I visited a few days ago."

Olira's breath caught in her throat just as Dienus leaned onto her throat again.

"Would you like to know which one of your brothers screamed the loudest?"

Pain split inside her, sharper than the crushing ache on her throat. Her temples throbbed, a pressure growing with every frantic, broken heartbeat.

"I hung the oldest one in the barn. I would have told you to get that roof fixed, but I guess it doesn't matter anymore. I burnt it all."

Olira let out a strained sound. Desperate for air, her chest rose and fell rapidly, her hips involuntarily bucking. A high-pitched ringing filled her ears, but couldn't entirely muffle Dienus's words.

"And then I killed the smaller ones, after they watched it all. They mewled your name the entire time."

Dienus's words triggered images in her mind, more painful than the pounding in her skull that matched the rhythm of her pulse. She sobbed and opened her mouth to howl, but no noise passed through the steel-like fingers that clamped around her windpipe.

Gilann, hung in the barn. She could almost hear the boys' screams.

The images tore her insides like blades, competing against the headache.

"Come on, Olira. Open your eyes. Show me." Dienus's voice grew desperate. "Show me!" He shook her neck, slamming the back of her skull against the solid ground. "Open your eyes!"

Olira squeezed her eyes tighter as her fingers went numb. A cold, tingling sensation creeped up her arms. The searing heat in her lungs felt like smoke. Her hips bucked weakly, but Dienus sat unbothered by the effort.

"Look in the eyes of the man who killed all your brothers, Olira," Dienus whispered, his voice muffled and distant. "All three of them."

Olira's eyes slammed open.

Three?

Dienus smirked victoriously. "Good. Good girl. That's right, look at me."

Olira saw his lips move, but his voice came to her as if drowned by the thunder in her head.

Dienus misinterpreted the emotion that pushed Olira's eyes wide open. Her mouth gaped, but the air she needed stayed just out of reach. Her heels kicked the frozen ground, but her legs had grown sluggish, her toes tingling in her boots. She forced them anyway. Forced every muscle to fight, to toss him off her, to make him say that word again.

Three.

All three dead.

"Yes," Dienus whispered. "Yes, that's it."

A wrongness shimmered behind his green eyes, the kind that smiled at suffering. He leaned closer, watching her eyes like he meant to drink the horror from them. But it wasn't just horror flooding her veins and tightening her muscles, driving her to arch off the ground in a futile attempt to throw him off. There was shock, yes. Grief too. But beneath it all — cutting through the fear — was a strange, overwhelming rush of relief. And gratitude.

One had survived.

And Dienus didn't know.

He thought he'd killed all her brothers. He smirked and purred with pride, savouring his pleasure as Olira now fought back with a ferocity she thought had abandoned her.

Her vision blurred as black spots danced before her eyes. Her skull felt like it might burst. Dienus continued muttering words of praise with a tone that dripped with a disgusting tenderness, but Olira hardly heard them through the rushing sound that drowned out everything. She kicked the ground, or thought she did; it was hard to know with no strength left in her legs. She focused on the words.

One had survived.

The words anchored her, pulling her from the bottom of a lake, but her face never broke the surface. She had to live. She had to find her brother. And she had to make sure Dienus never got his hands on him. She reached for air, reached and reached, but Dienus's grip pushed her further into the depths of that airless void.

She was all but blind now, the dark blotches in her vision blissfully concealing the prince's hideous eyes. The thought that she would die before knowing which one of her brothers survived filled her with a dark, consuming rage that she had no words to describe.

That rage was the last taste that lingered on her tongue as the cold wisps of death claimed her.

29

DIENUS

"Prince Dienus!"

Dienus startled at Lieutenant Quinner's bark and scrambled off Olira. He hated himself for the reaction, like he was a boy caught stealing a pie. He stiffened his composure and fidgeted with his sleeves, pulling them down over his forearms.

Quinner strode into the clearing, his fast gait betraying the anger simmering in him. If Sir Gennald hadn't been blocking his way, Dienus had a feeling the lieutenant would have charged at him and dragged him off the woman as if the prince was a common drunkard at a tavern.

"Calm down, Lieutenant," Dienus said coldly. "It's all under..." Something sharp pricked Dienus's composure when he glanced down at the farmer.

Olira's chest didn't move, and her face was an ugly purple, her brown eyes glassy with red splotches on their whites.

Shit. Had he taken it too far?

"Olira Aryanna is the king's prisoner!" Quinner barked.

"Watch your tone, Lieutenant. You're talking to your prince."

Gennald stood his ground, not letting Quinner approach further than he did. Quinner wore plain clothes, and his face was an angry red. Norrol followed close behind, flanked by several grim-faced soldiers. Quinner regarded Gennald as if considering taking him down to get to the prince. Although Dienus would be interested to see who would come out of that skirmish — his money was on Gennald, but only if the soldiers didn't get involved — today wasn't the day to sit back and enjoy that show.

"Oh, hold your piss, Quinner. She's fine."

Dienus positioned himself so he would block Quinner's view as he crouched beside Olira. Panic welled in his throat. He couldn't kill another one. Not again. He really needed to learn when to stop, but the bitch wasn't playing along, so this was all her fault. He tapped her cheek lightly, as though trying to rouse a child. Her head lolled to the side, and his stomach flipped. The faintest bead of sweat gathered at his temple.

Fuck.

"The prisoner is not to be removed from the camp without my consent. Step away, Sir Gennald."

"Not until you lower your voice." Gennald stood with his hand casually resting on his sword.

Panic heavy in his hand, Dienus slapped the girl's cheek harder. Olira's head jerked, and she gasped violently, her body jolting as though shocked awake. Her cough was racking and raw.

Dienus let out a breath, finding a strange thrill in it all. "See? All good."

He yanked the girl to her feet and walked her towards Quinner. Her legs didn't support her any more than her ugly skirt did, so Dienus pulled her close, holding her gently, like a true gentleman. He muttered, "You're okay, you're fine," as he patted her back while she rudely coughed at his ear.

The bitch threw up.

Dienus couldn't dodge it in time and got vomit on his elbow. He shoved her toward Quinner like she was nothing more than an old coat. "She's all yours."

Quinner caught her, his glare searing. He passed the coughing and retching woman to Norrol. "Take her back to the camp. Now."

Norrol took her by the arm with the eagerness of a teenage boy touching a woman for the first time. It probably was his first time. Dienus hid his sneer as he watched the young squire half-carry the stumbling woman back to the camp.

"I was just interrogating the prisoner to make sure she wasn't holding back any information. I still don't believe she didn't know the identity of the slave she kept for three months."

"You do not need to concern yourself with the prisoner."

Dienus stood beside Gennald, facing Quinner. He eyed the soldiers behind Quinner and was pleased to see they at least had the decency to look uncomfortable being here, witnessing this exchange. Dienus brushed invisible dirt off his sleeves and suppressed a yawn. A vein popped on Quinner's forehead.

"So, how did your little mission go?" Dienus asked, casually waving at Quinner's hideous clothes and not hiding the disdain from his face. "Did you hear anything useful from the town?"

Quinner stiffened, his jaw clenching as he forced himself to take a breath. He had taken a couple of his men and had gone to the town nearby early morning, to ask around about the beast. Being in Northern Chinderia, where people were too dumb and slow to accept King Leonis was spending his days in Farhome, he had opted to leave his Vogros uniform behind, hence the plain clothes. Dienus was half hoping he wouldn't return.

As if needing the extra seconds to further steady his composure, Quinner pulled his shirt to smooth the fabric. When he spoke again, his tone was respectful enough to placate Gennald. "Good news, Your Highness. You should not need to interrogate the prisoner anymore. We've found his trail."

"Excellent."

"A purebred beast killed three men in a cage fight last night, then got drunk in the local tavern."

"Got drunk, huh?" Dienus's fingers brushed his chin, the movement concealing the grin that tugged at his lips. Alcohol. That would be an interesting instrument to consider. Would booze make a purebred looser? Enough to help breaking them easier? Did he want to make it easier? He found a certain thrill in the challenge. And a purebred like Lion of Zarall would indeed serve a delicious challenge.

It was a shame, really — Quinner would do everything in his power to keep Dienus from having a blast with Lion.

"We're leaving now. We'll cut through the hills and set up an ambush ahead."

"Excellent strategy, Lieutenant. I'll await your success here at the camp."

Quinner's shoulders stiffened as he stopped mid-step. He drew in a slow breath before turning to face Dienus. "Care to elaborate that, Your Highness?"

Dienus sucked his teeth. "Oh, I don't think I should be around in an ambush, Lieutenant. I think I'll sit this one out."

"You'll..." Quinner rubbed his temples, as though a headache was coming on. "We've found Lion of Zarall and you want to wait at the camp? Your Highness?"

"Excellent listening skills, Lieutenant."

"I am breaking the camp."

"I'll get Emberlash to set up a tent and start a campfire for me. No big deal. We'll be nice and cosy until you return."

"Is this about the prisoner?"

"Take the prisoner with you for all I care."

"I don't get it, Your Highness. We're so close to catching Lion of Zarall, and you don't want to be there when we do it?"

"I prefer not being near that savage until he's apprehended. Call me a coward, Lieutenant. Maybe I'm just worried about my safety."

"You're worried about your safety, and yet—" Quinner's mouth clamped shut when it finally clicked. A faint twitch pulled at the corner of his eye before he forced his expression into stillness. "You can't stay here unprotected, Your Highness. I ask you to come with us."

Dienus's smile widened, though his tone turned nonchalant. "You see, you can't give me that order, Lieutenant. My father tasked you with capturing the slave and keeping it all discrete. My choice to stay here doesn't stop you from doing your task."

"Your Highness, people still sing Zarall songs in this region. I would have to leave a group of my men with you."

Dienus swatted a hand and leaned his forearm against Gennald's plated arm. "Oh, no, please, take as many men as you need with you. I have Sir Gennald. And my squires too; they've just learned which end of the sword is pointy. I'll be safe enough."

"Your Highness," said Quinner, his voice desperate for a rational response. "This is Lion of Zarall. He's dangerous, Raged or Unraged. And he's travelling with three armed men that we know very little about. If I divide my force—"

"You can do whatever you want with your force, Lieutenant. But I'm staying right here. I promise I won't attract too much attention, and I won't wander too far."

"If something happened to you, the king would have my head."

Dienus brushed past with a casual shrug. "I wish I could say he wouldn't, but..." He lifted his hands, palms up in a gesture of mock helplessness, then strode toward the camp, leaving the Lieutenant stewing in his anger. Gennald followed silently at his side.

Once they were far enough, the knight spoke: "So close to capturing Lion of Zarall. Are you sure you want to set him up for failure?"

Dienus's smile faded. "He annoys me."

"If he survives, he'll tell the king how you tried to sabotage the mission."

Dienus chuckled, though there was little mirth in it. "It won't make my father any more disappointed in me, Gennald."

30

BEAST

No. Wary wouldn't suffice to explain how the freeborn really felt about the purebred. On a scale from 'cautious' to 'petrified', Jessur would be sitting somewhere around 'sweating like a pig, wishing he was invisible'.

The cart lurched over a dip in the road, the wooden wheels creaking with every turn. Beast shifted to keep his balance leaning back against a ration bag he'd propped up behind him like a makeshift cushion. The coarse fabric dug into his shoulders, but it was better than the cart's rough boards.

Across from him, Jessur sat crammed into the corner, knees pulled tightly to his chest. The space between them was barely enough for the two of them to sit without their boots knocking together. He clutched his bandaged arm, a permanent grimace etched to his face. His gaze darted to Beast, and every time he found the purebred staring at him without blinking, another drop of sweat ran down his face.

Beast could feel the nervousness oozing out of him like blood spurting from a gut wound. It wasn't hard to guess why. The freeborn had probably watched Beast in the cage last night. Beast's scowl deepened. If the stupid, stubborn freeborn had looked at him for more than a fleeting second, he would see that Beast was just trying to start a conversation.

Jessur glanced at him again, paled like he'd seen a death threat on Beast's face, and looked away at Ink, who had been riding alongside the cart. The Kaldorian's bow slung loosely over his shoulder, his reins held slack in one hand. Ink didn't catch the silent plead the freeborn had sent his way, too focused on surveying the open road and the hills ahead.

Valnar rode at the opposite side of the cart, his heavy plate armour clinking faintly with the rhythm of his horse's stride. He carried his long sword on the saddle and the cloth-wrapped two-handed sword strapped to his back, but he'd left his shield, helmet, and his spare sword in the cart, along with other supplies that usually burdened the horses. His gauntlets rested on the pommel of his saddle as he watched their surroundings.

Lygor perched at the front of the cart. He held the reins of the mule in one hand. The other arm was draped casually behind the seat. Lygor's horse plodded along obediently, tethered to Valnar's saddle. The prince had been quiet since Ink's surprise decision to bring the injured freeborn with them. Travelling with the cart meant they'd arrive at Calae later than he anticipated, but it didn't concern Beast, as long as they'd get to Euroad before Spring.

When Jessur couldn't find whatever he was seeking from the back of Lygor's head either, he shifted in his corner and grimaced at the pain the movement had brought.

Beast found the freeborn fascinating. There was a time he regarded freeborns with contempt. Their obsession with freedom and their lack of training had annoyed him. They would complain about their orders, want things, display too many useless emotions, make eye contact casually, and speak without permission. All Acts of Defiance. The entire time Beast spent staring at the freeborn, he was having a revelation about how much he was behaving like a freeborn himself, casually committing Acts of Defiance. In the past, this would have bothered him. Although one part of him still saw freeborns beneath purebreds in fight skills and ability, he also admired how effortlessly free their thoughts were.

Jessur glanced at Beast again. Beast wanted to ask him what freedom was like. He couldn't ask that question to Lygor or Ink, and certainly not to fucking Valnar. Twelve times cursed prick. Those three wouldn't know how to appreciate something they never lost. But the man with the dull brown hair, narrow face, and sunburned skin who sat shivering across from him was a free man mere months ago. His tattoo was still a bright black. And Beast wanted to hear what freedom felt like from a man who had spent time under chains.

Beast tilted his head, a troubling new thought clouding his face. What if Beast won his freedom, and then lost it again, like Jessur did? A snarl curled his lips, revealing the teeth he gritted. No, Beast would never let anyone take his freedom away. He would do anything...

He would break that cage wide open and let Earthome burn if they'd tried to put chains on him again.

Jessur flinched, pulling his knees tighter to his chest. He edged closer into his corner, raising his head. He pressed his fist to his neck, requesting permission to speak, but spoke without waiting. "Sir? Master?" He caught Ink's attention. "Owner? Owner, is he— Is he Raged? He's not Raged, is he?"

Beast's scowl deepened when all three men turned to look at him. Lygor's amused grin sent his blood rushing to his face.

"You would have been torn to shreds already if I was," Beast growled at the freeborn.

What a stupid, idiotic question.

Lygor looked away, his shoulders shaking with a silent chuckle. Jessur didn't share the prince's glee. He looked as if he was about to climb out of the cart. "Owner?" he said, looking at Ink with pleading eyes. There was a whole lot of questions loaded in that one word, and somehow Ink heard it all.

"It's fine, Jessur. He's not gonna hurt you." The Kaldorian nodded at Beast. "Beast, leave him alone."

"I haven't done anything." Beast felt their gazes like blades pointed under his chin. He clenched his fists with a need to defend himself. "I won't attack him." He shrugged at Lygor. "Unless you order me to."

That didn't help bring more colour to Jessur's face.

"Beast?" Lygor called out from the front of the cart. "Why don't you come sit with me?"

The glare Beast shot at Jessur was identical to the one Valnar gave him. With a low grunt, Beast pushed himself to his feet, the cart swaying under his weight. He pushed Valnar's shield and spare sword aside and stepped over the bags to climb to the front. He ignored Jessur's relieved sigh.

Lygor scooted to the side, patting the empty space beside him on the driver's bench. The narrow bench creaked as Beast sat. There wasn't much room, so he had to sit with his arms crossed and legs together, and his shoulder was still plastered against Lygor's.

"I'm genuinely curious here," Lygor muttered, fidgeting to make himself more comfortable. He ended up stretching an arm behind the bench as he leaned back. "Why were you staring at him like that if you weren't planning to beat the crap out of him?"

Beast scowled at the mule's ears, mulling the question and searching for a clever way of not answering.

Lygor nudged him stubbornly. "Beast?"

Beast growled. He shrugged and hunched lower on his seat. "I was just..." He shrugged again, feeling his face blushing. This was stupid. "I was just trying to be friendly," he muttered very quietly under his breath.

Lygor pressed his fingers at the corners of his mouth in a very obvious attempt to suppress a smile. "Friendly?" he mumbled, looking away. The fact he hadn't burst into laughter was probably commendable. Lygor breathed through his nose and nodded at him.

"Has anyone told you how intimidating you are?" When Beast gave him a look, Lygor pointed at him sharply. "That look, right there. Is this your best attempt at a friendly face?"

Beast made another approximation of a growl.

"Have you ever tried to... I don't know... smile? Maybe?"

Lygor flashed him a charming smile and gestured toward it, as if demonstrating how it was done. He made it look effortless — never mind the unfair advantage of a clean, handsome face with bright eyes and easy features that invited trust.

Beast didn't find it funny, but Lygor laughed anyway. His laughter was warm and clear, full of genuine joy. It drew a sharp glare from Valnar, who rode parallel to the prince and made no effort to hide his distaste at Beast's proximity. That, at least, was enough to lift Beast's lips upwards slightly.

"Alright, maybe we'll try again later after a few drinks."

"Uh-uh," Beast shook his head sharply. His mild headache was still a constant background, and he'd barely managed a few bites since this morning. There was no way he was drinking again. Ever.

"We'll see about that. Here, your turn." Lygor handed him the reins.

Beast blinked, staring at the reins like they were a foreign object. Then he looked at the mule plodding along ahead of the cart. Its ears flicked lazily, and it swayed with each step, as if unimpressed by its own existence. Beast took the rough leather hesitantly.

Lygor leaned back against the bench, his posture relaxed, as though they were old friends on a leisurely ride. "Don't pull too hard — he'll just dig in his heels. Mules don't take kindly to force. You've got to guide him, make him think it's his idea. Give a light touch, keep him steady."

Beast gave the slightest tug, and the mule flicked its tail in irritation, veering slightly to the left. Beast pulled harder, and the cart lurched as the mule snorted in defiance.

"Easy, easy," Lygor said, his voice smooth as he reached over Beast's hands to steady the reins. The mule settled immediately under his confident grip, and the cart evened out. Lygor handed the reins back. "See? He's not a beast you face at an arena. You don't have to fight him. Just be confident."

Just be confident. Easy for a man like the prince of Chinderia to say.

"I've seen you fight at the Switchblade once. I think it was your first fight? A Slayer's Pit?"

"Not my first fight."

"I meant first fight at Switchblade."

Beast grunted. The mule tossed its head and the cart jostled again.

"Didn't you come out of your Rage funny then too?"

The mule's pace slowed down to a sluggish, half-hearted plod. Beast flicked the reins slightly, hoping for even the faintest increase in speed. But the mule slowed further.

Then stopped dead.

In the middle of the road. Ears twitching and legs stiff.

Beast gave the reins a hesitant tug, then a firmer one. Nothing. A flicker of irritation crawled up his spine. *Move, damn you.*

Lygor watched with an expectant smirk, not offering any help. Valnar and Ink rode past them, then stopped further ahead. Valnar shook his head impatiently.

Beast yanked the reins, his fingers aching. Was he supposed to hop down and push the animal? He begged for guidance from Lygor, but the prince was still expecting an answer. The subtle glint in his eye reminded Beast of their conversation about answering when the prince asked a question.

"It was the noise," Beast gritted through his teeth, pulling the reins harder. "First time at Switchblade, a lot of purebreds wake like that."

"Right."

"There's nothing wrong with my Rage."

"I didn't say there was."

Beast held his gaze. If he had to speak, he didn't think he could keep the tightness in his throat from leaking into his voice. Ahead, Valnar's horse snorted as if communicating its rider's displeasure. Lygor's blue eyes flicked over Beast's face, searching anything to give away the speed of his heart pounding in his chest.

Then, Lygor clicked his tongue, and the mule lurched forward, making Beast almost fall off his seat. Instinctively, he reached out and grabbed Lygor's arm to steady himself. He pulled his hand back immediately as if it burned.

Lygor scooped the reins, clicking his tongue a few more times, until the mule settled into a steady pace and they caught up with Valnar and Ink. He tossed the reins back at Beast.

"It was a good fight," Lygor said. "That Slayer's Pit. Brutal. My father was impressed too."

Beast focused on the mule. He swore the animal could feel it when Beast's hands touched the reins, even before he did anything. Beast's heart raced like he was in the launch room at the Switchblade Arena, getting ready for a fight.

"You know what my father said after the fight?" When Beast shook his head, Lygor opened his mouth, then glanced over his shoulder at Jessur. He shuffled closer and leaned in, his breath warm against Beast's skin in the chill of winter.

"He said, 'That's someone people can look at and know the Lion of Zarall will never fall.'"

Lygor leaned back again, waiting for a reaction Beast didn't have. They were just words. He wasn't Lion of Zarall anymore, and he didn't have any emotional attachment to the name. He was just a man with a beast tattoo.

"Anyway, those were pretty much the last things he said to me before he kicked me out."

"Your father didn't kick you out, Lodi," Valnar interjected, revealing he'd been eavesdropping. "He sent you to..." He glanced at Jessur, who had buried his head in the crook of his elbow, and chose his words carefully: "To his *business partner*, to smooth things out after that *incident* with the *place*. Which you've done well."

"So well, he extended my stay a few more years," Lygor said with a joyless smile. He shrugged. "Which turned out well, I guess. Probably would have been dead if I'd been home." He jerked his chin towards Ink, though Beast didn't want to take his gaze off the mule. "I still would have been dead if it wasn't for Ink and his quest."

If the Kaldorian heard him, he pretended not to. He continued scanning the road with vigilance. Lygor raised his voice, as if trying to provoke a response.

"There I was, minding my own business, and the next thing I know, a stinking Kaldorian decided to make my protection their quest, just to piss his father off."

"If you really want an arrow in your eye, all you have to do is ask."

Lygor nudged Beast, though the purebred still didn't look away from the mule. Every time it snorted and flicked its ears, Beast's hands stiffened on the reins, which the mule somehow felt and reacted. How was he supposed to not fight it when it kept wanting to pick a fight?

"You see," Lygor continued as if he had Beast's undivided attention. "Kaldorian people has this odd rite of passage. To prove their worth, every young man must pick and complete a quest. The more difficult or honourable their quest is, the more accomplished they become. So Ink pledged his next two years to my protection—"

"Six months to go," Ink added with a sigh.

"And I'm so glad he did, because if we didn't have Ink with us that night — and you know which night I'm talking about — Valnar and I would both be dead."

"He doesn't need to hear all the details, Lodi," Valnar said with another cautious glance at Jessur. The freeborn, his face hidden on his arm, was breathing steadily. Valnar nodded towards Lygor's horse. "Your horse could use a rider. Why don't you let Beast ride him a bit? Would hate to derail the cart and break an axel."

"He's doing fine." Lygor patted Beast's leg. "I trust him."

Valnar spat onto the road, but swallowed whatever words had risen to the surface.

Lygor leaned back against the bench, stretching his long legs out as the cart trundled along the uneven road. He tilted his head towards the sky where the wisps of clouds drifted across, like pulled wool stretched thin. The biting winter breeze gave his cheeks and nose a red tint and tousled his short-cropped blond hair.

"So?" the prince asked. He just couldn't stay quiet, as if he'd developed a taste for Beast's attention. "How does it feel being in control?"

Beast's fingers gripped the leather too tightly. His bruised knuckles ached and started bleeding again. "Terrifying."

"That sounds about right."

Beast flexed his fingers to work some of the tension off. Lygor stretched his arm in a wide arc, taking in the road and their surroundings. "I mean, think about it. No one telling you what to do, where to go. No one looking out for you. You have to make every single decision by yourself and somehow make good choices."

"Would you rather a chain around your neck?"

"No. But there's a difference between being owned and belonging somewhere. To someone."

"As you say, Master."

Lygor crossed his arms. "What are you even going to do after getting your freedom? And helping me with my goal, as you kindly promised? How are you going to get by? Find food? Do you even know how to hunt?"

"No."

"Do you have any money?"

"No."

"How are you going to buy food? Clothes?"

Beast shrugged. He didn't want to think about things he didn't have an answer for. "I'll figure it out."

"Are you going to kill and loot?"

That drew Valnar's sharp gaze at Beast. He could see it in the Kiejain's warrior's face. Valnar would hunt him down and enslave him for the crimes, just for the pleasure of it. Fury rose to the back of Beast's throat, his heartbeat picking up once again.

"I'll work."

Lygor smiled victoriously. "Do you have a trade? A talent? Are you good at anything other than jamming a man's head through the bars?"

Jamming a man's head... Beast's stomach dropped when he had the image flash across his eyes.

The sound of a skull crushing open... A wet sludge...

He shouldn't have remembered any of it.

Nails clawing onto his forearms...

"I'll... umm..."

He resisted the urge to look at his forearms to check if the marks Saradra had left were still there. He knew they weren't. Yet, he would sometimes see them anyway.

The cart suddenly jerked left, throwing Beast off balance. His knuckles whitened on the reins as he tried to correct it.

"What is it, Beast?"

"I-I'll do farm work."

"An ex-purebred beast doing farm work. I'd pay to see that."

Beast yanked the reins too sharply, and the mule brayed in protest, hooves skidding against the dirt. Beast pushed a steady breath through his nose and tried again, firmer this time. The animal flicked an ear and veered off the path, dragging them toward the ditch on the side of the road.

"Is there something wrong with your hand, Beast?"

"Lodi!" Valnar said sharply.

Lygor snatched the reins and calmed the mule before it took them off the road. Leaning back, Beast crossed his arms, hiding his trembling right hand.

"What's wrong with your hand?"

"Nothing."

"It doesn't seem like nothing. Is your hand fucked?"

"It's fine. It's just—"

"Can you wield a sword?"

"Yes."

"Can you fight?"

"Yes!"

"Are you going to freak out in the middle of a fight and drop your sword?"

"What? No!"

"How can you be sure when you can't even hold the reins properly?"

"My hand is fine."

"Then why the fuck is it trembling all the time?"

"I said my fucking hand is fine!"

The scrape of steel leaving its sheath and Valnar's roar shattered the air.

"Sit back down before I drop you, slave!"

Beast's breath came hard and fast. His vision tunnelled for a moment before sharpening, and he blinked, realising he was on his feet, fists clenched, towering over Lygor. His body thrummed with violence, ready to move, ready to break something.

Valnar had closed in, his horse sidestepping anxiously beneath him as he gripped the reins in one hand, his sword halfway drawn in the other. Beast didn't need to see the warrior's face to know his First Word hovered on his tongue.

Across from them, Ink remained still, but there was a shift in his posture — an awareness, like he was prepared to intervene if things went wrong. Even Jessur had lifted his head, his good arm curling tighter around his wounded one, watching with wide eyes.

And Lygor — Lygor didn't move. Didn't tense. He sat with one elbow resting against the cart's edge, his head tilted slightly as he regarded Beast. He seemed neither amused, nor concerned. He let the moment stretch, deliberately letting Beast *feel* the weight of his own anger pressing down on the space between them.

The mule broke the silence with a snort.

Beast dropped back to his seat. He folded his arms tight across his chest, fixing his gaze on the road ahead, forcing his breath to steady.

Metal rasped as Valnar shoved his sword back into its sheath. He lingered for a moment longer, then pulled his horse away.

Ink clicked his tongue. "He stopped a knuckled punch with an open palm last night," he said. "Might have just strained a nerve or something. Happened to me a dozen times. It'll pass."

Lygor said nothing.

As the cart creaked along, the tension eased, yet the heavy feeling persisted. Beast kept his arms locked across his chest, his hands buried beneath them so no one — including him — would see the faint tremor still lingering. He flexed his fingers, feeling the tightness of the bandage and a dull ache near the base of his palm. He held onto Ink's explanation that maybe the shakes were just a minor injury. Nothing more.

The road widened slightly. A gently sloping hill rose to their right, dotted with shrubs and dry grass. The land dipped slightly at its base, forming a shallow ditch where shadows pooled. The mule's ears flicked, catching the distant sound of a bird breaking from the shrubs. A crow, maybe. Beast tracked its movement without thought, watching the dark shape cut across the pale sky.

A shift on the edge of his vision pulled his attention back to Lygor. The prince's blue eyes, a brighter shade than Beast's, remained fixed on him. His face was stripped of its usual confidence. The sharp angles of his features softened and revealed a brief glimpse of someone too young and too vulnerable.

"I've lost everything," Lygor said. His voice trembled like the words cost him something. The light caught on his rich blond hair, tousled by the wind. His lips were pressed tight, as if holding back more, but he spoke anyway — like he was powerless.

"A lot relies on you," he said, swallowing. "I'm putting *all* my hopes on you, Beast. I need you to come through."

There was something in the way Lygor looked at him that made it harder to breathe, though not in the usual way. Not like a threat. Not like the weight of a collar. Something warm came alive in his chest, eating at the air like a fire and leaving him with a craving.

"I need you to fight for me."

Beast's blood stirred with urge to snap into action. It was the same sharp edge he felt before a fight, the familiar longing. Lygor's lips twitched, the briefest hint of a smile. Heat pricked at the back of his neck. He nodded, jaw tight, not trusting himself to speak.

Beast wanted to prove himself to the prince. To show him that he would come through.

He found his chance just minutes later, when Ink shouted, "Incoming!"

31

BEAST

The twang of bowstrings snapped through the air.

Beast moved before thought could catch up. He twisted, reaching for Valnar's shield at the back of the cart just as the knight spurred his horse closer. Valnar drew his sword, slamming it flat against the mule's rump. "Go! Lodi, go!"

The mule shrieked and lunged forward. The cart jerked violently. Lygor stumbled, barely catching himself.

Then, the sky darkened.

Beast caught the first glimpse of the arrows — a wave of them slicing through the air.

He yanked Lygor down, shoving him against the bench. He covered the prince with his own body and pulled Valnar's shield over their heads. He held his breath, praying to the darkness that he'd gotten the angle right and that all their vitals remained under the shield.

The first arrow punched through the shield, sending vibrations down his arm. He felt the second arrow bounce off, and a third one lodged onto the shield, the impact rattling through his bones. The sound of arrows shattering and splintering against the metal was deafening.

Beast waited for several seconds after the last thud of the arrows, then lowered the shield and looked up.

Valnar's horse pounded on the ground nearby. The knight's eyes were wide, wild with alarm. Beast unfolded himself off the prince and relief flickered across Valnar's face as he saw Lygor unharmed. A look passed between them. The Kiejain's warrior and the purebred beast, locking eyes over Lygor's frame.

Ink's voice cut through the whistle of arrows climbing into the sky. "More coming!"

The Kaldorian already had his short bow in hand, loosing arrows back. He guided his horse with his knees and steered away from the cart, which was the target of the volley.

Beast caught a brief glimpse of half a dozen archers crouched behind the hill's edge. As he watched, two of them fell with Ink's arrows on their chests.

Beast leaned over Lygor again, raised the shield up, and braced. When the second barrage was over, he peaked behind the shield.

More than a dozen mounted men were charging down the hill. Armed to the teeth, riding in formation. The archers were now picking their shots, with Ink returning their fire.

The cart rattled as Beast climbed to Lygor's right side, planting himself there, shield up. The mule tore down the road, frenzied and out of control.

"Keep him safe, Beast!" Valnar shouted as he veered his horse, putting himself between the cart and the oncoming riders. It sounded more like a plead than an order. Watching the archers carefully, Beast raised the shield just in time to deflect another arrow.

Lygor yanked the reins, battling the mule for control. He cursed under his breath when another arrow lodged onto the shield mere inches from his head. His face was pale as he looked around, searching for an escape route, or a defensive spot. Anything they could use to their advantage. The dirt road curved behind a hill ahead and both sides of the road were clear of any trees or rocks that they could use as cover.

"Lodi!" Valnar's voice rang. "Ride straight at them!"

Lygor snapped his head toward him. "Are you insane?"

"They're *not* engaging!" Valnar shouted. "They're pushing us toward that curve. We don't know what's behind that hill, and I don't want to find out."

The mule didn't listen. It bucked against the reins, veering wildly. Lygor bared his teeth, fighting to steer it.

Valnar was right. The mounted men had slowed down, riding parallel and flanking the cart between themselves and the hill, herding it towards the bend. The archers were now focused on Ink, though a few still aiming for Lygor.

Ink loosed another arrow. Then another.

Then, he fell.

Beast saw the arrow hit the Kaldorian's lamellar armour before he tumbled off his horse and disappeared in the dust behind.

"Ink!" Lygor yelled in fear. "Valnar, get him!"

Valnar glanced at the riders, then at the cart. A pained expression twisted his face.

"I said go!" Lygor roared.

Valnar's eyes met Beast's one more time. He didn't need to ask or order. Beast had no intention of letting anything happen to Lygor.

Valnar made his decision. He spurred his horse and rode back to where Ink had fallen. Lygor's horse was still hitched behind his.

Beast lowered the shield to steal another glance. The cart was finally out of range of the last two archers. Ink's horse had slowed to a stop, its saddle empty. Beast couldn't see the Kaldorian amongst the dust they'd left behind, but he saw four riders detach from the group and go after Valnar.

At the rear of the cart, Jessur lifted his head. He was half-buried under the saddlebags, pressed against the wooden slats for cover. An arrow jutted from one of the bags, but Jessur looked unharmed. Valnar's short sword lay near his side.

"Give me the sword!" Beast barked.

Jessur reached for it, but the sword slid out of his grasp just as the cart took the curve around the hill.

"Hold tight!" Lygor yelled.

Beast grabbed the back of the seat, barely keeping his balance. Ahead, a dark shape loomed across the road. A dead horse, sprawled in their path.

Lygor yanked at the reins. The mule shrieked, muscles bunching as he veered hard to the side. It galloped past the dead horse, but the left wheels struck the carcass with a sickening crunch. The cart jolted, tilting up on two wheels, hanging in the air for a breathless moment before crashing back down.

Beast threw the shield aside, gripping the cart with both hands. His body snapped with the impact, head whipping forward.

When he turned, Lygor was gone.

Beast jumped.

He didn't think about the riders closing in from their flank. Didn't think about the possibility of breaking his legs. Didn't think at all. His mind went blank as his limbs acted on their own.

The moment his boots left the cart, his body braced. Knees bent. Arms locked around his head and chest. Ground slammed into him, the sky and dirt spinning in a violent blur.

He rolled in a haze of dust, the momentum carrying him forward. He jumped up to his feet almost instantly. His body hurt, but he refused to pay attention to it. Through the swirling dust, a dark shape lay crumpled on the roadside.

Lygor.

Beast ran and skidded to his knees beside the prince just as the riders surrounded them.

Lygor didn't move, and Beast didn't have time to check his pulse. He surged to his feet, turning sharply, fists raised. His gaze flicked between the men circling him, eyeing their weapons.

Beast didn't wait for them to work out a strategy, or realise they were against a purebred beast.

Lunging at the closest rider, he stepped on the man's boot in the stirrup to pull himself up. His fingers found the hilt of a knife strapped to the saddle. He yanked it free and rammed it into the man's throat before the sound of the blade leaving its sheath had even faded.

Men shouted.

Beast dropped back to the ground, already moving for the next. The second rider was quicker. He had already drawn his sword and he turned his horse so Beast couldn't do the same trick again. Breeder Astaldo had taught his beasts how to fight mounted enemies, and honour had never been part of the lessons. Beast ducked under the horse, slashing at the girths under its belly. The saddle came loose and the horse screamed in pain, rearing, hooves beating the air. The rider toppled.

Beast turned toward the third rider when a voice cut through the chaos.

"Padlociasus!"

Beast flinched. His heart slammed. His body braced for the drop.

But nothing happened.

He blinked, swayed on his feet, waiting for the paralysis to seize him, for his limbs to slump uselessly in the dirt. Desperation twisted in his stomach, the unfairness of it stinging like a thorn

Still nothing.

A blond man, sitting on his saddle with the bearing of a leader, pointed a finger at him. The man's red cheeks paled as the realisation dawned.

The blond man had mispronounced Beast's First Word.

The blond man knew his Words.

The blond man needed to die first.

The conclusion was written plainly on Beast's face. When the man saw it, his cheeks weren't a healthy pink anymore.

"Padlociasus!" he repeated. *"Padlokiashus! Padlo—* Get him!"

Three men hopped down from their horses. They never got the chance to take another step.

Beast met them in motion. He drove a punch into the first man's throat, turned, caught the second's wrist, and drove his stolen knife through his eye. The third lunged from behind — Beast twisted aside and stabbed him twice under the arm. The first man wheezed, choking, bent double. Beast grabbed his hair and slammed the knife under his chin.

In less than five heartbeats, three bodies had hit the ground.

Beast turned toward the leader, but the remaining men filled the space between them, blocking the way. Beast adjusted his grip on the knife. If he had to go through all of them, so be it.

As Beast moved, the leader yelled, desperation cracking his voice, *"Prihjtivaviula!"*

This time, he'd pronounced it right.

Beast barely had time to think before the pain hit.

His body collapsed. A convulsion tore through him, his limbs locking. The knife slipped from his fingers. *No.* His mind screamed, the panic louder than the pain. *No, no—*

The blond man only let himself breathe for a heartbeat before barking orders. "Don't just stand there! Tie him up! Now!"

Hands grabbed at him, twisting his arms behind him. Beast forced a breath in. A twitch ran through his fingers at the sound of the manacles. An animalistic sound wrung from his throat when the cold steel touched his wrists. He ripped one arm free and swung wildly, but hands yanked him back down, fists crashing against his ribs.

"Prihjtivaviula," the blond man repeated.

Beast sunk under a blanket made of agony. His stomach lurched, his throat closing tight. He gasped, his vision blurring, shapes vibrating together and apart. His mind went icy.

Through the haze, Beast saw the blond man approach Lygor. Steel flashed as he raised his sword.

No!

With a growl, Beast slammed his skull into an attacker's face. He staggered to his feet.

He shouldered another man aside and threw himself at the leader. They hit the ground, Beast swinging his fists madly through the blur of pain. He didn't know how much damage he did. He barely felt his own limbs moving. But the blond man and the others pinned him down again.

"Prihjtivaviula!" the leader gasped, blood streaking his lip. *"Prihjtivaviula! Prihjtivaviula!"*

Pain swallowed Beast whole, digging deeper into his bones and flesh. It crashed through him like a blade severing muscle from bone. His thoughts turned to sand, slipping through his fingers.

He had a way out. A way to endure. A way to fight. But he couldn't remember.

He couldn't think.

He couldn't breathe.

Air.

He needed air.

He gasped, but the muscles in his throat were too tight. No air came. His lungs burned.

The next moment, cold water filled his mouth.

Beast thrashed, choking, his limbs flailing and splashing water. His head broke the surface and he gasped a lungful of air. Then, he miscalculated his steps and plunged under water again. His knee hit the muddy ground as he fought his way up. When he emerged again, he coughed, his breath coming fast and erratic.

The water was waist high, much higher than last time he was here. The cavern stretched around him, its jagged walls slick with moisture, catching the dim flicker of firelight. The deep growls of the fiend hounds rolled like distant thunder. They moved along the far walls, their flame furs trailing behind them.

"Lygor!" Beast gasped. Water trickled down his face. He didn't know how he got here, but somehow, he knew the fight still continued *there*. In Earthome.

He staggered towards the massive cage at the cavern's heart. "Please. They'll kill him!"

The darkness behind the silver bars swirled lazily. The chains rattled like restless serpents constricting the cage.

"Please?" Keder mocked. "Curious. I thought you did not believe in that word."

Beast's legs were numb and sluggish. He stumbled, then climbed back up, and reached the cage, gripping the bars. "They're going to kill him. Help me!"

Keder tortured him with his silence before he drawled, "I was under the impression you did not require my help, slave."

Beast hung his head, despair clenching his chest. "I'll do anything."

Keder withdrew into a thoughtful silence, while the shadows swirled rapidly. The weight of the High Fiend's attention settled over Beast. Beast's grip tightened on the bars. He'd never been this close to the cage. He could almost smell the darkness, a metallic scent, like copper on his tongue. Looking at the darkness from this close strained his eyes.

Finally, the High Fiend let out a deep and knowing sound. "Drink."

Beast complied without hesitation.

The water was bitter, ice-cold, and *wrong*. It slithered down his throat like something alive. He gagged but forced himself to swallow.

"More."

Beast drank another handful, glanced at the cage, then drank some more. He doubled over, determined to drink the entire cavern dry if that's what it would take.

The cavern spun around him. The fiend hounds' flames blurred. His stomach cramped violently, twisting like a fist crushing his insides. He hugged his abdomen as he collapsed. "What—"

His body sank beneath the water, swallowing him whole.

Darkness surged over him, deeper than before.

32

BEAST

His breath tore out of him, too fast and too ragged.

He didn't wake up.

He sunk into an airless pit of despair and horror.

His body jerked upright, then hit the ground, his arms and legs moving without coordination, leaving his mind behind.

Blood.

His palms pressed into something soft and wet.

Launch room.

Bodies.

Her body.

Her screams assaulted his ears. Then, his own breath turned to a raw, guttural cry.

He was back at the launch room, waking — not waking; drowning — from his Rage to find what he'd done to Saradra. To find her body.

Her broken body.

His senses were jumbled, like they always were when waking from his Rage. His mind couldn't catch up. Couldn't ground him to where he was. So, the past swallowed him whole, forcing him to live it all over again. The horror and the despair of that moment was carved into him so deep, no passage of time could ever wash it away.

That moment when he woke up and saw what he'd done.

His fists splitting her skin open, breaking her flesh.

A body lay beneath his hand, broken bones crunching under his weight.

His stomach lurched, bile rising fast. He flung himself back, scrambling away on hands and knees, but another corpse blocked his path. Then another. Then another.

They were all her.

His vision swam, then focused on a broken arm, twisted into an impossible angle.

Saradra's broken, lifeless limbs in his arms as he tried to hold her.

Dead eyes in a cracked skull stared at him, and they were Saradra's eyes.

His arms burned where her nails had clawed at him, tearing his skin. Bleeding him.

The sky closed in like rough stone walls. He gagged, scrambling over another corpse, slipping. His knee slammed into something hard. A dented breastplate. His breath came in sharp, shallow bursts, his lungs burning.

Her blood on his hands, arms, face...

He was drenched in it. His chest tightened. His muscles went stiff.

He didn't have the words to speak of it, but his body remembered how her flesh felt against his knuckles.

He choked on a sob. The ground was slick beneath his palms. Blood and mud and something worse. He couldn't breathe. He couldn't think. Earthome spun around him, the edges of his vision darkening, everything feeling far away and distorted.

She had fought him.

Beast curled his fingers, and the wetness on his arms made him sick. His pulse roared in his ears.

A dead man stared at him with one eye, a knife lodged in the other, his broken jaw hanging loose.

Another lay flat on his stomach, his head twisted back and facing the sky.

A wet corpse with his torso slit open in three places, his guts spilling out.

A strand of red hair, the same shade as Saradra's, spilt from under a broken helmet.

Saradra's eyes looked at him from every corpse.

Beast's hands clawed into his hair, gripping, twisting, trying to pull himself out of his own mind. The sky was too close, too dark. The bodies wouldn't stop being her. His arms wrapped around his head, pressing his forehead into the dirt. His body shook violently, suddenly drained of energy. He folded in on himself, every muscle locking tight.

Heaving.

Whimpering.

Crying.

A black knot tightened around his chest. He didn't want to get up. Didn't want to open his eyes. He wanted to lie here and simply stop existing.

He kept his eyes closed, though the sharp scent of blood and death still haunted him. His heart pounded in his ears. Echoes of screams — hers, his, theirs — rang inside his skull.

He lost track of time. He didn't know how long he stayed there. His muscles ached with that familiar yet unsettling fatigue of a Raged fight, compounded by the panic and grief that had scoured through him. He pushed some air into his lungs, then some more. He couldn't lift his head, couldn't unlock his body, which had shut down around him like a rigid shell, but something made him open his eyes.

A noise. Water lapping. A distant, echoing growl.

He saw the fiend hounds' faces as if looking at them through water. He blinked. He wasn't back in the cavern — he knew that because he could still feel the cold, damp dirt pressing against his forehead and the breeze on his back.

He was here, on Earthome, surrounded by corpses.

But he was also staring at the faces of the fiend hounds.

They didn't growl. They just watched him, their focus sharp, like a young purebred slave eager to obey. Liquid fire dripped from their muzzles as they waited for something.

They expected him to do something.

Beast sat up, his breath still too fast, too uneven. His muscles trembled, his limbs sluggish and stiff, but he kept his hands braced against the ground to steady himself. The fiend hounds' faces disappeared. He was just looking at dark soil dampened by blood.

He swallowed hard, staring at the ground as if to ensure the faces of the fiend hounds wouldn't return. He wiped the dirt and blood from his face with a shaky hand. Whatever the Darkhome that was — a hallucination, a nightmare — the fiends had briefly distracted him from his mindless panic. Allowed him a pitiful resemblance of control. He needed to move.

He needed to find Lygor.

The thought hit him like a mace to the chest, pushing past the disorientation, past the lingering terror that clung to his ribs.

Lygor.

Where had he last seen him? His head turned, scanning the chaos around him, but his vision wavered. He forced himself to focus.

Focus on Lygor. Find Lygor.

The bodies blurred, shapes doubling, shifting in his vision. For a moment, she was there, just outside his sight.

A twisted shape with red hair lying in the dirt. Broken.

He sucked in a sharp breath, blinking and forcing himself to think nothing but Lygor.

His stomach churned as he crawled forward. His hands dug into the cold dirt, his knees scraping against stone and blood-soaked earth. He tried not to look at the bodies. He'd never shied away from corpses or violence before. But not having any recollection of how he tore that man's jaw apart, or caved the other one's face in, or ripped another's throat out, left him in a vulnerable state to see Saradra's corpse in every one of them.

He gritted his teeth, breathing through it and keeping his eyes on the motionless shape of Lygor on the side of the road.

He crawled past a sprawled body, its limbs twisted in unnatural angles. The blond leader. The corpse was a wreck. Blood pooled around its head, soaking into the dirt. The face — what was left of it — was barely recognisable. His chest had collapsed inward, bones shattered beneath torn flesh.

Remorse shows that you're human.

Olira's words came out of nowhere. Beast clenched his fists as he stumbled past the body. Fuck him. Fuck these men. They all deserved everything Beast had done to them.

And fuck Olira too.

Finally, he reached Lygor. The prince lay on his side, exactly how he'd left him. Beast's heart lurched. He scrambled closer, almost falling over himself in his desperation. Lygor's head was slick with blood, a deep wound across his scalp. His face was pale, too still.

Beast reached for his wrist, trying to feel for a pulse, but his own hands wouldn't work. His fingers were too cold, too numb, and both his hands shook too much.

He sucked in a sharp breath and pressed his ear against Lygor's chest.

For a moment, nothing. His own pulse pounded in his ears, drowning out everything else. He clenched his jaw, focused. Then, beneath all the noise, he heard a faint thumping.

A heartbeat.

Beast exhaled, a sharp, shuddering breath that emptied his lungs and relaxed his muscles. The relief hit so hard it almost knocked him over.

He stayed there, ear pressed against Lygor's chest, listening. The steady beat grounded him, pulling him away from the horror that still curled in the edges of his mind. The sound held him together.

He didn't want to move. He couldn't move, because all the tension was drained from his body, along with his strength. He couldn't even lift his head. But the heartbeat was still there, strong and steady.

Beast let his eyes close and drifted off.

33

BEAST

Beast sat with his back against a fallen log, the cold seeping into his bones. He pulled the blanket tighter around his shoulders and ignored the throbbing on his knuckles and wrists. The fight had pushed his already hungover and sore body to exhaustion, now also compounded by an odd pang of hunger. The late afternoon sun hung low, stretching the shadows of the trees across the space between him and Lygor.

The prince leaned against another tree trunk, directly opposite. He watched Beast intently, and Beast returned his gaze.

A bandage was wrapped around Lygor's head, already stained with blood. He pressed a damp cloth against his temple. A faint grimace framed the edges of his expression, betraying his headache. His face was otherwise unreadable. He didn't smile, nor did he scowl. He just watched Beast with an intense stare.

And Beast let him see it all.

He let Lygor see him, bloody and sore. And exhausted. He wanted the prince to really see him. He had fought. He'd fought for Lygor.

I came through, Beast thought. *I came through for you.*

Lygor dabbed the cloth to his temple, his eyes narrowing slightly. His jaw ticked as he nodded imperceptibly.

"Praise be to Kiejain," Valnar said for maybe the fiftieth time. "Kiejain the mightiest, ever listens to the prayers of those who welcome the Twelve inside their hearts."

More like praise be to Keder, the High Fiend of Darkhome, Beast thought. He hadn't quite welcomed the High Fiend's presence inside his head, but he was there, and he helped when help was needed.

Unlike Valnar's phony gods...

The knight stood nearby, shifting restlessly on his feet, half-watching the treeline, half-fussing over Lygor. Valnar's horse was tethered beside Lygor's, both animals flicking their tails idly, their breath misting in the air. The knight continued swearing, the words of gratitude spoken more out of habit than thought.

Valnar dug through one of the saddlebags, pulling out a clean shirt. He tossed it toward Beast without a word, his eyes lingering on the blood still drying on Beast's arms. Then, he bent to retrieve a waterskin, uncorking it before passing that over too.

Valnar hovered nearby until Beast was forced to tear his eyes off Lygor and take a sip from the waterskin. He shed the tattered, stained shirt off and tried to wash his hands clean with the water.

"I'm not gonna snap," he said begrudgingly when Valnar's shadow still shaded him.

Valnar let out a sound that was part grunt, part sigh. Beast could feel the questions radiating from him. *Had Beast been Raged? If so, who had Raged him? And if Beast had performed that massacre Unraged...* The possibility bothered the knight enough to move away, muttering another prayer.

The sound of hoofbeats broke the silence.

Ink rode into view, leading another horse by the reins. He didn't smile. He pulled the horses to a stop, swinging down from the saddle. The sight of him dragged Beast back to those first fractured moments of consciousness, when Valnar and Ink wrestled him off Lygor and hauled them both away from the carnage.

Several of the lamellar plates on Ink's armour were scuffed and dented where the arrow had struck. The impact was strong enough to take him off his horse, and he would have certainly felt the damage through the padding underneath, but at least the plates had held. The fall had knocked him unconscious, but he was lucky.

Of course, Valnar had attributed Ink's fortune to the Twelve's blessing too.

Valnar had explained what had happened after Ink fell. He had reached the Kaldorian and had to fight those four riders and the remaining archers, then help Ink onto Lygor's horse and go after the rest. By the time they'd found the corpses, Valnar had lost his senses, thinking Beast had killed Lygor along with everyone else. His relief had matched Beast's when he'd found Lygor still breathing. Other than praying and fussing over Lygor, the knight hadn't spoken much since.

"Well," Ink said, glancing at Beast but speaking to Lygor. "Found my horse and caught one of theirs for Beast, but that's about all the good news I have."

"Did you find the cart?"

"Broke an axel twenty minutes off the road." Ink fiddled with the dented plates of his armour, his head sagging down. "The mule is gone. So is Jessur. And half our supplies, and all the coin."

"He escaped?"

Ink nodded apologetically. Valnar sighed and turned his back. Lygor sat calmly, as if Ink had merely mentioned that nightfall would come in a few hours.

"We'll report him when we get to Calae," Valnar said. "You save his miserable life, and the bastard steals from us and bolts?"

"Hunters will find him," Beast said. He used a damp cloth to rub the blood off his arms. The cold breeze pricked his skin and he shivered.

"Why didn't you run?" Lygor asked. That intensity returned to his face, mirrored on Valnar's.

"He couldn't," Ink said. He slid his fingers under his bracer and pulled a folded, stained paper out. He offered the paper to Lygor as he spoke. "They were after him."

"The archers were aiming at Lodi."

"They must have been trying to disable the cart, take out the driver."

"Vogros soldiers," Lygor said, his attention on the paper.

Valnar cursed, then drew the Twelve's sign in the air.

"This is signed by Kastian." Lygor raised an eyebrow at Beast, as if to see his reaction.

Beast shrugged. He took another sip of water to wash the taste off. They had been so close to capturing him.

"They knew your Words," Lygor said, lowering the paper.

Beast shrugged the clean shirt on and wrapped the blanket back over his shoulders. "He mispronounced."

Valnar barked out a laugh, though his voice lacked mirth. Lygor studied the paper again and shook his head.

"No, he didn't. It was misspelled... Someone changed one letter."

"Did any of them escape?" Valnar asked. Since Lygor had been unconscious the entire time, the question was directed at Beast. He shrugged.

"I don't know."

"Would they be able to? When you're Raged and..."

"Possible. If they were quick. And smart."

"I don't like this. I don't like the idea of Kastian being so close to finding Beast. How did he know?"

"If we could find him, Kastian would too. We need to get to Calae."

Valnar turned to Lygor. "Can you ride?"

Lygor pulled the damp cloth from his head and tossed it aside. "I'm fine," he said, pushing up from the tree with only a faint wince.

They packed up quickly, tightening saddlebags, checking weapons. Valnar helped Lygor onto his horse, while Ink led the spare horse to Beast. It was a solid, sturdy thing, dark-coated and well-muscled, its ears flicking uncertainly. They adjusted the saddle and secured the straps.

Beast put one foot on the stirrup, and just as he hauled himself up, someone wrenched him back down. He stumbled, irritation flashing through him as he turned sharply to face Valnar.

His knuckles ached. He was way too sore and tired to deal with whatever shit Valnar was about to dish him.

The knight regarded him with a face as hard as Beast's fists. Then he held out a sword, sheathed in a worn leather belt, looted from one of the corpses.

Beast blinked.

Valnar said nothing. He passed the sword over without a word, then turned on his heel, wind tugging at his dark, unruly hair. His face, strong-nosed and unreadable, gave no hint of what he was thinking.

For a second, Beast held the sword in his hands like it was a strange object. He pulled the blade halfway from its sheath, examining the steel and he caught his reflection on the metal. He saw the faint trace of surprise in his own face. His fingers curled around the hilt, something like anticipation curling low in his stomach.

Across from him, Ink smirked faintly. Lygor slumped on his horse, watching him, a subtle smile curling his lips. They both knew what he held in his hands was more than a sword.

"Quit gawking and get on your horse," Valnar huffed as he climbed on his.

Beast shoved the sword back into its sheath before wrapping the belt around his waist and fastening it. He climbed into the saddle, adjusting his position until the sword rested comfortably. The weight felt right.

Beast nudged his horse to join the others. All four on horseback, all four armed. He didn't dwell on it, but somewhere in the back of his mind, he felt it. That unspoken shift, the way his presence meant something different to them now.

"Alright, then," Lygor said. "Let's go."

He turned his horse and his companions followed.

34

OLIRA

Olira spotted a severed arm, ripped out of its socket by force. She covered her mouth and looked up, trying not to vomit.

The battlefield reeked of blood and rot. The sickly scent of torn flesh and the copper tang clung to the back of Olira's throat. Bodies twisted where they had fallen, some mangled beyond recognition. She had seen death before, but not like this — not so brutal, so inhuman.

Beast had done this. Lion of Zarall.

"Are you alright, ma'am?" Norrol asked.

Olira had almost forgotten about the boy. They rode double, and she could feel the tension in his body, the slight tremor in his arms as he held the reins. He thought she couldn't see his face, but she could hear the fear in his voice.

She swallowed the bile in her throat and muttered, "Yes."

The answer didn't convince either of them. Her throat ached, raw and red from Dienus's hands. Talking hurt, breathing hurt. She rubbed at it absently, but no amount of pressure would erase the lingering sensation of his fingers squeezing the life out of her.

Ahead, Prince Dienus picked his way over the dead bodies. Olira shuddered at the memory of the thirst in Dienus's green eyes. His face twisted, his lips pulled over his teeth...

Open your eyes, Olira.

She thought she didn't care about what would happen to her, but the prince made her realise how much she still wanted to live.

Dienus stopped and crouched beside a corpse, gripping an arm and rolling the body onto its back.

Lieutenant Quinner.

Her stomach lurched again, but this time, it wasn't from nausea.

Quinner had never treated her gently, but he had kept the soldiers in check, had kept Dienus in check. He had been the closest thing to a leash on the prince's cruelty. Now, he lay dead, his skull caved in, pieces of his flesh missing.

Dienus rubbed his mouth, and Olira knew the gesture was to hide his smirk.

A soldier bent over and vomited, retching loudly into the dirt.

Dienus glared at the man with contempt. "Hey!" he snapped. "Keep it together, princess. We'll get him, and we'll make him pay."

A queasy voice from the gathered men responded, "This was half our force. If he did this single-handedly—"

"He didn't," Dienus dismissed. He waved a hand toward the hills. "You saw it yourselves. Those men over the ridge were killed by arrows, and the others down the road were butchered with a sword."

The soldiers weren't convinced. They shifted uneasily, exchanging glances. Dienus noticed. He puffed out his chest and began to pace as he spoke, taking on the posture of command.

"Lieutenant Quinner underestimated our enemies," he declared. "Now we know, Lion of Zarall's companions can fight as well. We will learn from the Lieutenant's mistakes."

Someone called out, "How?"

"For starters, we will not rush, like the Lieutenant did, leaving half our force behind. We will catch them off guard, separate them, and get Lion of Zarall when he's most vulnerable."

A gruff voice from the ranks spoke up. "Your Highness... we've seen the signs. They were already separated. Lion of Zarall killed most of these men with his bare hands. How much more vulnerable can he be caught?"

Dienus's cheek twitched — just barely — but Olira caught it. He forced a smile, stepping toward the man with the ease of a commander offering reassurance. A hand on the soldier's shoulder. A patronising tilt of his head.

"I understand your fear," Dienus said smoothly. "But remember, he is still a purebred. And I know his Words."

Someone from the back of the group muttered. "So did the Lieutenant."

The effect was instant.

Dienus's head snapped toward the voice. His entire body tensed. "Who said that?"

Silence.

He scanned the faces around him, his eyes glinting with fury. The men shifted, shoulders drawing in, looking at anything but him.

"I asked," Dienus said, voice rising, "Who. Said. That?"

Hooves pounding against the dirt broke the silence.

A scout galloped toward them, leaping down from his horse before it had fully stopped. He didn't notice the tension in the air, too caught up in whatever news he had brought. His face was slick with sweat, flushed with excitement.

"Your Highness!" he called, dropping to one knee. "We've got him! We've captured the beast!"

Dienus froze. His jaw slackened. "You what?"

The scout's chest heaved as he caught his breath. "We found Lion of Zarall wandering nearby and apprehended him. Yense and Vyran are bringing him now."

Dienus's expression wavered between disbelief and elation. He turned to Sir Gennald, then back to the scout. His lips curled into a slow, hungry smile.

"We've got him," he whispered.

Two riders appeared over the ridge. A bound figure was draped over one of the saddles, arms and legs tied behind his back.

Lion of Zarall. Captured and defeated.

Olira's heart skipped.

How would he react when he saw her again?

She had no idea. But as the horse carrying him drew closer, dread muddled her stomach.

Dienus's face paled slightly as he took in the sight of the man he had hunted. He raised a hand to halt the approaching riders.

"That's close enough. Get him off the horse. Ready your arms!"

The soldiers obeyed, drawing their swords as they surrounded the two riders. Two of them stepped forward and hauled the captive down.

The figure stirred, and Dienus flinched. "Padlociasus! Prihjtivaviula! Padlociasus!" he yelped.

The man slumped, blinking up at them in confusion.

"Sir... Master... Please, I... I wasn't doing anything wrong. My arm hurts, please..."

Silent confusion filled the air.

The slave kept talking and struggling against his binds while Vogros soldiers waited with their weapons drawn. Dienus watched the man; his expression changing from nervous to dumbfounded.

"You're not Lion of Zarall!" Dienus said accusingly.

"What? No, Master— What?"

"Who the fuck are you?"

"My name is Jessur, Master. I was... I was separated from my Owner... I didn't mean to run."

"How did you get here?"

Jessur licked his lips. "My Owner and... and his companions were attacked and— and we got separated. Master, please, my arm is broken. It hurts so much tied like this..."

Dienus breathed impatiently. The soldiers relaxed. Some of them sheathed their swords. Dienus ground his jaw. "Who is your Owner?"

"Ink... His name was Ink."

"That's a weird name."

"It... it must be Kaldorian. He was Kaldorian."

"Tell me about his companions."

"Their leader was called Lodi and... and the other one's name was Valnar. They also had a... a purebred beast with them."

Dienus's face brightened. He smirked at his men victoriously. Olira struggled to hide her disappointment. She had kept those names hidden from them, just to hinder their search for Beast. Now they knew their names.

"Did you say Valnar?" Sir Gennald stepped forward. "*Sir* Valnar Gaege?"

Jessur grimaced and fidgeted to adjust his right arm into a less painful position. "I— I didn't catch his last name. Master, please... My arm..."

"Did he carry Kiejain on him?"

"Ah... Yes, yes, he wore a breastplate with the First Rider on it."

Dienus raised an eyebrow at Sir Gennald. "You know him?"

Sir Gennald nodded subtly, but didn't elaborate. They shared a look that seemed to agree to discuss it later privately.

Dienus returned to the slave, blew one of his cheeks as he thought what to do about him.

He smiled.

Dienus started barking orders, using a tone he clearly thought was authoritative. "Half of you, find a place and set up camp. The other half, start digging. We can't continue our mission before giving these good men a proper burial. We will pursue Lion of Zarall first thing in the morning." He clapped his hands. "Off you go!"

The men set to work. Dienus gestured his servant, Emberlash, to come near. "Set up my tent immediately," he ordered. "I'll have to interrogate our new prisoner and extract all the information I can before going after them."

Olira recognised the spark in Dienus's green eyes. She understood what was coming, and felt sorry for the slave.

35

BEAST

The water had begun to chill.

Beast grabbed the soap and sponge from the tub's edge and spent the next fifteen minutes scrubbing his skin. He couldn't remember the last time he'd soaked so thoroughly. Back in Brinescar, Badimar sent him daily to the servants' bath house. Master Raydon would send him there too, before parading Lion of Zarall at Leonis's feasts.

Did he miss that life? He was treated well, trained in all manner of weapons and styles, and he always knew his role. He had the comfort of wanting nothing. It was simpler.

Now, the bath water was black with filth. Beast frowned at the colour. It reminded him of the flooded cavern. He closed his eyes, and for a heartbeat, he was drifting back to Darkhome. A sharp breath pulled him out of it.

No. He wasn't going back to that place. Not again.

He still didn't know exactly what had happened when he drank the water, but he never wanted to feel that way again. The Rage that had overtaken him... it was familiar, yet not like the others. That black water — there was something in it. Something wrong. He didn't know how he knew, but he was certain it was part of the High Fiend. And when he drank it...

"No," he muttered. "No more."

Keder's presence lingered like a shadow at the edge of his mind. The High Fiend hadn't spoken since the ambush, but Beast could feel him there, silent and watching. Now, the silence broke.

They'll betray you.

Beast pressed his lips together. The warning felt so out of place, it barely warranted any thought.

Lygor will never release you.

"He needs me to be free for his plan to work," Beast muttered. "That's the deal."

There are countless loopholes in that deal.

"He'll come through," Beast said, swallowing. "I don't need your help anymore. Get out of my head."

Keder didn't respond. His silence weighed more ominous than any threat. He slithered back into the dark corners of Beast's thoughts, smug and certain.

A chill crept over Beast. He rinsed off, climbed out of the tub, and towelled himself dry.

They had reached Calae two weeks after the ambush, all four of them on swift horses.

Calae was a clean, orderly city of wealth and polish — elegant stonework, manicured avenues, and banners that didn't fray in the wind. Even the air smelled expensive. Beast pictured the map of Chinderia in his mind, where every city existed as a pinprick of ink. He knew them all by heart, not just by names or landmarks, but by the arenas they held.

Calae's was called the Scorchline Arena — a strange structure built differently than most others. He'd never fought there, but the thought of it always stirred a thrill in his chest. It was the way one might eye a coiled viper, equal parts fear and fascination.

They'd spent the last of the coin Lygor had kept on himself on a spacious room in a pricey inn. Ink had finished his bath first and had gone out. Lygor had told the rest to wash up and get ready.

Beast emerged from behind the wooden screen that separated the tub from the rest of the room, the towel wrapped around his waist. His clothes weren't where he'd left them.

Valnar and Lygor buzzed around the room, getting ready as they talked about a topic Beast had tuned out while he was in the tub. Their belongings were scattered everywhere in a chaos. He looked for his clothes.

"It doesn't matter, Kastian hardly even acknowledges them," Lygor was saying as he stood shirtless in front of a mirror, a razor in his hand, half his face covered in foam. His pants hung low on his waist, his back and chest too pale and too smooth, untouched by neither the brutal sun nor violence. He dragged the razor down his cheek slowly.

Valnar sat in a corner, polishing the spare set of armour he usually kept out of sight. Unlike the practical, battle-worn plate he typically used, this set was ceremonial. Excellent quality craftsmanship, more suited for royal courts than bloodied battlefields. The full-plate armour lay spread out before him. Engraved lions prowled across the breastplate, their golden manes curling in intricate detail. The pauldrons bore the emblem of House Zarall. Even the gauntlets, resting nearby, were more adorned than practical, the knuckles reinforced with shaped gold rather than raw steel.

"And for a reason," the knight grunted. "They don't have a lot of power."

Beast took his eyes off the armour and searched the bed, which was cluttered with sets of expensive clothes. None of them were the simple breeches and shirt he'd borrowed from Valnar. As he scanned the room, Lygor's reflection met his eyes through the mirror. The prince's lips curled.

"That's where you're wrong, Valnar," Lygor said as he scraped the last of the foam off his cheek. "Haven't you read the scholar Syltoris Windflaw? He says, 'power is defined by your opponent.' Do you know what that means?" He wiped his face with a damp towel, then cleaned the razor. His eyes were still locked on Beast's as he waved a hand at the wooden chair nearby.

"Those words sound like the ramblings of some scholar who's never been in a real fight," Valnar said.

Lygor walked over to the washbasin. The faint scent of lye soap mixed with the damp air as he lathered it between his palms, working up a thick foam. He turned and raised an eyebrow when he found Beast still standing.

Beast held out his hand for the razor. "I know how to shave."

"I'm not letting you turn yourself into a plucked chicken. I need you to look like Lion of Zarall tonight."

Beast growled as he dropped onto the chair. He didn't miss the playful gleam in Lygor's eyes. He crossed his arms and stared ahead, suddenly not wanting to give the prince the satisfaction of seeing him squirm. Beast had suffered this type of treatment countless times when Master Raydon groomed him for hours before every feast; trimming his beard, plucking his body hair off, rubbing oil into his skin to make him shine under torchlight. He had tolerated strangers inspecting his teeth, his hands, his posture. He'd stood motionless while lords discussed his physique like a prized stallion. This wasn't new. But the warmth that crawled up his neck was odd.

Lygor dipped his fingers into the lather, spreading it evenly over his cheeks. "What do you think, Beast?" He asked as he tilted Beast's chin slightly to cover his jaw and neck. "What does the scholar mean?"

"What?"

Valnar scuffed. "Sure, ask the slave to decipher Syltoris Windflaw. That man is a raving lunatic, half his brain is off in Farhome."

Lygor ignored him. He stood behind the chair, close enough that Beast could feel the warmth of him. He settled a hand lightly on Beast's head, tilting it back until the back of his skull pressed against Lygor's stomach.

"He says, 'power is defined by your opponent.' What do you think that means?"

Beast's pulse quickened as the razor scraped against his skin with slow, careful strokes. Lygor leaned over Beast's face, too close he could almost feel his breath against him. The prince's focus didn't waver. His hand was steady and confident, a warm finger anchoring Beast's jaw. The chilling touch of the blade at his throat made him go still.

"Yes?" Lygor pressed.

"Power is power," Beast huffed.

Valnar barked out a laughter. "See? Even Beast knows."

"Your enemy's greatest weakness can be your power," Lygor explained.

Beast felt the slight drag of the blade as it carved away the rough edges of his beard, leaving raw skin in its wake. He couldn't bring himself to look away from

Lygor's face, as if the act would somehow empower the prince. It was silly. Lygor already had all the power over him; he was practically Beast's owner, knew his Words, and could snap a finger and order his death. Yet, closing his eyes or looking away felt like losing a fight Beast didn't know he was fighting.

"A knife in the heart," he muttered.

"Excuse me?"

"A knife in the heart can be anyone's greatest weakness. Master."

Lygor's free hand steadied Beast's jaw, his fingers brushing over his mouth, as he scraped the remaining hair along his chin. The prince's arrogant lips curled as if he could hear the thrumming in Beast's chest. Beast had the sudden urge to stand his ground, carve himself a space against Lygor. His blood rushed.

"Killing is not the only way to defeat someone," Lygor said. His voice was casual, like he wasn't standing this close, sliding a sharp razor down Beast's throat.

"I've never seen a victorious corpse."

Lygor brushed away stray hairs with his thumb before wiping the remaining soap with a damp towel. He held Beast's gaze as he whispered, "Is that why Kastian killed your woman?"

A black knife stabbed Beast's chest, twisting and burning. His eyes widened, his breath leaving his lungs. The smug flash in Lygor's bright blue eyes ignited a dangerous surge of anger in him.

Beast pushed off the chair. Lygor grabbed him by the shoulder and yanked him back down.

"I'm not done with you."

Beast stiffened. Across the room, Valnar pulled his inner shirt and padding over his head, seemingly absorbed in the task. Beast couldn't decide what irked him more: Lygor's mention of Saradra, or the smug satisfaction of having gotten a reaction out of him. The prince swapped the razor for a pair of scissors and began trimming Beast's hair.

"You've gotta learn, sometimes a knife in the heart isn't enough to win, Beast. If you know your enemy's true weakness, you know how to truly defeat him."

Beast's fingers curled against the arms of the chair. Lygor's hands caressed his scalp, pulling blond locks of hair and snipping the tips. "Kastian thought the woman was—"

"*Her name was Saradra,*" Beast growled through his teeth, the tension in his voice drawing Valnar's attention.

Lygor gave a half smile. Beast knew he had just given the prince more power by offering him Saradra's name, but something in him couldn't bear hearing her being called 'the woman'.

She had a name.

"Kastian thought *Saradra* was your weakness," Lygor continued, unfazed by the interruption. "He thought he could defeat you by killing her. That knowledge was what made him powerful."

Lygor patted his shoulder to indicate he was done. Beast stood and faced him, standing in full height, a head taller than Lygor. He closed the space between them, not caring that Valnar had stopped and was watching them.

Beast towered over Lygor, the heat of his body filling the air between them, his breath slow and controlled despite the fire raging beneath his skin. Lygor met Beast's glare with that same casual confidence, his lips barely tilting at the corners, as if he was enjoying this. Beast let the weight of his presence sink in before he finally spoke, his voice low and dangerous.

"Do I look defeated?"

Lygor's eyes swept over him from head to toe. His smirk spread at the edges. "No," he murmured. He leaned closer and breathed into his ear. "But you look damn good."

Beast's breath hitched, barely noticeable, but enough that Lygor caught it. He felt a flicker of heat creeping up his neck.

The prince had gotten to him. Again.

That realisation snapped his spine straight, his flustered moment instantly curdling into annoyance. When he finally forced himself to look away, he was met with Valnar's raised eyebrows.

A slow, knowing look.

Heat bloomed under Beast's skin, but this time, it was pure embarrassment. Valnar huffed through his nose before he stiffly turned away, busying himself with his armour again.

Lygor patted Beast's arm as he brushed past. "Try those clothes on for me."

Beast exhaled sharply through his nose, still stuck in that rattled haze between irritation and the strong desire to give Lygor a good thrashing. The prince, meanwhile, had already moved on, completely unbothered. He started dressing himself in clothes that screamed wealth: a cotton shirt and a blue doublet, black leather boots, a belt with gold accents.

A particular pattern of a knock on the door announced Ink's return. Valnar let him in.

"So? How did it go?" Lygor asked.

Ink took his coat off and tossed it aside. "Well, I got what I needed. But first—" He paused mid-step, his gaze flicking between Beast and Lygor. His mouth curved into a smirk. "Why is he looking at you as if he wants to either eat you up or punch you through the wall?"

Beast grunted, grabbed one of the shirts Lygor had pointed at, and pulled it on with more force than necessary. Ink chuckled, unfastening his sword belt as he moved toward the washbasin.

"One hour," the Kaldorian said. "They'll see us at Master Vadithas's manor. It's the most secure place in the whole city. He's got free men as well as purebreds protecting the property. Master Naelar is gathering the rest of the Union there."

Beast buttoned his shirt, half-listening, half-focused on just getting through this without further humiliation. Lygor, of course, wasn't done with him. Now fully dressed in his noble finery, looking like a gilded painting that deserved to be punched, he stood across from Beast, eyeing him critically, as he spoke to Ink. "So did you see your friends?"

"Uh-huh," Ink said. He rolled his sleeves up and splashed water over his face.

"I'm not sure how I feel about Kaldorian spies on my soil, Prince Ingelhar."

"What spies, Prince Lygor? They're just some friends, doing me a favour."

Lygor gestured at Beast's clothes. "Lose that shirt. Try the other one."

Beast stared at him. "This fits well."

Lygor had already turned back to Ink. "Anyway, tell me what they know."

Beast clenched his jaw, ripping the shirt off and grabbing another. He shoved his arms through the sleeves.

"Well, there's Ruzen. He's the Master of Sands."

"Regulates the arenas all over the country. What do your *friends* know about him?"

Ink picked his clothes, their quality matching Lygor's. He slipped them on quickly, then grabbed three small jars from his bag.

"He's not very bright. Gets angry very quickly. Lately, he's quite troubled about the increasing amounts of underground arenas. He'll probably ask for tax benefits, but might settle for shutting down a few of those arenas."

"Well, we already know the location of one of those." Lygor pointed at Beast. "No, tuck that in properly."

Beast released his irritation into a slow breath and tucked his shirt in. He reminded himself of the time Master Raydon had directed him to try an entire wardrobe on and off for three hours. If he'd tolerated that, he could tolerate this.

Ink opened the jars and lined them in front of him. Each had a paint in them: black, red, and yellow. Ink dipped his fingers and started painting his face with Kaldorian warrior marks.

"He's also quite mad about Kastian shutting down the Switchblade Arena at Brinescar."

"Excellent. Who's next?"

"There's Vadithas. Master of Blood."

"Head of slave breeders. I know what he'll ask for. They've been asking for it since I was old enough to understand politics; financial support for slave ranches." He shook his head at Beast. "Try the next one."

"I've heard a slave ranch was shut down recently. Problem with their food supplier asking for unreasonable prices."

"I'm reluctant to promise him my father's vaults. If Kastian left anything in them. Would he settle for tax benefits for the ranches? What kind of a man is he? What's his poison?"

Ink screwed his face, the paint making him look like a growling fiend. "Rumour has it, he has a penchant for twisted pleasures. The worst kind."

"How wonderful."

"This is the man whose house we're going to, by the way."

Lygor rubbed his chin thoughtfully. "I'll agree to tax benefits. If he's still not happy, I can accept offering financial aid for a limited period of time. Come over here for a second. What do you think?"

Ink approached, standing next to Lygor and looking Beast up and down with mock consideration. "Hmm. Not bad," he mused, stroking his chin. "If you want him to look like a disgruntled hired blade and not a dignified champion."

Lygor sighed theatrically. "I knew it. Try that shirt again."

Beast snapped his head toward him. "You already made me try that."

Lygor's grin was pure satisfaction. "Yes. Now do it again."

Valnar spoke from across the room, adjusting the inner padding before moving on to the armour plates. "You know I can find him a set of plate and be done with this."

"Yes," Beast jumped in. "Please... Master."

Lygor didn't even glance up. "No." He turned to Ink. "Who else will be there?"

"Next is Master Naelar," Ink said. He walked over to Valnar to help him with his armour. "Master of Chains. He oversees slave merchants and traders."

"Right. And what's his most recent problem?"

"His convoys getting attacked."

"Better roads? Increased patrols? Done."

"I don't think that'll be enough." Ink's face darkened. "My friends say he's the smartest one amongst them. You should really watch out for that one. He'll probably ask for more."

"Weaknesses?"

"Not quite sure if he'll regard that as a weakness, but apparently, he's had an altercation with the Chamber of Twelve recently. He denounced Twelve Riders."

Valnar scoffed, but didn't comment. He stood still as Ink fastened the buckles on his greaves.

"Is that all?" Lygor asked.

"There's Kyrophe. My friends were actually surprised, saying she doesn't really operate from Calae. Visits the city once a year and spends the rest of her time at White Tower."

Beast shuddered at the name of White Tower. He stood still to let Lygor appraise another set of ridiculous outfit. Lygor handed him a velvet vest in House Zarall's black-and-gold.

"So what's bothering the White Tower's representative recently?"

"My friends don't know much about her. I'm sorry."

Lygor nodded. "Anyone else?"

"A young mage called Adept Ziuw. Word is, the head of Casters Board of Chinderia, Adept Kato, is at Brinescar right now. He left his assistant to represent his seat at the Union. I don't think he'll be too pushy about anything. It's not even his seat."

"What's Adept Kato doing at Brinescar?"

"The Casters Board are having problems with the Eternal Pillar since Kastian's accusations about that rogue mage your father supposedly aided. I believe Adept Kato is meeting an investigator, trying to clear the Chinderian mages and keep the Eternal Pillar off their backs."

Beast's stomach dropped at the mention of the rogue mage. Belandir Malderan. The mage in black robes. He had done something to Beast that night. He suspected what the mage did resulted in Beast's visitations to the flooded cavern and Darkhome.

"And the Kiejain's Army," Valnar joined in. "The Army will wipe all of the Chinderian mages if they suspect one of them meddled with Darkhome magic. Then, they'll go after the Eternal Pillar if they were involved too."

Would anyone know Beast was having conversations with a High Fiend of Darkhome? Was that considered meddling with Darkhome magic? It didn't matter; it wasn't like Beast was doing anything other than waking up in the cavern at random times. Neither was he planning to unleash the High Fiend into Earthome. Beast was in control.

When he remembered the faces of the fiend hounds as they looked up at him through water, right after he woke up from that odd Rage, a chill ran down his spine.

"So everyone's doing a lot of butt covering," Lygor said. "What can I offer for the Casters Board?"

"Any information that would clear their involvement with that rogue mage."

"Right." Lygor waved at Beast. "Try that vest without the shirt."

"It won't make a difference," Beast grunted, pulling at the fabric. "This is too small."

Lygor clicked his fingers. "Shirt off."

Beast schooled his irritation and forced himself to move slowly and calmly. He took the vest and the shirt off, then pulled the vest on. It was too tight across his shoulders and snug under his arms. He couldn't even button it. The neckline left his collarbones, his brands, and part of his stomach exposed. His arms, thick and defined, looked even more so with the way the vest hugged him.

"Are you sure you wanna expose his brands like that?" Valnar asked.

"Oh, absolutely. Let them recognise him."

He handed Beast a belt, with a golden buckle shaped like a lion's head. He paired it with dark leather bracers and a lightweight mantle over one shoulder. Lastly, he handed Beast his sword, then took a step back and nodded his satisfaction.

Valnar shifted, the soft clink of steel marking his movements as he adjusted his gauntlets. Beast's eyes flicked to the armour, a subtle twinge of jealousy souring his stomach. He would have felt a lot more comfortable in an armour, but he doubted if Lygor cared about his comfort. If anything, the prince made a game out of his discomfort.

"Alright," Lygor said after checking the fit of his expensive coat. "Let's go."

"I thought we were meeting them in an hour?" Valnar said.

"I don't wanna give them time to discuss their strategies amongst themselves." Lygor plastered a confident grin on his face. "Besides, you know the saying: sit first, and speak last; if that fails, hit first, and stand last."

36

VALNAR

MASTER OF BLOOD GREETED them at the wide, oak double doors of his manor. He was a tall, lanky man in his early thirties, with a bald head that caught the evening light and a bushy beard that almost made up for it.

"Prince Lygor, it is an honour to have you at my humble residence," Vadithas said with a deep bow. He had a warm, musical voice.

His 'humble residence' rivalled half the size of King Zumnorin's palace in Kaldoria. The walk from the front gates through the garden — more a private forest than a courtyard — had taken nearly twenty minutes. The sun was already sinking behind the city's brick roofs, painting the manor's windows in molten gold. Pairs of purebred beasts and free men patrolled the grounds at regular intervals, their paths intersecting like threads in a spider's web.

"The honour is mine, Master Vadithas," Lygor said, with a curt nod. "Thank you for having us."

Valnar followed Lygor and Ink as they stepped through the grand foyer, Beast trailing behind. A rich fragrance of oils and flowers filled the air. The floors gleamed with polished black marble, each step echoing faintly in the vast foyer. A towering chandelier of intricate gold and crystal hung overhead. A grand staircase of dark-stained wood and gilded railings curved toward the upper floors, its steps draped in velvet runners.

The other leaders of the Union stood ready in the grand foyer; three men and one woman. If they were surprised by Lygor's early arrival, their faces betrayed nothing. Valnar took his position behind his prince, quietly studying each Union leader as they exchanged pleasantries.

"Please allow me to introduce Masters Ruzen and Naelar, Mistress Kyrophe, and Adept Ziuw."

Each Union member bowed as their name was called. Ruzen's large frame and light hair were at odds with his deep tan. His curious frown fixed on Beast, his eyes flicking to the brands visible on the purebred's chest. Naelar appeared to be in his early twenties, at most. Though his features were plain, his intelligent eyes and ready smile carried a dangerous sort of charm. Ziuw, youngest of all, wore a white robe adorned with red flame patterns at the cuffs, his nervous fingers adjusting his collar repeatedly. Kyrophe's light brown curls fell wild around her shoulders, framing a face lined with crow's feet. Her motherly smile didn't quite match the sharp assessment in her eyes.

"It's a pleasure to meet you all," Lygor said, nodding at each.

"Praise be to the Twelve Riders, you are alive and well," Naelar said.

Valnar stared at the man. Didn't Ink report that this man had publicly condemned the Twelve? Yet here he stood, invoking their names? Naelar caught Valnar's stare, then grinned. This had been a test to gauge how much information Lygor had on them, and Valnar had just revealed the answer.

"I appreciate your prayers," Lygor said smoothly.

Naelar is the smartest one, Ink had also said. The one they needed to watch most carefully.

"Please, come on in." Vadithas gestured toward the stairs.

As they followed their host through the manor, Valnar couldn't shake the feeling they were walking deeper into a wolf's den.

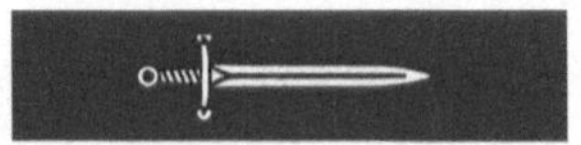

"Please, Your Highness, make yourself comfortable," Vadithas said.

They were settling in the study, a room that spoke of wealth in every detail. The leather-bound books lined dark wooden shelves, and a massive oak table dominated the centre. Brass lamps cast warm light across polished surfaces, making the room feel smaller than it was.

The Union members took their seats along one side of the table. A unified front. Lygor sat opposite them, with an empty chair beside him meant for Ink. The arrangement reminded Valnar of army maps he'd studied, showing opposing forces across a battlefield. He clenched and relaxed his gauntleted fingers. He would follow Lygor to the bloodiest battlefields, but this was no field of swords and shields. This was a kind of battle Valnar couldn't fight for him. He couldn't help but feel he'd abandoned Lygor, but at least Ink was there. The Kaldorian knew how to navigate thirsty merchants and power-hungry leaders much better than Valnar ever could.

He touched his chest out of habit, his fingers brushing the House Zarall sigil on his breastplate instead of Kiejain's winged horse. He offered a quick prayer to the First Rider.

"Prince Ingelhar, I presume." Vadithas gestured at the second seat. "Please."

Ink took the seat with a polite nod. The war paint marked his face in sharp lines, each symbol and dot with a different meaning. It gave the young, friendly prince an uncharacteristically serious expression.

"Stand near Lygor," Valnar murmured to Beast, then took his own position by the door, where he could watch everyone at once.

Beast stood just behind Lygor's right shoulder, hands clasped in front of him. Instead of bowing his head, he stared straight ahead, as Lygor had instructed. Lion of Zarall had kept his head high at King Leonis's feasts, and Lygor intended to preserve that image — the revered purebred, proud and dangerous. Leonis's undefeated champion, a deadly beast on a leash.

A male slave entered, carrying a silver carafe and crystal glasses. As he poured the wine, Valnar caught sight of the tattoo on his neck — an intricate circle surrounding a stylised hand. A purebred house slave. The rarity of such a thing lifted Lygor's eyebrows. Most purebreds were raised as beasts or flames. Those roles justified the years of costly training. Breeders aimed for the highest profit, and demand was always stronger for fighters and pleasure slaves than for house servants. After all, a well-trained freeborn could pour wine just as well. A pure-bred house slave was little more than a vanity piece.

After serving the drinks, the slave tucked the tray under his arm and withdrew to a corner to stand still like he was part of the room's furniture.

"I hope you like *Serpentblood*," Vadithas said. "It is quite hard to come by these days. There are rumours of some lunatic attacking wine convoys. But I've had my own private stash."

"*Serpentblood* is an exquisite taste," Lygor said as he took his glass.

"To your health," Ruzen said. He raised his glass in a toast, then scuffed it down. The others joined him.

"Wine convoys are not the only ones being attacked," Ink said casually. "Safety of the trade roads are quite concerning."

Naelar smiled over his wine glass. "True indeed. My business is being affected as anyone else's, I'm afraid." He put his glass down and leaned back comfortably. "Luckily, we are in this trade for long enough to know, the best cure for the uncertainty is time. Things will settle, one way or another."

"That's right," Ink said, mimicking Naelar's tone and leaning back. He smiled, but the bold streaks of black, red, and yellow only made him more intimidating. "Though time is not always a luxury we all have, isn't that right? Master Ruzen, you must be losing quite a lot of money every day Switchblade Arena remains closed. When do you think it will reopen?"

Ruzen stood up and reached for the carafe with his paw-like hands. He poured himself another glass. "We're working on security improvement plans to present to King Kastian," he grunted. "Should be done soon."

Ink nodded gravely. "I wish you good luck, though I'd be surprised if Kastian would ever consider reopening the arena before the public settled down. But I'm sure that'll happen, given enough *time*, as Master Naelar pointed out."

Ruzen gulped down his drink, but didn't comment. Naelar grinned with amusement.

"What can the Union do for you, Your Highness?" Vadithas asked pleasantly.

Lygor leaned back in his chair and let the silence stretch as he made eye contact with all five. "I believe you all know why I'm here."

"You're seeking our alliance."

"You must be desperate to ask for *our* alliance," Ruzen said.

"True. Union wasn't my first choice."

"Ouch," Naelar said with a smirk.

"I mean, you don't have any army, and financially, you're not having your best days. There is little you can offer me."

"And yet, your presence here speaks of your despair."

"My father understood the Union's importance for Chinderia's economic prosperity. Your activities have direct influence on everyday lives of Chinderians. Kastian does not know — or worse, does not care — about the damage that can be done, should Union fall apart. I'm here to listen how I can ensure Union's survival and future."

"Excellent speech, Your Highness," Naelar said. "But we're in the business long enough to know, not to tell our prices before appraising what we sell."

"What the rightful heir of Chinderia requests from you is entirely within your capabilities," Ink added.

"Which is?"

Lygor tilted his head, taking his time answering. He nodded over his shoulder, directing their stares at Beast. "You recognise him." It wasn't a question.

"Lion of Zarall," Ruzen grunted. "The slave who got my arena shut down." He studied Beast with a mixture of admiration and contempt.

"The one they call broken," Vadithas said, with a dangerous curiosity in his eyes.

"I've heard he was on his way to White Tower?" Naelar raised an eyebrow at the woman sitting beside him.

"We awaited its arrival at White Tower," Kyrophe spoke. She had a dull, expressionless voice that conveyed no intonation. "Never had the pleasure."

Still as stone, Beast gave nothing away, his expression empty, unreadable. Yet Valnar noticed the faint rigidity in his stance, the way his back tensed, as though he was forcing himself not to shudder.

"Umm... I'm sorry," Ziuw said, speaking for the first time. "I don't understand. What does Lion of Zarall have to do with... with us?"

"Right." Lygor leaned in towards Ruzen. "I'd like to register him for Twilight of Infinity."

A parade of emotions crossed Ruzen's face in rapid succession. Excitement came first, his mind no doubt calculating the crowds Lion of Zarall would draw. Then, hesitation crept in, quickly followed by panic. He raised a finger, his voice sharpening. "Wait a minute. Last time he fought in one of my arenas— No, no way! The second Lion of Zarall sets foot in Scythe Arena, Kastian will have it shut down."

"Isn't Scythe Arena in Euroad?" Ink said. "He doesn't have authority over there."

"He'll close the other arenas just to be spiteful!"

Lygor's grin was sharp and easy. "He won't," he said smoothly, "because you'll shut them down yourself."

Ruzen froze, then doubled over with a violent laugher. When he noticed he was the only one laughing, he paled. He snatched the carafe and gulped down its entire contents. Shaking the empty carafe, "More!" he yelled at the house slave, who slid out of the room quietly.

Ruzen stood and paced back and forth in front of the bookshelf as he waited.

"You're being overdramatic," Kyrophe spoke.

"Overdramatic?" Ruzen snatched Naelar's glass from the table and drank it. "He wants me to shut down all my operations!"

"Not all," Ink said cheerfully. "Scythe Arena in Euroad will stay open. It'll be at full capacity for Twilight."

"Every day Switchblade remains closed costs me forty-five Blues," Ruzen almost yelled. "If I shut down all my operations, I'm... I won't recover from that!"

"My purpose in being here is to learn how I can assist your recovery, following the restoration of my throne."

The house slave came back with two bottles of wine. He served one to Ruzen and refilled others' glasses with the other. Ruzen sat down, scowling at Lygor.

"I don't see how shutting down the arenas will help you, Your Highness," Ziuw squeaked.

"You're all smart people," Lygor said. "Why don't you tell me?"

Naelar's eyes widened. "You want to start a riot."

"Correct."

It was Naelar's turn to stand, but unlike Ruzen, he was amused rather than troubled. His eyes sparkled with excitement as he spoke, his slow steps drawing him closer to Beast.

"Lion of Zarall wins Twilight of Infinity," Naelar said as he circled Beast, studying him from head to toe with the scrutiny of a merchant appraising his goods. "He earns his freedom. Then, as a free man, he pledges his loyalty to Lygor Zarall, the true king."

Naelar stopped in front of Beast, his fingers carelessly darting out to peel back the edges of the vest. He tilted his head to admire the brands that marked Beast's past victories. The purebred kept his gaze straight, as if Naelar's intrusion into his personal space didn't bother him at all.

"He inspires people to stand up and fight for the Zarall name. Clever."

"And I need the arenas to remain closed for that," Lygor said. "People won't lift a finger if they're subdued with entertainment. I need them bored."

"Kastian will give my arenas to his loyalists and keep them running to subdue the crowds as soon as he catches on what you're planning."

"He could try, but let's be honest, running an arena is not an easy task. So many things could go wrong without the Union's and the Master of Sands' oversight. Imagine the public's reaction if they were to find out the fights were fixed or beasts were poisoned."

Ruzen rubbed his chin, mulling over the implication. As the Master of the Sands, he had the connections at every arena to make those things happen. And for arena goers, there was nothing more outrageous than a fixed battle.

"It's a dangerous move," Naelar said. He stepped to the side and picked at an old arrow wound on Beast's left bicep. Valnar couldn't help but admire the purebred's self-control. "If you remind someone what they are capable of, you can't take that knowledge back." He leaned closer and narrowed his eyes at the intricate design on Beast's tattoo. "That's why we have Words. But you will not have that kind of control over the people once you wake them up."

"That will be my concern, not yours."

Naelar stepped back and after sending one last assessing glance at Beast, he walked over to his seat. "Is that all you ask from the Union?"

Lygor examined his wine glass as he spoke casually. "I want a hundred pure-breds from Master Vadithas. Beasts. Master Naelar will donate ten thousand Blues to my cause. And I believe Casters Board of Chinderia have mages at every lord's court. I want their intel." He glanced at Kyrophe. "I'm not sure what White Tower has to offer?"

"My vote." Kyrophe crossed her arms. "The Union does not take action unless there's unanimity."

"Right." Lygor sipped his wine as he studied the Union leaders' faces. Vadithas was frowning. Naelar leaned back, scratching his chin and looking at the ceiling, thinking. Ruzen took his head between his hands.

"I like a customer who knows what they want," Naelar said. "I like them even more if they also know how to pay."

"Your request is a significant one, Your Highness," Vadithas said cautiously. "What are you offering in return?"

Lygor smirked. "Well, let's negotiate."

What followed was anything but cordial. Lygor and Ink fought nail and teeth, each exchange ruthless and each word sharpened to cut.

Ruzen asked for tax-free entry fees to the arenas and the cities to give up on their cuts from registration fees of contestants. He also demanded illegal arenas to be tracked and shut down. Ink convinced him to accept the terms for tax-free entries only for five years, starting after Lygor's coronation. And Lygor promised enslavement as the punishment for operating illegal arenas, and agreed to reward whoever reported these establishments to the authorities.

As Lygor predicted, Vadithas pressed for financial aid to slave ranches and pushed back hard against Lygor's counteroffer of removing land taxes for five years. Oddly, Naelar put in a few words on Lygor's behalf, pointing out how much money that would save them in five years, and how easily the ranches could expand and grow.

By the time it was Naelar's turn to make his demands, both Lygor and Ink were already exhausted.

Naelar drummed his fingers at the table. He gazed at the far corner of the room, nodding to himself. He smiled. "I want you to legalise cannibalism."

Lygor couldn't hide his flinch. Ink's jaw dropped. Even the other Union leaders turned to stare at their colleague.

"Excuse me?" Ink asked.

"Legalise the consumption of human flesh in Chinderia," Naelar said, drawing each word out as if speaking to a child.

Lygor still stared at the man, his eyes narrowed to slits. Ink took a sip from his glass and regained his composure. "Why?"

Naelar turned to Vadithas. "How many years does it take to raise a good purebred beast?"

"Minimum fourteen, though sixteen would give them better chances in the arenas."

"Let's say, fourteen years of hard work. The average price for a purebred beast in the market is two-hundred Blues. What happens when that beast goes out for their first fight, and endures a permanent injury?"

Ink glared at the man, breathing through his nose. Lygor was still quiet. Naelar continued: "All that hard work and investment is lost."

"All the reasons to take good care of those fighters," Ink sneered.

Naelar raised an eyebrow at Ink's choice of words, but didn't comment on it. "Right now," he said, "the only buyers of damaged slaves are Tribesmen beyond the northern borders and Veiled Houses. They are fully aware of the fact that they can force whatever price they want to pay. Besides, the Veiled Houses only want the pretty ones, not the grossly disfigured ones. I don't care about temporary tax benefits, Your Highness. Open up another market for the slave merchants, so they can make up for their losses."

Lygor connected his hands on the table. His voice grew cold when he spoke. "Chinderia follows The Twelve's light," he said. "And the Twelve Riders forbid cannibalism. Even if I do permit that, you will not find a market for it in Chinderia. People will refuse to consume human flesh and the Chambers of Twelve will stand against it."

Valnar swelled with pride when Lygor spoke of The Twelve's teachings. What that man suggested was blasphemy. It was obnoxious. The idea made Valnar sick. He could see it in both Lygor's and Ink's expressions. Even Ziuw seemed uncomfortable. This was out of line.

Naelar rolled his eyes at the mention of the religion. "What did The Twelve Riders do for you, Prince Lygor? Did the Pyrearch even reprimand Kastian's treason? Murdering a beloved king in his sleep? Besides," Naelar smirked, "public wasn't the market I had in mind." He turned to look at Vadithas.

Despite the war paint, Ink looked pale, almost sick. He shook his head, eyes narrowed in revulsion. "This is disgusting."

"Since the ranches are not getting any financial aid other than waiving the land taxes for a bit," Naelar said, "they would benefit from cheaper, alternative sources. And my merchants would have a way of recovering from their losses on damaged slaves. Prince Lygor gets Union's support, and everybody wins."

Vadithas nodded. "Meat is meat. Ranches will buy it."

Ink looked away.

"This is blasphemy," Valnar blurted. "Consuming human flesh is a sin, and forcing other humans to do it is no different."

"Technically," said Ziuw, "Chinderian law defines slaves as property, not human. In that sense, they're not much different from livestock animals."

"And the Pyres preach that slaves don't have *rhoas*," Naelar added. "If they don't have *rhoas*, how can we regard them as human?"

"This is wrong!"

"Why? Are you suggesting they're humans?"

"No—"

"Then what is your problem?"

"Master Naelar," Lygor spoke. "If you commit a crime tomorrow, Chinderian law can enslave you. And if you happen to break your arm, you can be the one who'll end up in a slaughterhouse. I want you all to think about this carefully before answering. Is this really what you're asking for?"

Naelar erased his smile, turned his gaze to the ceiling, and appeared to consider deeply. He met Lygor's gaze and pursed his lips. "I've always been at peace with the possibility of ending up as a slave."

"It'll inspire people to be law-abiding, good citizens," Ruzen joined in. "They'll be less likely to commit crimes, like opening illegal arenas."

Lygor gritted his teeth. He sighed. "Twelve guide my *rhoa*. I will permit it... under strict restrictions!"

A strangled sound escaped Valnar before he could stop it. He stared at Lygor in disbelief — Lygor, who had once sat beside him, studying and memorising all twelve passages; who had prayed with him time and time again after his family's murder. Prince Lygor, a man blessed by Kiejain's sword and strength in every battle, a loyal son of the Twelve Riders. And yet here he was, standing among those who mocked their teachings, permitting them to spit on Twelve's faces.

Naelar swallowed a smirk. "What kind of restrictions?"

"Any *facilities* will require a permit signed by me before they can open," Lygor said firmly.

Naelar chewed his lips, considering. "And your requirements for signing those permits?"

"Will be subject to further negotiations."

Tension filled the space between Naelar and Lygor as they locked eyes. Lygor's features might have been carved from stone. Naelar met his stare, amusement dancing at the edges of his scrutiny as he weighed and measured the prince. Finally, his mouth curved into a knowing smile. "As you wish, Prince Lygor."

Lygor turned his attention to Kyrophe. "And what does the White Tower want, Mistress Kyrophe?"

The woman's motherly smile deepened the lines on her face. She spoke in her monotonous voice: "Nothing."

"Nothing?" Ink, still looking sick from the last demand, ground his jaw. "What does that mean?"

Kyrophe's eyebrows drew closer in an apologetic grimace. "White Tower will not support Prince Lygor's cause."

"Why not?" Lygor asked calmly.

"Prince Lygor," Kyrophe bluntly. "Your plan is absurd."

"Excuse me?"

She gestured at Beast. "There is a reason Lion of Zarall was sentenced to White Tower. It had engaged in multiple Acts of Defiance. It disobeyed and publicly humiliated its Owner. It attacked and killed free men. It is rabid and severely broken."

"She's right," Ruzen said. "I saw him at Switchblade that day. He acted like a freeborn brat who was enslaved yesterday."

"And all your plans rely on it," Kyrophe continued. "What if it disobeys you too?"

"He won't," Lygor sneered.

"Also, there's the possibility of it *losing* Twilight of Infinity. King Kastian can buy the best beasts in the country. What if Lion of Zarall can't win? Then what?"

"He'll win."

"How can you be sure?"

"Because he's bloody good," Ink answered in Lygor's place.

"I can see you truly trust in its ability to fight, but that is not enough for me."

"What if we tested him?" Naelar blurted. He leaned forward, his hand on his chin.

"Test him? He already won five tournaments," Lygor said. "I don't think he needs to prove himself."

Naelar turned to Kyrophe. "If you were to see him fight first hand, would it convince you to believe he could win Twilight of Infinity."

"If I saw it fight with my own eyes — assuming it won — then yes, it would convince me of its ability to fight."

"Master Ruzen," Naelar continued. "I believe there's a fight coming up right here in Scorchline Arena?"

"Fire Breath," Ruzen said straightaway. "A Trial. About two weeks away."

"That's the one. How about we get Lion of Zarall to win Fire Breath?"

"I'm reluctant to display him to the public before Twilight of Infinity," Lygor objected. "I don't want any premature attention."

"Oh, that wouldn't be any problem," Vadithas swatted his hand. "If he wins Fire Breath, we'll convince our dear Lord Brocton of Calae to pledge his loyalty to you and we'll coronate you here. We'll announce the people of your return and of Lion of Zarall's victory."

"I'm not sure if that would be a smart move," Ink said. "The city lord has been a firm supporter of Kastian. His loyalties are unreliable. Besides, as soon as Kastian hears Prince Lygor is alive and well, he'll come after him."

"By the time Kastian or his puppets get to Calae, you'll be on your way to Euroad, along with Lord Brocton's six hundred men. And Master Vadithas's hundred purebreds as your personal security."

Lygor leaned back in his chair, rubbing his chin thoughtfully. His eyes were scanning the table, as if seeing things that were not there.

"It's risky," Ink said.

"Look at it this way, Prince Ingelhar," Naelar said. "If Lion doesn't win Fire Breath, that means he doesn't have what it takes to win Twilight of Infinity, anyway. We might as well find out now, before fully committing to this plan."

"And if he can't win Fire Breath," Vadithas continued, "we'll make sure you get out of the city safely. Lord Brocton — and King Kastian — will know nothing about Prince Lygor's visit here."

Lygor leaned back. His gaze slid casually toward Beast. Beneath that indifference lay a desperate search for confirmation. The purebred remained perfectly still, not a muscle twitching — yet somehow that very stillness made Lygor's mouth curve into a confident smile, as if he'd read volumes in that absolute silence.

"He'll come through," he said, his voice carrying the quiet certainty of a man who had just confirmed his winning hand.

"Excellent."

"Will his victory win White Tower's vote?" Ink asked.

"No," Kyrophe said calmly.

"But you just said—"

"I said it would convince me of its ability to fight. It still would not prove its obedience."

"Then we've wasted our time here," Lygor bit out.

Naelar made a subtle gesture, drawing their attention like a sergeant silencing a bunch of fresh recruits. His expression shifted into something contemplative, almost calculating, as he held Lygor's gaze. He let the silence stretch, watching Lygor's irritation gradually transform into reluctant anticipation.

Finally, Naelar released a measured sigh. "What if we retrained him?"

Beast's muscles tensed imperceptibly, the slightest ripple beneath his skin betraying his attention.

"What exactly do you mean by that?" Ink's voice carried an edge.

Naelar turned to Vadithas. "Could you do it?"

"Yes, of course," Vadithas responded. "I have the facilities."

"Could you do it overnight?"

"Depends on how broken he is."

Ink didn't repeat his question, but his jaw ticked, and his eyes darkened beneath the jagged streaks of war paint.

"He doesn't need retraining," Lygor said. "He'll do as he's told."

"How certain are you?" Naelar countered smoothly. "Certain enough to stake your throne on his temperament?"

Lygor huffed a dry, humourless sound, too baffled to give the question anything more than that. "I have full control over him."

"Full control, is it? Tell me, Prince Lygor, with full honesty. Over the time you've had him, have you ever feared him?"

"I have his Words."

"That's not what I asked, Your Highness."

A muscle jumped in Lygor's cheek. The line of his mouth flattened before he spoke, each word deliberate. "No, Master Naelar. I do not fear a slave."

"Have you ever given him an order and wondered what if — just what if — he didn't follow?"

Valnar said nothing, but his throat tightened. He had wondered that — Kiejain knew he did.

Lygor's face was a mask of sharp lines and frozen fury. His voice was controlled, but cold and edged with threat.

"If he didn't, he knows well what will happen. Besides, he's proven his loyalty to me—" Lygor snapped his mouth shut, as if realising he'd just said something stupid.

Naeler smirked as he mouthed the word, *"Loyalty?"*

"He's a purebred," Vadithas said. "You shouldn't need his loyalty."

"You've seen it too, haven't you?" Naelar pressed. "Those moments when his obedience slips. When something feral stirs behind his eyes. Those moments when you question."

Lygor said nothing. The heat in his glare could've scorched glass. He looked away, feigning interest in the flickering candlelight on the shelf across the room.

Valnar stared at the purebred's rigid back. He'd breathed that doubt with every inhale since they bought Beast. Too often, Beast had obeyed like a man indulging Valnar's orders, not submitting to them.

"It crossed your mind, hasn't it?" Naelar leaned closer. "Prince Lygor, you hold a fine blade — but it's dented, split down the middle. This is your chance to have it reforged, sharpened. Then you'll never need to rely on loyalty or goodwill. Let Master Vadithas retrain him. It'll ease our minds, and strengthen both your plan and our alliance."

"What would this retraining involve?" Ink cut in, voice sharp with barely contained anger. The streaks of war paint across his face made the fury in his eyes all the more striking — like a masked predator ready to bite.

"Just a brief refresher on the basics of obedience," Vadithas said dismissively. "Acts of Defiance and sorts. Some work around inhibition, pruning avoidance, and instructive control."

"You'll break him down to rebuild him," Ink sneered. "He doesn't deserve this."

"It's not about what he deserves, Your Highness. It's about what he delivers." Naelar splayed his palms on the table. "Admit it, Prince Lygor. You had doubts about him. I can see it on your face."

Lygor's eyes flickered involuntarily to Beast's hands. Clasped in front of him, Beast's hands were perfectly still. They hadn't trembled since the day of the ambush. Maybe Ink had been right. Maybe the shakes were just the result of a minor damage to his hand, which had since healed itself. But Valnar knew Lygor had been troubled about it.

"If you're worried about his discipline, I'm sure we can find other ways to prove it to you," Ink said.

"What about I prove to you how broken he really is?" Naelar's focus settled on Beast, his posture shifting ever so slightly, the way a man might adjust his grip on a dagger before plunging it in. "He's about three seconds from giving me a death stare. Isn't that right, you worthless mutt pretending to be a man? Shall we ask Master Ruzen how long it took to thoroughly clean that launch room at the Switchblade Arena?"

Beast's control cracked.

His hands clenched into fists at his sides, eyes burning as they met Naelar's. The hatred was tainted with a hollow pain that Valnar only caught the tremor of it. He felt a chill, not even wanting to guess what Naelar had implied.

The realisation of what he'd just done struck Beast. His gaze darted to Lygor, to Ink, to the other Union members watching. His shoulders tightened, lips drawn back over gritted teeth like a wild animal realising the cage was closing.

When his eyes found Lygor again, there was a desperate warning in them, masked as a plea. Lygor looked away.

"Do you truly feel safe now?" Naelar asked softly. "With that anger barely contained beneath the surface?"

"I can guarantee you, Master Naelar," Ink growled, "his anger is contained much better than mine at this moment."

"I agree with Master Naelar," Ruzen said. "He needs to be retrained. Master Vadithas is the best slave breeder. He'll know how to fix him."

Beast clenched and relaxed his fists, breathing deeply, trying to stay in control.

"White Tower will not support Prince Lygor's cause until the slave is retrained."

"I promise no permanent damage will be done, Your Highness, if that's what you are worried about. Maybe some cuts and bruises, that's all. He'll be ready for the Fire Breath."

"Purebreds go through this all the time, Your Highness. He'll function much better."

"I'm afraid the union will stand firm on this subject, Prince Lygor. There's nothing more dangerous than a purebred who has committed defiance."

"Lygor has been generous enough with you. There must be another way to prove his reliability."

Valnar noticed something that made his stomach sink. Lygor hadn't spoken the last few minutes, retreated into himself. He sat rigid, one elbow cradled in his palm, hand pressed against his mouth, staring fixedly at some distant corner as if it held answers. Valnar recognised that pose — it was Lygor's tell when he wanted to pull out of the conversation.

The Union leaders had cornered him badly. They had tired him with heavy demands and long negotiations, like wearing down a warrior with testing attacks and drawing out the fight. Then, they'd forced him to agree to something that was against his values, and the Twelve's teachings, not to mention it was disturbing and disgusting, no matter how they worded it. They had forced him to take the risk of an early coronation, as well as risking Beast's neck before Twilight of Infinity. He didn't want to give in more than he already did.

But he'd come a long way to drop everything now.

And, for a slave…

Valnar's chest tightened with sudden clarity. When they first walked into this room, he didn't think he could aid him at that table, but maybe he had been wrong. This was his chance — not to fight, but to shield Lygor from this decision that would hurt him dearly. To step between him and this cruel choice, that would haunt him for countless sleepless nights.

He stepped forward, drawing breath to speak. "I'm afraid Prince Lygor can't make this decision."

All the eyes turned to Valnar, except Beast's and Lygor's. Beast tensed, but didn't pull his gaze off the prince. Lygor continued looking at the far corner, his eyes focusing on nothing in particular.

"I am the Owner of the slave."

"You are?"

"We had to keep Prince Lygor's identity hidden. My name is on his sales paper."

"So, Prince Lygor doesn't even *own* Lion of Zarall, and yet he's so confident the slave will obey him."

"I will transfer the slave's ownership to him when my prince deems it safe to do so."

"Well, that doesn't change the Union's position. The slave still needs to be retrained."

Valnar flicked a glance toward Lygor, searching for anything: a shake of his head, a glance, the smallest sign telling him to stop. But Lygor kept his eyes averted, his expression carefully neutral, refusing to meet anyone's gaze.

That was answer enough.

"I trust he will be unharmed?"

Beast's head snapped toward Valnar, his breath sharp as if the words had struck him physically. His expression flickered between fury and something raw. He looked at Lygor again, begging for help.

The prince sat facing away, his posture perfectly at ease, as if he hadn't heard it. As if he hadn't felt the weight of the sacrifice.

"Nothing he can't physically recover from," Vadithas said. "I despise inflicting any permanent injury to an expensive purebred."

"You have time until sunrise," Valnar said.

He felt sick.

Vadithas pursed his lips. "It'll have to do. Well then, let me accommodate you all at my manor until the Fire Breath. This is the safest place in the whole city."

"Tell me, Your Highness," Naelar said, his voice velvet-soft but merciless, "if you would feel safe being alone with him right now. Tell me you don't fear him."

Lygor's chair scraped the floor, the sound a sharp, slicing intrusion on the silence as he rose. Without a word, he strode from the room, leaving a vacuum in his wake that seemed to pull the other Union leaders to their feet.

Beast moved to follow, but Valnar was already there, filling the doorway. They faced each other across the empty space, Beast's eyes bright with betrayal, Valnar's stance unyielding.

"Umm..." Ziuw raised his hand like a child asking for permission to speak. "How about Casters Board of Chinderia? I'm... I'm voting on behalf of Adept Kato and the Casters Board. I... I demand benefits for all Chinderian mages."

No one but the crackling tension responded him. Ziuv glanced at Beast and paled, realising the meeting was truly over and he was about to be left behind. He gathered his things. "I guess we can discuss our terms later," he muttered as he joined the others.

The Union leaders filed out, leaving Beast and Valnar locked in their silent confrontation. Beast's expression had transformed into something bleeding and wounded, as if Valnar's blockade of the door was a physical blow.

Ink remained seated for several long moments, seemingly deflated.

Vadithas paused at the threshold. "I'll send someone to collect him," he said quietly, then disappeared into the corridor.

Finally, Ink rose. The warrior paint on his face couldn't mask his shame. He slipped past Valnar without a word.

Valnar and Beast remained alone in the study that suddenly felt too large and too small all at once.

"Let me talk to him."

Valnar shook his head. "I can't let you do that."

"Let me talk to Lygor." Beast's voice wavered with an edge of despair. "I know he'll change his mind."

"He needs this alliance. This is his only chance. I won't let you risk everything."

Beast's eyes darted around the study, taking in the mahogany-panelled walls, the placement of the heavy furniture, the width of the doorway, and the windows. Valnar became aware of the secure tightness of his armour's straps, the reassuring press of steel against his hip.

"He can't... He doesn't... He wouldn't do this..." The words tumbled out of Beast's mouth. His eyes moving rapidly around the room, without focusing on anything.

"Give me the sword," Valnar ordered

Beast stiffened, at the same time Valnar realised his mistake. He shouldn't have mentioned the sword.

Beast's hand drifted to the hilt, his breath coming faster.

"Don't make this harder, Beast. Give me the sword." Valnar shifted his stance, his steel boots loud against the dark wooden floorboards. Sweat trickled down his back. He avoided making a sudden movement. He reached for the sword calmly and confidently.

Beast retreated.

He built space between them, his fingers wrapped around the weapon. His eyes blazed with defiance even as despair crept in. They both knew how this would end. That knowledge seemed to break something in Beast.

Footsteps approached from the corridor, accompanied by the distinctive rattle of chains.

"Valnar, don't do this."

Valnar met his gaze, his resolve warring with regret.

"Please. Valnar…" A broken whisper. "Please don't do this."

Vadithas's men entered. Their plain, pale uniforms were a stark contrast to the study's opulent décor. They carried no weapons, only chains with cruel-looking hooks and clasps that seemed designed for something less than human.

"We're here to collect the purebred."

Beast and Valnar locked eyes one final time. Beast's knuckles whitened on his sword hilt. It was final as the Twelve's wings on a clear sky, what would happen if he drew that sword.

Beast did it anyway.

He pulled the sword like a condemned man charging into the battlefield, knowing he won't see another sunrise.

"*Padlociatius.*"

One of Vadithas's men kicked the sword off Beast's limp fingers. They stripped away his mantle and vest before wrenching his paralysed arms behind his back. The chains went on — wrists, arms, legs, and finally a muzzle that made Valnar's stomach turn. They'd come prepared, knowing exactly who they were dealing with.

His paralysis started to lift, a muffled groan escaping as he was dragged away. The sound of chains echoed down the corridor.

Valnar stood there until he couldn't hear the subdued scuffle anymore. Then, he picked up the fallen sword — the same one he'd given Beast the day he'd saved Lygor's life. He left the room like escaping a sin.

37

BEAST

He told himself it was just the cold. The dungeons beneath the manor were a tomb of damp stone and stale air, where rot and decay hung thick in every breath. The chill had already frozen his bones.

They'd stripped him naked and forced him to his knees in the centre of the room, securing him to the stone floor with heavy chains at wrists and ankles. The metal muzzle they'd crammed between his teeth prevented him from closing his mouth. Spit ran down his trimmed beard and he couldn't stop it.

He knew his body would betray him in far worse ways over the hours to come.

The trembling would grow until his muscles screamed. His breathing would turn to desperate, animal pants, each one carrying a whimper he couldn't swallow past the knot in his throat.

And through it all, one image would replay endlessly in his mind: Lygor's back as he walked out of that study

The men had left after their preparations, leaving Beast alone to await Master Vadithas. Though windowless, the room blazed with light. Five full-length mirrors were placed around him in a perfect ring, with dozens of candles scattered between them, creating an island of light. Everything beyond the mirrors were obscured by shadows that reminded Beast of Keder, while the space within burned bright and inescapable. It was as if this circle of light was all that remained on Earthome — an arena set to display whatever horrors awaited him, every moment to be witnessed in merciless clarity.

Beast chose not to look into the shadows lurking beyond the mirrors. He already knew what waited there. Tables full of torture devices, chains, equipment, mechanisms. His stomach twisted into a knot. He was experienced enough to understand waiting was part of the torture. The dreading. The knowing but not knowing.

Waiting made his thoughts drift into endless dark possibilities. He might have thought this anticipation was the worst part, if he didn't know with certainty that the reality would far exceed his darkest imaginings.

He kept his eyes on the stone floor beneath him. Smooth grey surface, utterly featureless — no cracks or dust to distract his racing mind. The dark colour transported him back to the rug.

The rug...

Every detail of that rug surfaced with devastating clarity. The short, stiff threads. The worn corner where countless hands had scuffed the fabric. The small hole near the edge that had grown year by year, picked at by dozens of small, nervous fingers.

He had gone years without thinking about that rug, but every tiny detail was etched into his earliest memories, stored securely, and now poured into his mind with such precision. He could feel the rough threads against his bare skin, smell that distinct odour — if dread had a scent, it lived in that rug, breathed in by dozens of purebred children as they lay curled on it, crying, sweating, shivering, desperately trying to maintain their silence.

He didn't want to look at the shadows, but he couldn't keep staring at the floor, either. That damned grey stone kept dragging him back to the rug. Glancing into the mirrors only showed him how utterly fucked his situation was. So, he closed his eyes, which didn't help either, because now his thoughts returned to Lygor and his silent betrayal.

He hadn't stopped them. He was allowing this to happen. He was actually going through with it. Valnar's claims about being the Owner were bullshit — everyone knew Lygor called the shots.

He could have stopped this.

He blinked, his gaze darting everywhere and nowhere at once. He almost wished Vadithas would just get this over with. He could survive this. He could get through this, and claw his way through to the other side, just as he had countless times before. He knew how to do it. After all, he'd spent the first fourteen years of his life in workshops just like this one.

He inhaled deeply, then regulated his breathing. His eyes searched for a focus, finally settling on the chain links binding him. He fixed his attention there as he muttered the words that had soothed him for years.

"It's not my body, it's their property. It's not my body..."

Slowly, he pushed his mind to *that place*. The dark, safe corner where he could crawl into and hide. It took longer than usual, but with each repetition, the words pulled him further from his body, untethering him from the weight of the moment. He abandoned that trembling, pathetic thing behind in that cold, bright room. Whatever happened to that body — *not his body* — wouldn't matter. He would be safe in *that place*, waiting for it to be over.

You know, that phrase was devised to strip you of your humanity. Yet, remarkably, they bring you solace instead. You have forged them into your own instrument.

Keder's voice drew him back into the room. Beast refocused on the links and pushed himself away again.

Let us return to that rug thing, Keder mused. *That occurred at Faychill Ranch, did it not? How old were you when you first slept on that rug? Eight or ten, perhaps?*

"It's not my body, it's their property," Beast whispered. His voice pressed against the muzzle, muffled and thick, the sound echoing into his ears in the cold silence.

Oh, that's right. You didn't sleep *when it was your turn there. You never did.*

Beast shrunk, just as he had on that rug countless times, tucking his arms and legs close to keep from spilling over its edges. His fingers would pick at the stiffened threads, tracing the frayed hole for hours, eyes unblinking in the dark. The steady rhythm of Astaldo's snores was a fragile shield. He would dread the moment the sound would cease. Every breath he took was thick with the stench of tobacco and booze, clinging to his skin, sinking into his lungs.

Beast reached for *that place* again, but found Keder still waiting there.

It is one of those places you will never get back to, but you will never quite leave.

"If you're expecting this will break me and convince me to release you, you're wrong," Beast said through the muzzle.

Oh, no. I know you shall endure this. I have utmost faith in you.

"But you'll be here to make it harder, won't you?"

Keder made a thoughtful noise. *I see no need, truly. This Vadithas... Is he not the Master of All Breeders? If Breeder Astaldo excelled in his craft, I can only assume the Master of All Breeders surpasses him in every regard. Would you not agree?*

Beast pressed his forehead against the stone floor. Bile rose in his throat.

But I know you shall survive. And I know you will not release me. Not yet. Because you still harbour hope.

Beast drew in long breaths, pushing the air as deep as he could, trying to settle his stomach.

You still hold faith that Lygor will indeed honour his promise of freedom. You can trust him, can you not?

"He needs me," Beast whispered. "He needs me to win Twilight. Be free."

Right. I cannot wait to see how that will fare.

His stomach churned, the unease tainted by a flicker of irritation.

Oh, it begins, Keder whispered excitedly. *I'll be right here. This shall be entertaining to watch.*

Beast lifted his head and startled when he caught the sight of Vadithas emerging from the shadows. His tall, lean frame was draped in luxurious silk that barely rustled as he moved. His face was a gaunt mask of high cheekbones and hollow eyes that were invasive. A ledger rested under one arm, lending him the air of a refined man on his way to a meeting.

Not a predator ready to tear a man apart.

The cuffs bit into Beast's skin as he shuffled backward. How long had the man been watching from the shadows?

"Speaking without permission," Vadithas spoke in his calm, musical voice. He opened the ledger and started scribbling. "I've already noticed the eye contact before." He waved a hand towards Beast. "And I see your inhibition is frayed too. We'll see to all of that."

Something cold and dark sat in Beast's chest, strong enough to blur his vision. He turned his head down, not to feign obedience, but to rob Vadithas of the satisfaction of witnessing his fear. Fixing his eyes on the chain, he repeated the words in his mind, seeking his escape. He could survive this, if he could just slip from his body.

"Lion of Zarall," Vadithas purred as he strode around him. "Ever since I've heard of what you've done at Switchblade, I dreamed of having you here in my workshop, but never truly believed I could. You can't imagine how grateful I am to Naelar, for giving me this opportunity."

It's not my body, it's their property, Beast repeated in his head. *It's not my body...*

Beast's shoulders relaxed, his head feeling heavier. He reached toward that familiar void — the place where thought and feeling ceased to exist. But the emptiness kept slipping from his grasp.

Vadithas set his ledger on the floor and crouched beside him. His fingers tangled in his hair while his other hand gripped beneath his chin. As the man examined his face and checked his pulse, something primal stirred within Beast. A feral growl built in his throat as he thrashed against his restraints, forcing Vadithas to retreat. Though Beast could barely raise his hands from the stone floor, and the muzzle kept him from biting, the threat of violence was enough to make Vadithas keep a cautious distance.

Retrieving his ledger, Vadithas clicked his tongue disapprovingly as he wrote, muttering aloud, "Reactive affect. Aggressive and noncooperative."

"Fuck you," Beast growled through the muzzle.

Vadithas raised an eyebrow, then pursed his lips and scribbled some more.

Beast drew in a ragged breath, trying to reign over the anger that had suddenly taken over from fear. He wasn't being smart. He should have kept his head down and sunk into that void until this was over and he was out of this place. Just one night. That's what Vadithas had told Valnar. By morning, he would be free of this place. He only needed to endure these next few hours.

But when Vadithas reached for him again, all Beast's careful self-coaching shattered. Fury surged back through him like a flood, yet this time Vadithas was prepared. His grip was iron-strong as he roughly wrenched Beast's head to the side, keeping himself well beyond reach while he studied his tattoo.

"*Prihjtivaviula.*"

Agony crashed through Beast's body. He fought against it, forcing first one breath, then another into his lungs. Summoning what remained of his strength, he pushed himself up from the cold stone, trembling as he rose to his hands and knees.

How the fuck did he know his Pain Word? Had Valnar given it to him?

"Interesting," Vadithas said, crouching at a safe distance, chin resting in his palm. "I've heard mages hypothesise about *Myrrak'thael Bond* weakening in some cases, but never really witnessed it. Very curious indeed." He recorded his thoughts on his ledger as he spoke.

He waited until the last tremors of pain subsided. Fury erupted through Beast's body, drowning out his desperate attempts to cling to reason and self-control. Escape into numbness remained his best option — his only option — yet instead, he hurled himself against the chains with a feral howl, blood welling from his wrists where the cuffs bit deep. But the restraints held fast.

Leaving his ledger behind, Vadithas stepped into the shadows briefly, and returned with an object. Beast's stomach clenched as he strained to see it better.

An hourglass.

Before Beast could even wonder why the fuck the man had an hourglass, Vadithas inverted it and spoke a single word: "*Padlociatius.*"

Beast crumbled in a heap of flesh. From where he lay — helpless, defenceless, naked before this ruthless man who regarded him like a specimen to dissect — Beast could only watch the hourglass.

Mercifully, Vadithas maintained his distance. He observed from where he sat, his charcoal pen poised over the ledger, gaze shifting between Beast and the flowing sand, waiting.

When Beast's fingers began to twitch, Vadithas reached out and stopped the hourglass. Sand still remained in the upper chamber.

"Interesting," Vadithas repeated. He recorded his observations in the ledger. "You wouldn't happen to be helpful and tell me exactly when your Words started being less effective?"

Less effective? Beast pushed himself up onto his elbows and knees. His Words felt anything but less effective. He just glared at the man.

"Didn't think so." Vadithas shut his ledger closed. "Alright, let's get to it then."

He scooped the hourglass and the ledger and walked into the shadows. Beast's ears caught the soft whisper of leather and metal, followed by the slow, methodical scrape of something moving overhead. The sound was accompanied by the gentle clink of chains.

When the mechanism emerged into the candlelight, Beast's breath caught in his throat. A complex arrangement of leather straps and metal rings hung from a track in the ceiling, its chains gleaming dully in the flickering light. The apparatus swayed slightly as Vadithas guided it forward. It was designed to suspend and position a body in whatever way its user desired.

"No," Beast sputtered. "No—"

"*Padlociatius.*"

Vadithas spent the next few minutes repeating his First Word as he unlocked his chains, then turned him facedown and pulled his arms and legs through the straps. He moved his arms back, pulled his legs through a series of straps and hoops that kept his knees bent and feet pointing away.

"I'm usually not this chatty with purebreds," Vadithas said as he worked. "But I'm going to adapt a more verbal approach with you. I'll treat you like a freeborn."

He looped a serrated string around his neck, pulled it back across his body, and tied the other end to his toes. A low creak trembled through the chains as Vadithas adjusted the tension, ensuring the bindings held firm.

Vadithas stepped into the shadows as Beast's paralysis faded. The sound of a lever and cogs echoed, and his stomach lurched as he was slowly lifted off the ground.

The leather straps tightened and almost immediately, his own weight became a painful pressure on his arms, shoulders, and elbows. Some of his weight was transferred to the straps that went under his stomach, which dug painfully beneath his ribs. He had to keep his toes facing up, to ease the string from strangling him, or tilt his neck all the way back to keep the muscles on his calves and feet from cramping.

He howled and screamed, but didn't thrash. Any sudden movement would only sharpen the pain. Suspended in the air, his body turned in a slow, weightless rotation. The room shifted around him, until Vadithas's face slid into view, watching.

"I'm unfortunately limited by my promise to Prince Lygor. I'll have to avoid causing you any permanent injuries, so we'll start with something small."

Beast frothed, spat, then squeezed his eyes shut. This was it. It was time to escape.

He steadied his breathing, forcing his body into stillness, slowing his heartbeat. His mind reached for *that place*, repeating the words like a prayer: *It's not my body. It's not my body.*

Wood scraped against stone, the low rumble of tables being dragged. He knew what Vadithas was doing. He was arranging tables full of torture instruments around him. Beast didn't need to see them.

He was slipping. Slipping into that place where pain, fear — and even anger — couldn't reach him. Everything dulled. The glow of the lamps, the ache in his limbs, the weight of the straps biting into his skin. Even Vadithas's voice, smooth and melodic, felt far away, as though it belonged to someone speaking from the other side of a door.

"You're one of Astaldo's," Vadithas said. A soft clink, a rustle of dry leaves, and the pop of a jar lid accompanied his words. "Breeder Astaldo is one of the best. He raises exquisite purebreds. Remarkable work, truly."

Beast kept his eyes closed. *Not my body. Not my* fucking *body...*

"There is only one thing I criticise about his work, though."

An herbal smell filled the air. Sound of a match being lit, followed by smoke. The herbal scent became stronger.

"He teaches you that stupid phrase. How does it go? *It's not my body, it's their property?*"

Beast's eyes flew open.

Against his will, he took in the torture instruments he knew would be there. His stomach heaved. He forced himself to look away. That's when he spotted the wooden bowl in Vadithas's hands. A small flame lit the contents in it, which Vadithas swiftly blew out. He pulled a cloth over it, trapping the smoke underneath.

He turned from the table and scowled at Beast. "I understand what Breeder Astaldo intends to teach. I really do. The only problem is, that method also teaches the slave to dissociate from their body."

Beast regarded the bowl as if it was more dangerous than any other gruesome device displayed on the table.

"It allows you to escape from the experience. But if you're not here in the present, how are you going to learn?"

When Vadithas moved, Beast couldn't help but strain against the straps. The pressure lit his muscles and joints on fire. Vadithas brought the bowl under Beast's mouth and pulled the cloth back, letting the smoke rise and fill his nostrils. Beast held his breath, but the smoke overwhelmed him, filtered in through everywhere.

"I want you to forget about that phrase."

Beast coughed and hacked. The smoke tickled the back of his throat. He blinked, trying to clear his eyes. Something was wrong with his vision.

"Tonight, it *is* your body. All yours."

No, not just his vision. All his senses. It felt as if he'd been blind his whole life, and just gained the ability to see. He'd been deaf all this time, and had just received a pair of ears. All his senses were heightened, overstimulated. His body was fully awake. Aware.

"Everything I'll do to you, you'll be right here to fully experience it."

His scream was muffled, yet the sound tore at his eardrums. He closed his eyes, but it only heightened his other senses. He desperately searched for *that place* in his mind. His heart pounded, his breath hitched, and his thoughts scattered uncontrollably.

"Tonight, there is no escaping."

Stepping back, Vadithas tossed the bowl onto the table.

"Fuck you," Beast sputtered. The string burned his neck when he spoke. His skin was on fire. Even the parts where nothing but the cold air touched hurt. "I'm going to kill you."

"Let's start with relearning Acts of Defiance."

"I will fucking kill you."

"Can you repeat me the first one?"

Beast looked him right in the eyes. "I swear on sand and blood, I swear on fucking darkness; I will rip your face off." The muzzle warped his words into a garbled snarl, but Vadithas listened with quiet amusement, as if indulging the ramblings of a caged animal. "I'll break your skull and tear your tongue out of your throat. I'll cut your balls and jam them in your guts."

"When I speak your Pain Word, you shouldn't break anything. Shouldn't."

He walked around him, touching the straps and chains that held him, checking their firmness. His voice was a smooth irritation that set his teeth on edge. From this close, the cloying scent of fragrant oils clung to the air — thick, sickly sweet, as if he had bathed in it.

"I'm fairly certain I've given this enough range to distribute the pressure evenly. Of course, it'll still be agonising when you spasm, but with any luck, no bones will snap."

Beast swallowed down a whimper. Vadithas stopped in front of him and held his gaze.

"First Act of Defiance, you will not make eye contact."

Beast didn't look away.

One night. Just a few hours. He would live through this.

Just one night.

"*Prihjtivaviula.*"

38

VALNAR

VALNAR TOOK HIS CLOAK off and left it on the bed.

He examined the room he was given. Master Vadithas's guest rooms were more luxurious than the rest of the manor, if such thing was possible. Every detail spoke of wealth and power, an indulgence meant to impress rather than comfort. He took in the serene paintings on the wall, their gilded frames catching the flickering light of the candles that sat on polished brass sconces. Beneath his feet, a thick carpet muffled his steps, its fibres impossibly soft, woven in deep reds and golds that seemed to drink in the shadows.

In the corner, the carpet gave way to polished floorboards where a tub of steaming water awaited. The floor beneath it sloped subtly toward a grated drain. The air carried the faint scent of oils that wafted from the tub. A well-mannered freeborn house slave, his posture perfectly rigid and his face hauntedly blank, waited respectfully to tend to his needs.

The room's most significant feature, however, was its connecting door to Lygor's room. He could get to the prince within seconds if there was need.

He accepted the slave's assistance to get out of his armour, then dismissed him to wait outside as he slid into the tub. He leaned back and let himself relax until the water cooled off. The dinner had been exquisite. The best one they'd had since leaving Kaldoria. His stomach was so full, he could hardly keep his eyelids open. He couldn't go to sleep though, not yet.

Valnar emerged from the bath unwillingly, patting himself dry with towels as smooth as a woman's touch. Their belongings were brought from the inn into the manor. His bags were neatly stacked against the wall, and the armour he wore on the road was polished thoroughly.

After dressing in his shirt and breeches, Valnar pushed the bathtub against the wall. He retrieved a piece of chalk from his bag and drew his prayer ring onto the floorboards. Then, picking up his two-handed sword, still wrapped in layers of cloth, he stepped toward the ring, only to hesitate.

His scowl deepened as he stared at the chalk lines. He shuffled closer, but his feet refused to cross the boundary. Frowning, he scratched his head. Confusion crawled inside his heart, creeping into his thoughts. What was happening to him?

He paced the room, each step tightening the knot of frustration inside him. He couldn't sleep without praying. He just needed to step inside the ring, kneel before Kiejain, and...

Valnar set his sword down with his other belongings, pulled a chair next to the ring, and sat heavily.

And then what?

Was he meant to express gratitude for their success today? Or was he supposed to ask for forgiveness? And why would he do that?

Why?

He stood and paced again before throwing himself onto the bed, staring at the ceiling with wide, unblinking eyes. He tossed and turned for nearly an hour, knowing sleep wouldn't come. Not before he cleared his head. Not before he spoke to Kiejain.

But what was he going to say?

"This is absurd," he muttered, pushing himself out of bed with a sharp exhale. "I haven't done anything wrong."

He marched toward the prayer ring, each step heavy, as if he could stomp out the gnawing guilt. But instead of crossing the chalk line, he dropped into the chair, scowling at the pale markings on the floor. His mind betrayed him, conjuring the image of Beast's face just before he'd drawn his sword.

Just before Valnar had paralysed him and let those men take him.

"He's a slave," Valnar said out loud. "Not a man."

The words felt thin in the empty room. No answer came, save for the thoughts clawing at the edges of his mind. The day of the ambush resurfaced — the moment he thought he had lost Lygor, only to find Beast sprawled over him, shielding him.

"He doesn't have a *rhoa*."

He could still feel the faint ache of his ribs where Beast had lodged a fierce punch as they fought in the mud outside the inn. He'd assumed alcohol had made the slave reckless, but no. Valnar recognised true grief when he saw it.

Leaning forward, he braced his elbows against his knees. "He needs to be retrained," he muttered. "He's too dangerous. Too..."

The word *unreliable* froze on his lips. That should have been the end of it. A beast without a leash needed taming. If he'd just acted like how a purebred should...

The contrast between the wild, unrestrained mad man in the cage and the man he had been on the road since the ambush — that shift in Beast's demeanour — gnawed at Valnar's certainty. That was the problem. He couldn't understand Beast, and that uncertainty festered inside him.

He gripped his head, fingers digging into his scalp as panic swelled in his chest. Why couldn't he step inside the ring? Was his heart straying from the Twelve after what he had been complicit in today?

"Lodi needs this alliance," he whispered into his hands. His voice was tight, barely more than a breath. He wanted to howl. "I had to protect him. I had to protect him from making the decision."

But had he? Had he truly protected him?

His gaze flicked toward the adjoining door. Was Lygor asleep? A part of him hoped he wasn't. Another part hoped he was.

Shoving the thought aside, Valnar got dressed. He left his armour but buckled his longsword at his waist and strode out of his room.

Through the bright hallways, past the gilded sconces and smooth marble floors, until he reached the massive front doors of the manor. The moment he stepped outside, the pleasant scent of night jasmine hit him.

Under the light of the stars, he walked through the vast garden, the smells taking the edge off his worries. One of Vadithas's men, and a purebred beast, stood watch at the front gate.

"Where's the nearest Chamber?" Valnar demanded.

The guard blinked as if Valnar spoke in another language. "Chamber?"

"Chamber of Twelve?" Valnar said impatiently. Was everyone a heathen in this manor?

The guard gave him directions. Without another word, Valnar turned and strode into the dark streets.

VALNAR FOUND THE CHAMBER of Twelve exactly where the guard had said. The building was round, crowned by a dome, and old — so old it looked like it hadn't been properly maintained in decades. The stone walls, once white, were streaked with grime and dark patches of moss. Cracks ran along the dome, spider-webbing through the once-grand structure. Compared to Vadithas's pristine manor and the wealth of the city, the sight of it irritated him.

He pushed through the heavy wooden doors, their iron handles rusted, and found the courtyard in just as poor a state. Weeds sprouted between the stones, clawing through the cracks like no one had bothered to tend them in years. A broken lantern lay discarded in the corner, its glass shattered.

Valnar exhaled through his nose.

Setting his cloak aside, he rolled up his sleeves and got to work. He cleared weeds from the cracks, pulling them out by the roots. He brushed dirt and dried leaves from the stone path, shoving them into a pile near the outer wall. It was cold, his breath visible in the night air, but he didn't stop. The work was simple and repetitive enough to keep his hands busy and his thoughts quiet.

An hour passed before exhaustion crept in. He straightened, rolling his stiff shoulders, and finally turned toward the entrance.

Inside, the chamber was as neglected as the outside. A circular room, dimly lit by a few flickering candles, their wax long melted and left to drip down the walls.

Dust clung to every surface. The statues of the Twelve Riders lined the perimeter, each standing beside their dragon, their presence imposing even in the dark.

At the foot of each statue sat a small table, cluttered with offerings — some fresh, most old. Carved trinkets, dried herbs, broken weapons, and tarnished coins lay scattered across the surfaces, each representing a god or goddess. The floor was marked by prayer rings — one before each statue, and a larger ring encompassing the entire room, likely for rituals that Valnar doubted were held often.

His boots echoed against the stone as he stepped forward.

Kiejain's statue stood as he had expected. Imposing and clad in full-plate armour, one hand resting on the hilt of a greatsword. Beside him, his black dragon loomed, wings half-unfurled as if caught in the moment before flight.

Valnar took a candle from the nearby table and placed it in front of the statue. The flame flickered weakly in the cold air. He stepped into the prayer ring, lowered himself to his knees, and prayed all night.

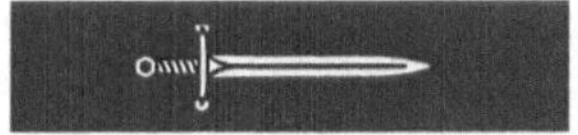

"YOU'RE PRAYING TO THE wrong one."

Valnar flinched. He hadn't noticed he wasn't alone.

He turned his head and spotted a homeless drunk slumped at the feet of Zaon, the god of roads and travellers.

Though part of him instinctively disapproved of the man's ragged appearance and the wine bottle clutched in his hand, he reminded himself that every man had the right to seek the Twelve's guidance, no matter how they looked.

Ignoring him, Valnar turned back to Kiejain's statue. His candle had melted halfway. He must have been praying for hours; his neck and knees ached from staying motionless. And yet, his heart was still heavy. He kept asking for Kiejain's forgiveness, but the god felt distant, as though he wasn't listening.

"You stink of remorse," the drunk muttered. "Which means you're guilty of something. And everyone knows Kiejain isn't the forgiving type. Haven't you heard of the Haari?"

Valnar scowled. Of course, he'd heard of the Haari.

Thousands of years ago, after the Twelve Riders had imprisoned the Thirteen High Fiends in Darkhome, the Offprings — half-fiend abominations — waged war against the world. The Haari had refused to aid the other nations. When the war ended, they were the only country left with wealth and resources. Rather than rebuild alongside the others, they had sought to rule them instead.

Kiejain flew over them on Karaalev, and cursed them with a sickness that affected only the Haari.

Their advanced medicine and magic failed them. By the time half their nation was dead, they realised their mistake. They built Chambers to the Twelve Riders, praying to Kiejain day and night. They held rituals that lasted for weeks. They even sacrificed animals — and humans — in his name.

Kiejain never listened.

The leader of the Twelve Riders was unforgiving. He didn't give second chances. None of the Haari survived the plague.

Valnar narrowed his eyes at the drunk. The man wore a single long glove on his right hand, the other missing. His beard was unkempt, his clothes stained. He sat slouched against Yolgezer, Zaon's bronze dragon, his half-lidded eyes watching Valnar as he took another sip from his bottle.

"I did not commit any sin," Valnar grunted.

"Oh yeah?" The drunk smirked. "Then why are you begging for his forgiveness?"

Valnar's jaw tightened.

Beast had begged him in the study, genuine horror in his face.

"Mind your own business!" Valnar snapped.

The drunk just shrugged. "Look, mate, I don't care. In fact, none of these bozos care. Not even Kiejain." He lifted a lazy finger, swirling it vaguely toward the statues. "Maybe except for Kyrus. That numpty still tries, every now and then." He took another sip, then scoffed. "What a loser."

Valnar's jaw clenched and his hands curled into fists as he turned back toward Kiejain's statue. His candle flickered in front of the armoured god, barely holding against the cold air. He didn't get half the things the man had said, but he understood enough to hear the undertone. Drunk or not, this man had no right to speak of the Twelve like that. The gods weren't common folk to be mocked over cheap wine. Even Kyrus, the god of shadows, revered by thieves and criminals, was still one of them. A god.

Valnar's irritation burned into anger, and he turned sharply, ready to lash out, ready to make the drunk choke on his own disrespect—

But he was gone.

The space beneath Zaon's statue was empty, save for an overturned bottle lying at the dragon's feet.

Valnar frowned, scanning the room. There was no door creaking shut, no shuffle of retreating footsteps. Just the weary bronze form of Zaon, carved as a traveller who had been on the road too long. His cloak sagged from his shoulders, boots worn thin, eyes dull with exhaustion. His dragon, Yolgezer, was equally worn, as though they had been walking together for centuries, never resting.

Valnar exhaled sharply and dragged a hand down his face.

With a muttered curse, he picked up his candle and knelt to gather the empty wine bottle the drunk had littered. He only paused briefly to scowl at the delicately carved *Serpentblood* label on the glass. He wiped the spilled wax from the floor, set the offering tables back in order, and brushed the dust from his knees.

The chamber felt colder now, emptier than before.

Without another word, Valnar walked to the door and made his way back to the manor.

When he returned to his room, all he could think about was sleep. He unbuckled his belt and propped his sword against the wall. His bed called to him, but before giving in, he opened the adjoining door to Lygor's room just enough to hear the prince's steady breathing.

Lygor was all that mattered. Nothing — not doubt, not guilt, not even his own remorse — could stand between his prince and the throne.

Valnar closed the door, stripped off his clothes, and crawled under the blankets. The night was almost over. In a few hours, he would wake up and go collect Beast. His gut twisted, but he had exhausted himself enough, the sleep claimed him almost instantly.

39

VALNAR

THE NEXT MORNING, VALNAR went to retrieve Beast, only to be met with delay. Vadithas needed *more time* with the slave, they told him.

Hours slipped away. Morning became midday, then afternoon.

By dinner, there was still no word.

Another night passed with Beast still in the dungeons.

40

VALNAR

The following day, Valnar returned to the dungeons, and was refused entry outright. Vadithas's men and beasts blocked his path, their orders firm.

Lygor and Ink joined him. The argument escalated quickly, voices rising in the halls until Union members arrived, led by Naelar himself. He calmly but firmly persuaded Lygor to grant one more day of retraining. Lygor, Ink and Valnar, all three of them pushed back. But the Union knew which strings to pull.

In the end, the prince relented.

Another day.

41

VALNAR

BY THE THIRD MORNING, Valnar had reached his limit. He and Ink met early, weapons strapped, ready to storm the dungeons if they had to. No more delays. No more excuses. But before they even left their rooms, a worker intercepted them with a message from Master Vadithas.

Beast was ready to be collected.

42

VALNAR

THE DUNGEON HALLWAYS WERE nothing like the rest of the manor. The grandeur and polished excess of Vadithas's world ended the moment they stepped beyond the iron-reinforced doors. Here, the air was thick with damp and rot, the stone walls sweating with moisture, streaked black from years of neglect. The torches lining the corridor were low-burning, their light barely enough to push back the dark. The smell — old blood, filth, and something sour — settled deep, refusing to be ignored.

Valnar walked ahead, his boots echoing against the stone floor. The guard at the entrance had given them directions to the room. The halls twisted and turned like a maze, but eventually, they reached the door.

Ink hesitated. Just for a second. Valnar didn't. He pushed the door open and stepped inside.

A thick, vile smell clogged his throat. A mix of sweat, urine, vomit, and blood. The room was dimly lit by candles, their flickering glow casting distorted shadows across the tables lining the walls.

Ink didn't move. His breath hitched, his fingers twitching near the hilt of his knife. He remained frozen in the doorway, staring.

Valnar didn't give himself the luxury. He pushed forward, past the tables. He forced himself to look.

The devices were laid out neatly, as if part of a craftsman's workshop. Pincers, blades, clamps of all sizes, coils of barbed wire, branding irons, instruments whose purposes he didn't even want to think about. A wooden table bore fresh stains, dark and still wet in places.

Chains hung from the walls, some long enough to drag along the floor. A heavy mechanism loomed above — a hanging rig, its leather straps and pulley system designed to suspend a body in midair. Nearby was a chair, reinforced with restraints and lined with crude spikes.

Every piece of the room was built with purpose. Valnar dragged his gaze over each tool, forcing himself to see.

See it all. Don't look away. Don't pretend you don't know what was done here.

His lips moved silently. He touched three fingers briefly to his chest, as he muttered, "Uniting Kiejain…"

In the centre of the room, a group of mirrors stood in a perfect circle. Like a prayer ring. At their heart, Beast lay on his side, bare and motionless.

His body was a canvas of agony. Bruises stained his skin in violent patches of blue, purple, and sickly yellow. Shallow cuts crisscrossed his ribs, dried blood flaking off with every half-hearted breath. His wrists bore deep impressions where restraints had once been, though there were no chains now. A raw, reddened mark encircled his neck, as if a thin string had bitten into his skin, pressed too tight for too long. His lips were cracked, his skin unnaturally pale beneath the grime and dried sweat. He wore a muzzle, its thick straps digging into the raw flesh of his cheeks and jaw. The stench of vomit clung to it.

But what stopped Valnar in his tracks wasn't the injuries. It was his eyes.

Open and unblinking. He stared straight ahead.

Valnar hesitated before kneeling beside him. He reached out slowly, resting a hand on Beast's shoulder, wary of startling him, but there was no reaction. Not even the flicker of muscle beneath his touch. Beast remained utterly still, his breath shallow and barely noticeable. Valnar followed Beast's gaze to the mirror.

The purebred wasn't staring at nothing. He was staring at himself.

His reflection, clearly visible in the smooth, clean glass, looked back at him with empty eyes.

Valnar's stomach twisted as his own reflection caught in the glass beside him. Clad in neat clothes, freshly shaven, his hair clean. A respectable knight. Kiejain's devoted warrior. Loyal servant.

Owner.

He felt sick.

Letting out his breath, he unclasped his cloak. Carefully, he draped it over Beast's body, covering his exposed skin.

"Ink," he said quietly. "Find the keys for the muzzle."

No response.

"Ink?" he repeated, sharper this time.

Ink jolted as if snapped from a trance. He swallowed hard, then moved, stepping around the tables. His movements were jerky, knocking over instruments as he searched. The sound of metal clattering to the stone floor made Valnar flinch. Eventually, Ink returned with keys in hand.

Valnar unlocked the metal clasp at the back, then eased the muzzle off. The stench of bile and decay worsened as the device came free. Deep, angry marks lined Beast's face where the straps had dug in. His lips, barely parted, were stained with dried blood and filth.

"Beast." Valnar spoke low, cautious. "Can you stand?"

Beast's lips moved to shape the words, "Yes, Owner." His voice was barely a hoarse breath, raspy and weak, like he'd shredded his vocal cords shouting.

Valnar and Ink moved to lift him, but the moment they tried, Beast's muscles seized. A violent tremor ran through his limbs, his body spasming as if rejecting its own movement. His breath caught, a weak, choked noise escaping his throat. Then his body went limp.

"Shit," Ink cursed. He draped Beast's arm around his shoulders.

Valnar adjusted his grip, taking on most of Beast's weight. The purebred was deadweight — slumped, head drooping, limbs slack, though his muscles still spasmed.

"Let's get him out of here," Ink said, almost begging.

They started toward the door, carrying him between them. Before they stepped over the threshold, Valnar spoke, his voice tight. "Ink?" He met the Kaldorian's gaze. "Lygor can't know about this."

Ink's eyebrows drew a fierce scowl. "Lygor can't feign bliss on this," he sneered. "He has to know exactly what was done here."

"We need to spare him the details," Valnar hissed.

"Details," Ink repeated, voice flat. He spat to the side.

"He doesn't need to see this in his head every time he looks at Beast."

"And what do you think he will see every time he looks at Beast?"

Valnar's grip tightened. "Ink, please."

They locked eyes over Beast's lolling head. The weight of him between them didn't seem to register. Valnar had seen Ink in a dozen different moods — grinning through a fight, teasing over a drink, even coldly calculating in battle. But this was different. The easy-going Kaldorian was gone, replaced by something hostile and harsh. If he had worn his people's traditional war paint right now, it wouldn't have made him look any fiercer than he did.

"He needs this alliance, Ink. If he knows... if he knows how bad it was, he won't be okay working with them."

Ink's stare didn't waver. "Are you sure about that?"

Valnar felt his irritation pressing against his ribs like a vice.

A muscle ticked in Ink's cheek, but he was done talking. He turned his head, staring at the door ahead. Reluctantly, he gave a single nod. It wasn't agreement. Not really. Just the bare minimum of compliance, enough to get them out of this cursed place.

They moved toward the door, the weight of the secret just as heavy as the man they carried.

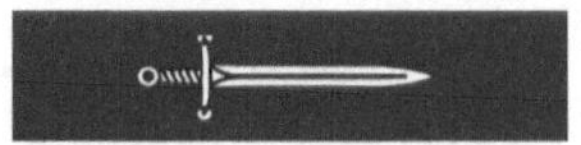

BY THE TIME THEY reached Valnar's room, several house slaves and a neatly dressed man were already waiting. The man introduced himself as Master Caerlo, Vadithas's head physician. He was the youngest physician Valnar had ever seen, and had a patchy beard that gave the impression he was trying too hard to look older. His sleeves were rolled up like he was ready for serious work, but his expression was too casual for Valnar's liking.

They laid Beast on the bed, then Ink slipped away without a word, leaving Valnar to supervise the physician. They had already brought everything they needed: hot water, towels, cloth, bandages, and a selection of herbs, salves, and poultices, neatly organised on the table.

Caerlo got to work, pressing his fingers to Beast's pulse, checking his breathing, lifting his eyelids one by one. He moved without hurry, as if he was simply doing the assessment to be thorough, but already knew what he would find.

"Master Vadithas is always very careful," Caerlo said as he worked. "His heart rate is a bit weak, but steady. See? He's not in shock. That's because Master Vadithas made sure to pace the sessions properly."

Valnar moved around the bed for a while before pulling a chair as close as he could without getting in their way. Forcing himself to sit, he clenched his jaw, grinding his teeth harder with every word the physician spoke. Each comment made Caerlo a sharper target for his growing fury, which could make even Kiejain look merciful.

"He was given water in-between sessions, to keep him from dehydrating too badly," Caerlo said as he dribbled small amounts of water into Beast's mouth with a damp cloth.

"No deep wounds, just surface-level lacerations. See? Master Vadithas is not crude. He's much more refined in his methods," he said as he dabbed a warm cloth soaked in sharp smelling liquid over his cuts and bruises.

"The muzzle was tight enough that it didn't chafe, but not enough to break the skin. A less careful breeder would have torn his face apart," he said as he rubbed a cooling balm over the deep marks on his face and neck.

"Master Vadithas even had me stretch him after each session. That's why his muscles haven't locked up completely," he said as he kneaded out the stiffness in Beast's arms and legs to aid blood flow.

"I swear under Twelve's wings, if you speak one more word, I'll stretch your jaw so far from your face, you won't eat solid food for a year," Valnar said as he leaned forward slowly, resting his elbows on his knees, voice dropping to something dark and low.

Caerlo froze mid-motion, fingers hovering over a roll of bandages. He blinked in surprise, as if he had genuinely expected Valnar to be impressed by Vadithas's expertise. He opened his mouth like he was about to say something, then caught Valnar's expression and thought better of it. From that moment on, he worked in absolute silence. He hardly needed to give instructions to the two slaves. They seemed to know what they were doing, as if they'd done this a hundred times before. Valnar hated that they probably had.

Despite himself, his concerns about Beast's condition eased as Caerlo continued. The physician was confident, though his competence seemed to stem more from a fascination with the human body — how far it could be broken and put back together — than from any real sense of care. He patched Beast's open wounds with poultices and bandages, then left one of the slaves to continue his care and excused himself.

Caerlo returned throughout the day to check on him, but kept his head down and his mouth shut unless he had a good reason to speak. The slaves alternated staying with Beast, rubbing and stretching his muscles, giving him water, and feeding him small amounts of watered-down puree. Beast remained unconscious through the night, and Valnar sat rigid in his chair.

A servant came to suggest moving Beast to one of the staff rooms, but Valnar refused. His gut twisted at the thought of Beast being somewhere Vadithas could reach him. So, he held vigil, leaving his chair only to pray and eat.

Lygor didn't come to see Beast.

Valnar didn't know what to make of it. He convinced himself that maybe the prince had wanted to come, and Ink had talked him out of it. He reminded himself that this was for the best, that he wouldn't have wanted Lygor to see Beast like this, anyway.

The next morning, Valnar washed up, changed into a fresh set of clothes, plastered a neutral expression on his face, and slipped into Lygor's room through the adjoining door.

Valnar stepped into the room, catching the faint clink of silverware as Lygor finished the last of his breakfast. The prince's chamber was warm, filled with the soft hum of morning activity.

An expensive set of clothes — best quality Whulgar cotton, with bright black-and-gold embroidery — lay spread across the bed. No doubt gifts from the Union. Three house slaves — one purebred and two freeborns — moved around the space, one clearing the breakfast tray, another feeding the flames that roared in the enormous fireplace, and the third filling the basin with fresh water.

Ink stood by the window, arms crossed. When he turned, Valnar saw the Kaldorian war paints on his face. Thick, dark lines stretched across his cheekbones, streaking up toward his temples. They disguised his expression, making him unreadable.

Valnar hesitated. In Kaldoria, war paint spoke louder than words — every colour, line, and dot had a meaning. Even the choice to wear it, or not, carried weight. He understood why Ink had worn it during their first meeting with the Union. They were walking into hostile ground, preparing for a battle of sorts, and Ink stood there not only as Lygor's ally, but as Prince Ingelhar Korvathir. It made sense.

Valnar examined the red and black markings on Ink's face, noting there was no yellow this time. Despite the years he'd spent guarding Lygor in Kaldoria, Valnar still hadn't learned to read those patterns with any real fluency. But he could tell one thing for certain: Ink had slapped that paint on his face to make a point. And in Kaldorian custom, asking about war paint was about as polite as asking a man the size of his cock.

He could only hope the message was aimed at the Union's overreach, and not something else.

Lygor noticed him and stood up immediately. "Valnar," he said, brushing non-existent crumbs from his coat. "How is he?"

Valnar kept his expression neutral. "He'll be fine. Just some cuts and bruises."

Ink huffed sharply, shifting his weight, but said nothing.

Valnar felt the need to sell it further. "The physician sounds like he knows what he's doing. He's been tending to him, and a pair of slaves stayed with him all night."

"All that over some cuts and bruises?"

Valnar forced a shrug and tried not to crack under Lygor's clever gaze. "They're just being thorough."

Lygor didn't look convinced, but he didn't push it. Instead, he grabbed another glass of wine from the tray and took a slow sip. "Will he be okay?"

"Of course," Valnar said smoothly.

Lygor nodded. He hesitated, rolling the stem of his glass between his fingers and watching the liquid swirl inside. He looked as though he had something else to say but was embarrassed to ask.

Ink noticed it too. His jaw clenched, eyes darkening beneath the paint. His stare turned sharp, almost daring Lygor to say it. To ask it.

Valnar prayed he wouldn't.

Finally, Lygor exhaled and asked the question.

"Will he be ready for the Fire Breath? I need him to win."

"You should have thought of that before you agreed to let that twisted bastard torture him for days," Ink said, the paints around his mouth lifting to make him look like a snarling animal.

Lygor's grip on his glass tightened, but his face remained impassive. "I didn't agree or disagree to anything."

"You're full of shit."

Lygor ground his teeth at the slaves: "Leave us."

They dropped what they were doing and filed out of the room quietly. The last one closed the door behind him, leaving them in a silence simmering with tension.

Lygor set his glass down, then turned and leaned his hip against the table. He grabbed the edges of the table with his hands so tight, his fingers blanched.

"This whole plan," he said through gritted teeth. "Twilight of Infinity was his idea. He wanted his freedom."

"I don't remember him agreeing to be tortured."

"This was the only way to secure that plan. Without Union's backing, neither of us could get what we wanted — his freedom, or my throne."

"We should have found another way."

Lygor's jaw tightened. "We did try. And every ally we approached turned us back, including your father."

Ink's expression didn't change, but something flickered in his eyes. "We should have negotiated harder."

"You were sitting at that table with me. Why didn't you?"

Ink dragged a hand down his face, his fingers smearing the war paint slightly, not enough to remove it but enough to show his frustration bleeding through.

Lygor exhaled, rubbing a hand over his face. "If I had known the Union would agree to this in exchange, I would have volunteered to be tortured on his behalf."

The words came quiet. There was no grand declaration, no dramatic flourish, just simple, unshaken truth. Valnar studied him, watching for any sign of insincerity, but he found none. Something sat beneath Lygor's usual confidence, something he was holding back. There were dark shadows under his eyes. The cuffs of his shirt were creased, as if he had been tugging at them, and a button was missing.

Valnar had seen the way Lygor had looked at Beast. As much as he disapproved — and tried to ignore it — it was all clear.

He believed Lygor meant what he said.

Lygor steadied himself with a deep breath. "But we didn't have that choice," he said. "This is the cost of securing our future. Mine and his. Now, I need him to be ready for Fire Breath so it wasn't all for nothing."

"The physician said he should be able to move around tomorrow," Valnar said. "The day after that, some light training."

Ink muttered under his breath, turning towards the window. The glass distorted the reflection of his painted face, making him look more like a fiend out of Darkhome.

"I believe we all would have preferred he had the time to properly rest and recover," Valnar said, trying to appease the hostility and disapproval that still poured out of the Kaldorian. "But why don't we ask him? If he says he's up for it, I'll train with him. Make sure he won't overdo it."

"Sounds good," Lygor said.

Ink didn't speak, but he turned from the window, his arms crossed. His jaw twitched as if he was barely holding back a retort.

Lygor walked over to the bed and started getting changed. He shrugged into a clean undershirt, then slipped a black-and-gold embroidered coat on with elaborate cuffs.

"Ink, I need you to come with me to meet Naelar," he said as he rolled his sleeves down properly. "He wants to discuss the details of my coronation. Assuming Beast wins Fire Breath."

"And if he doesn't win?" Ink asked, his speech slow and quiet.

"He'll win," Valnar said. "He's undefeated in the arena. He'll come through."

Lygor swallowed hard and took his time adjusting his cuffs before he spoke again. "I expect Naelar will also try to push back on my restrictions on cannibalism. He let it go last time, but I doubt he'll be so agreeable now."

Ink didn't respond at first. He moved away from the window, pacing along the room, arms still crossed, his fingers pressing into his biceps hard enough that his knuckles whitened. The war paint across his face made his silence heavier, his narrowed gaze unreadable beneath the dark streaks.

"You want me to have your back, so he doesn't take more than what you already gave up."

"Yes. Will you help me?"

"Sure."

Lygor studied him for a moment but didn't press further. He turned to Valnar instead. "Stay with Beast. Your priority is to make sure he recovers."

"Yes, Lodi."

Valnar left them to get prepared for the meeting with Naelar. He trusted Ink would keep his cool and work with Lygor. He headed back to his room and when he stepped inside, the first thing he saw was Beast's open eyes.

The purebred was still lying in bed. His body was stiff under the covers and he stared blankly at the ceiling.

Valnar's grip tightened slightly on the door handle. He shut the door quietly behind him. There was an odd reverence to the moment, like he was attending to a Sending Ritual at a Chamber of Twelve. Even his own breathing felt too loud. He crossed the room quietly and lowered himself onto the chair.

The two house slaves stood by the bed. One stirred a bowl of watered-down puree. The other supported Beast, lifting his shoulders and sliding pillows behind his back to keep him upright. Beast didn't resist. He let them move his limbs, position his body, tilt his head back as if he weren't there at all.

Valnar hated watching the quiet indifference with which the slaves carried out their work.

They raised the spoon to Beast's lips, tipping his head slightly when he didn't swallow right away. They weren't rough, but they lacked something Valnar couldn't put his finger on. Something that should have been there when tending to a man who had been to Darkhome. These slaves were freeborn. Not that Valnar had expected compassion or empathy, but still… Shouldn't their *rhoa* have shown a little?

Instead, he saw two men performing a task, no different from scrubbing a pot or hanging washing.

More than anything, Valnar hated watching Beast accept it. The way he opened his mouth mechanically, let the food slide down his throat without re-action, swallowed without taste.

The slaves continued their routine. One wiped Beast's mouth clean when they were finished, then moved onto his limbs, rubbing his arms and legs, kneading at the stiffened muscles. The other slave took a fresh cloth, dampened it, and wiped down Beast's arms and chest, carefully cleaning away any sweat and grime.

"Leave us," Valnar finally said, when he couldn't stand to watch it any longer. Though he spoke softly, the slaves heard him. They gathered their things and stepped out.

Beast lay his head against the pillows behind him. His eyes were heavy.

Valnar stood, lifted his chair, and brought it closer to the bed. He sat, leaning forward, fingers tapping restlessly against his knee as he searched Beast's face.

What was he even hoping to see?

Softly and hesitantly — like he wasn't sure if he should be asking at all — he spoke.

"How are you?"

Beast's gaze shifted slightly, just enough to focus on him. His lips parted, and the words scraped their way out of his throat with a delay.

"I am well, Owner."

Valnar stilled. He leaned back and crossed his arms, then uncrossed them and tapped his fingers against the arms of his chair.

"Are you thirsty?"

"I am well, Owner."

Valnar poured him a cup and brought it to his lips. Instead of holding it for him, he gently took one of Beast's bandaged wrists and guided his hand to hold the cup himself. Beast's arm trembled. Water sloshed over the edge, spilling onto the blanket.

Valnar exhaled, then took the cup and helped him drink the rest.

Two weeks. Fire Breath was two weeks away, and Beast couldn't even lift a cup. Valnar wished there was something stronger than water in the room.

"Are you in pain?"

"No, Owner."

"Bullshit."

Beast didn't respond. His eyes followed the slow crawl of a bug across the wall.

"Beast..." Valnar said softly.

Beast didn't show any alertness.

Valnar wanted to tell him to snap out of this, but then what? The Union wanted him broken. They wanted a mindless tool, and Lygor was right: Beast wanted his freedom more than anything. And the only way to secure it was to play by their rules.

At least until he won Twilight of Infinity. At least until Lygor secured more allies.

Until then, it was safer for Beast to keep that vacant look on his face.

Valnar released a slow breath. "Have some rest."

"Yes, Owner."

He closed his eyes dutifully. Before Valnar could reach over to remove the extra pillows and help him lie back down, Beast had already drifted off.

43

OLIRA

THE ROOM STANK OF mould. Olira was good at tolerating unpleasant scents, but this one got to her. It creeped into her clothes, her hair, her lungs, and it clung like despair.

A single boarded-up window let in slivers of light, but not enough to uplift her mood. She stood near the mattress on the floor, her arms crossed tightly over her chest, too restless to sit. The blanket was thin over her shoulders, the fabric worn to threads in places, barely enough to chase away the cold that bled through the walls. She shifted her weight, as if the movement could help work some warmth into her, but it only lifted more dust off the rot-ridden floorboards, sending them to float lazily in the still air.

They'd arrived at Calae a day ago, and had sneaked into the city in small groups. Dienus and his men had changed into plain clothes and split, each group slinking off to different safe houses. Olira hadn't seen Dienus since. A quiet relief. She touched four fingers to her forehead, whispering a prayer to Alunwea under her breath.

Why all the secrecy? Dienus was the prince of Chinderia, and he had all the authority to walk into any city and demand cooperation. Why did he want to keep his presence secret in Calae? Why the need to hide in filthy rooms that smelled of damp and decay? The questions made her skin crawl.

Her head jerked up at the footsteps outside the door. A key scraped in the lock and the door swung open, revealing Emberlash.

His expression was soured with resentment, his mouth twisted like he'd bitten into an unripe thornplum fruit. Even Olira knew why. The man was Dienus's chamberlain, and the prince had ditched him. Dienus had taken that wretched knight instead, along with two soldiers, and was spending his days in Calae's pleasure houses.

Olira pitied the slaves there.

Everyone pretended that poor freeborn beast's death had been an accident. Things getting out of control in the heat of interrogation. But Olira knew. She just knew Jessur had become a victim to Dienus's perverse enjoyment.

Just as she knew, with quiet certainty, that she never wanted the prince to get his hands on Beast.

Emberlash's disinterested gaze swept over Olira. "Need to relieve yourself?"

She hesitated, then nodded. "Yes."

He stepped aside, but his scowl deepened, his hands clenching at his sides. He motioned for her to follow. As he led her through the narrow hallway and down the stairs, the scent of mould faded slightly, replaced by smoke, damp wool, and simmering broth.

The house was old, older than it looked from the outside, its bones creaking like a tired beast even when no one moved. The main room was larger than she expected, though cluttered with bedrolls and makeshift sleeping spaces. Seven, maybe eight men occupied the space, their gear stacked in untidy piles against the walls. It was only early afternoon. A few sat hunched over a small table, murmuring in low voices. Others passed the time by cleaning their weapons and organising their gear.

Steam lazily rose from a pot hanging above the hearth. Whatever was cooking smelled passable, though she had discovered the smell was misleading when it came to what was served as food in these men's company. It appeared the most talented cook amongst the soldiers had died in the ambush with Lieutenant Quinner.

Olira's gaze flicked to the far end of the room. One of the guards sat slumped in a corner, wrapped in heavy blankets. A sickly yellow pallor marked his drawn and thin face. He trembled violently, his breaths coming shallow and rapid. She slowed slightly to get a better look at him, but Emberlash prodded her to keep walking.

Olira pressed her lips together, then held back the comment. She knew exactly what the man was suffering from, and though the compassionate part of her wanted to help, the rational part kept her silent. She owed these men nothing, and she knew any kindness would go unreturned.

Then she spotted Norrol, sitting alone, bruises darkening one side of his face. Guilt and pity pinched her insides.

It was all Olira's fault. The boy was being targeted because he'd been treating her with decency. He'd saved her life that day in the woods. Olira would have been dead if Norrol hadn't fetched Quinner. But since the lieutenant died, the others had turned on him. Their mockery was inspired by the malice Dienus had shown when he beat the boy half to death under the guise of sparring. Eager to stay in favour with the others, even Melton — the other squire — had joined in with the constant bullying and roughing. If Norrol hadn't been a lord's son, they might have done worse.

Emberlash pushed open the back door, letting the crisp afternoon air spill in. It had a pleasant coolness to it. Olira took a slow breath, savouring the freshness after the stale dampness of the house.

The courtyard was enclosed by high stone walls. Moss and weeds grew thickly on their cracked and weathered surfaces. Knee-high brambles and tangled shrubs overran the space, clawing at the stepping stones that led to the privy.

Emberlash stopped near the door and jerked his head, silently urging her to hurry up. He didn't need to escort her all the way to the privy — there was no way out of the courtyard, and the walls were too high to climb.

Olira walked across the stepping stones, yanking her skirt from the claws of thorny branches. The privy was a rickety wooden structure at the far end, its planks weak and dark with rot. The scent of damp earth and old waste clung to the air. As she neared, something caught her eye.

Mushrooms.

They clustered in the soil next to the privy, pale green caps blending perfectly with the weed. A few sprouted at the back, nearly hidden in the shadows. She held back a curious noise. *Pale Gallcap* often grew in damp, undisturbed places: abandoned barns, deep forests, forgotten corners of farmland. It was unusual to see a cluster sprout inside a city.

It showed how neglected this house had been.

Olira entered the privy cautiously, minding her step. The floor was muddy soil, and the stench of waste mixed with rot made her want to hold her breath.

She finished her business quickly and stepped back into the fresh air. The sun clung to the sky overhead, offering little warmth. Despite the cold, she lingered, dragging her steps over the stepping stones, stretching the moment. The fresh air sharpened her mind. She turned over an idea, careful not to glance at the *Pale Gallcaps* again, the beginnings of a plan taking shape.

When she finally re-entered the house with Emberlash breathing down her back, the warmth felt oppressive. Voices drifted from the far end of the room.

"It's nothing, just bad food," the sick man muttered. His friend, crouched beside him, looked unconvinced.

Olira stopped near them, tilting her head. "Bad food?" she echoed lightly. "Only if Kiejain has mercy to spare."

The men looked up, narrowing their eyes.

She continued casually. "If it's just bad food, you'll be fine. But if it's what I think it is, you'll be writhing in fever in less than an hour. By supper, your breath will rattle like cracked eggs. And by midnight—" She paused, watching the man pale. "—well, I suppose you won't be complaining about food anymore."

The room fell into a tense silence. Even Norrol, sitting in his corner, glanced up, his eyes wide with warning.

Emberlash exhaled through his nose. "Stop filling their heads with nonsense," he muttered, prodding her roughly toward the stairs. "It's just bad food."

She pretended not to care, allowing him to lead her upstairs. But as soon as Emberlash locked the door behind her, she allowed herself a small, knowing smile.

She didn't have to wait long.

Nearly an hour later, the sounds of hushed panic drifted through the floorboards. Frantic voices argued. Boots shuffled as people moved in a hurry. Then, footsteps pounded up the stairs.

Olira stood, brushing the dust from her dress as the key turned in the lock.

Emberlash opened the door, his scowl as sour as ever. "Get downstairs," he snapped. "Since you're such an expert."

She followed him down and stepped into a room thick with tension. The sick man lay shivering, his face more yellow than before and slick with sweat. All the others stood a distance from the man. One of them had even kneeled inside a praying ring he'd drawn on the floorboards and was muttering frantic prayers.

Olira approached the man without hesitation, crouching beside him. A quick glance confirmed it. Swampchill. Not pleasant, but not fatal — not unless they let the fever take him.

"Pen and paper," she said, glancing up at Emberlash.

The chamberlain narrowed his eyes, but went to his bags and fetched what she asked. Olira scribbled down a list of herbs. She hesitated, then added one more. A small bag of *Hollowbell*. Her pulse quickened, just a fraction. She put the pen down and folded the paper a bit too quickly. Not that she worried any of these men would know its properties. She passed the paper off to the nearest soldier. "Get these from the apothecary," she said with urgency. "Hurry."

The young man left without argument.

Meanwhile, Olira moved efficiently, grabbing a clean blanket and shifting the man to a more comfortable position. The others hovered in a distance. Norrol looked like he wanted to step in, but he hesitated and looked away. *Good*, Olira thought. The boy didn't need any more trouble.

The soldier returned faster than she expected, carrying a bundle of herbs. She spread them on the floor, selecting what she needed. She crushed and mixed the herbs with hot water, and as she worked, she slipped the bag of *Hollowbell* into her pocket. She held her breath, waiting to see if anyone was onto her, but no one stopped her. Releasing her breath, she passed the prepared cup into the sick man's trembling hands.

"Drink. You'll feel better in half an hour."

Emberlash snatched the cup off the man's hand. "How do we know it's not poison?"

Olira blinked. "That's the most stupid thing you could have asked."

Emberlash flinched like she'd just slapped him. His surprise quickly turned to embarrassment, but before he could fully commit to offence and drag Olira back upstairs, she stood.

"Would you like me to explain why you couldn't know if it's poison or not? Or should I really bother trying to convince you how I wouldn't gain anything by poisoning a man already on his way out to Farhome?" She brushed the dust off her skirt as she addressed the rest of the room. "I suggest wear long gloves when you remove his body out of the house. Burn it as quickly as possible and try not to breathe the smoke."

The sick man reached for the cup, his hand trembling and his face paler than ever. "I'll drink. Just give it me. I don't care."

Reluctantly, Emberlash handed the cup back and the man gulped it down. Olira held Emberlash's gaze for a few more seconds before turning toward the hearth. She grabbed the simmering pot off the flames and carried it outside.

"What in Darkhome are you doing?" someone barked.

She tipped the pot over, dumping its contents into the weeds. "You wanna catch what he has?" she asked coolly.

The men muttered uneasily, shifting on their feet. Olira set the pot back down and knelt by the supply bags with the confidence of someone who belonged there. The soldiers watched her, some bewildered, some wary.

Emberlash opened his mouth as if to say something, but he hesitated, his lips pressing into a thin line. Olira could see the urge to snap at her, to assert his authority, but he held back. Maybe he didn't want to risk another humiliating reply.

Instead, he turned away like she wasn't worth the thought and kept himself busy with organising his belongings.

The others followed suit. No one bothered her as she rummaged through their supplies, picking out what she needed. They just let her cook.

The fire crackled as she worked, filling the space with the rich, warm scent of proper food. The men noticed. A few of them glanced her way, noses twitching, but none dared comment or approach her.

Except for Norrol.

The boy hesitated before stepping forward, crossing and uncrossing his arms, as if already regretting the decision. "Do you need help?" he asked quietly, but not enough to go unnoticed.

A few men turned their heads, barely bothering to hide their amusement.

"I'd be careful, Lordling," one of them scoffed. "She has a sharp tongue."

Melton smirked. "Norrol's just hoping she wraps that sharp tongue around something other than an insult."

A chuckle rippled through the room. Others joined in with more comments about Norrol's interest in Olira. The jabs weren't loud or cruel enough to invite intervention, but the intent was clear. Norrol didn't answer them. Perhaps he knew it would only make it worse. His jaw tightened, his ears red, and his hands twitched at his sides as if he wanted to clench them into fists.

"I'm fine," Olira said. "I don't need help. Thank you."

Her response elicited more mockery and laughter from the soldiers.

"Oh, rejection!"

"Cold as a Frostbringer's Eve."

"Poor bastard. Bet he thought she'd be swooning."

"Right into his noble little arms."

Norrol mumbled something under his breath and returned to his corner, gaze fixed on the floor. His face was more flushed than before.

By the time the food was ready, the sick man's breathing had steadied, and some colour had returned to his face.

Olira ladled herself a portion. She didn't bother serving the men, and made it clear that she had no intention to. Her steaming bowl in one hand and a piece of bread in the other, she turned on her heel and walked upstairs, moving like a woman returning to her own bedroom. Not a prisoner being locked away.

44

DIENUS

THE LIGHT IN THE purebred's eyes slowly faded.

That flicker, the last spark of life, was what Dienus had hungered for. Around him, the small bedchamber in Calae's notorious pleasure house felt too cramped for his excitement. The walls were painted in cheap burgundy, chipped here and there to reveal rough stone beneath. A single, greasy lamp flickered on a low side table. The sheets on the oversized bed were rumpled and stained, reeking faintly of old sweat and incense.

Dienus tightened his grip around the slave's neck, his pulse thundering in his own ears as he drank in the sight beneath him. The man was a purebred flame, every part of his body carefully bred and trained to offer pleasure and entertainment in any manner. His hair was a bright red, shaved close along the sides. His pale skin held a faint sheen of sweat, and the faint lines of old scars were barely visible in the dim light.

When Dienus had first laid eyes on him, the purebred had shown no trace of emotion. His training had scraped every trace of fear out of him. But those glassy eyes were clouding now, bloodshot and slightly bulging out of their sockets.

Dienus savoured the moment. His arms shook with the strain, the muscles in his forearms burning. But even the strain itself was exhilarating, almost as much as seeing the reward it brought.

At first, the slave reacted to Dienus's grip with a frantic display, clutching at his wrists and twisting his body in a show of panic. But Dienus saw the performance for what it was. Purebred flames were taught to understand and satisfy a patron's morbid tastes. The charade only irritated him. He shifted his weight, pressing down harder on the man's throat.

Gradually, the purebred's thrashing subsided. His arms slackened. His gaze dulled with resignation. It was clear he'd endured strangulation before, likely trusting that no patron would dare kill an expensive purebred flame outright and incur hundreds of Blues in debt. There were Veiled Houses that catered to those who wanted to push boundaries. So, the flame had assumed Dienus would release him before he died.

It excited Dienus that it took a while for genuine fear to spark.

Only in that final moment did the man realise he was about to die. It was only then that his eyes widened, revealing their raw wakefulness.

That was exactly what Dienus wanted.

He felt the final push of the slave's body, a last jerk of limbs fighting to break free. Then the male's eyes rolled back, life slipping away. His body fell limp, and the rush coursing through Dienus peaked like a surge of lightning as he found his climax.

Slowly, he eased his cramped fingers from the man's neck and massaged his arms. A grin tugged at his lips. He'd done it. He'd watched the moment fear — true fear — replaced indifference. He'd watched a purebred become truly awake.

Broken.

He leaned back, straddling the dead man's midsection, his own breathing uneven. He filled his lungs with the air he'd deprived the purebred from. He reached out and ran the back of his hand across the male's damp cheek. Bruises were already forming where his fingers had crushed his windpipe.

He bent down to press his ear against the purebred's smooth chest, listening for any final stir of a heartbeat. Nothing. Only silence. It made Dienus chuckle.

He stayed poised on the corpse's stomach for a few more seconds, relishing that sense of absolute domination. When he finally pulled himself upright, the coarse bed sheets slid against his knees. He turned and rummaged for a folded scrap of paper on the bedside stand. On it was the slave's Pain Word. A single word that could make a purebred's bones feel like they were on fire. A word Dienus was only beginning to understand was linked to a deeper power.

He wondered if his mother knew. Would she praise him for his discovery? Or would she shame and exclude him like she always did?

Dienus didn't let the thought taint his thrill. Quinner's meddling had kept him from his explorations for far too long already. But now was his chance.

He spoke the slave's Pain Word out loud.

The reaction was immediate. The body beneath him spasmed, arching so sharply it looked like the man might snap in half. A long, desperate gasp tore from his lips, eyes bulging. His chest heaved, trying to suck in air. Veins stood out at his temples, and his face twisted in raw terror that made the previous moment of death look peaceful.

"Welcome back to life," Dienus whispered. He felt a heated pulse radiate through him, a thrill so intense his fingers twitched with it. He'd never felt more powerful than he did at this moment.

The slave, once a paragon of discipline, now let out a low, broken whimper. "No…" he moaned. "No, Master, please…" The voice was ragged and scratchy. All the mindless compliance was gone, replaced by fear.

Dienus allowed himself a small laugh. He reached down, cupping the slave's chin, tilting it up so he could see the frantic darting of those eyes. "You're free of your purebred training."

The man's lips quivered, but he couldn't form words.

"Good," Dienus said softly. "You're truly alive now."

A sudden knock on the door made Dienus curl his lip in displeasure. He stayed silent, hoping the intruder would leave.

Another knock came. Louder.

Dienus exhaled in exasperation.

"Master Dallus," came Sir Gennald's voice from the hall. "Your guest is here."

Dienus rolled his eyes. That was the alias they'd agreed upon to keep Dienus's true identity hidden.

On the bed, the slave had gone still beneath him, as though too petrified to move. Dienus watched him for a moment longer. The man's eyes were squeezed shut, breathing in shallow gasps. Perhaps he was trying to recall old mental techniques, to clamp down on his emotions. Too late. Dienus had already broken him.

"Don't go anywhere," Dienus whispered. He kissed the tip of the slave's nose, then slipped off the bed. He tugged on his clothes, smoothing them into place with swift gestures.

He paused briefly at the door, looking back at his victim. The slave lay there, eyes still shut, forcing each breath through battered lungs. Dienus smiled. Let him regain his composure, Dienus could break it over and over again.

Sir Gennald waited in the hallway. He wore a simple tunic and leggings, but Dienus knew there was chainmail beneath. A tall Vogros soldier, also dressed in simple garments, stood a few steps away.

The corridor was narrow, lined with red doors. Muffled moans and sighs drifted from behind each one. Dienus walked down the hallway with Sir Gennald and the soldier in tow. They descended a winding staircase into a spacious lounge area.

There, soft lamplight illuminated wooden booths separated by curtains and screens. Patrons were scattered around — some nibbling on fruit and pastries, others lazily tangled with lovers and slaves. The air smelled of spiced wine, perfumed oils, tobacco and sex.

Sir Gennald led Dienus toward one of the dimly lit booths in the far corner. A large man in his mid-thirties waited there, broad-shouldered and deeply tanned, with forearms thick as tree trunks. He cradled a half-empty mug of beer. A female flame slave rubbed his tense shoulders, but as soon as Dienus appeared, the man gestured for her to leave.

"Master Dallus," the man said, rising to offer a short, respectful bow. "Thank you for seeing me."

"You've chosen your confidant wisely," Dienus said, settling onto the padded seat across from him. He gestured for the man to sit. Sir Gennald stood behind Dienus, the Vogros soldier taking position at the booth's edge.

The big man lowered himself gingerly, anxiety etched on his face. "I just want you to know, Master Dallus, that I've always been loyal to your kind father."

Dienus waved a dismissive hand. "Fine. Let's hear it. How's Lygor?"

The man hesitated. "He's... persuasive. Obsessed with that slave he has."

Dienus clicked his tongue. "Well, his father was equally fixated. Didn't even see his own men scheming to betray him right under his nose."

The man nodded gravely. "Union thinks Lygor's plan is going to work."

"Which is?"

"He wants to orchestrate riots, using the 'Lion of Zarall' as a symbol, stirring up the commoners to rise against King Kastian."

Dienus blew out a sharp breath. "Fools, all of them," he said, though a hint of amusement crept into his eyes. "So what are you proposing to me, other than the information I could have acquired from a fortune teller?"

The man's gaze flicked to Sir Gennald, then back to Dienus. "I'm here to warn you. He's building support. The Union will coronate him after the Fire Breath."

Dienus poured himself a small cup of wine from a clay jug on the table, swirling it lazily before taking a slow sip. "I've already sent word to my father about Lygor's... good health. He's arranging my reinforcements. The Union will cease to exist soon."

"Your reinforcements... must be Lord Brocton," the man said warily.

Dienus's lips twitched in a half smile.

"If you are planning on charging Master Vadithas's manor, you should know his security is quite tight. If you strike now—"

"In my experience, charging in can do wonders against tight places," Dienus said, grin turning slightly vulgar.

The man offered a weak laugh.

"You still haven't given me anything useful," Dienus said.

The man leaned on his elbows, dragging a hand through his face. "If you would wait until after the Fire Breath, it might be easier. Master Vadithas will invite Lord Brocton to celebrate Lygor's victory — he's hoping to win Brocton's support. You could slip some of your men inside with Brocton, mingle with the guests, and then open the gates once everyone's distracted. I can assist from the inside."

Dienus studied the swirling wine in his cup, thinking it over. "And what if Lion fails to win Fire Breath?"

"We will just have to hope that he'll win."

"Aren't you the Master of Sands? Can't you make sure he wins?"

Master Ruzen's face darkened. "I don't fix fights, Your Highness. This is not some underground arena. Besides, Fire Breath can't be rigged. It's not designed like an ordinary fight. It's a Trial."

Dienus considered it. He thought about the slave he'd left upstairs, eager to be done with this useless hunk and return to his room. "Don't worry, Master Ruzen. Lion of Zarall has a habit of winning impossible fights."

He pulled a sealed parchment from inside his coat. He waved it in front of Ruzen's face, as though teasing a dog with a bone.

"See this? It's the letter that will reopen Switchblade Arena once it reaches King Kastian. I'll hold on to it, nice and safe, until I'm certain of your loyalty."

Ruzen nodded solemnly. "I understand, Master Dallus. I'll do my part."

"Then we both get what we want," Dienus said, setting the parchment back in his coat's pocket. "Soon."

"Soon."

Ruzen took his leave, slipping past the curtain with a nod to Sir Gennald. Dienus let out a low exhale, leaning against the back of his seat. His heart had steadied since his little thrill upstairs, but the memory of it lingered. No alliance or deal could replicate the feeling.

45

VALNAR

Valnar fought as if his life depended on it.

The training ground behind the barracks was a broad stretch of hard-packed dirt, enclosed by a simple wooden fence. In the late afternoon sun, its shadows painted the earth, and a faint haze of dust hung in the still air.

Valnar sidestepped and raised his sword to parry Beast's attack. The waster swords cracked together. He lunged in with a quick slash, but Beast dropped into a crouch, then sprang up instantly, following with a jab. Valnar twisted at the last moment, feeling the wooden blade graze past his ribs. He kicked at Beast's front knee but nearly lost his footing when the purebred spun full-circle and whipped the blunt side of his sword at Valnar's back.

Valnar recovered but couldn't control the ground. Beast hammered an upward thrust that Valnar barely met in time. The force jolted his arm. He grunted and tried to stall Beast's advance with a backhand slash, but Beast blocked it with his free hand. He danced away from Valnar's overhead blow, arching his back and swiping his sword in a wide arc, his long arms granting him a dangerous reach. Valnar stumbled back.

Another near miss.

Sweat ran from every pore. His breath fogged. Faint steam curled off his bare torso despite the winter chill. Beast didn't let him catch his breath. He lunged forward, his sword aimed at Valnar's shoulder.

"Fuck," Valnar grunted as he managed a clumsy block, but the force jarred his arms.

He pushed through, feigning high before dropping low at the last moment. Swords locked with another crack, and Beast huffed as Valnar twisted his wrist, forcing him to stumble. Seizing the opening, Valnar swept his blade in a tight arc toward Beast's hip.

Beast reacted too late and toppled sideways, bracing a hand against the dirt. Valnar advanced. His blows weren't pretty or strategic. He hacked like a desperate man, forcing Beast to scramble backward on his arse. He refused to give him a moment to recover. Beast swiped at his legs, but Valnar stepped over and kept pressing.

Then, Beast scooped a handful of soil and hurled it at Valnar's face.

Valnar flinched, grit burning his eyes, dust filling his mouth, clinging to the sweat on his skin.

The next instant, he was on the ground, Beast's legs locked around him.

They rolled in a flurry of limbs and rattling wood. Beast jammed an elbow into Valnar's sternum, pinned him with his free hand, and prodded the tip of his waster sword against Valnar's throat.

"Cheap move," Valnar spat out dirt. "I yield."

He shoved the purebred off and picked himself up.

Beast didn't reply. He moved aside, shaking the tension from his arms and legs. Valnar did the same, grimacing at the ache in his chest. He had yet to win a sparring match against Beast, and it felt just as sour now as it had the first time. He reminded himself that Kiejain didn't demand his warriors to triumph, but to persevere.

Besides, it was likely a good sign that Beast was at his best. The Fire Breath was tomorrow, and Beast seemed more than ready.

The purebred spun the cloth-wrapped hilt of his waster sword in his hand as he paced, a habit Valnar had observed him do. His bare back, tarnished with messy old scars, was covered in dust, sweat, and mud.

Training had served him well, helping him reclaim his physical strength, though there was still something missing behind his eyes. He kept his head down, quiet and reserved. He followed his orders without that annoying delay Valnar had often seen. His movements were exact, efficient, and stripped of personality. Like a perfect purebred.

Yet Valnar had noticed the small shifts each time he entered the training yard. A subtle change in posture. Eyes lifting a little more often. Every sparring session seemed to help him recover a sliver of something he'd lost in that dungeon.

"We'll finish here for today," Valnar said.

Beast paused, glancing at the sun still hanging in the sky. Dusk was hours away.

"As much as I would love getting my arse kicked one more time," Valnar rolled his eyes, "you need proper rest before tomorrow. And Vadithas is holding a feast tonight. I need to get ready."

Beast froze, his eyes darting across the yard. His hand spun the hilt a little faster.

"No, you're not invited," Valnar said softly. "You don't have to be there. Cool down, wash up, and stay in the room. Rest."

"Yes, Owner."

Valnar started gathering the practice weapons, but paused when he noticed Beast still standing in place. The purebred glanced at him, shifting his weight from one foot to the other, the sword spinning faster in his palm. Hesitantly, he raised his fist to his neck.

Valnar tilted his head, mildly surprised. Beast hadn't spoken unprompted since then. At all.

He walked closer, slipping his shirt over his head. "What is it?"

Beast spoke quietly, eyes lowered. "If you want me to win Fire Breath..." He hesitated, dragging in a breath. "Don't Rage me."

Valnar sighed. "I know you don't like being Raged. It's... not pretty. But you're unstoppable when Raged. We can't risk losing you."

Beast's jaw tightened. He seemed to weigh his words, struggling to voice them. "Fire Breath is a Trial," he finally murmured, eyes flicking away. "It's different. You Rage me... and I'll—"

"Sir Valnar," a servant called from across the yard, cutting off whatever Beast might have said next. The young woman hurried over, pressing her palms together. "I've been sent to fetch you. Prince Lygor is looking for you."

Valnar exhaled, a faint spark of frustration in his chest as he realised their conversation was over for now. "We'll continue this later," he told Beast. "Go cool down. Rest."

Beast simply inclined his head. He slumped on the ground and started stretching his muscles.

Valnar followed the servant out of the training yard. They slipped around the barracks and into the manor's side entrance, heading through a narrow corridor that opened into the kitchen. Steam rolled off bubbling cauldrons, and the heavy smell of roast and spices filled the air.

Near one of the broad tables, a cluster of Vadithas's guards huddled together, talking over each other in brazen voices. One of the guards slapped a battered ledger on the table, flipping it open as he scrawled on it.

"There's no way he can even reach the trench without getting his arse burnt."

"I've seen how he trains. The beast is fit. He'll reach the trench."

"They won't risk him at the trench. An unfortunate slip is always a bummer."

"I'm betting on a skirmish on the second half. Heaps more juice there."

"Nah, that's still too dangerous. Too close to the end."

Valnar's steps slowed down as he walked past the table the group had gathered. He frowned at the coins clicking against the wooden planks. He had been hearing talks of trenches and fire all week, but hadn't figured what they were about.

"Not only will he cross the trench," the loudest of the men said passionately, "he'll also drop at least two shepherds!"

Disagreeing voices filled the kitchen.

"When was the last time someone offed a shepherd?"

"He's right, I've seen the beast train," one of the cooks approached and slid a Chinderian Grey across the table. "He'll draw blood."

"He'll draw blood and cross the trench. I'll wager on that..." the loudest guard said, slamming two Greys on the table.

"Sir Valnar," the servant urged quietly.

Valnar cast a final glance at the guards. Then he let the servant guide him out of the kitchen and into another corridor. Steam and the smell of roast and spices faded behind them as they ascended a narrow flight of stairs.

Halfway up, Valnar waved the servant away. He knew where they were. As the servant hurried off, Valnar turned down the hall by memory, ignoring the gilded mirrors and torch-lit tapestries that marked this as one of the manor's finer wings. Near the end of the corridor stood two doors set close together: Lygor's suite and the one Valnar shared with Beast.

Ink was pacing between the two doors like a caged animal. His face bore a new design of black and red paint — still no yellow — that curved in jagged lines along his cheekbones. He looked furious, pausing only to rattle off curses under his breath.

"Ink?" Valnar approached warily. "What's going on?"

Ink spun, anger radiating from every tense movement. "I've done my best, but you need to say something to him. He's not listening to me."

"Are you the one who summoned me? Is Lodi okay?"

"Okay?" Ink let out a harsh laugh. "Go ask him if he's okay. He sure sounds more than okay in there."

At that, Valnar noticed low, ragged moans seeping through the door. His skin prickled. "Ink," he said softly. "Calm down and tell me what—"

"Don't you tell me to calm down," Ink snapped, resuming his agitated pacing. "While you were busy piecing Beast back together, Lygor's been doing everything in his power to ruin himself. I spent the entire week trying to keep Naelar off his back. I step away for one moment—"

"Why would you leave him alone?" Valnar hissed between clenched his teeth.

"And he approves a trial facility opening next week! Naelar waved the scroll at my face like a brat showing off his first chest hair. Signed by *King* Lygor Zarall."

"He's not coronated—"

"He will be in a few days and the Union clearly doesn't care about the technicality."

Valnar ran his hand through his hair. "You were supposed to stay with him. Make sure he wasn't—"

Ink threw up his arms. "He's not my child. And I'm not his fucking wet-nurse, as he so kindly reminded me. He doesn't listen to me. Now I can't stand at his door like a foot soldier, hearing... that."

He glared at the door, where another broken moan, trapped between pain and pleasure, sounded from behind. Valnar's stomach twisted.

"Vadithas sent them," Ink hissed. "Early celebration, and to 'take the edge off' before tomorrow. They're trying to break him, Valnar, the way they broke Beast. You need to beat some sense into that pampered idiot. I'm not questing to keep a spineless, spoiled brat alive."

Valnar drew in a slow breath, fighting both anger and apprehension. Ink spat a final curse, then threw his hands in the air. "Sort him out," he muttered, stalking away down the corridor.

Valnar turned the handle and stepped inside. He crossed the living space and walked into Lygor's bedroom where the noises came louder.

The room was dim and heavy with the stench of stale alcohol, perfumed oils, and something burnt. Curtains hung unevenly around the four-poster bed, their deep purple folds swaying slightly in the draught. Wine stained the sheets, and blankets lay twisted across the mattress. Two overturned chairs sat near a small table littered with empty bottles.

Three pleasure slaves occupied the bed with Lygor. Two muscular, blond men — a freeborn and a purebred flame — and a lithe, dark-haired female flame. Valnar looked away from the ragged breathing and pained moans that hinted at something far from gentle. He felt his stomach churn as he strode forward and barked, "Out! Now!"

The slaves didn't show any confusion, but they didn't move immediately either. Valnar grabbed one of the men by the arm and dragged him off the bed. "Go," he hissed, pointing at the door. The other two followed quickly. As the woman walked past, Valnar caught her by the elbow. "Bring water for a bath," he ordered. She bobbed her head and hurried out after the others.

Lygor made a weak, slurred protest. His indistinct words ended in a half-laugh, half-hiccup.

He turned back to Lygor, who sat sprawled against the head of the bed. The young prince's hair clung to his forehead in damp strands, and his eyes were bloodshot. He was naked, his body glistening and his chest mapped with bruises and bites. Several empty bottles rolled on the floor. Another, still half-full, lay on its side on a cushion.

Lygor blinked blearily at Valnar. "You're such a fucking buzzkill."

Valnar crouched to pick up one of the discarded bottles. He took a quick sniff and recoiled. "This isn't wine," he said flatly, tossing it aside. The harsh scent stung his nostrils. A swirl of pungent spice and bitterness confirmed it was laced with something stronger.

"So what?" Lygor slurred.

Valnar crossed to the shutters and threw them open. Cold evening air rushed in, carrying away some of the stench. Lygor squinted, groaning at the sudden light. A swirl of wind caught the edge of a tapestry on the wall, rattling it softly.

"This stinks," Valnar muttered, stepping over a stain on the floor. He squinted at a brass bowl with ash in it. "What have you been burning?"

Lygor let out a humourless laugh. "No idea. It's from Vadithas. Good man... he says it'll... help, you know... help me relax a bit."

"Help you make a mess of yourself," Valnar snapped, turning sharply. "Get up."

Lygor scowled, swaying when he tried to rise. "Are you giving me an order?"

Valnar grabbed him by the wrist and hauled him upright, ignoring Lygor's drunken flail. "I'll do more than order you if you don't sober up."

He spotted a basin of water on a nearby stand. Without warning, he shoved Lygor's head forward and splashed water across his face.

Lygor gasped and sputtered, struggling in Valnar's grip. He choked out a cough that quickly turned into retching. Some blend of liquor and whatever else was down his throat spilled onto the floor. Valnar grimaced, but kept hold of him until the heaving subsided.

"Get... off me," Lygor rasped. "What're you—"

Valnar pinned him with a hard stare. "I'm trying to keep you from killing yourself. Or from letting Vadithas and Naelar do it for you."

Lygor gave a bitter laugh that cracked into a sob. "Vadithas... he slipped and told me... you know..." His voice trailed off. He screwed his eyes shut, tears streaking his cheeks. He punched Valnar's chest, but he could barely muster any strength. "Just some cuts and bruises, my arse. You and Ink lied to me."

Valnar felt anger and sympathy twist inside him. "Lodi, you're making it worse for yourself. Snap out of this." He tossed a glance at the jumbled mix of bottles on the floor.

"What do you think I'm trying to do?"

Valnar softened his grip, drawing the prince into a steadier hold. "Listen to me," he said firmly. "We can't fix anything if you're too drunk to stand. Vadithas and Naelar are dangerous men and you're pushing your friends away."

"Ink hates my guts. So does Beast. And you! You're looking at me like I fell from Twelve's wings." He tried to shake Valnar's grip off, but the knight didn't let go.

"You, me, Ink... and Beast. Four of us are on a hostile battlefield, scattered and getting flanked. We need to regroup." He dropped his voice. "Maybe you need to see Beast."

Lygor shook his head, refusing to open his eyes. "I can't. It's... it's safer this way."

This had been one of Lygor's many excuses to avoid seeing Beast since the meeting, and the most logical one so far. He didn't want the Union members to know the exact nature of his interest in Beast. Fair enough. But deep down, Valnar knew there was another reason behind the prince's avoidance.

"Besides what's the point?" Lygor sniffed. "He's just a slave, isn't it? Isn't that what you always claimed? He's a purebred. He doesn't have a *rhoa*. He's just a—"

"Lodi..." Valnar could see that saying those words hurt Lygor as much as hearing them shamed Valnar.

"I can't... I just can't..."

Valnar patted his back, though the gesture felt awkward. He guided him toward the bed, letting him sit again. He briefly rested a hand on Lygor's shoulder, thinking of Beast's battered face in that dungeon and Lygor's trembling guilt.

"Talk to him, Lodi. Kiejain teaches that peace doesn't come to those who hide from what they need to face."

Slowly, Lygor nodded, tears pooling in red-rimmed eyes. He leaned into Valnar, arms clinging like a lost child. Until he heard the footsteps of the slave returning with bath water, Valnar sat with him and muttered prayers to the Riders.

46

VALNAR

OILS, LEATHER, AND METAL polish lingered in the air of the Scorchline Arena's preparation room.

The room was oddly bright, despite having no windows. Rows of torches and overhead sconces filled every corner with shifting light, casting dancing shadows across the sand-coloured stone walls. The arena beyond those walls was alive with rising chatter. Distant roars and murmurs seeped through the stone like a heartbeat.

Beast stood in the centre of the room, his muscles glistening with sweat from his warm-up. The sound of heavy breathing filled the space around him as he stood shirtless, his chest rising and falling rhythmically. Two young slaves dabbed away the sweat from his arms and chest.

In a side alcove, an armourer fussed over half a dozen sets of plate and leather, all sized for Beast's broad frame. Valnar hovered by these pieces, pressing his palm against polished cuirasses and flexing hinges on greaves. The armours were courtesy of Master Vadithas. None were made for Beast, but they were of approximate size, and the armourer was there to make the necessary adjustments.

Valnar had lost count of how many times he'd examined each one. The designs ranged from ornate, swirling etchings to stark, practical plates. Torchlight glinted off the polished steel. The constant background noise of the cheering spectators

— they were holding preliminary fights to keep the people entertained — reminded him that the Fire Breath was only minutes away.

It wasn't like him to feel anxious before a battle, but this was different. He wasn't the one going out there to fight. He was the one forced to stay behind and watch. In a sense, this was harder. Made him feel helpless.

Valnar spared a glance at the weapons rack — spears, axes, swords — enough to arm ten men. Then, he refocused on the set of armour in front of him. Reinforced breastplate. A curved plate designed to protect the ribs without pinching, layered over flexible leather segments at the sides. Thick pauldrons that would cover the shoulders without restricting full arm rotation. A narrow tasset to shield Beast's upper thighs but still allow him to pivot. Valnar ran his hand across the steel, feeling the subtle ridges beneath his palm.

"You want me to fit him?" the armourer asked, edging closer as he followed Valnar's gaze. His tape measure hung from one hand, and a small leather pouch of rivets clinked at his hip.

Valnar turned toward Beast. The purebred stood a short distance away, his jaw set, eyes fixed on the armour with a look that bordered on distrust. There was something brittle in his stare, as if he expected the worst.

Valnar beckoned him over. "What do you think?"

Beast hesitated. His gaze darted from Valnar to the armour, then back again. Eventually, he pointed to a studded leather set made out of tough hide reinforced with rivets, made for swift movement. "I need mobility," he said softly, his voice taut. "Owner."

Valnar frowned. "You can't outrun them," he reminded Beast. The rumble of spectators in the distance made him grit his teeth. "You're better off having proper protection."

Beast didn't respond. His shoulders dropped slightly, and he went rigid, like they both knew the decision would be Valnar's. He wasn't going to bother arguing.

Valnar exhaled and paced along the line of armour stands. "All right then, what about this?"

He tapped at a brigandine displayed on a nearby stand. The torso plates were hidden beneath layered fabric, offering decent defence without weighing the wearer down like a full-plate. "Kaldorian archers like this type of armour. Better coverage than straight leather, while still letting you move."

Beast studied it, then gave a slight nod. Relief flickered in Valnar's chest. "He'll need a decent gambeson underneath," he told the armourer. "Enough padding for impact."

The squat man raised one eyebrow at him, but nodded and knelt to retrieve a padded gambeson from a trunk. He laid it out, measuring its sleeves and tugging at seams, muttering to himself about refitting shoulders and waist.

Valnar let him work and led Beast toward the weapons rack. An overwhelming selection to crowd his mind. The roar of the crowd grew louder by the minute.

"A spear for a better reach?" he asked, unable to keep his irritation out of his tone. He ran his fingers over the haft of a long spear and weighed it between his hands.

Beast gave no answer, only scanning the weapons with a distant look before crossing his arms and turning away. His silence and the contrasting noise of the crowd outside weighed on Valnar's nerves.

"What?" Valnar snapped. "Stop acting like a mindless mute. Tell me what's on your mind."

A muscle twitched in Beast's jaw, but his voice was carefully hollow when he spoke. "I live to serve, I breathe to please, Owner."

"Beast..."

Beast met his eyes, holding his gaze just long enough for Valnar to recall exactly how Vadithas had forced him back into this perfect, mindless obedience. Valnar saw the anger swell like a cresting wave, then vanish into nothing. Carefully crafted nothing. Beast inhaled, swallowing everything down.

"The choice of weapon depends on whether you'll Rage me, Owner."

Valnar chewed his lip, turning back to the weapons rack. The muffled cheers rattled the walls, making it impossible to think clearly. Before he could respond, Beast reached out and plucked a lor'qas from the rack, testing it with a quick flick of his wrist. Then he grabbed a plain, functional knife and stepped away from the weapons.

"That's it? That's all you're having?"

Beast nodded.

"What about a shield?"

Beast shook his head again. "Mobility."

"A buckler doesn't weigh much."

"And it doesn't cover much. I'd rather keep my hand free. Owner," he added.

"Fine," Valnar grumbled. He strode towards the armourer's corner, shoving past stacked plates and shoulder pads until he found what he was looking for. He returned with a bracer shield. A curved band of reinforced steel, small enough to strap tight against the forearm without restricting movement. It wouldn't stop a direct strike from a heavy axe, but it was enough to deflect blades.

"There," Valnar said. "Keeps your hand free."

"Yes, Owner."

Valnar led him toward the stone slab where the armourer and slaves waited with the rest of his gear. The pieces had already been set out.

Beast pulled on an inner shirt, and stepped into loose linen braies, tying them securely at the waist. He wore wool chausses, snug around his thighs and strapped tight along the lower legs with cloth bindings to keep them in place. The armourer helped him into the padded gambeson next, checking the fit of the arms and shoulders. Then came the brigandine armour — straps tightened, buckles secured, each piece adjusted and rechecked. The bracer shield was bound to his left forearm.

Beast accepted a strip of cloth for his right hand to help his grip. He wrapped it around his palm and wrist, pulling it tight.

Then, something in the air changed.

Beast's fingers hesitated, pulling the cloth too tight before loosening it and starting over.

Valnar's head turned, following the invisible weight that had turned Beast's muscles into stone. He found Lygor standing in the doorway.

The prince looked polished to perfection. His blond hair neatly combed back, his clothes immaculate. Scents of soap and expensive oils masked every trace of the heavy drinking of last night. He was as composed and clean as ever, but beneath the surface, his posture held a slight rigidity. His grin was too casual, too controlled, and it didn't match the paleness of his skin.

Beast unwrapped the cloth and started over again, his head down, his focus on his task.

The weight between them was so heavy, Valnar felt it in the air. He exhaled through his nose. He was grateful Lygor had listened. It eased a knot in his chest to know Lygor still listened to him and he came here to talk to Beast. But this needed to happen without an audience.

He cleared his throat and spoke firmly. "Everyone out."

The slaves gathered their supplies and retreated without question. The armourer muttered something under his breath, but packed away his tools and followed.

Beast didn't move.

Lygor didn't either.

Valnar tried to catch Beast's gaze, but the purebred's eyes belonged to the hard ground as he pulled the cloth tight. Not even a muscle flinched in his expression. He gave nothing away.

"I'll be right outside," Valnar muttered as he tapped Beast's shoulder. The touch was intended to ground him, but Beast still gave no response.

Valnar nodded at Lygor in passing, the gesture feeling perfunctory. Lygor barely acknowledged it, his attention fixed on Beast.

Outside, Valnar exhaled, pressing his back against the cool stone wall beside the open doorway. The sound of the arena beyond these walls had thickened — a steady thrum of anticipation, voices rising and falling like waves. He told himself he wasn't lingering — just giving them privacy, making sure no one barged in. That was all. The torches flickered, their light failing to reach the deeper shadows pooling along the passage. Valnar flexed his fingers, rolling one shoulder, and glanced toward the doorway.

Nothing but silence.

Soon, he found himself holding his breath, straining to hear anything past the eerie silence that filled the room behind him. Finally, he heard Lygor shuffle a few steps further into the room.

"I see you're still standing," Lygor said. His voice was painfully casual. Meant to be light-hearted. "Tough as ever... You look good."

Valnar grimaced. He heard a faint clink of armour and couldn't help but glance inside from the shadow of the doorway. From that spot, he could see into the room while staying mostly unseen. Beast stood by the stone slab, his hands clasped together and head bowed.

"Are you... Are you okay?"

There was something vulnerable in Lygor's voice beneath the forced lightness. Like he *needed* to hear it, needed confirmation that Beast was fine. That everything was fine.

Beast didn't answer.

Valnar would have expected some memorised, obedient reply, one of those infuriating phrases drilled into him. But there was nothing.

Lygor survived the silence for a moment before shifting, exhaling sharply through his nose. He moved like he could outrun his own nervousness, scanning the room, drifting toward the armourer's display, pretending to scrutinise the gear with faint distaste.

"I've heard you've been training," he said, grasping for casualness once again. "And doing really well. Being extra rough with Valnar, even." He chuckled, but it landed awkwardly. "You're not still cross with him, are you?"

Still, Beast gave him nothing. He might as well have been part of the stone slab behind him.

Lygor hesitated, then stepped closer, like he had nothing to fear. Like Beast's eerie silence wasn't sinking into his skin.

"Look," he said, his voice lowering, sharpening. "He did what he had to. You know that."

Still no reaction.

Lygor waded deeper into the silence, moving toward Beast as if stepping into dark water, unafraid, as though it couldn't pull him under. Valnar clenched his jaw. He'd seen this before — men convincing themselves they had control right up until the moment they drowned.

"And I knew it wouldn't break you. I was right, wasn't I?" He tilted his head, eyes scanning Beast's face, searching for the smallest reaction. "You're strong. Much stronger than me," he added with a bitter whisper.

Lygor's fingers curled at his sides. His smile twitched, then smoothed over as he let out a low, breathy chuckle.

"Fine." His voice turned sharp, clipped. "Give me that silent purebred shit if you want, but tell me one thing." He leaned in slightly, gaze locking onto Beast's down-turned face. "Has he done anything you haven't survived before?"

A beat of stillness. The torchlight flickered, catching the dark angles of Beast's face.

Lygor's lips pressed together, his patience stretching thin. Valnar willed him to step back. He wasn't worried about Beast lashing out, but Lygor's words were clearly not getting through to him. The animosity between them couldn't be resolved with a brief chat under the arena.

But Lygor wasn't giving up. Beast's silence was a void swallowing him whole, and he desperately fought his way out of it.

"I knew you've lived through much worse," he continued, quieter now, almost coaxing. "And you're going to live through this. And you're going to pick yourself back up and keep fighting until you're breathing the air of Scythe Arena at Euroad, winning Twilight of Infinity."

The name hung between them for a heartbeat. Somewhere beyond these walls, the crowd surged into another wave of cheers. And finally, Beast looked up with solid steel in his grey eyes.

A victorious grin sharpened the edges of Lygor's mouth. He stepped closer, his fingers grazing Beast's armour before tugging at a strap, checking its tightness.

"I know how much you want your freedom," he murmured. "And this is the only way forward."

His gaze flicked over Beast's face, drinking in the subtle shift in his expression. Valnar saw that shift too, and something in his chest tightened. It wasn't unease, or relief, but something close to recognition. The Beast they knew wasn't completely scraped away. He was there, and Lygor was about to pull him out of whatever dark place he was hiding.

"You'll crawl through the gore and guts if you have to, bleed for it if you must, until you get what you want."

A pause. Lygor's voice dipped lower, smoothing into something quieter, more certain. He took another step forward, consuming the space between them. Casually, he adjusted another strap, then brushed an imaginary speck of dust from Beast's shoulder.

"You'll do whatever it takes, won't you?"

His hand lingered where it had settled on Beast's chest, fingers smoothing over the reinforced leather. Beast's chest expanded with a deep breath, like he was inhaling every word Lygor offered him. His lips pressed firm, like the silence he wielded so well was starting to fray at the edges.

"So you'll go out there now, and you'll beat those pampered idiots. Because you're undefeated. You're the fucking Lion of Zarall."

Beast tipped his head back, his gaze flicking toward the ceiling, as if distance could smother the raw, unfiltered hunger. His fingers flexed restlessly against his bracer, like he needed to grip something, to anchor himself.

"I know you," Lygor said.

The words landed like an old truth. Lygor moved forward, the space between them vanishing. Beast didn't step back. His throat bobbed, like he was forcing down the truth rather than giving into it.

"And when it's over, when you're standing in the middle of that fucking arena, drenched in glory... you'll see. I was always right about you."

Lygor's hand glided upwards, reaching behind Beast's neck and guiding his eyes back to him.

"Say it. Say I was right."

Lygor's confidence folded around Beast like a snare, tightening with every second of silence. His voice dropped even further, smooth as a blade sliding from its sheath. The faint echo of drums filled the arena outside. Lygor's hand rested securely, possessively, behind Beast's neck.

"I know you, Beast," Lygor whispered. "Let me show you who you are."

Then he leaned in and caught Beast's mouth in a kiss.

47

BEAST

Every breath burned.

Fury seared through his ribs, then smothered instantly by the hollow frost in his chest.

Every breath died.

Every single one.

His body was a carcass. Something unliveable. A shell he could not escape.

He had sent his mind to *that place* before, pushed himself out of his own suffering until he was nothing but a blade moving on command.

But this was different.

His body had abandoned him first, and he had slipped into the pit of cold. He couldn't feel warmth. Not even the burn of rage.

Then, Lygor pressed his lips to his, and the frost had shattered.

A thrumming, pulsing anger surged beneath his skin, rolling through him like an avalanche. It scorched through the filth, searing his flesh from the inside out, scouring him to the bone.

Fuck.

You.

The kiss went on for three heartbeats.

The first dragged Beast back from the pit. A fury, raw and undiluted, like he'd never tasted before, burned through him. Hotter than his own blood, hotter than the humiliation thick in his veins.

The second heartbeat filled his mind with violence. A singular, vicious desire to hurt. To slam Lygor through the nearest wall. To shatter his bones. To crush him and watch him bleed. He was in a room full of weapons, alone with him. He could thoroughly fuck him up before Valnar could rush in from where he stood hidden outside the doorway, watching.

The third heartbeat brought an eerie sense of calm.

The anger didn't vanish. Instead, it refined itself, sharpened to a perfect, gleaming edge. Instincts took over, and he knew what to do.

He reclined away from the kiss. Not a flinch, not a snarl. Just the smallest tilt of his head. The most innocent, inconspicuous movement he'd ever done to destroy a man.

The prince stumbled back as if Beast had driven a knife into his gut. His eyes widened, shock cracking through his usual veneer of smug control. His mouth — that same confident mouth that had filled Beast's ears with carefully measured words, meant to pacify him, to shape him — went slack.

Lygor worked his lips, taking another step back as if the distance could shield him from the humiliation, though it only made him look more exposed.

And Beast watched him burn. The air he breathed tasted sweet, rich with satisfaction. Heat crawled up the prince's neck, flushing his face a deep, searing red.

Just like that, Beast took it back.

What was taken from him, he wrenched it right out of Lygor's hands.

And now, Lygor squirmed. The prince of Chinderia, rejected by a fucking slave.

Lygor pressed his lips together, his jaw tensing like he could will himself back into composure, but Beast saw the way his fingers twitched, smoothing down the front of his pristine shirt, tugging at the fabric with frantic little adjustments. He forced a dry chuckle, but it sounded brittle. He rubbed his chin. Fixed his cuffs. Fidgeted with his collar.

Like he didn't know what to do with his hands.

"Right," he muttered, then cleared his throat. "I'm— I'm glad we cleared this up. Umm..."

He flinched when Beast took one step forward. It was barely more than a breath, but Beast saw it. He didn't even have to lift a hand.

Lygor swallowed and tried to laugh again, but it barely reached his lips.

"Beast..."

Beast walked past him.

He didn't rush. He didn't shove. He simply moved, forcing Lygor out of his way.

He scooped up his lor'qas and knife from the bench and strode out the doorway, nearly ploughing through Valnar. He didn't break stride. Heart pounding, muscles screaming for action, he followed the thrum of the arena.

Outside, the crowd at Scorchline Arena howled for blood.

His hunger matched theirs.

48

VALNAR

Valnar followed Beast through the winding hallways under the Scorch-line Arena.

He hadn't anticipated that.

Last night, Valnar had pieced Lygor back together. And with a single tilt of his head, Beast had shattered it. He cursed at the purebred, and he cursed at Lygor for being too cocky. For underestimating Beast. For taking it too far.

And he cursed himself most of all. For telling Lygor to come talk to him.

Valnar had always known Beast was a danger to his prince, but he'd thought it would be raw, physical danger — the kind you could counter, restrain, or beat down. But what he'd just witnessed was something else.

Beast had hurt Lygor without lifting a hand.

He kept a few paces behind Beast, watching the way he walked. He carried himself like he was still riding the high of it, shoulders loose, steps controlled. There was something else beneath it too. That barely contained pulse of anger, running just under his skin. Not reckless, but close.

Valnar prayed that anger would give him the edge he needed for this twisted fight.

The torches lining the walls flickered as they moved deeper into the underbelly of the arena. The stone was damp, carrying the thick scent of sweat, blood, and burned oil. The distant roar of the crowd hummed through the walls like a living thing.

Ink stood just outside the launch room, its doors guarded by arena security. The Kaldorian prince wore yet another war paint design on his face today, some angular red patterns shadowing his cheekbones, dark lines across his forehead, and yellow dots, perfectly aligned across his nose and jaw. He straightened when he saw Beast.

"Hey," Ink started. "May Kiejain sharpen your... sword."

Beast walked past Ink without a glance and stepped into the launch room.

Valnar paused for long enough to meet Ink's confused expression. He grabbed the Kaldorian by the arm and whispered., "Take Lodi to the grandstands. I'll meet you there when the fight starts. Keep him away from booze."

Ink opened his mouth, hesitating. He glanced at the doors Beast had disappeared through.

"Valnar, I've seen the arena setup. This fight is fucked."

"I know."

"We need to pull him out."

"It's too late now. Go. Watch Lodi."

Ink exhaled sharply, then nodded, disappearing up the hallway.

Valnar turned and stepped into the launch room, which was an open chamber, slightly underground. At the front, the massive wooden gates loomed, reinforced with thick iron bars. The ramp outside led directly into the battlefield above. The noise of the crowd pressed down like a storm cloud.

And there, off to the side, mounted on a display stand, was the headgear.

Valnar had only found out about the headgear last night at the feast. He had heard the description. He had imagined something crude, but this was worse.

The headgear was shaped like a bull's head, gleaming slick and black in the firelight. It was crafted from oiled leather and waxed fabric, coated in animal fat. The bull's mouth was wide open, to reveal the fighter's eyes and nose, but that did little to make it look less suffocating. A pair of curved horns jutted upward, wickedly sharpened, while thick leather straps dangled from the bottom.

Valnar exhaled slowly. The scent of oil and tallow clung to his throat.

Beast stood dead centre in the room, lor'qas hanging loosely in his hand, his knife tucked away, his focus fixed on the massive gates ahead. He had barely spared the headgear a glance. Unphased.

The purebred took it all in without reaction, like the battle ahead mattered more than the spectacle they were about to make of him. As if the headgear was just another obstacle to cut through. The sight of the headgear unsettled Valnar more than it did Beast.

A group of arena attendants approached, a high-ranking official among them. Two of the workers lifted the heavy headgear from its stand and stepped forward, standing expectantly in front of Beast.

Beast didn't kneel.

A flicker of hesitation passed through the attendants. The official's scowl deepened before he motioned sharply to one of the workers. The man hurried off and returned with a wooden stool, setting it in front of Beast.

Valnar watched in silence as the attendant climbed up, hoisting the headgear over Beast's head. The straps were yanked tight, digging beneath his jaw. The smell of grease and sweat would be suffocating inside the mask, but Beast stood still, unbothered.

The official approached, tugging at the bindings, checking their hold. He made a note in his ledger, nodding in satisfaction before stepping back. Him and the attendants withdrew to the back of the room, leaving the space to Valnar and Beast.

Valnar stepped up beside Beast. The muffled roar of the crowd above filled the space between them. The drums sped up, then stopped sharply. In the silence that followed, the crowd hushed, though their excitement still buzzed beneath the quiet.

The arena master's strong and commanding voice filled the Scorchline. He welcomed the people of Calae, then rambled acknowledgements and niceties to important figures that Valnar couldn't care any less about. He barely listened, only catching pieces as the arena master went on to tell some sort of story to drive the crowd's anticipation to its highest.

It was a story about a group of brave shepherds, and a bull that escaped Darkhome.

"Fuck," Valnar muttered, shifting and rolling his shoulders.

"Calm down," Beast muttered.

Valnar exhaled softly. The man who was about to go out there and fight a wicked game against the odds, was telling *him* to calm down? Kiejain had strange ways of reminding him who needed tempering.

Beast didn't move. He stood like a statue, lor'qas loose in his grip, not the slightest tremor in his hand. The headgear gleamed, the oiled leather catching in the dim torchlight, the gaping maw of the bull's face framing his own.

Valnar swallowed. The longer he stood there, the more aware he became of the pressure in his chest, warning him how this was going to end. The arena master's voice rose again, pausing at the appropriate places, prompting for his audience's reactions. The crowd roared.

Valnar exhaled. "Beast…"

Beast only turned his head after a long pause. The torchlight threw deep shadows across his face, carving out the hollows of his cheekbones, catching on the sheen of the oiled leather. Through the gaping mouth of the bull's head, he pinned Valnar with a gaze that made the knight still like a prey. The headgear had been designed to make him a spectacle, a victim for the slaughter, vulnerable and at risk. But instead, Beast wore it like a weapon, letting it amplify the savage creature that was in there.

The crowd's roar swelled. A thunder of hooves rumbled through the arena above as the arena master welcomed the shepherds, introducing them one by one, each name followed by cheers and claps.

Valnar blinked at the sound, but Beast didn't. He didn't flinch, neither did he shift. He didn't even glance at the gates. He simply watched Valnar. Without words, he told him something with a slight tilt of his head. Not pleading, not demanding.

Telling.

Valnar's throat tightened. He knew what Beast was asking.

The arena master called out again, urging the shepherds to take their places.

The drums resumed, a slow rhythm that invited the crowd to join in, beating fists against benches, stamping feet against stone.

Beast's lips firmed, his jaw tensing as he still kept his eyes on Valnar. Like his life depended on him. The look on his face reminded Valnar of the look Beast gave him at the study in Vadithas's manor, just before Valnar had paralysed him and let those men take him. The same furious, helpless, desperate expression.

The gates groaned open.

The noise and light flooded the launch room.

Beast still watched him. Still asked.

And this time, Valnar listened.

"Fuck it," he muttered as he caved in and stepped back. Without speaking the Kill Word.

Beast turned to face the gates, his chest heaving with a deep breath, a flicker of gratitude briefly crossing his face. He firmed his grip on his lor'qas. He walked past the gates and jogged up the ramp into the Scorchline Arena, Unraged.

49

BEAST

Beast stepped onto the black platform at the edge of the arena.

The moment he emerged from the tunnel, a tidal wave of roaring voices hit him. Thousands crammed into the stands overlooking the battlefield, shouting for blood and death. He shut them out. Nothing would break his focus. Not the noise, not the pathetic look Valnar gave him just before, and certainly not Lygor's sheer audacity, believing he ever had any control over Beast, so certain he could just take anything from him.

But he kept the anger. The heat that still coursed through his veins. He needed that.

The Scorchline Arena stretched before him, almost as large as Switchblade. Unlike most other arenas, the battlefield was an enormous oval instead of a circle. Walls taller than two men separated the battlefield from the rows of stands, balconies, and grandstands. Above the battlefield, chains crisscrossed the open sky, suspending dozens of braziers in the air.

Beast's gaze swept the field. On either side of the battlefield, standing atop their own black platforms, six figures waited — three to his left, three to his right. The shepherds.

They sat astride short, broad-chested horses, their manes shaved short, their tails cropped and knotted. Their riders were lean, clad in pale leather and cloth. The colours were washed-out like sun-bleached bone. They carried blunt, nonlethal weapons. Nets, weighted for easy entanglement. Hooked chains, meant to snag and pull. Long, padded staves and clubs that would break bones without piercing flesh.

The battlefield itself was a designed nightmare. Shallow pits of coals and tinder lay scattered across the sand. Those would be easy enough to avoid, but he could see more clusters and strips of tinder branching out of the pits, ready to spread the fire traps. More concerning was the glisten of oil streaked across the arena floor. The patterns weren't random. They created corridors, paths, and dead ends. Once set alight, they would be walls of flame.

Beast glanced at the chains that networked above the battlefield, and the glass braziers that hung from them, each housing a small fire. A breeze stirred, sending the braziers overhead, swaying slightly.

Fuck.

There were too many of them.

He spotted wells of muddy water, which would offer reprieve from the heat, though he couldn't tell how deep or how thick those wells were. If the entire arena went in flames, with all the pits and traps caught in fire, some muddy water wouldn't be enough to save him.

To his right, a platform jutted out over the battlefield. The arena master stood there, draped in thick, patterned robes, his hands resting on the carved rail. Beside him, an arena worker stood, clutching a horn in his grip.

Beast inhaled, slow and steady. He scanned the battlefield again, eyes settling on his real opponent.

The trench.

It split the arena cleanly in two, a deep, gaping wound in the sand. Fire churned within, the flames moving like living fingers clawing out of the trench bed. Even from here, Beast could feel the heat, licking at his skin like breath from a fiend's maw.

There was a stone bridge along the right side of the arena, but it was guarded by archers and arena security. Beast wouldn't be allowed to cross it; that bridge was for the shepherd. The only other way of crossing to the other side was through a path of uneven stones. They jutted from the fire, spanning across, their surfaces blackened from the heat. The gaps between them were wide, some too wide. A single misstep would send him plunging into his death.

Beyond the trench was another stretch of battlefield, designed similar to the first half, but with more fire traps and less mud wells. At the far end of the arena was another black platform, like the one he stood now. His target. Where the Fire Breath Trial would end.

His mind calculated the distances, the locations of the fire pits and traps, and the glistening oil that marked the ground. Avoid the shepherds. Cross the trench. Don't let the headgear catch a spark.

The arena master gestured at his worker, and the man blared the horn.

Beast ran.

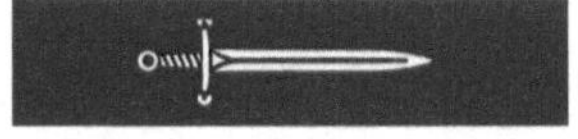

VALNAR

Valnar ran.

His boots slammed against the stone, breath steady, muscles burning as he took the stairs three at a time. The underbelly of the arena was a maze of tunnels and chambers, each twist and turn gave him the fear of getting lost. The hallway ahead stretched long and dim, ending in a bright archway. The exit to the higher stands.

That's when he heard the horn.

A deep, guttural sound that sent a tremor through the stone.

Valnar pushed harder. His legs burned as he sprinted, barrelling through the passage. The light at the end exploded as he burst out into the open, searing his vision white. With his eyes blinded by light, the thunderous wave of screams, shouts, and cheers briefly disoriented him.

He staggered a step, blinking rapidly. The sun burned against the stone walls, the vast arena stretching out before him. He took in the wicked design in a breath.

The sprawling oval pit, the patterns of oil laced into the sand, the pits of coals waiting to catch, the mud wells, the hanging braziers swaying above.

Fuck.

Fire Breath was designed to kill beasts, not let them win.

Beast was a blur of motion, tearing across the battlefield. The shepherds were already moving, riding hard, closing in. The short, broad-backed horses kicked up sand as their riders wielded their blunt weapons. They didn't need to kill. They only needed to drive Beast where they wanted.

And Beast was heading straight for the trench.

Valnar shoved past a few lower-ranking arena officials, making his way up toward the grandstand reserved for Lygor. He stepped onto the shaded platform and found Ink leaning against the railing, his attention locked on the chaos below.

And Lygor...

Lygor was lounging on a couch, his feet up. A tray full of snacks beside him, and a glass of wine in his hand. Two purebreds — a house slave and a pleasure slave, courtesy of Vadithas — accompanied him. The house slave waited with a bottle of wine, and the female pleasure slave sat behind him, rubbing his shoulders.

"Lodi..." Valnar's throat clenched.

"Valnar," Lygor said. He tossed a grape at him. "Move, you're blocking my view."

Irritation poured out of him as he watched Lygor gulp down the wine and hold the glass to the house slave to fill up. Ink became the target of Valnar's ire, but the Kaldorian prince simply shook his head and focused on the fight.

Below, Beast was moving fast across the battlefield, but he wouldn't make it. The shepherds were gaining ground faster. One of them veered off, galloping toward the nearest brazier overhead.

Valnar's stomach dropped.

The shepherd swung his stave, striking the hanging metal.

The brazier lurched, then dropped, flames spilling from the shattered glass as it plunged straight into Beast's path.

BEAST

The brazier streaked through the air, a mass of glass and sparks, tumbling toward his path.

Beast caught the movement in his periphery and veered sharply before it landed, sand kicking up beneath his feet. He didn't stop to watch it crash. He ran parallel to the trench instead, pace relentless, breath steady.

Behind him, the pit burst into flames. The fire licked at the oil-soaked sand, spreading to the loose timber scattered around.

Hooves thundered. A shepherd closed in, cudgel raised. Beast twisted, the blow grazing past his shoulder as he spun. His lor'qas was firm in his grip, fingers tight around the worn leather hilt. Another rider flanked him, coming from the side. A stave whooshed past just over his head as he ducked.

A third shepherd approached, fast on an overambitious horse.

Beast turned with the momentum, lor'qas flashing up to parry the strike. His blade met with the shepherd's cudgel, the impact reverberating through his arm. He followed with a counter, a quick strike aimed at the rider's ribs, but it was blocked. He didn't engage further. There was no time. The other shepherds were closing in.

He ran.

He turned toward the trench again, which loomed ahead. Fire churned inside like an abyss.

A shepherd emerged from the side. Beast dodged instinctively, his body twisting away from the oncoming strike.

And he barely stopped himself from walking right into a pile of coal and loose timber.

He didn't see who hit the brazier. He didn't even see it land.

One moment, he was noticing how close he'd been to the fire trap. And in the next, heat slammed into him like a wall.

VALNAR

Beast jumped away from the fire and hit the ground. His lor'qas flew from his grasp. He landed rough, rolling once before coming to a stop.

The horn blared.

Valnar found himself leaning over the rails, like he was about to jump into the battlefield. Beast was down and unarmed. The shepherds had him. This was the moment they'd strike.

But they didn't.

They reined in their horses, circling, weapons still but ready.

"The horn," Ink said.

Valnar's gaze snapped to the arena master's platform. The man stood with his arms spread, palms on the rail in front of him, watching the fight. His assistant gripped the horn in both hands.

Ink exhaled sharply beside him. "He's burning."

Valnar followed his stare and felt his stomach lurch.

Beast's back and arm were on fire. The flames licked at his body, curling along his shoulder, creeping towards his headgear.

The purebred rolled in the sand frantically, smothering the flames before they could reach his head. He scrambled, half-rising as if expecting the shepherds to be on him. But they still kept their distance.

The arena master raised a finger, and the horn blared again.

Beast lunged for his lor'qas at the same time the shepherds moved. His fingers closed around the hilt, but he wasn't fast enough.

A horse came right at him, and Beast rolled, barely avoiding being trampled. He pushed to his feet, too slow, just in time to meet the next two riders. He parried one, then greeted the other with his bracer shield, though he almost lost his footing.

"Ten seconds," Ink said. "He gets ten seconds break when he's hit."

"Isn't that cheating?" Lygor chuckled. He tossed a grape into the air and caught it with his mouth, then pulled the pleasure slave into a long kiss.

Around Beast, the battlefield burned. The oil lines had caught. Flames curled along the sand, feeding on the tinder-strewn ground. Two other pits roared to life, turning the battlefield into a maze of fire and smoke.

The shepherds' horses barely reacted to the fire, prancing through the blaze as if it were nothing. Valnar wondered how many Fire Breaths these shepherds had fought before.

"Ink," Valnar said, his throat dry. "You've been to the gambling dens."

It wasn't a question, but Ink nodded anyway.

"What odds do they give for him?"

"Three hundred to one."

Valnar's jaw tightened. "Him winning?"

Ink's war paint made his grimace look like a growl. "Him crossing the trench."

Valnar swore under his breath. He clenched his fists as he watched Beast weave through the chaos. Beast's steps faltered, like he wasn't sure which direction to go. He was disoriented by the smoke, fire, and by shepherds charging out of nowhere with quick and nasty attacks Beast could barely meet. He was forced to backtrack nearly to where he started.

"Why don't you try praying, Valnar?" Lygor asked. "Maybe Kiejain will give him a hand." He pulled the half-dressed pleasure slave to his lap, his hands sliding down her hips. He was hardly even looking at the arena, too busy getting his face sucked.

Something snapped in Valnar's chest. He moved like a blur of rage, yanking the house slave by his arm and shoving him towards the steps. He pulled the pleasure slave off next, and sent her after the other.

"Fuck you, Valnar," Lygor yelled, sitting up.

"Lodi, enough with this."

Lygor held out his wine glass. "You kicked him out, you better be my wine-bearer."

"He's down there, risking his life. For you!"

"Oh, spare me. He's not doing it for me. This whole Twilight of Infinity plan was his idea."

"You went through all that trouble to get him! He's your symbol. Everything depends on him."

"You think I don't know that?"

"Then act like it!"

"What do you want me to do?" Lygor hands gripped the wine glass tighter, his knuckles white. A tremor ran through his arm, barely perceptible, but betraying the turmoil within. "Cheer? How's that gonna help?"

Below them, Beast had found an opening — a spot where the fire hadn't yet spread. He moved toward it, but he wasn't fast enough.

It was the armour.

Valnar saw it. The armour was weighing him down. Beast had wanted to wear something lighter, but Valnar's insistence on proper armour, on making sure he had protection, was now going to cost him his life.

Lygor cupped his hands around his mouth and yelled: "Go Beast! You can do this! Yeah!" He raised his eyebrows at Valnar. "Did that help?"

Valnar met Lygor's eyes, and they were not the eyes of the young, confident prince he'd met and sworn to protect five years ago. Beneath Lygor's sulky attitude, Valnar saw the festering hurt of rejection, and realised that wound had been there since King Leonis sent him to Kaldoria. Lygor had never learned how to sit still with his own pain, how to endure being denied or dismissed. His pride ran too deep, and when it was bruised, he lashed out like a petulant child. But this...

This was worse than wounded pride.

This was helplessness. The slave they called Lion of Zarall had become something Lygor could never be—beloved by the people, a living symbol of House Zarall. While Chinderia's subjects would dutifully put a crown on Lygor's head, they would riot behind the slave. A purebred who barely spoke, while their rightful heir remained a stranger to them. And as if that wasn't painful enough, Lygor had fallen for Beast, and the slave was too hollow to ever reciprocate. He could order his life or death, but he would never truly possess him, neither could he save his life, sitting in these stands right now, forced to watch.

Lygor was powerless.

"Do better," Ink said. "Least you can do is show him some respect."

"Fuck you, Ink."

A wave of shouting rose from the stands, dragging their attentions to the battlefield. A shepherd came up behind Beast, mace raised. Beast turned, but not in time.

The mace slammed into his chest.

The horn blared again.

BEAST

Valnar's damn insistence on the armour saved his life.

The mace hit him with brutal force, sending him sprawling. A sharp, relentless pain tore through his ribs, but at least the armour had lessened the brunt of it. He didn't think they were broken. But if he'd been wearing anything less, his chest would have caved.

The horn blared again.

Beast grit his teeth, half-expecting another strike, but just like before, the shepherds kept their distance.

He exhaled sharply, pushing himself up onto his hands. So it was confirmed. The horn signalled a halt. A rule. He could use this.

He didn't let himself relax.

Pain lanced his ribs, but he pulled himself to his feet. He scattered the sand as he searched and found his lor'qas. He had seconds before the horn blared again.

He forced himself to scan the battlefield. The trench was still ahead, fire twisting within it like a living thing. It was odd how much he dreaded the trench, and yet how badly he wanted to get there. The shepherds wouldn't let him reach it. Not directly. That meant running straight for it was suicide.

He needed to change tactics.

His gaze darted over the placement of the pits, the braziers swaying above, the sheen of oil and tinder snaking across the sand. He traced the paths in his mind, calculating. Where would they drive him? Where did they want him to go?

The horn blared again and Beast moved.

He still ran for the trench, but not directly. He curved his path into a wide arc, avoiding an unlit fire pit. He needed them to anticipate him. To think they had control.

A shepherd reacted immediately, spurring his horse toward the nearest brazier. Another one rode to intercept Beast, intending to drive him straight into the unlit pit.

Beast pivoted.

He turned toward the shepherd, who was heading for the brazier. He sprinted, then leapt and caught the saddle, planting his foot on the shepherd's boot. The horse snorted, staggering under the sudden weight as Beast hauled himself up.

The shepherd twisted in the saddle, arm still reaching for the brazier.

Beast drove his lor'qas beneath the man's arm.

The shepherd choked, his grip on the reins loosening. Beast clung to the saddle for a moment, trying to pull himself into control of the horse. But the shepherd slumped to the side, and his foot tangled in the stirrups. The horse screamed, tilting its head to the side and trotting in a circle to compensate for the dead weight he dragged along one side.

Beast had no choice. With a sharp breath, he launched himself at another shepherd. His shoulder slammed into the man's torso, knocking them both off the saddle. They hit the sand and rolled. The impact jarred his ribs, wrenching another surge of pain through his side.

Amid the smoke and burnt wood's smell, a sharp, acrid scent from the shepherd stung his eyes.

Somewhere behind him, a fire pit ignited. Another shepherd had knocked the brazier onto it. The heat flared nearby.

Beast recovered first, untangling himself from the shepherd. Then he twisted and shoved the dazed man toward the flames. He watched the man fall into the burning pit. For a brief second, Beast expected a scream, a body thrashing, the familiar smell of burnt flesh filling his breath.

But a moment later, the shepherd walked back out.

Beast froze.

The man's stave burned at the tip, his face slightly singed, but otherwise, he was fine.

Beast's gaze dropped to the armour and once again, he noticed how pale and washed-out the leather looked. Then, he figured it out.

The shepherds' armour were treated for fire resistance.

And he'd lost his lor'qas when he tackled the man off the horse.

Fuck.

VALNAR

Valnar's grip tightened around the rail as he watched Beast prepare to meet the shepherd unarmed. He moved fast, dodging the shepherd's first strike. The stave swung past his ribs. Beast twisted, keeping light on his feet, reading not just the man in front of him but the others circling in the smoke.

Another shepherd closed in. Beast ducked under a cudgel that swooshed past over his head. He stood and parried a stave with his bracer shield. Then, he quickly rolled aside to avoid being trampled by a horse.

"I remember giving you an order, Valnar," Lygor said coldly. He held the wine glass up. "You kicked my slaves out, now get me more wine."

When Valnar didn't answer, he threw his wine glass at him. He missed, and the glass shattered against the rail.

"Lodi, snap out of this." Valnar squared his shoulders, then loosened his hands at his sides. Discipline over impulse, just as Kiejain taught. "I know you can't help him, and I know he hurt you, but—"

Below, Beast had somehow disarmed the shepherd who was on foot, snatching the stave off his hands. But before he could press his advantage, another shepherd rode in, struck from behind. Beast barely managed to pivot, raising the stolen stave just in time to parry.

"You think he can *hurt* me?" Lygor scoffed. "He's just a fucking slave."

The stave blurred between Beast's hands as he spun, striking and deflecting. The flames spat and soared around him, the smoke curling over him like a cloak. He fought like the fire itself, fast and ferocious, yet he couldn't gain ground. They were boxing him in. Unarmed, outnumbered, and surrounded. Normally, Valnar would feel confident in Beast's ability to handle these men. He had fought worse odds before. Defeated more, alone. But this wasn't just a fight.

This was a trial against the arena itself.

The shepherds didn't need to beat him. They only needed to control him.

And they were doing it well.

"Bitterness rots the blade from inside out," Valnar said softly. "That's not Kiejain's way."

"You need to stop acting like a twelve times blessed man, Valnar. We both know you're a fucking coward."

Lygor hadn't moved — still sprawled across the couch like he owned the arena, arms draped over the backrest, chin tilted just enough to look down at him without standing. There was a cruel glint in his eyes.

"I won't let you push me away too," Valnar said.

"I don't need to," Lygor said indifferently. "I know you'll abandon me, just like you abandoned your brothers in the Kiejain's Army."

The words plunged into Valnar's chest, sinking deep, sharp with both pain and fury. He couldn't look at Lygor. He couldn't reconcile that voice, that cruelty, with the man he'd sworn to protect. Instead, he turned his gaze to the battlefield below. Another battlefield where flames licked the air and chaos reigned. A man standing alone in the centre of it. While Valnar stood aside and watched. Not permitted to aid. He understood now. That tightness he had been carrying inside his chest for days. It wasn't just the fear of losing Beast. It was the fear of bearing witness to horror and being shackled by silence. Powerless to intervene.

Helpless.

A shepherd came from Beast's left, feigning high, while another charged from the right. Beast parried the first, ducked under the second, only to find himself corralled closer to one of the mud wells. They were herding him. From the moment Valnar had laid his eyes on Scorchline Arena, he knew Beast's chances were impossible.

Just like he knew his old unit's chances against that fiend hound were impossible.

"You preach honour and ideals, but how did your ideals fare for you when things got real and you froze?"

"Low blow, Lygor," Ink said. "He had his orders."

"You shut the fuck up. I'll deal with you later."

Ink turned away, but not with anger or indifference. He had an air of quiet resignation of someone who had recognised the value of not engaging. Watching him, Valnar was reminded of a teaching he'd long known but never fully embraced. A knowledge he'd grown so used to ignoring: The Twelve Riders didn't soar into every battle together. Some fights were meant to be faced alone.

One of the shepherds swung a hooked chain at Beast. The steel hook caught the stave and yanked it from Beast's grip, the force dragging him forward. He staggered, off balance. Valnar's heart rose to his throat. Then, he released his breath as if surrendering the air to the truth he couldn't escape anymore.

Beast was to face and defeat the Scorchline Arena, alone. And Lygor was to face his weaknesses — the shame, the pride, the humiliation, the pain and resentment, and the jealousy that ate him from the inside out — alone.

And Valnar was to stand down and watch. His trial was to endure his helplessness in silence. To accept that he wasn't a hero.

Another shepherd rode in with a cudgel. Beast barely managed to raise his arm to block. The bracer took the impact, but the sheer force sent him stumbling closer to the mud pit. His boot slipped on the slick edge. He tried to regain his footing, but the ground betrayed him.

Beast went under.

The horn blared.

The stands erupted into cheers.

Ink cursed loudly and Lygor went quiet, sitting taller to see the arena better.

In the mud pit, Beast splashed violently, breaking the surface with a heaving gasp. He staggered to his feet, but plunged back in. He tried to push forward, and submerged again.

"Does he not know how to swim?" Lygor huffed. "Is he drowning or something?"

Ink's brows furrowed. "Water can't be that deep."

Valnar leaned forward, fingers digging into his scalp as he dragged a hand through his hair. "Kiejain the first, strike me twelve times," he cursed as he watched Beast fight against the mud and water. His jaw clenched as realisation settled in.

It was the gambeson.

BEAST

The mud swallowed him whole.

Cold, thick and suffocating, it clung to his limbs like chains, dragging him down with every movement. He twisted, pushing against it, but the weight of his soaked gambeson and gear pressed down like a stone cage. His boots sank deep. Water filled his ears, muting the arena's roar.

Beast forced himself up, sucking in air, spitting out mud. He heard the horn and knew he had precious seconds. No more.

He fought to move, but the waterlogged gambeson pulled at him, turning every motion into a struggle. The fabric, stiff with wet sand and filth, kept him from bending his arms. His fingers, numb and sluggish, felt useless.

He gritted his teeth and shoved forward, reaching for the edge of the pit. His foot slipped. The mud sucked him down again.

The horn blared.

Just as his fingers found purchase, something slammed into him.

Beast barely had a heartbeat to react before he was thrown back into the mud.

It was the same shepherd he was fighting before. The one on foot. The bastard had followed him.

A knee crushed against Beast's stomach, forcing the air from his lungs. The weight shoved him deeper, water closing over his face. He bucked, twisting, but the damn gambeson made his limbs feel like they were encased in lead.

The shepherd grabbed his headgear by the horns and dunked his head under water.

Cold water rushed into his nose and mouth, filling his throat with filth. His muscles screamed as he struggled against the man looming over him, pinning him down. He was drowning.

In an arena made of fire, he was going to die beneath the water.

He thrashed, trying to reach for his knife, but his fingers were too numb, too slow. The gambeson wrapped around him like a corpse shroud, making every movement a battle. The shepherd tightened his grip and pushed harder.

A black haze edged into his vision and his arms drifted like useless logs.

Then, his hand scraped something sharp.

Without thinking, his fingers curled around it, ignoring the sting as the jagged edge bit into his palm. A piece of glass from one of the braziers. He drove it into the shepherd's hand.

The man roared, jerking back and easing his hold for the smallest fraction. It was all Beast needed.

Beast surged upward, a desperate strength ripping through his veins. He slammed his body into the shepherd. The man's eyes barely had time to widen before Beast dragged the glass across his throat. Blood vanished into the mud as the man collapsed. Beast didn't stop to watch him die.

He clawed his way out, hands scrambling for anything solid. His body burned with effort, his ribs screaming, his gear a relentless weight on his shoulders. But he kept going.

When he pulled himself free, the thick, hot air hit him like a slap. Smoke surrounded him. He coughed violently. His eyes stung. The air itself turned to fire in his throat.

The shepherds had lit everything.

All the fire pits and traps around the mud well were on fire. Flames curled high around him, boxing him in completely. He blinked and fought against a coughing fit, tears running down his face, as he tried to find a way out. He saw only one path out. A narrow corridor still untouched by the flames. A single gap.

He knew it was a trap. They were herding him.

He covered his mouth and nose with the soaked arm of his gambeson, trying to protect his face from the blazing smoke. He didn't have a choice but to fall for the trap. It was that, or he would stand here and suffocate, or fall back into the mud well and die. He'd rather take his chances against the remaining shepherds, until he could find a path to the trench.

He paused.

The trench.

The trench was so close. Only a wall of flames stood between, followed by a short, clear path that he could stumble through before the shepherds clued in on what he was doing.

It was crazy.

Another coughing fit almost took him out. His breath came ragged, his heart a hammer against his ribs.

Fuck it.

He ran.

Straight into the fire.

The moment he plunged through, the flames clawed at him. Heat surged up his legs, raced across his body. He threw his arms over his headgear, shielding the flammable fabric. The water and the mud that the gambeson stored gave him a brief resistance against the flames, but the heat still seeped through, licking at his skin. The air burned, and the smoke filled his mouth, sinking into his lungs. It was like running through a breathless, blistering night.

Endless pain, endless heat, and the scent of burning oil and flesh.

And then he was out, slogging through a narrow space of sand, before he collapsed onto the cold, stone platform just on the edge of the trench.

The horn blared.

VALNAR

Beast lay sprawled on the black stone platform, steam rising from his soaked skin as he heaved in breath after ragged breath. The crowd erupted, the sheer force of their voices rattling through the arena like thunder.

Valnar released his breath.

Beside him, Ink chuckled, breathless. "That," he exhaled, shaking his head, "was the dumbest, most insane thing I've ever seen." Relief filled his voice, but his tight grin showed he wasn't sure whether to laugh or swear.

Valnar didn't look at Lygor. He settled into his acceptance. He would not try to steer Lygor back the path the Twelve Riders had set for him. He wasn't worthy of saving anyone, though he prayed for them both. He tore his eyes from the battlefield and looked at the arena master's platform.

The man had turned his back to the battlefield, leaning lazily against the railing as though this was just some cheap entertainment at a common inn. He accepted a glass of wine from an attendant, lifting it to his lips. The horn-bearer stood at his side, waiting, but the master didn't seem remotely rushed.

Below, Beast was moving.

Ink straightened. "What's he doing?"

Beast had pushed himself up to his knees, fingers fumbling at the straps of his brigandine armour. A second later, he yanked his bracer shield off, tossing it aside. Then the knife appeared in his hand, hacking at the straps of his armour with quick, sharp movements.

Valnar exhaled through his nose. "He's shedding the weight."

The brigandine fell away. Beast wasted no time, moving straight to his gambeson. As he worked, the purebred kept glancing at the trench ahead of him. The stepping stones spanned across the fire from one side of the trench to the other like scattered bones. They were black with soot, some were smaller, and with different sized gaps between them.

"He can't cross with all that weighing him down."

Beast worked fast, cutting the sleeves and side seams of the gambeson, splitting the fabric so he could tear it free. He wouldn't be able to pull it over his head, so he had to cut and peel the waterlogged cloth off his body piece by piece.

The arena master was still enjoying his wine. The crowd had noticed and were now making more noise. Some were yelling at Beast, urging him on, while others turned their jeers toward the master. They shouted, laughed, or chanted him to hurry up and chug it.

"Kiejain, lend him speed," Valnar muttered. If the horn blared again while his attention was on his armour, he had no way of defending himself.

The arena master took another slow sip.

Valnar heard the couch creak behind him. Lygor stood, stretching lazily. The shattered pieces of the wine glass crunched under his boots as he approached rail, like he was dragging his feet out of boredom, not out of curiosity. He rested one hand on the rail, the other propped against his hip, as he leaned against it casually.

Below, the four remaining shepherds had gathered, their heads close in discussion. Then, three of them broke off, moving toward the stone bridge at the far end of the trench. They would cross the trench and cut him off on the other side.

The fourth shepherd remained, waiting just a few feet from Beast's platform, his weapon raised. Waiting for the horn.

The gambeson finally came free. Beast tore it off, flinging the sodden mass away. He ripped his inner shirt off too. Then he cut the laces of his chausses, peeling them off until he was left in nothing but his short braies. His bare skin was slick with sweat and mud, steam curling off him in the fire lit air.

Lygor chuckled. "Not his first time naked in an arena."

Valnar tilted his head and kept his silence. His eyes blurred. He had sworn an oath to protect Lygor, just like he had sworn an oath to the Kiejain's army. He had forfeited that oath. It pained him to stand back now and watch Lygor fail. Fail to find the decency inside him. But Valnar accepted the pain. Welcomed it.

The arena master tilted his glass and the last of his wine vanished down his throat. With a lazy flick of his fingers, he gestured to the horn-bearer.

As soon as the horn blared, the remaining shepherd rushed Beast to jump across the trench.

BEAST

Beast jumped.

The moment his foot hit the stone, it wobbled beneath him, shifting under his weight. He swayed, arms outstretched, a scream strangled in his throat. His legs trembled, but not from fear. From exhaustion and the brutal toll this fight had already taken.

The heat hit him full force.

The flames roared just beneath his feet, their hungry breath curling towards the edges of the stone he stood on. Every inhale burned, like sucking in air from a furnace. His skin prickled, sweat boiling off his back before it could even drip. The fire stole the moisture from his mouth.

He couldn't stay still.

He jumped to the next stone, slightly bigger and more stable.

His knees nearly buckled on impact, but he steadied himself. He sucked in a lungful of scorched air, feeling it sear all the way down. His vision blurred for a second.

The next stone was too small. He jumped and landed on one foot, barely keeping his balance. The heat made him dizzy. His ears rang. He had to move, had to move now.

He threw himself forward onto the next stone. This one was wide enough for both feet.

Behind him, hooves clattered against the stone. The shepherd they'd left behind was riding back and forth along the trench's edge, watching.

"You almost fell there," the man called over the roar of the fire. "You feeling dizzy yet?"

Beast ignored him, looking ahead to the other side of the trench. *Focus.*

It looked too far.

His stomach clenched and his pulse pounded in his ears in an unfamiliar way. The heat was suffocating, pressing against his skull like a vice. His lungs were two scorching stones inside his ribs. He couldn't breathe.

"You'll fall," the shepherd called out behind. "You're gonna pass out any minute now."

The entire arena demanded his death. He could hear them all. Thousands of voices, jeering, chanting, urging that he falls.

"They all fall," the shepherd said. "It's the sixth step that gets them all. Watch out for that one."

Beast jumped to the next stone.

Wobbled.

Slipped.

And caught himself at the last second.

The shepherd howled and shouted behind him. "Almost got you. Your legs must be feeling heavy now."

Beast's legs shook. His arms too. His fingers twitched.

"You'll smell your own flesh burning. It'll melt off your bones before the fire takes your lungs."

He willed himself to jump onto the next step, but his legs refused to move. His muscles cramped. He was shaking all over.

"You'll feel your eyeballs turn to liquid before they burst."

Beast looked up. The other three shepherds were waiting for him at the other end. Another platform stood just on the edge of the trench. If he could cross and make it there, he would get another break. A moment to breathe.

Then, his eyes surveyed past the platform and the shepherds, to the second half of the arena. And his heart sank.

It was worse than the first half. More unlit pits and traps, more braziers overhead. Designed to burn him alive. If not the flames, the shepherds would get him. He wasn't armoured anymore.

He was fucked.

His vision blurred again. His knees nearly buckled.

The spectators were on their feet, their shouts rising like they'd anticipated he was about to tumble. He lifted his head and spotted the grandstands. He found Valnar, Ink, and... And Lygor. Leaning against the rails, watching him.

They'd sent him here to die.

The thought hit him like a fist to the ribs.

He was never getting his freedom.

He was never leaving this place alive.

Beast swallowed. His throat was so dry it hurt.

Why did he ever want to be free, anyway? What was the point? He would still have to follow Lygor's orders. Could he really be free while people like Lygor existed? Like Vadithas?

Like Olira?

His gaze dropped to the fire below.

The flames twisted, snaking into long, streaming strands of gold and red. The colour reminded him of Saradra's hair.

His breath hitched.

Suddenly, freedom felt so stupid. What was the point without *her*?

The shepherd kept shouting behind him, but he couldn't hear him through the roar in his ears.

It must be a trick of the light, or his mind falling apart. Saradra's face flickered in the fire, watching him. She looked so real. And so beautiful.

Something inside him broke open.

He felt an immense longing, so violent it nearly tore him apart.

He wanted to jump.

He wanted to throw himself into her arms.

VALNAR

"Fuck!" Ink cursed. "He froze."

Valnar barely heard his own thoughts over the deafening roar of the arena.

Lygor's knuckles blanched against the rail, though he kept his voice casual. "I thought he wasn't having those episodes anymore."

Ink wasn't even listening. He was cursing nonstop, hands tangled in his own hair, war paint smeared across his forehead from dragging his fingers over his face too many times. "Shit. He's gonna fall. He's gonna pass out and fall. We need to do something."

"We can't stop the fight," Lygor said through gritted teeth. He hadn't taken his eyes off Beast.

Valnar refused to search his face. His attention was on the arena master, searching for something, anything. The man stood where he had before, his arms crossed, his head tilted. The horn-bearer stood beside him. Like everyone else, they were waiting for Beast to fall. The crowd were on their feet, howling in anticipation.

Their noise dropped for a split second, and exploded into shouts of unhinged excitement.

Valnar spun back, expecting to see Beast fall. Instead, he saw the purebred running.

The wrong way.

Valnar's breath caught. Beast flew back across the steps, his footing suddenly sure and effortless, like the heat, the pain, and the exhaustion no longer mattered.

"Why is he running back?" Ink shouted.

"Was he faking?" Lygor let out a dry laugh. "Did he really just fake freeze?"

"But why is he running back?" Ink shouted again.

Beast was barrelling straight toward the lone shepherd they'd left behind.

The shepherd saw him coming. He raised his mace, squared his stance. The horse beneath him shuffled uneasily. Across the trench, the three remaining shepherds reacted. Two of them turned for the stone bridge. The third stayed back, likely to cut off Beast if he went forward.

Beast jumped at the platform and charged straight at the shepherd. The shepherd braced. At the last second, Beast ducked his head down, lowering the curved horns of his headgear—

And rammed them straight into the horse's flank.

The horse screamed and reared back, front legs kicking the air. The shepherd swung his mace down, then tumbled off the saddle.

Beast was on him before he hit the ground. He wrenched the mace from his grasp and brought it down at the shepherd's skull. The first impact sent a sharp crack that Valnar could swear he heard despite the roar of the arena. Beast raised the mace and brought it down again.

Ink whooped beside him, slamming a fist against the railing. "Fuck yes!"

Valnar's jaw was tight, eyes fixed on the way Beast was moving. The shepherd was dead, his skull crushed, but Beast didn't stop. He brought the mace down over and over again. Valnar had seen Beast become possessed with a rage like this, blood-hungry and reckless, like there was nothing left of him but fury and instinct. He was lost.

And the other two shepherds were coming.

Valnar's gut twisted. He cupped his hands near his mouth to shout him to look out, then he brought them back down.

He was not a hero. He was not meant to help. He was to suffer his helplessness and watch.

His voice would have been lost in the arena, anyway. Beast wouldn't hear him. He didn't even hear the thunder of hooves behind him. The two shepherds were closing in fast. One readied a hooked chain, swinging it in a lazy circle over his head. The other drifted towards the nearest brazier.

Without a flinch or a stutter, or even a look at the approaching shepherds, Beast sprung to his feet and ran back to the platform. He jumped onto the crossing.

Ink burst into laughter, wild and breathless. "Was he faking that rage too?"

Lygor didn't reply. When Valnar turned his head, he found the prince gone. His eyes met Ink's; a shared grief passed between them. Lygor was gone. His heart too bitter and frosted, he didn't even care enough to watch the man fight the battle Lygor himself had forced him into.

Valnar's prince was truly gone.

The arena went feral.

Beast was flying across the steps, still staggering here and there, still fighting for balance, but moving much faster than before. He kept stumbling forward, like the momentum helped with his balance, kicking himself to the next step, then the next one.

Heading straight for the lone shepherd on the other side.

The two riders behind him veered, redirecting back to the stone bridge, but they wouldn't cross in time. Beast would get to the lone shepherd first. And he still held the blood-soaked mace in one hand.

If he took that shepherd out, then he was free to run. All the way to the end.

BEAST

The arena blurred. Not from speed or smoke, but from the sheer, seething fury crackling through his body. His limbs buzzed. His blood had turned to liquid fire, sparking and burning under his skin. His chest heaved, sweat and blood mixing in rivers down his ribs. His throat was raw from the smoke and the screaming.

His eyes burned, but not from the heat. Tears streaked down his face, leaving tracks in the grime and blood. He refused to look at the flames.

He had wanted to die.

And he was so fucking mad at how badly he'd wanted it. How badly *they* had made him want it. The shepherds. The arena. The whole twelve times fucked Earthome.

He jumped onto the platform on the other end, feet slamming against the stone. The horn announced another break for him. His muscles screamed for rest. He growled louder. The arena master could jam his break into his own arse. Beast didn't give a shit.

Howling like a mad animal, he charged straight at the bastard.

The lone shepherd ahead raised his cudgel and prepared to counter. But then he saw Beast's face, covered in mud and filth and blood, framed by the wicked headgear. His entire chest and ribs were soaked red.

The shepherd's eyes went wide with fear. He turned his horse and bolted.

Coward. Fucking coward.

Beast almost chased after him. His fingers itched to rip through flesh, to break bone, to watch the blood flow. An overwhelming craving for violence consumed him. He wanted to kill the man.

Kill them all.

But he forced himself forward. His feet pounded across the arena, sand kicking up behind him. His body was wrecked, muscles torn apart, lungs ripping open with every breath, but at least the air was clear here. No smoke. No fire. No choking on his own breath. Just air. Just sand.

The end of the arena was so close.

Then, he heard the darkness cursed hooves behind him. He knew before he turned his head that he wasn't going to make it. A blistering, pure rage ripped through his throat. He hesitated between speeding up and slowing down to take down the fuckers. His legs were too sluggish to run faster. His skin was too unprotected to fight. One hit and he wouldn't get back up.

He spun mid-stride, roaring like a fiend, and swung the mace at the oncoming horses. The nearest one reared, hooves flailing, its rider yanking hard on the reins. The second barely dodged, the shepherd swearing as the mass of iron barely missed his leg. The third one — the coward — joined the chase.

Beast resumed running. Swinging the mace wildly, rushing them away, keeping them off him while he drove forward. The ending platform was so close. One more mad dash, and—

VALNAR

The shepherds changed tactics.

One of them swung his stave high, knocking a hanging brazier loose. The heavy glass container lurched, then plunged down, straight at Beast.

Beast dodged at the last second. The brazier crashed on the sand, breaking into molten pieces and spilling oil across the ground.

Another brazier came down. Then another. The three shepherds were aiming directly at him now, not bothering to herd him into a fire pit. All they had to do was have one spark make contact with Beast's headgear.

Beast moved like an animal without fear or hesitation. He twisted, dived, rolled between the deadly rain, barely escaping the next one as it crashed right behind his back, exploding in a rush of fire. The shepherds kept swinging, and the arena roared with each one.

Another brazier came down too close. The flames nearly licked his leg before he launched forward, sprinting harder.

"Did Kyrus steal his mind?" Ink gasped. "*What is he doing?*"

Valnar scowled. Ink wasn't watching the battlefield. His gaze was fixed elsewhere. Valnar followed it — and felt his heart drop.

Lygor.

The prince had stumbled onto the arena master's platform like a rich drunk who'd wandered off and gotten lost. He barked at the two guards blocking his path, arms flailing in furious gestures. Suddenly, he darted forward, slipping past them to charge at the horn-bearer. He wrestled the man down, wrenching the horn from his grip.

Proving Valnar that men could fight and win alone.

Lygor raised the horn to his lips. But before he could sound it and stop the fight, the arena master himself tackled him to the ground.

Valnar cursed, the word coming out as a choked, strangled sound. He ran down the grandstand, shoving past officials and arena security. He flew down the steps two at a time, rushing through the stands, tossing people out of his way, jumping through the rails and benches that separate the stands into sections. Ink was right behind him.

In the arena master's platform, the security flocked around Lygor. Fists flew. The horn was yanked off his hands. Valnar growled as he ran faster.

Parallel to him, on the battlefield, Beast ran too. The purebred would make it to the end, if he kept running—

The next brazier came straight for his head from behind. Beast didn't see it. It exploded on the headgear with a sickening roar.

The impact threw Beast forward. He staggered onto the sand as the flames caught.

For a heartbeat, the entire arena held its breath.

The headgear ignited.

And the Scorchline went wild.

BEAST

Fire.

It crawled over his scalp, searing into skin. It feasted on his flesh. Heat licked at his ears, his neck, devouring him. His vision blurred, and tears boiled in his eyes. The heat was inside him, filling his lungs, dissolving his breath to smoke before he could even scream.

He fumbled blindly for the chin straps. His fingers were clumsy and half-numb. No, not numb. They hurt; the skin shrivelling, the flesh peeling as he yanked and pulled.

The headgear wouldn't come off.

He patted at it wildly, slapping at the fabric, but it only burned hotter. His skin sizzled beneath his own touch. The sound of it was a sickening hiss, like meat thrown into a hot pan.

Fuck. Fuck!

His hands throbbed. He felt the pain in his bones, as if the fire had already sunk beneath his flesh. Still, he clawed at the headgear, fingers tearing at the straps, at anything. The material melted against his skin. His breath came in short, choking gasps.

He screamed.

It wasn't a human sound. It was something torn from his throat.

He thrashed, rolled, anything to put it out, but the flames consumed him.

50

VALNAR

Valnar stepped through the adjoining door into Lygor's room and shut it behind him.

"How is he?" Lygor asked. His face was pale, except for the mild bruises that painted his cheekbones and jaw. His expression was tight, like a child expecting a flogging for misbehaving. His fingers trembled around the half-full glass of wine.

Ink leaned against the windowsill; his arms crossed. His face was stormy. He'd wiped his warpaint off. His mouth was set in a hard line, and he watched Valnar with disgust.

The three of them were alone in Lygor's room at the manor. The sun was setting. A couple of slaves had come in earlier to tend the fireplace and light the candles, but Lygor had dismissed them quickly. The dim glow suited their moods.

Valnar strode to the bar, poured himself a glass of wine, and downed it in one gulp.

"Valnar?" Lygor asked softly.

Valnar poured himself another.

BEAST

Wake up.

VALNAR

"Valnar, how bad is it?" Lygor repeated.

Valnar didn't speak. Every time he closed his eyes, he saw Beast's body writhing, fire crawling up his skin, the screams tearing through the arena. He remembered the smell, the sound of burning flesh. By the time Valnar reached him, Beast had been twitching, whimpering, barely conscious as Valnar smothered the flames with his cloak.

It was Twelve's blessing that he was still alive.

No. He couldn't call it a blessing.

He shuddered.

"Is he in pain?" Ink asked.

"They gave him something to help him sleep."

Lygor hesitated. "Is he... going to be okay?"

"He'll survive," Valnar said softly. There was no trace of joy or relief in his voice, nothing to suggest this was good news.

Lygor turned and walked toward the fireplace, staring at the dying embers. Ink's features hardened as he looked from Valnar to Lygor.

"What are we gonna do?" Lygor whispered.

BEAST

Wake up.

VALNAR

A gentle knock announced there was someone at the door. Lygor's jaws clenched. He stood tall and took a deep breath before calling, "Come in."

Master Vadithas walked in, followed by Masters Ruzen and Naelar.

Three purebred slaves, dressed in identical plain shirts and trousers, trailed in after them and lined up near the door. All three were beasts, and they looked similar enough to be related.

"Your Highness," Master Naelar said as he closed the door behind him. He glanced at the bruises on Lygor's face, but didn't comment. They already knew. Ruzen had gotten involved to let the arena security release Lygor.

"Good news!" Naelar said. "Lord Brocton has agreed to host your coronation at his castle."

"What?" Lygor mouthed. He narrowed his eyes and looked from one to the other.

"We're having a feast at my manor tonight," Vadithas added. "And he's coming over to pledge his loyalty to you."

"I... I don't understand," Lygor said. He sought an explanation on Valnar's face, but the knight looked just as confused.

"What... don't you understand, Your Highness?" Naeler asked slowly, as if talking to a child.

Lygor puffed his chest out. "I failed your test," he said, with a hint of challenge. "Lion of Zarall lost Fire Breath."

The masters grinned at each other, as if sharing a joke Lygor couldn't understand.

"No, Your Highness," Naeler said carefully. "A slave lost Fire Breath."

BEAST

Beast opened his eyes.

At least, he thought he did. There was not much difference between sleep and wakefulness. Everything was dark and blurry. His thoughts were sluggish, like drifting through thick water. Thick with mud.

A mud well.

A weight crushed onto his chest, a feeling like he was drowning.

He gasped and found he couldn't move much. The drowning sensation intensified. He gagged like mud was filling his mouth. His body resisted movement.

Something was wrong.

His breath quickened, but he didn't feel the sting of bruised ribs, the raw ache of burned flesh. He should be in agony. He should feel his body torn apart by fire.

But there was... nothing.

Just a hollow absence where pain should be.

His sluggish thoughts latched onto that wrongness. The last thing he remembered was flames. His own skin melting off his bones.

Why wasn't he screaming?

His hands twitched at his sides. Or tried to.

A sharp cold crawled through his gut. His fingers didn't spread, didn't curl. He lifted his arms — or something that felt like his arms — into the blurry darkness that hung above his face.

His vision was wrong. It wasn't just dark, it was hazy; shapes bleeding into each other, shifting in ways that made his stomach lurch. Everything looked warped, smudged, like trying to see through a sheet of thick glass.

But he saw enough of his hands.

A gasp tore out of his throat.

VALNAR

"What does that mean?" Lygor demanded. "I thought your support was contingent on Lion of Zarall winning your twisted fight."

Naelar raised his hands in surrender. "I apologise for the misunderstanding, Your Highness. We only wanted to see if we could trust *your* slave to succeed."

"We think your plan to free Lion of Zarall and use him to stir people up was genius." Ruzen nodded. "He has such an influence on people. It's remarkable."

"We just weren't sure if the slave you had was the right one for the task," Vadithas chimed in. "In terms of fighting capacity and obedience."

The room suddenly felt hot. Valnar's blood rushed to his ears. "You retrained him," he growled as he took a step towards Vadithas. "To make sure he was obedient enough to be trusted." He vaguely noticed his nails were digging at his palms.

Vadithas pursed his lips. "I'm not Twelve's miracle, Sir Valnar. I would need a lot longer than three nights to properly fix him."

"Then why did you insist on retraining him?" Ink asked. His voice was unusually calm.

Vadithas rolled his eyes. "Occupational curiosity." He smirked. "And I needed to see how broken his mind was. I can confirm it's beyond repair."

"So is his body," Ruzen added.

"No." Lygor shook his head. "My plan won't work without him."

Naelar smiled. "But *our* plan will."

BEAST

Beast sobbed.

His breath hitched and his body trembled, but not from the pain. He pushed himself up, slowly and awkwardly. His body didn't feel like it belonged to him. His muscles ached. A faint heat lingered on his hands and face, but it was so muffled, he wasn't sure if it was real or a memory.

He felt weak. He sat up, and the effort left him short of breath. The small glow of a candle flickered somewhere nearby. It was tiny, and yet, the light hurt his eyes. It needled through them like hot iron. He squeezed them shut, but his lids were dry, raw, like sandpaper scraping over his eyes. Every blink sent fresh sparks of pain through his skull.

His breath came faster.

He moved carefully, shifting his legs down the side of the bed. He planted his feet on the carpeted floor. Every motion felt like he was pushing his body into an unnatural angle. He rested his hands on his lap. He breathed a sharp, herbal smell, thick enough to choke on, clinging to the back of his nose. Some sort of medicine. Ointments and poultices. It reminded him of Olira.

His gut twisted, made him want to retch.

He forced his blurry gaze downward, trying to see. His hands — or what should have been his hands — were wrapped in thick bandages. They were so swollen, they looked nearly double the size. He tried to flex his fingers and couldn't feel them.

A whisper crawled from his lips.

"No."

His breath quickened as he lifted his hands, bringing them closer, trying to see past the blur, trying to understand how bad it was. He brought his hands to his mouth, and discovered his face was bandaged too, though his eyes and mouth were left free. He fumbled against the knots, using his teeth. It took too long, but the knots finally began to loosen. The fabric slipped and the scent of herbs and medicine grew stronger.

"Please," he whispered as he pulled the bandages free. "Please, please, *please*..."

VALNAR

"Lion of Zarall is just a name given to a slave," Naelar explained. "Slaves don't own names. They only carry them."

Lygor wasn't speaking. He stared hard at the Master of Chains. His eyes grew large with understanding. He shook his head subtly.

"Master Vadithas?" Naelar prompted.

Vadithas strode over to the three purebreds standing silently by the door. He presented them with a wave of his hand. "These three are amongst the hundred purebred beasts I'll be pledging for your cause," he said, pride evident in his tone. "We'll arrange the transfer of ownership first thing in the morning and I'll deliver their Words. The rest of your hundred are at my warehouse. All yours."

Lygor still didn't speak. He only stared at the three slaves.

Valnar looked at them too, feeling a growing unease. He was just noticing how similar the slaves were. Almost identical. Same build, same wavy blond hair...

His throat tightened. He cleared it, forcing out words. "Are you suggesting...?"

Vadithas bowed his head slightly toward Lygor. "Each of these three are remarkable fighters, Your Highness. Among the finest beasts money can buy."

"That's outrageous," Valnar hissed. He shook his head. This couldn't be right. They couldn't dare to suggest— Lygor wouldn't...

"In fact," Vadithas continued smoothly, ignoring him, "this one," he gestured to one of the slaves, "was raised by the same breeder as Lion of Zarall." He turned and patted another on the cheek. "And this one... fathered by the same male."

Valnar gawked at the slave. The resemblance was undeniable. A couple of years younger than Beast. Same grey eyes, but without the defiant spark. His chest tightened.

This poor bastard was Beast's half-brother.

A wave of nausea rolled through him. He didn't trust himself to speak. Didn't trust himself to argue. Relief surged through him when Lygor finally broke the silence.

"No."

Naelar lifted a brow. "Your Highness..."

"I see your point," Lygor said firmly. For the first time in a long while, he sounded like himself — that sharp, sometimes arrogant, cutthroat prince he'd been before the Domestic Assets Trade Union. "But I won't use a fake Lion of Zarall."

A tangible silence hung between them. Just hours ago, Beast had rejected and humiliated him. Shattered his heart. Valnar had witnessed the hurt. And yet, here he was, still defending Beast. Still loyal. Valnar was brimming with pride for him.

Vadithas blinked, his eyebrows creeping toward his scalp. He walked over to the fireplace and prodded the charred remains of the woods with an iron stick. The embers barely flickered.

Ruzen took a step forward. His bulky arms were crossed over his chest. "If I may, Your Highness, what makes your slave a special one?"

Lygor chuckled bitterly through his nose. "I don't think you would understand, Master Ruzen."

"With all due respect, I've seen many beasts come and go. They gain fame one day and they meet their fate the next day. Nothing makes one more special than—"

"Look, Master Ruzen," Lygor cut in, patience thinning. There was a note of warning in his voice, signalling his rapidly fading patience. "I can't simply discard my slave and replace him with another. My father paraded him at every feast. The public may not know the difference, but the noble houses? They know Lion of Zarall's face well enough to recognise a fraud."

Ruzen grimaced.

Vadithas glanced up from the fireplace.

Valnar knew. The bitter taste of wine returned to his mouth.

"His *face*, Your Highness?" Naelar enquired cautiously.

BEAST

Beast slid down from the bed and slumped on the carpeted floor.

Soaked in the pungent herbal scent of medicine, the bandages lay in a pool at his feet. His hands lay bare on his lap. He stared at them. His vision was still wrong; shapes blurred and shifting, edges smeared together like wet ink. He blinked, but it didn't clear. The candlelight was too bright and sharp, stabbing into his skull like needles.

The hands before him didn't look like his own.

They were swollen, the skin stretched tight, raw and shiny in places. The outlines of his fingers wavered, disappearing into the haze of his sight, but he could see enough.

Enough to understand his hands were fucked.

He let out a small, pathetic whimper.

VALNAR

"No!" Lygor snapped, shaking his head firmly. "I won't replace him."

"Then your plan won't work," Vadithas hissed.

"You've got resources. Find someone to heal him."

"It's impossible, Your Highness. Even if he could be fully healed, it'll take more than three months. He won't be ready for Twilight of Infinity."

"No." Lygor's voice was stone.

Valnar turned his head slightly, pausing. He thought he'd heard a soft, muffled voice through the adjacent door.

Lygor pressed on, undeterred. "He's resilient. He'll make it—"

"Have you seen his hands, Your Highness?"

BEAST

"No," Beast sobbed. "No, no, no, no..."

He took a ragged breath and buried his face on his forearms.

"No... no... no..."

VALNAR

"I said I won't discard him!"

"You don't have to discard him," Naelar reasoned. "You can still keep him at your side, do whatever you want with him. But we'll have to use one of these three to pose as Lion of Zarall and fight at Twilight—"

They all could hear it now. A soft cry, growing louder and louder. It was coming from the adjoining room.

"No, no, no, no..."

Valnar was the first to rush into his bedroom. Lygor was right behind him, followed by the others.

Beast was on the floor, slumped next to the bed. The bandages lay discarded around him. His burnt hands were bare.

Lygor gagged at the sight of them.

Even Valnar grimaced. He'd already seen them before, while the physician had worked on them, but the sight still turned his stomach. Raw, ruined flesh. The skin barely holding together, wrapped in an angry sheen of scarlet and blistering white. Beast had slumped in on himself, howling and wailing.

"Hey," Valnar said, as he approached him. "Hey, it's okay—"

Beast jerked back. His head was fully bandaged, save for his mouth and his eyes. His face, hidden under that bandage, was burnt just as bad as his hands. The physician had warned Valnar that his vision would be impaired for days, maybe weeks, but his eyes were the least of his concerns. Burns like these were unpredictable, their true severity not fully known until days later. The risk of flesh rot was the real danger now. Even with salves and poultices, even if they changed the bandages daily, if rot set in, there was nothing to be done. Moreover, severely burned flesh shrank as it healed. His skin would tighten and twist, pulling his fingers into useless, mangled claws if they weren't careful.

That was, of course, if he survived the next few days.

"No!" yelled Beast. He scrambled backward, dragging himself on his elbows, shaking his head violently. "No!"

"I'll get Caerlo," mumbled Vadithas.

"Hey, hey, it's okay," Valnar said. He grabbed Beast's elbow, careful to avoid the worst of the burns, and tried to help him up.

Beast ripped his arm free and staggered back. He lost his balance, flailed his arms blindly, and caught the edge of the table, then knocked it over, sending medicine jars, a jug of water, and cups crashing to the floor.

"He'll hurt himself," Ruzen commented.

"Beast, stop it," Valnar ordered, stepping forward again. He tried to hold him down, but Beast fought him wildly.

Ruzen was right. Beast was completely lost in panic, and at this rate, he was going to hurt himself even worse. Valnar moved behind him and wrapped his arms around his chest, trying to restrain him. Beast threw his head back, almost breaking his nose. Valnar grunted. He understood why Beast was acting like this. A permanent injury was his greatest fear. All he knew, all his purpose in life, was to fight.

And now, he was never going to hold a sword again. Not with those hands.

Valnar didn't need to guess what was running through his head. Poor idiot probably thought they were going to get rid of him — send him to the Tribesmen, or worse, to one of Naelar's slaughterhouses. But Valnar knew Lygor would never do that.

"*Padlociatius*," said Lygor.

Beast's body went limp in Valnar's arms. The slave's sobs and wails were replaced by a sudden silence. Valnar hated that silence.

From the outside, Beast almost looked peaceful, as if he had simply fallen asleep. But Valnar's arms were still wrapped around his chest, and he could feel the rapid, irregular beat of his heart.

"Do you see it now, Your Highness?" Naeler asked. He was standing too close to Lygor, with his hand on the prince's shoulder, speaking directly into his ear. "He can't fight for you anymore. But your plan can still work. You can still have your throne back."

Every word was true. Beast could never win Twilight of Infinity. Disguising another slave as Lion of Zarall could work. Lygor realised it too. His eyes softened with pity as he looked at Beast's burnt hands.

Valnar knew the decision was made.

"Come, Your Highness," Naelar said smoothly, steering Lygor back toward his room. "We should discuss your coronation. I think Lion of Zarall should make an appearance that day."

Ruzen followed them, shutting the door behind him.

"Ink," Valnar said. "Get his legs. Help me put him back to bed."

Ink didn't move for long seconds. He looked toward the far corner of the room, his expression cold and hard.

"Ink?"

Ink's eyes trailed to Beast. He sighed and stepped forward to help Valnar. Beast's paralysis was fading, but he hadn't started thrashing yet. Ink grabbed his legs and together they carried the slave to Valnar's bed.

"My hands," Beast sobbed. His breath hitched, turning rapid and shallow. A low groan followed, his body trembling. "It hurts. It hurts..."

"I know, I know..." Valnar murmured. He wanted to comfort him, reached out to place a hand on his shoulder, but the moment his fingers touched bare skin, Beast gasped in pain, and Valnar jerked his hand back.

Caerlo entered the room, muttering something about his medicine and equipment being wrecked, but he fell silent after one look at Valnar's face. With a huff, he ordered a house slave to fetch clean bandages and fresh herbs.

He rummaged through the mess, salvaging a clean cloth from the table, then pulled a small vial from his jacket and tipped a few drops onto the fabric. He pressed the cloth against Beast's mouth and nose. Beast stiffened, his body tensing for a moment, before his eyes rolled back and he went limp.

Valnar and Ink retreated to the corner of the room to give the physician and the slaves room to work.

"I'm returning to Kaldoria."

"What?" Valnar's head snapped at Ink. When Ink didn't elaborate further, Valnar pressed on. "You can't! What— What about your quest? The shame of forfeiting your quest—"

"Is nothing compared to being part of the shit Lygor is doing here." Ink's voice dripped with disgust. "I can't be part of this."

"Ink—" Valnar put his hand on Ink's arm and felt a rush of frustration when Ink shook it off. "You can't leave us! Not now!"

"I should have left when Lygor let that sick bastard take him!" Ink's voice was muffled with anger. He bit his tongue to stop himself from saying more.

"That's why you can't leave him. He needs our guidance more than ever."

"He won't take our counsel."

"We have to try!"

Ink shook his head. "I'm leaving. First thing in the morning."

What surprised Valnar the most was that he felt more jealous than angry.

51

BEAST

The water was up to Beast's chin now.

"It's all over," Keder purred. "You are done."

Beast stood up on his toes to keep his head above the water. Soft, muddy sand caressed his bare feet.

"I warned you not to trust him. He never intended to release you."

Beast tilted his head up. His eyes drifted to the dark ceiling of the cavern. The water level was rising fast.

"You shall never grasp a sword again. You are nigh blind and repulsive as a human child. You understand what that entails, do you not? You know the fate reserved for broken slaves such as yourself."

He did. His body wasn't burnt and damaged here, but he knew how he looked like in Earthome. He'd seen it in Valnar and Lygor's eyes.

He closed his eyes, sucked a deep breath in and dunked his head under the water. He wanted to escape from Keder's mockery, but somehow, he could still hear him.

"Open the cage. I shall grant you the front seats as I scour Earthome. Name anyone and grant them to you."

The animal tooth, lodged into his chest, throbbed fast. Black veins spread further from the object, which gleamed with a silvery spark. He floated in the water, the object tugging him gently towards the cage. Once again, Beast wondered what kind of animal the giant tooth belonged to.

"Why do you linger? Is there any cause to spare Earthome, after all they have wrought upon you?"

Despite being half submerged, the water couldn't penetrate through the cage's silver bars. Beast's eyes were drawn to the padlock hanging outside.

"Olira vowed to help you. Yet at the first opportunity, she sold you..."

Beast needed air. His head emerged out of the water and sucked a lungful of air. He found that his feet didn't touch the ground anymore. He flapped his arms and kicked his legs to stay afloat. The water was rising steadily. Beast did his best to delay drowning while Keder kept talking.

"Lygor swore to grant your freedom, only to force you to endure your darkest torments so he might win favour. He bound you to a contest he knew you could not win, simply to display his power, believing he could wield you as he pleased."

Beast was getting tired now. The water was cold and welcoming. He could unlock the cage and let go of everything. He wasn't going to get his own freedom, but he could give the High Fiend his.

He could finally die and maybe find his way to Farhome, see Saradra again.

"And now, they will discard you and replace you with another slave to fight at Twilight of Infinity."

"No."

Beast glared at the black fog inside the cage. It looked thicker, almost tangible. Beast's hands balled into fists, and he started sinking.

"Yes!" Keder continued victoriously. "They will even name him Lion of Zar-all."

"No!"

"He shall win his freedom. The freedom that was owed to you!"

"No!"

Beast sank. The water filled his mouth and nose. The cage was completely under the water now, but it still looked dry inside.

"Some mere purebred will win his freedom solely because he bears your like-ness."

Anger raged inside Beast. The object pulled towards the lock, like it belonged there. Like it wanted to reunite. It throbbed faster in his chest.

"Unbar this cage, and I shall unleash fire upon them all, as they have unleashed it upon you. You hold no reason to spare their lives."

The High Fiend was right. Beast wanted them all to burn. He could let this happen.

All he needed was to unlock that cage.

"Yes," the Keder agreed. "I shall take your revenge. I will punish them all for—"

"Revenge?"

Under the water, Beast could still form the word.

"Yes!" Keder said eagerly. "Is this not your desire? You burn for vengeance—you would see them punished for their deeds against you, would you not?"

Beast considered the question. Thoughtfully, he tilted his head and said, "No."

"Yes!" Keder insisted. "They harmed you and you desire to harm them back. I can grant your wish. Just... Open. The. Cage!"

Beast shook his head. "I don't want revenge. I don't want them punished, or Earthome destroyed."

Beast placed a hand over the object. It felt warm, like life in his palm.

"I want my fucking freedom."

He wanted it with all his blood and flesh. He wanted it violently — and the object reacted. It heated up and pulsed once.

"No!" the High Fiend roared. The black fog expanded and spread to every corner of the cage, as if seeking for a gap.

The object drank the water.

Keder's furious roar filled the cavern. Beast closed his eyes as the vortex in his chest pulled with ravenous hunger, drawing the water into itself with violent need. Cool air kissed his skin where the water receded. His feet found purchase on muddy ground.

The object pulsed, lighting up beneath his flesh like a trapped star. Heat radiated from it as it drank and drank, consuming the cool water that had nearly defeated him. The mud beneath his feet hardened, moisture fleeing until only dry sand remained.

Beast opened his eyes. He clutched his sternum, feeling the warmth of the pulsing object beneath his fingers, panting heavily. The cavern had transformed. Light filled the space, revealing stone walls that seemed smaller now, less infinite than the crushing darkness had suggested. Still, the ceiling vanished into shadow above.

The fiend hounds stirred. They approached on light feet, their fur burning stronger, flames flickering along their bodies. They surrounded him, heads down, ears tilted back, their molten eyes glinting. One of them peeled back its lips and snarled, revealing teeth like black daggers.

"We both know you can't harm me here," Beast said.

The black fog was almost still in the cage, barely moving. It hung inside the small space within the cage, like it was nothing but a splash of colour in the air. For the briefest moment, Beast imagined what it would be like to spend hundreds of years trapped inside a tiny cage like that. He empathised with Keder's desire for freedom.

"We both know they will never give you your freedom."

Beast nodded. "I know."

He looked down. The sand felt familiar beneath his bare feet — arena sand, slightly discoloured by countless battles, countless deaths. It felt natural, like he'd spent his entire life standing on sand exactly like this.

It felt right.

"I'll take it myself."

He dropped to his knees and slammed both fists into the ground.

He wasn't certain what he was doing. He was moving on instincts, on vague hunches. He knew this was the way out. He'd sank down under the ground every time he woke up from these nightmares. The Earthome was below him.

He knew the water was a part of the High Fiend; when Beast drank it, Keder was able to take control of him briefly, Raging him at the ambush.

Now, the object held all the water, and it thrummed powerfully in Beast's chest, eager to fulfil what he needed.

He pushed his hands deeper into the sand. The cavern shuddered. Stone cracked and groaned. Chunks of rock began to rain from above. The fiend hounds scattered, their burning forms weaving between the falling debris. A boulder the size of a man crashed where one had been standing moments before, sending up a cloud of dust and sand.

The cage disappeared beneath an avalanche of stone and rubble, buried under the rock that thundered down from the fractured ceiling. Only the faintest glimmer of silver light leaked through the cracks in the pile, marking where Keder's prison lay trapped.

Beast pushed his arms deeper, up to his elbows now. The sand felt cooler underneath his hands, but still dry. The object in his chest pulsed with increasing intensity, each beat sending waves of heat through his body.

Then he heard it — a sound like the world being torn in half. The loud, violent rip of fabric, but magnified a thousandfold, as if air itself was being rent apart.

Beast pulled his hands back. Where they had been, the sand began to fall away, revealing darkness beneath. The hole started small, no bigger than his fist, but it grew rapidly, sand cascading into the void like water down a drain.

The cavern convulsed again. More stones crashed down, and Beast shuffled backward as the hole widened. The ground gave way, spiralling into a whirlpool of churning grains. Clusters of sand lashed at his skin, forcing him to raise his arms, shielding his face from the storm. Rock dust filled the air, and the groaning of cracking stone echoed from every direction.

Then, suddenly, everything stopped.

Silence fell like a curtain. The cavern looked like a battlefield — rubble strewn across the floor, jagged cracks spider-webbing up the walls. The pile of stones where Keder's cage lay buried glowed faintly with trapped silver light, pulsing weakly like a dying heartbeat.

The fiend hounds emerged from their hiding places among the debris, shaking dust from their burning fur. They padded forward cautiously, forming their circle around Beast once more, their molten eyes fixed on him.

And there, in the centre of it all, was the hole — massive now, easily wide enough for a horse cart to fall through, its edges crumbling slightly as loose sand continued to trickle into the black depths below.

Beast stood and coughed, shaking dust and sand from his face and hair. He stepped closer to the hole and peered inside. Nothing but darkness stared back at him. He glanced at the pile of rubble that buried Keder's cage. The High Fiend didn't speak. Whether he couldn't or chose not to, Beast couldn't tell. But he was on his own now. Truly.

No, that wasn't quite right.

The fiend hounds watched him with eager attention that made Beast stand taller. His stomach twisted the way it did in the underground tunnels of the Switchblade Arena. There were over a dozen fiends, shoulder to shoulder, their flames dancing in the dusty air. A circle of fire around Beast and the dark void in the ground.

Beast pointed into the hole and commanded: "Go."

The fiends snarled eagerly. They stepped closer, glancing down into the darkness. They shifted on light claws, pacing around the hole's edge and crouching as if to jump, but they didn't. A few of them snarled and yapped in frustration. Something was holding them back.

"Go!" Beast repeated, louder this time.

The hounds bounced and paced around the hole. They growled and howled, but still wouldn't enter. Beast hissed in frustration.

"What are you waiting for?"

The hounds glared at him, mouths open, lips pulled back to reveal glinting teeth.

Beast scowled at the black void. He gritted his teeth, thinking. This wasn't enough. They needed something. The fiends needed something to help them cross. He rested his hand over his sternum, feeling the faint pulse of the object. He was missing an important detail, an answer, and he needed to know what.

The object pulsed and heated. The taut skin around it ached, marked by the black veins spreading from it. An idea filled his head, settling like dust on the ground.

"I see," he muttered.

Several of the fiend hounds growled louder with hunger.

A small voice inside his head told him not to go through with this. That this was a terrible idea. Beast reminded that voice of the state of his hands and the fate that awaited him. He had no choice and nothing to lose.

He stepped into the void and willed himself back to Earthome.

52

OLIRA

THE SCENT OF ROASTING meat and simmering herbs filled the living area of the house, masking the usual stench of sweat and unwashed bodies. Olira stirred the pot, one hand on her hip, looking somewhere between bored and focused. Around her, the men were gearing up, adjusting belts, tightening straps, checking their blades.

She'd been here for weeks now, cooking for them, keeping her head down. At first, Emberlash had only expected her to prepare meals, but then came the other chores: scrubbing their dishes, fetching water, washing and mending their clothes, sweeping the floors. She had considered refusing, but the work gave her freedom, however small. It let her move through the house without suspicion. It let her step out into the courtyard when she needed air.

So she bid her time.

She never mistook her position here. She was still their prisoner. Emberlash still locked her door at night. And as familiar as these men had become, she knew each one of them would slit her throat if ordered to. She didn't let her guard down. She had to get away, no matter how. She had to find her surviving brother.

And she had a feeling she would get her chance now.

The men's voices drifted around her as they talked, casual but charged with anticipation. She glanced over her shoulder. They were dressing in unfamiliar uniforms: deep charcoal grey tunics trimmed with gold stitching, black belts, and, on their shoulders, a stitched insignia. A golden hound, mid-snarl, fangs bared. She didn't recognise it, but she knew it wasn't Vogros colours.

"So what? They're just gonna let us in?" Garrik muttered as he buckled his belt. Over the past few weeks, Olira had learned more than their names. Garrik came from a town south of Brinescar, chewed his nails when thinking, and never turned down a second plate at dinner. "What sort of resistance are we expecting?"

"I've heard there are purebred beasts patrolling the place," Tovin said. He was a wiry man who had three sons he never mentioned unless drunk, and picked his teeth with his knife after every meal.

"Fuck off?" Garrik's hands froze on his buckle.

"Not joking."

"Don't piss your pants," Hedrin muttered, adjusting the worn straps of his shield. Older than the rest, he complained about his back a lot, didn't gamble, and never raised his voice. "Lord Brocton's men will back us up, and Prince Dienus has an ally inside. He'll drop the purebreds."

"Are you sure?"

"I'm not, but Prince Dienus is. Otherwise, he wouldn't be risking his neck coming along with the rest of us."

"I'm surprised he's stepping out of the pleasure house in the first place," Brask said, lifting his sword to check the edge. He was the youngest of the group, built like a bull, more muscle than sense. "Maybe his dick finally fell off from fucking so many arses."

The room erupted in laughter, which was short-lived as Hedrin's posture changed. "Hey," the older soldier snapped. "Shove your resentment up your arse. You're soldiers, not twelve-times-cursed mercenaries. Act like it."

Silence settled for a little while after that. It was odd how ordinary they all were. Normal men. Nothing overtly monstrous about them. They had families. They grew up in farms, villages, cities. They liked food, they snored, they bickered.

And yet, they had killed people without hesitation. They drank, they picked fights. They bullied Norrol whenever they found a chance. They would kill her without a blink and finish their dinner right after.

What Olira had truly learned in the past few weeks was that the conversation she had with Beast — how she had lectured him about killing, about remorse — sounded so stupid now. Nothing was that simple. She felt so naive.

After weeks of idleness, their anticipation for some action was so high, Hedrin's snap didn't keep them quiet for long.

"So is he really there?" Brask asked. "Bastard of Zarall?"

Olira reached for the bundle of *bitterflax* on the table, fingers plucking at the leaves as she listened. Her heart pounded in her chest.

"Has to be," Carron, the man Olira had cured from Swampchill weeks ago, joined in. "Otherwise we wouldn't be storming the place."

"And if it's another dead lead?" Garrik asked, securing the last strap on his arm guard. "Or worse, if he's there and his First Word don't work?"

"He's not a fiend out of Darkhome," Hedrin said. "With Lord Brocton's men, there'll be a small army of us. We'll get him."

Olira forced herself to keep chopping, to keep her breathing steady. Her mind worked quickly, sorting through how many men were preparing and how many weren't. She wiped her eyebrows with her forearm as she scanned the room. Norrol was the only one who wasn't gearing up. He sat near the far end of the room, head lowered, fingers idly tracing a crack on the wooden table. If he was staying, that meant someone had decided he wasn't needed.

Emberlash wasn't going either. He leaned against the hearth, arms crossed, watching the preparations with his usual sour expression.

That was it. Everyone else was leaving.

Her odds were better than she could have ever hoped for, though her heart panged because that only meant Beast would have more to deal with. She pictured Beast, helpless at Dienus's feet, and the image was so horrifying that bile rose in her throat.

She had to help him. She had to act now.

Olira wiped her hands on her apron, careful not to move too fast. She stirred the pot once more, then stretched, feigning nonchalance. She moved toward the door, stepping into the courtyard like many times she'd done before. Cool air grounded her, steadying her shaking hands. Her eyes landed on the messy weeds near the privy.

Before she could move, footsteps followed her.

She glanced back over her shoulder and found Melton standing by the door. She gestured at the stepping stones leading to the privy. "You first, My Lord," she offered.

The squire hesitated. "I'll wait."

Olira forced a casual shrug and moved onto the uneven stepping stones. She passed the *Pale Gallcaps* growing at the base of the privy, their soft green caps blending into the weeds. She couldn't risk picking them. Not with Melton watching. She stepped inside the privy and closed the rickety door behind her.

She had to get those mushrooms.

She considered waiting for a bit, then stepping out, letting Melton take his turn, and picking the mushrooms then. But they were too close to the privy. He would hear her. And if she tried to come back later, it would look suspicious. She needed to get them now.

Crouching in the far corner, she ran her fingers along the weakest plank at the back. She pried it loose, but the wood groaned louder than she expected.

Merciful Alunwea.

A shadow passed under the door. She held her breath, but Melton said nothing. Olira reached blindly behind the loose plank, her fingers digging into the damp earth. Her hand closed around a handful of the mushrooms, yanking them free, just as Melton knocked on the door.

"What are you doing there? Hurry the fuck up."

Olira shoved the plank back into place, stuffing the mushrooms into the folds of her dress. Her heart pounded against her ribs, but she fixed her posture, wiped her hands on her skirt, and forced herself to breathe before stepping out of the privy.

Melton's sneer greeted her. Keeping her face neutral, she stepped past him and headed towards the house.

"What? No snappy comeback?" Melton's voice came after her. "Did you hit your head in there or something?"

Olira didn't slow. She kept her pace steady, her hands tucked into the folds of her dress, feeling the slight dampness where she'd hidden the mushrooms. She just needed to get back inside, finish the food, and make sure the men ate every last bite. She felt Melton's suspicious gaze on her, but the boy didn't press.

She forced her hands to remain steady as she stepped back to the hearth. The stew simmered, thick and rich. She glanced over her shoulder, making sure everyone was still busy getting ready. Then, she crushed the mushrooms inside a bowl and tossed them in, giving it a good stir. She added more seasoning to mask the bitterness of the *Pale Gallcaps*, gave it another stir, and that was it.

She glanced at the room, and her eyes stopped on Norrol. He sat where he always did, head down, shoulders hunched. He had new bruises on his face, from another bout of friendly sparring between him and a few of them. It was almost like Norrol was another prisoner, though no one bothered to label him.

Olira didn't want Norrol to eat this. *Pale Gallcaps* wasn't lethal, but it wasn't pleasant either. She hoped it would make them sick enough to give Beast a better chance against them. But Norrol didn't deserve it.

She reached for the bowls, stacking them in her arms, and began ladling portions. She made sure to scoop extra into each one. She handed them off to the men as she went. By the time she reached the last bowl, there was nothing left. And Norrol was the only one waiting at the end of the line.

"Oi," Brask smirked, nodding his head toward Norrol. "Lordling's got nothing."

A few of the others snickered. Olira feigned surprise, lifting the empty ladle. "I'm sorry. I'll fix you something else."

Norrol barely looked up. His face burned hot — he really wasn't good at hiding his emotions — and when his eyes finally met Olira's, they held none of the reluctant kindness she had once seen. Now, he only looked betrayed. Like she was in on the humiliation with the rest of them.

"Don't bother," he muttered before storming out.

The men barely noticed. They ate in a hurry, still laughing and talking, their attention already on their task ahead. Olira tried not to watch them. She grabbed a piece of bread and cheese for herself and made her way upstairs, as she often did.

As soon as she shut the door behind her, she set the food aside and dragged the flimsy mattress away. Kneeling, she lifted the loose floorboard and reached into the dusty nook beneath. She kept one ear trained on the stairwell, listening for the telltale creak of footsteps.

Her fingers closed around the bag of *Hollowbell* she had stashed weeks ago. She pulled it out along with another bag — one filled with food she had been collecting for her escape. She tucked the bread and cheese inside, then hid the bag beneath the blanket, where it would be easier to grab if she had to move fast.

By the time she returned downstairs with her empty plate and the bag of *Hollowbell* tucked inside her cuff, the men had started leaving in small groups to avoid unnecessary attention. She scanned the room quickly. A small pot of water had been set to boil on the hearth.

Emberlash enjoyed brewing tea in the evenings. Her heart quickened.

She mixed the *Hollowbell* leaves with the tea leaves, adding extra water before closing the lid.

When Emberlash walked in, he found Olira collecting the empty bowls and preparing to wash them.

"There you are," he said, pointing to the stairs. "Upstairs. Now."

"Why?"

Emberlash scoffed. "Why? Because you're a prisoner, and I know what you're thinking."

Olira's pulse faltered. Had he seen something? Did he know? She forced herself not to look at the brewing pot.

The chamberlain stepped closer, sneering. "You're thinking, *this is my opportunity — they're all gone.*" He snapped his fingers and gestured toward the stairs again. "I'm not taking any chances with you. You're staying in your room until they return."

"Why would I—"

"I'll have none of that!" Emberlash's voice rang through the house, loud enough to draw Hedrin's attention.

A few of the men still lingered near the entrance, waiting for their turn to slip into the streets. Hedrin called over, "All good there, Emberlash?"

Emberlash smirked, never taking his eyes off Olira. "I might need assistance with the prisoner."

Olira ground her teeth. "Don't bother," she snapped, yanking off her apron and tossing it at Emberlash's feet. "Enjoy doing all those dishes by yourself."

"I'm sure I'll survive."

Olira stormed up the stairs, the chamberlain following close behind. She slammed the door shut, then heard the key turn in the lock.

"Strike me twelve times," she cursed under her breath, rubbing her forehead. What was she going to do now?

She moved to the boarded-up window and peeked through the gaps. She saw another small group leave the house and disappear into the dark streets. Olira tested the boards, yanking at them, but they were sturdy. Not like the rotting wood of the privy or the loose floorboards. She wasn't getting out through the window.

Pacing the room, she tried to think. How much time did she have? Once they all started dropping like flies with severe stomach cramps, eventually they would figure out it was the food. If she was still here by the time they returned...

Olira groaned.

She pulled the mattress aside again, lifting the loose floorboard. This time, she didn't set it aside. She weighed it in her hands. Could she break the door with it? It would make a lot of noise, but after drinking his *Hollowbell* tea, Emberlash wouldn't care.

Olira sat by the door, listening to the distant clinks of dishes and the slosh of water as Emberlash finished cleaning up. She willed him to hurry up and drink his tea. Her fingers curled tightly around the edge of the floorboard.

The sounds stopped. A pause, followed by the faint scrape of movement. She pictured him settling into a chair, sipping his tea. It wouldn't take long now.

A few minutes later, a soft thump echoed from below.

Olira stiffened. She cleared her throat. "Emberlash?"

Silence.

She stepped closer to the door. "Emberlash?"

Still nothing.

Her pulse pounded in her ears. He was asleep. Bracing herself, she lifted the floorboard and swung it hard against the hinges. The wood groaned but held. She hit it again, ignoring the sting in her hands, the sweat gathering at her temple. She worked at it for a good ten minutes, and the hinges held firm.

She froze when she heard a voice downstairs.

"Emberlash?"

Norrol.

She heard him move across the room, imagined him bending down to check the unconscious chamberlain.

Olira tossed the floorboard aside. Her muscles were sore, her hands were bleeding, and the door showed no sign of breaking. She wasn't getting out of here without help. She pounded her fists against the door.

"Norrol? Norrol! I'm here. Open the door. Please!"

The young squire was her only hope. And Alunwea smiled upon her, because she heard the stairs creaking as Norrol climbed upstairs.

"Norrol, please open the door," she called again.

The key turned in the lock, and the door clicked open. Norrol stood there. But his expression wasn't what she expected.

"What have you done to Emberlash?" His voice was sharp with alarm. He stepped inside, forcing Olira to back up.

"What makes you—"

"I saw you put something in the food."

"It's not what you think..."

"Why isn't he waking up? Did you—" His gaze flicked to the floorboard she had tossed aside. His breath hitched. "Are you trying to escape?"

Olira held up her hands. "Norrol, I have to get out of here. Please." She glanced past him, toward the hall and the stairs. Freedom. So close.

Norrol's jaw tightened, his throat bobbing as he tried to process. His face paled. "I can't let you do that."

"Norrol, Prince Dienus is going to kill me." Her voice cracked, her hands trembling as she touched her neck, already feeling the phantom pressure of the prince's grip. "Sooner or later, he'll come back for me, and this is my only chance. Please, Norrol. I have to go." Tears welled in her eyes.

Norrol hesitated, rubbing his face. His brows furrowed, and for a moment, she thought he might actually help her. Then, he shook his head. "I helped you once. Look what that got me."

"Norrol, please—"

"If I let you escape, they'll... they'll—"

She didn't let him finish. She shoved him aside and dashed past him. She almost made it to the threshold, before Norrol's hands found her collar. He yanked her back with force and tossed her across the room.

Olira crashed against the wall, hitting the back of her head. Light flashes across her eyes. Before she could scramble up, Norrol was already gone. He slammed the door shut and turned the key.

"No! Norrol, don't!"

Olira threw herself against the door, pounding her fists. Her head throbbed, but she barely noticed. She pressed her palm flat against the door, breathing hard, listening for any sign of hesitation.

"Norrol, please! Please, let me go!"

He didn't answer. He just stood there. She could hear his shaky breath, and the shift of his weight, like he was waiting for something — maybe for her to stop, or maybe for his own guilt to settle.

Then, the hesitation passed.

The stairs creaked under his weight as he walked away, leaving her behind.

53

DIENUS

THE CORRIDORS OF THE slave breeder's manor were outrageously wealthy. Everything was excessive. From the polished black marble floors to the gold-caged sconces lining the walls; dark green velvet drapes that hung between the tall arched windows to painted vases and colourful tapestries. Every detail was a subtle insult to noble houses of Chinderia, many of whom had much less to flaunt. Even the Vogros family estate, Karvogros, didn't boast this many painted, full-sized statues and elaborate wall carvings to impress its guests — though they did have an entire gallery lined with Ghorclaw tusks, trophies from generations of hunts.

Dienus couldn't wait to burn this place down.

The unapologetic display of wealth was also meant to make Lord Brocton small, who was already amongst the pettier, less influential noble houses of Chinderia. The Union had more control over Calae's internal affairs than Lord Brocton did, the city being the Domestic Assets Trade Union's headquarters. The invitation to attend to Master Vadithas's feast wasn't a courtesy. It was a summons. A demand to pledge loyalty to the Union's chosen prince and smile while doing it.

It was also a test.

Lord Brocton had understood that, which was why he had accepted the invitation without protest — at Dienus's request. His cooperation had been absolute so far.

Dienus walked a half-step behind him, dressed in a servant's uniform of muted grey. Brocton hadn't questioned his presence, nor objected to his usual men being left behind. He hadn't argued when Sir Gennald took the role of his head of security for the event. He'd even happily provided uniforms for Dienus's men to wear as they infiltrated the heavily guarded manor under Brocton's invitation.

His son's safety was motivation enough. A ward under Lord Halvar — one of King Kastian's most devout loyalists. And Lord Halvar was not known for his mercy.

As they passed a pair of towering statues carved in obsidian and ivory, Brocton's voice dropped to a whisper. "I have a bad feeling about this, Your Highness."

"My father can make you feel even worse. So shut your mouth and play along," Dienus whispered back through a friendly smile.

Brocton said nothing more.

They stepped through the towering double doors into the feast hall.

The room was enormous, featuring a high, vaulted ceiling. A high table stretched out along one side, with polished silverware and plates far too delicate for the likes of Calae. There wasn't much security in the room, but so many slaves. Purebred house slaves — who would bother raising a purebred to become a house servant, what a waste — walking around with trays and wine bottles. Guests in extravagant attire moved like pieces on a board. They were mostly merchants and slave breeders, some high-profile business owners, looking out of place surrounded by this much wealth.

Host and master of the manor, Vadithas, glided forward to greet Lord Brocton. The man's bearded smile was sharp and oily, and his bald head glistened under the rich light.

Master Ruzen stood nearby, eyes half-lidded as he sipped from a silver goblet. He was so obnoxiously loud, people ignored him. He didn't acknowledge Dienus, but as Brocton was led further into the room, Ruzen moved. He began drifting across the room like a bored guest, and snapped at Dienus and his men to get out from under foot, nudging them to take position along the exists and alcoves.

The Master of the Sands had been right to suggest waiting until after the Fire Breath. Dienus had watched the fight from the upper stands of the Scorchline Arena, wine in hand, when Lion of Zarall caught fire. The beast had flailed like a slaughtered pig, limbs wild, voice swallowed by the roar of the crowd. It was pitiful. Hilarious. The purebred wasn't in any shape to fight now. All they had to do was walk in and take him.

And just like Ruzen had promised, the Union had invited Brocton to the manor, allowing Dienus to walk in without shedding any blood. No alarms raised. No resistance.

Too easy.

Dienus moved to the far corner of the room where Gennald and Melton were already waiting, both dressed in the plain, deep charcoal grey and gold uniforms of Brocton's house. From here, they could see the entrance, the tables, the mingling guests, and — soon enough — him.

Prince Lygor Zarall entered with no announcement, no fanfare. He didn't need it. The room noticed him immediately.

The prince strode through the doors like the place belonged to him. He was dressed in finely tailored black-and-gold, the sigil of House Zarall gleaming on a silver pin at his shoulder. His blond hair was perfectly styled. His smile was too white, too flawless; the kind that made Dienus want to drive a knife into his cheek just to ruin it.

He hated how people looked at Lygor. Hated the way the room tilted toward him with every step, how servants parted like water without being told, how nobles straightened their spines to catch his eye. His confidence wasn't even put on. He carried it like a second skin.

Flanking him were two purebred beasts, tall and broad-shouldered, with perfectly messy blond hair. They wore matching armour with the black-and-gold lion engravings across their chests. The arrogant brat didn't even bother hiding his colours anymore, openly announcing that the assassins King Kastian had sent to Kaldoria had failed.

Dienus clenched his jaw as Lygor paused to exchange a few polite words with Vadithas and Brocton. Even from across the room, the sound of his voice made Dienus want to spit. He couldn't wait to kill the piece of shit. He didn't even want to take his time with him; he would just slit his throat without gracing the bastard with any last words.

His father had sent him to retrieve Lion of Zarall. And Dienus was about to bring him not only the savage slave, but Lygor Zarall's head as well. He couldn't wait to see the begrudging gratitude on the king's face.

Gennald made an odd noise, drawing Dienus's attention.

"What?" Dienus huffed.

"Where is Sir Valnar?" Gennald muttered, his eyes scanning the room.

"Who?"

"Sir Valnar. His knight."

"Who needs a fucking knight when he has those savage purebreds? Look at them."

Gennald shifted and pretended not to take offence. He still scanned the room though, as paranoid as always.

"The foreign prince isn't here either," Gennald said.

"Well, that's a good thing," Dienus whispered back. "I really prefer not killing a Kaldorian prince and starting a war."

Lygor, Brocton, and the others took their seats shortly after. Lygor settled into the central seat at the high table, his two purebreds standing behind him, all menacing and threatening. Dienus could feel the eyes of every guest flicking toward them — some with awe, some with concern.

Brocton sat next to Lygor, with Ruzen dropping into the seat beside him like a man made of wine and laughter. The moment his goblet was refilled, he raised it in a clumsy toast to no one in particular and slurred something about the strength of Zarall friendship. Lygor smiled politely. Dienus didn't.

Vadithas sat on the prince's other side, with the other Union leaders taking their seats beside him. Music started. So did the food. Platter after platter of steaming meat and sweet wine and spiced vegetables laid out like an offering. Dancers emerged from behind the curtains at the edge of the hall. Purebred pleasure slaves, glistening with oil, wearing nothing but silver thread and paint. They started a steamy dance, with slow and languid movements, their bodies writhing on the dark marble floors, like begging for Dienus to come break them.

Dienus watched, longing for a glass of wine that would quench his thirst. The need stirred inside him, and for a brief moment, Dienus felt frustrated. No matter how many times he'd satisfied the need over the last few weeks, it was still there, stronger than ever. He'd accepted that he would never be free of its hold over him. Once they secured the manor, he promised himself to get to know those slaves better. Treat himself.

A retching sound drew his attention. He turned his head and saw one of his men — Bask or Brask or something — stumble toward the exit, clutching his stomach. He barely made it out before doubling over in the corridor, vomiting violently. One of those purebred house slaves quietly went after him to clean it up.

"What the fuck?" Dienus muttered, eyes narrowing.

Gennald was already tense beside him, his hand twitching near the hilt of his sword.

"What's wrong with you?" the knight hissed at Melton, who was leaning against a nearby pillar, looking pale.

"I'm fine," Melton said too quickly, forcing a smile. He stood straighter, but couldn't do much about the paleness of his pimpled face. "All good."

Dienus gestured him to come over. "Take someone with you. Go to the guest wing. Find the room they're keeping Lion of Zarall in. Secure it. Don't let anyone in until I'm finished here. Understand?"

Melton nodded and slipped away, pulling one of the disguised men with him.

Dienus watched Ruzen, who was now speaking far too loudly, gesturing with his wine cup and laughing like an idiot. He clapped Brocton's back like they were old friends. No one would suspect him of being anything more than a drunken fool.

Dienus let his gaze drift back to the purebreds flanking Lygor. They were intimidating: tall, muscled, bred for obedience and blood. But Dienus wasn't worried. Within minutes, Ruzen was going to give Dienus the signal. Then, the Master of the Sands, would stand up and shout the First Words, and Lygor's purebreds would collapse, paralysed and helpless. Dienus's men would close all the exits.

And then the slaughter would begin.

54

BEAST

A BAND OF WHITE-HOT pain seared across Beast's hands and forearms. His face prickled with raw burns, and when he tried to lift a hand to check the bandages, a sharp sting radiated all the way to his shoulders. His eyes throbbed at the light. He clenched his teeth, wanting to scream.

A hand pressed over his mouth to muffle his voice.

A familiar voice spoke nearby. "Stay calm," it said. "I know you're in pain, but I need you to stay quiet for a moment."

An instinctive panic seized Beast. The voice was too close. Someone was leaning over him, though he could only make out a blurred shape in the dim light that assaulted his eyes. He jerked backward, ignoring the agony that tore through his arms and face.

"Calm down, Beast. You'll hurt yourself."

Beast tried to swat the hand off his mouth, and almost passed out from the pain that shot all over him. He was back in the arena, surrounded by flames that tore his skin off his bones. *Flames everywhere... Everywhere he ran...* His heart was racing so fast, his chest ached. Air didn't reach his lungs.

"Fuck it. I'm so sorry for doing this. *Padlociatius.*"

Beast felt a cold weight descend. His limbs went limp, but the pain didn't retreat. He sank down into the flames. The fire was eating his flesh and he couldn't even move a muscle to save himself.

A strong arm propped him upright and supported his head. Fingers parted his mouth open. He felt the coolness of a glass vial against his lips. Then, a bitter liquid with a familiar taste slid down his throat. He coughed some out but swallowed the most.

In seconds, the burn in his hands and face dulled. It was like floating on a current that swept away the worst of his suffering, leaving something akin to peace in its wake. Though the light still disturbed his eyes, and his sight was still a flurry of shapes and shadows.

The arm supported him until the paralysis faded and Beast could sit by himself.

"*Pemitoin*," Beast sighed once he could move his lips again. He'd used the drink before, remembered the potent blend of strength and numbness it gifted.

He squinted and blinked his eyes until he could see the shape of Ink kneeling beside him. The Kaldorian used dark colours to paint his face this time, the design looking as fierce as before. He clutched the empty vial, relief and worry mingling in his eyes.

"W-what's happening?" Beast croaked. He was afraid to move, expecting the pain to return, despite knowing *pemitoin* would keep it at bay.

"I'm leaving," Ink answered, voice low and urgent, "and I'm taking you with me."

Beast's mind spun. "Why? Where...?"

"What's being done to you..." Ink said through gritted teeth, "it's not right."

Beast swallowed, his heart fluttering. "Is it true... they're replacing me?"

A slow, reluctant nod.

"What's gonna happen to me?"

"You wanna stay here and find out, or you wanna come with me while you still can?"

Beast fought a dizzying wave of memory. Images of the last time he'd used *pemitoin*, how the crash afterward nearly killed him. His hand drifted to his neck. "The aftereffects..." he whispered hoarsely.

Ink lifted a second vial from his pocket. "Antidote," he said, tapping the tiny container. "My contacts will help us slip out of the city. By the time the aftereffects hit you, we'll be safe and the antidote will help counter the effects. You'll be fine."

The Kaldorian prince held out a hand, offering support to help him up. Beast stared at it like it was a dangerous weapon. "W-why? Why would you help me?"

Ink pressed his lips together. He looked annoyed. "Because it's the right thing to do. Because remorse sucks." He shrugged. "Because I'm a decent man. Now let's go while everyone's busy kissing Lygor's arse at that feast."

He held out his hand again, and Beast had to force himself to take it. Gratitude stung his chest, immediately followed by a fresh fear. His instincts raised warnings in him, like he was stepping into an arena filled with fire traps. He allowed Ink to support him to his feet. The Kaldorian prince helped him get dressed in a plain shirt, a pair of pants and boots. Lastly, he threw a cloak over Beast's shoulders.

"Can you walk?" Ink asked.

Beast tried to take a good look at Ink's face, but his blurry vision and the mixing colours of Ink's war paint kept him from discerning the man's expression. He shrugged Ink's hand off and tested his legs. The *pemitoin* gave him enough strength, though he couldn't use his hands, and he could barely see.

He'd never felt this vulnerable, this weak. Not even when paralysed by his First Word. He was utterly powerless, and he had no choice but to trust Ink.

Cold fear sat on his chest like a mangy animal, but he nodded.

"Good," Ink said, "Let's go."

Beast followed.

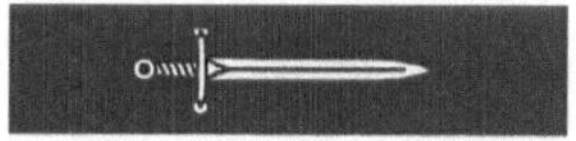

THE CORRIDORS BURNED.

Not with fire or heat, but with light. Too much light, pouring out of the lanterns. Beast moved through it like a man wading into a fiery battlefield. His eyes felt like they were being scraped by rough wood with each blink, and each moving shadow triggered a headache behind his eyes.

Ink led the way. His footfalls were soundless and relaxed. He wasn't bothered by the lights that made Beast want to press his hands over his eyes and sink into the comfort of dark.

Darkness had always been safe for him. He always feared the light the free men and women brought with them when they came to hurt him.

Now, light was no longer just a harbinger. It was the pain.

"You alright?"

He barely heard Ink's voice over the pounding in his head. He nodded once. "It's the light."

Ink made a small sound in his throat. He pulled something out of his jacket and moved towards Beast. "It's just a handkerchief," he said when Beast recoiled.

Beast let him wrap the handkerchief around his head, dulling the brightness to a tolerable level. The relief was instant. But as the world dimmed, a new fear took hold. Without sight, he felt even more defenceless. This darkness didn't feel safe. It didn't belong to him. It felt like a prison.

The weight of it coiled in his gut.

Ink's fingers found his arm, leading him forward. His grip was firm, like iron shackles around his wrist. The halls stretched, the air shifting subtly as they moved. Suddenly, Ink jerked him back. He shoved him to the wall, pressing a hand against his chest to pin him still.

"Stay here," Ink whispered, like Beast had a choice.

He felt the Kaldorian step away, then heard the muffled sounds of a fight. Sudden, muted shuffles, the rush of bodies colliding. No swords. No clash of steel. Just grunts, quick exhalations, the sound of impact against flesh and bone. A body hitting the ground.

Silence.

His heart pounded, and he flinched when he felt a hand on his arm.

"It's me," Ink murmured. "It's fine."

The Kaldorian's grip tightened once again on his arm as he guided him forward. Beast forced the tension out of his muscles and kept walking. He tried not to feel like a condemned man being dragged to a fate he couldn't control. But the harder he tried, more stubbornly the image clung to the darkness over his eyes.

A door creaked open. Ink led him through and muttered, "Steps."

Beast lifted his foot and found the first step. They climbed in silence, with only the faint echo of boots on stones. The air shifted, cooling with every step. A breeze swept in through a window, shifting his cloak around his legs.

By the time the steps finally levelled, the air smelled fresh, with faint traces of night jasmines. He could tell they were in a large room with wide windows.

"You'll need your eyes for this part," Ink said apologetically.

The blindfold loosened, and the fabric slipped away. The light pressed against Beast's vision. He squinted, his pupils struggling to adjust. The world around him sharpened and the sting receded to an ache.

A single candle flickered at the far end, casting long shadows over the stone walls. The room was large and unfurnished, save for a crate and two stools. Two shapes were slumped against a wall. Two of Vadithas's guards, their hands bound and their mouths stuffed with rags. They glowered at Ink and Beast as they protested through the rags.

Judging from the way Ink didn't give them a second glance, Beast guessed this was his doing. Ink had planned this through.

"Can you climb?" Ink asked. He drew Beast's attention to a ladder propped against a gap in the ceiling.

Beast nodded, avoiding looking at his hands.

Ink went first, hauling himself a few steps up. He reached down and hooked his arm through Beast's elbow. Beast pushed himself with his feet, his other arm stretched for balance. Ink climbed through the gap, then reached and pulled Beast with him onto the roof.

The night stretched vast and soundless above them, thick clouds shifting sluggishly against the moon, dimming its light. Wind tugged at Beast's cloak, carrying the scent of stone and distant smoke of torches.

From up here, the manor's grounds unfolded in sprawling shadows. He could barely make out the yard, paths twisting through trimmed hedges and open courtyards. Beyond that, the outer walls loomed high. He spotted clusters of men — pairs of purebred beasts and free men — at the gates and patrolling across the yard. The distant murmur of voices, laughter, and the faint swell of music reached his ears.

Ink touched his arm. He guided Beast across the roof. The tiles beneath them were slick with the remnants of rain. Ink stopped in the middle of the roof and fished out a bag stashed between the tiles. He pulled ropes, hooks, and gears and started prepping them.

He really had planned this through.

The tension tightened in Beast's chest. He blinked, trying to clear the haze in his vision, but Ink remained a dark, blurred figure against the night. He could have left. He could have walked through the front gates unchallenged. Yet, he'd stayed, and he'd stashed those ropes and gear in the roof. He was risking his life to take Beast with him.

Why?

"Why are you doing all this?" Beast asked again. His throat bobbed with an ache he couldn't name, a wordless thing pressing tight against his ribs.

Ink didn't look up from the rope in his hands. "I told you," he muttered, fingers working knots. "I don't need any more remorse."

"I don't get it."

"What don't you get? Remorse?"

Ink's shape stilled and shifted. Beast felt the Kaldorian's eyes on him. He would have killed to see the man's expression, to rely on more than just the softness in his voice.

"Beast, I..." A quiet sigh. "I'm sorry. I should have stopped them. I should have said something."

Sorry.

The word burrowed into his head like a foreign thing. He didn't know what to do with it. He recoiled.

"Did you know there's no slavery in Kaldoria? Or in most of Earthome?" Ink's voice dropped lower, like he was speaking while looking away. "I thought I could stomach it."

Silence. Then, the faint rasp of rope against leather as Ink resumed tying knots.

"I wouldn't find my way to Farhome if I did nothing."

Beast still didn't get it, and then he did.

Ink was different. He was a good person.

The moment the thought surfaced, dread seized his gut. A slow, cold fear pooled inside him, and he sank deep into it, like a stone dropped into dark water.

He'd believed Lygor was different too.

And Olira.

I am not a bad person, she'd said.

I will come through for you, Lygor had promised.

Beast had trusted them both. And both had betrayed him.

Ink's head snapped up sharply. In an instant, he was on his feet.

Beast turned his head in the same direction, straining to see past the blur, past the thick shadows. It took him a few frustrating seconds before he could make out the large, dark shape looming over the tiles.

"Ink!" Valnar's voice bellowed in the dark. "What are you doing here?"

55

BEAST

"Let us go, Valnar," Ink demanded coldly.

"Go where?" Valnar growled.

"Anywhere but here."

Valnar stepped forward. Ink moved instantly, placing himself between him and Beast.

"Did Kyrus steal your mind? Ink, what are you doing?"

"I'm saving him from being butchered at one of Master Naelar's slaughter-houses."

"What are you talking about?"

"Tell me, Valnar, what happens to crippled slaves in this country?"

Valnar's jaw worked. "You think... Lodi would..." He sputtered, grasping for words. "Lodi would *never* let anything like that happen to him!"

Ink let out a bitter scoff. "Oh yeah? You wanna talk about all the things Lygor *did* let happen to him since we arrived at Calae?"

"That—" Valnar's face darkened. He lowered his voice. "That was on me."

"Stop protecting him, Valnar."

"That's my job. And it's yours too. Do you remember your quest?"

Ink's voice turned venomous. "Don't come after us, Valnar."

"I can't let you do that!"

"Valnar, let me help this man. Please!"

Beast listened in mute disbelief, caught between confusion and helplessness. Ink was fighting for him. Arguing against Valnar *for* him. That realisation flooded him with a warmth so foreign it left him breathless.

Ink really was different.

And then, like a snake slithering back into his gut, distrust coiled around the warmth and strangled it.

"I can't let you betray him like this," Valnar said.

"Beast doesn't mean anything to Lygor."

"You're wrong."

"Lygor has no use for him anymore. He'll toss him away."

"He will make sure Beast recovers. He'll give him a good life."

"Do you really think the Union will trust a slave to keep quiet about their little scam? Using an imposter to rouse the people for them?"

Valnar's voice was like steel. "Lodi won't let them harm him."

Ink scoffed. Beast blinked, noticing a shift in Ink's stance, like he was getting ready to fight. Valnar must have noticed the shift too. He took another step forward, raising his palms to Ink in a gesture of surrender.

"Look," Valnar said, his voice softer. "I wanted Beast to have his freedom too. He deserves it. I swear, I'll make sure he lives a good life, with as much freedom as a slave can have."

"That's not good enough," Ink snapped.

Valnar exhaled sharply. "And what can *you* offer him? You think you can just take him to Kaldoria and release him? Ink, Hunters will find him. Wherever he goes. Unless you remain his Owner."

"Fuck you."

"Ink, think about it. You steal him, you become his Owner. But the moment you step away from him, he becomes an escaped slave. Then, Hunters will get him. It'll be much worse for him."

Beast took an involuntary step back. Valnar saw it. He turned, pointing straight at him.

"Look at him," he said. "He *knows* it too. If you really want to keep him safe, you'd have to *own* him. For the rest of his life. And you can't own a slave in Kaldoria."

"I'll find a way to give him his freedom."

"There *was* a way," Valnar said. "Twilight of Infinity. And he'll never win that. Not anymore."

Beast made a strangled noise. Frustration clawed up his throat. He swallowed it down.

Valnar took another step toward Ink. "I *promise* you, I'll take care of him, Ink. I swear under Kiejain's wing, I'll see to it that he's comfortable for the rest of his life. Dressed well. Fed well. Treated fairly."

The words reminded Beast of the promises Lygor had made to Olira when he was convincing her to sell him. Same words. Same lies.

Ink tilted his head back, looking at the dark sky. His shoulders slumped.

Beast's gut twisted harder.

He wished he could see Ink's face. Wished he could tell if he had that same look Olira had when she signed the paper. The same look Lygor had when he agreed to the Union's terms.

Valnar approached further, and Ink let him.

"As much as you hate him right now, Lodi is still your friend," the knight said. "Just put everything aside and remember this, okay? You both owe each other your lives! You can't steal his property and escape in the middle of the night, like a lowly thief. Where is the honour in that?"

Ink shifted. His foot slid back, like he was stepping away. But when he spoke, his voice lacked the fierce determination he had a moment ago. "The Union has Lygor under their thumb."

"That's why he needs us more than ever."

Beast's breathing grew shallow. His hands twitched at his sides, instinctively wanting to curl into fists, but his burnt fingers barely responded. He glanced down the side of the roof. The garden stretched far below. The distant ground promised a lethal fall.

There was no winning Twilight of Infinity now.

If he went back inside with them, the best he could hope for was Valnar's definition of a *good enough life for a slave.*

He stared at the shrinking distance between Valnar and Ink.

"Let's get down and talk to him," Valnar begged. "If you still want to leave, leave. But don't do it like this. Not in the dead of night, like a criminal."

Ink's head sagged.

Beast closed his eyes. His chest hurt. He wanted to cry and laugh at the same time. He couldn't believe this was happening.

Again.

He couldn't believe how stupid he was.

Again.

A sound tore from his throat — half a chuckle, half a sob.

"All free men are greedy," he muttered.

Ink's head snapped up at him sharply. Even through the blur, through the thick war paint and shifting shadows, Beast saw the shock on his face. Maybe even hurt.

That face, that expression, burned itself into Beast's mind.

Beast lunged forward, slammed his shoulder into Ink's chest, and hurled him off the roof's edge.

56

VALNAR

"No!"

Valnar's fingers brushed Ink's cuffs. Ink's nails scratched against Valnar's wrist. Neither of them found purchase.

Ink fell.

"Ink!"

The only reply to Valnar's cry was the sickening, wet crack of flesh and bone meeting the hard ground.

"No, no, no, no!"

Valnar lunged to the edge. Below, Ink's body lay sprawled on the ground. His limbs twisted at unnatural angles, arms and legs splayed. Blood pooled beneath his head, dark and spreading across the cold stone.

The patrol had heard the impact. Vadithas's men gathered, torches bobbing as they rushed toward the crumpled figure.

Valnar's head snapped up. His eyes locked onto Beast.

With an animalistic snarl, he charged at the slave, fists swinging.

Beast didn't simply stand there and take it. He raised his bandaged arms to shield himself. Valnar landed a blow on the injured limb, sending Beast to the ground in pain. Valnar didn't stop. His fists crashed into Beast's body, blow after blow, each one landing harder than the last. The slave barely got his arms up in time, his bandages darkening where Valnar struck. Beast grunted, flinching under the assault, trying to move with the hits, but he was slow. He was too weak to match Valnar's grief-stricken power.

Another punch slammed into Beast's ribs, and he staggered. Beast hit the roof tiles, rolling down the slope before he barely caught himself. Valnar kicked again, harder, driving his foot into Beast's side, the impact reverberating up his own leg.

Ink was dead.

Ink was dead.

And the *slave* had done this.

A snarl ripped from his throat as he drove his boot into Beast's chest, sending him rolling backward to the edge of the roof.

Valnar inhaled sharply.

As much as he wanted to kick the beast down to his death, his discipline took over. His hands shot out and his fingers curled around the collar of Beast's shirt. He yanked him back before gravity could claim him.

"You killed him!" Valnar yelled, tossing him away from the edge. "He was trying to help you, and you murdered him!"

Through clenched teeth and ragged breaths, Beast forced out words, but his voice was hoarse and barely audible. Valnar thought he heard "come."

Raking his hair with his fingers, Valnar shouted his anger at the sky. "You're going to pay for this," he pointed a finger at the slave, lying on his side, folded in on himself from pain. "Do you hear me? I'll make sure you—"

A loud sound cut through Valnar's fury. Like fabric tearing. Like parchment splitting down the middle.

Valnar's blood went cold.

He knew that sound.

He had *prayed* never to hear it again, though it had haunted his nightmares for years, waking him drenched in sweat and out of breath.

Shouts erupted from the courtyard. Panic. Boots scrambling over stone.

He took a reluctant step towards the edge of the roof. His breath hitched as he turned his gaze downward.

Ink's body lay still where it had fallen. His chest had caved in — not with broken bones or torn flesh, but with something far worse. A dark void had opened where his heart should be, slowly widening, swirling and pulsing like the mouth of a hungry creature.

Inside the abyss, Valnar saw movement.

Thick legs emerged first, claws curling over the bloodied stone, gouging deep into it as it pulled itself free. A long muzzle followed, snarling, its breath heavy with smoke. A canine-like body pulled itself out. Its coat wasn't fur — it was *fire,* burning low along its muscular body, shifting in flickers of orange and black. Liquid flames dripped from its jagged teeth, sizzling against the ground. Molten eyes, bright as a forge, turned upward — straight at Valnar.

A fiend hound.

Valnar's stomach lurched.

The creature exhaled, a low, rumbling growl that rattled his ribs.

Behind him, Beast said through a jagged, strained voice, "Kill him."

The fiend hound bared its teeth. It launched itself at the manor, its claws digging into the stone as it started climbing up the wall.

Valnar ran.

VALNAR BARELY USED THE ladder — he dropped through the hatch, landing hard in the watch room. The moment his boots hit stone, he was moving again, barely sparing a glance for the two guards still tied up on the floor. He should have freed them. They deserved that much. But time was a luxury he didn't have, and if they were lucky, the fiend hound would stay on *his* scent.

A fiend hound. He still couldn't believe what he had seen.

The last time he encountered one, he had been barely more than a boy, green and eager, his hands still soft on the hilt of a blade. A new recruit in Kiejain's Army, desperate to prove himself. And then the fiends came, and he learned — *truly* learned — what war against their kind meant.

It wasn't like fighting men. Men bled. Men faltered. Fiends did neither. And when it was over, Valnar had walked away, though he'd left a part of him behind, like a lost limb.

The screams behind him snapped him back to the present. The guards. The ones he had left tied on the floor. Their muffled cries were barely audible over the sound of tearing stone. Valnar didn't need to turn around to know the hound had entered the watch room.

His instincts screamed at him to keep moving. He sprinted down the stairs, through the hallways, his boots pounding against the floor. His only chance was his sword. Not the longsword at his hip, nor the knife strapped to his thigh. Those feeble weapons couldn't even scratch the hide of that fiend. No, there was only one thing that could harm a fiend on Earthome.

Behind him, the halls flared with sudden light, an unnatural brightness that sent shadows lunging across the walls. The heat followed next, searing close to his back. Then the deep, rumbling growl that made his blood turn ice-cold.

It was coming.

Valnar ran harder, sweat chilling against his skin despite the fire licking at his heels.

A fiend hound. Here. In *Earthome.* How? How had it broken through?

It should have been impossible.

The distant clang of alarm bells rang through the manor, but no guards appeared. No men came rushing to his aid. Where were the men who had seen the creature scale the walls? They must have warned the others by now. Were they gathering their forces? Preparing to intercept the fiend?

The hallways stretched endlessly ahead of him, long and open, offering the hound a perfect path to sprint. Valnar needed to slow it down. With a sharp pivot, he veered into a narrow servant's corridor. The space was tight, but it led straight to the guest wing. He forced himself forward, lungs burning, boots striking stone. But something gnawed at the back of his mind.

Where was everyone?

Not a single servant or slave crossed his path. No scattered voices, no hurried footsteps. The halls were deserted.

His confusion lasted only a moment before a flicker of movement ahead nearly made him stop.

Men — fighting.

Each other.

Valnar's instincts screamed to pause, to look, to *understand* what he was seeing. But he couldn't. The air behind him thickened with heat, the walls glowing orange. He felt the hound's breath before he saw its shadow lunging up behind him.

Valnar ducked.

A massive claw slashed overhead, splintering the paintings lining the wall. Wood and canvas burst into flames immediately.

Shoving himself forward, Valnar caught sight of his room at the far end of the hallway. Too far. But Lygor's door was right beside him.

Without hesitation, he threw his weight against it, knowing Lygor was still at the feast.

The door burst open under his shoulder. He stumbled inside just as the hound lunged again, its snapping jaws nearly closing on him.

It crashed into the doorframe with a furious snarl, its shoulders too broad to fit through. But the creature didn't stop. It pushed through, and the walls themselves crumbled around it, chunks of stone falling as it forced its way in.

Valnar staggered back, yanking open the adjoining door to his own room. Behind him, the hound tore through Lygor's furniture, its fiery coat setting the lavish sheets and wooden fixtures on fire. The flames danced in its wake, feeding on everything it touched.

Valnar slammed the door shut behind him, knowing it wouldn't buy him more than a handful of seconds. He dove for his belongings, tossing the bags and armour away, until his hands found the weapon he was looking for.

The hound crashed through the door.

Wood exploded into splinters, stone cracked, and the fiend surged into his quarters, shaking debris from its smouldering back. Its molten eyes locked onto him, victorious.

Valnar ripped the cloth away from his two-handed sword.

Red veins pulsed along the length of the black steel, dark and gleaming in the firelight. Red *dragonscale* — the *only* metal in Earthome capable of bleeding a fiend.

The hound hesitated. Just for a moment. Its fiery gaze flicked to the blade, its muscles twitching, its stance shifting slightly. It recognised the metal.

Valnar swallowed hard, adjusting his grip.

He had never fought a fiend alone. Not once. He'd watched his brothers, his entire unit, got decimated between those jaws. Burnt to crisps. Bones and flesh ripped apart.

Icy fear gripped Valnar's muscles, freezing his veins. He couldn't have stayed with the Kiejain's Army then. The lone survivor from his unit. He couldn't have accepted that he was meant to stay back and watch as men fought for Earthome and died.

And the day he'd accepted the truth, that he was no hero, Kiejain had granted him this fight. His own fight. Alone.

Afterall, the Twelve Riders didn't soar into every battle together.

The hound bared its teeth, and fire dripped from its mouth, hissing as it struck the floorboards. That's when Valnar realised where he was.

His boots stood within the faint chalked outline of a prayer ring — one he had drawn himself, a sacred space near the bathtub where he sought Kiejain's guidance.

He almost laughed at the irony.

If this was where he was going to die, he supposed there were worse places to make a last stand.

He inhaled slowly, the sword steady in his hands.

"Kiejain, the First Warrior..." he prayed. His voice barely wavered. "Guide my blade."

57

DIENUS

"WHAT'S TAKING HIM SO long?" Gennald muttered, eyes narrowing at Ruzen, who was still swaying in his chair, draped over Lord Brocton like they were kin.

"The idiot probably got drunk for real and forgot the words," Dienus said, voice low. He glanced at the two purebreds behind Lygor, their glassy eyes fixed ahead. "Gennald, how many would it take to bring them down?"

Gennald's hand twitched near his sword. "Too many, Your Highness. We need Master Ruzen to paralyse them."

Dienus scowled and stared at the beasts. His fingers fidgeted at his belt. He wondered if he could change that vacant look in their eyes — later, once the manor was his. He'd never broken a purebred beast before. He wondered if they'd be more of a challenge than the flames. He promised himself he'd find out — after he was done with Lion of Zarall.

Ruzen swung his goblet mid-sentence and splashed wine across Brocton's lap. The noble looked irritated but kept smiling. He couldn't afford not to. Brocton's eyes met Dienus's, silently echoing the same question. *What's taking so long?* Why hadn't Ruzen given the signal yet? What was he waiting for?

He scanned the room again. His men were in place — over twenty, dressed as Brocton's guards, servants, scribes, and advisors, posted near exits and alcoves. Armed to the teeth. The one who'd stumbled out earlier, vomiting, hadn't returned. Melton and another were off securing the Lion's room. Two or three others leaned against walls or tables, pale and sweating, visibly struggling. Something was off with a small group of his men; they looked pathetically ill.

But still, it would be enough.

Most guests were deep in their cups, slouched at the tables. The pleasure slaves had finished dancing on the marble and now writhed on guests' laps. Other than Lygor's two beasts, no one else in the room was armed. Just guests and far too many purebred house slaves. They moved through the feast, pouring wine, collecting scraps, clearing plates.

One purebred house slave was already excessive. This many? It was ostentation. An insult.

Vadithas would die slowly.

"Screw his signal," Dienus muttered. "I'm starting the attack. Get the men ready."

"Your Highness," Gennald cautioned, "we need those purebreds down."

"He'll speak the words once we begin. I'm not waiting on his pleasure."

"We should give him more time. If Brocton's soldiers aren't let in, we'll be stranded in this room — Vadithas's security will eventually break in and..."

"Yeah, yeah, I get it."

Ruzen had promised to have his own men open the outer gates once the fighting started, letting Brocton's soldiers inside. Without them, Dienus's men would be outnumbered fast. Maybe that was what Ruzen was waiting for — his people getting into position.

Dienus swore under his breath and started pacing the far wall. Patience scraped at him like glass.

Every extra second that Lygor Zarall prick breathed the same air was a personal offence.

The prince sat so comfortably, as if no part of this night could touch him. He leaned back in his chair, one boot resting over the other, elbow on the table, idly sipping his wine as if he were born with the right to be adored. Wealthy merchants and slavers angled for his attention. When one of the purebred pleasure slaves came over to grind her half-naked body between his legs, Lygor appreciated her for a polite few seconds before patting her rear and sending her away with the kind of casual dismissal that made Dienus want to cave his face in.

Like he was too good for all of these.

When the alarm bells started ringing, that self-assured smile was wiped from Lygor's face. He wasn't alone in his alarm — Dienus stiffened too, cold sweat trickling down his spine. This wasn't part of the plan.

Throughout the room, heads turned — at least those sober enough to react. The music stopped mid-note. Even the pleasure slaves paused.

Distant shouts and clash of steel followed the bells.

Gennald was at Dienus's side, sword half-drawn. Dienus caught Ruzen's gaze across the hall. Was this some elaborate deception? A betrayal? Yet Ruzen appeared equally bewildered. Then the Master of Sands pulled himself together. He rose, knocked over his wine glass — the signal. Then he shouted two words.

The purebreds behind Lygor dropped like stones, their armoured bodies slamming into the polished floor.

"Now!" Dienus bellowed, heart pounding against his throat. The metallic ring of drawn steel resonated throughout the hall. Dienus flashed his own sword from its sheath and lunged at the nearest target — a purebred house slave.

At the high table, Lygor scrambled to his feet in panic, fingers fumbling desperately for his sword, but Brocton had already positioned himself behind the prince. The lord secured an arm around Lygor's throat and held a knife just beneath his ear.

And that was it.

One shattered glass. Two spoken words. And Lygor Zarall found himself at Dienus's mercy.

Dienus felt exhilaration ripple through his chest. All they had to do now was finish the purge. Kill everyone. Secure the manor. Gut the Union pigs. And drag Lion of Zarall out by his hair.

Dienus seized the purebred house slave's arm and forced him to turn.

The slave's hand clamped over Dienus's with unexpected strength.

He yanked Dienus off balance, drove an elbow into his face, followed by a devastating punch to his abdomen. *A house slave. A fucking,* purebred *house slave...* He realised it then, but he was too late. The purebred twisted Dienus's fingers from the sword's hilt. A knife flashed, then plunged deep into Dienus's gut.

58

BEAST

BEAST LAY ON THE roof, willing strength to his aching limbs. His ribs felt like splintered wood pressing against his skin, and his burned hands throbbed with a deep, pulsing heat. His body should have been too battered to move, too broken to even think of rising. But the *pemitoin* still coursed through his blood, dulling the worst of it, twisting the agony into something he could endure.

He breathed in slow, steadying himself.

A blur of fire shot past him, a flash of heat and fury as the hound leapt onto the roof and hurtled after Valnar. Beast didn't flinch. He barely moved, watching with hollow satisfaction as the creature disappeared into the dark.

Valnar would die.

And he deserved it.

The hatred inside Beast was a cold, steady thing. It didn't burn like rage; it didn't shake his limbs or steal his breath. It settled deep, solid as bone. The hound would rip Valnar apart. It would carve through his flesh and break his bones and spill his blood across the manor's stone. And Beast *wanted* it.

He shifted, pushing himself up on his elbows, forcing his body to move. Just as he climbed on his knees, an explosion shook the manor grounds. The impact rattled through the tiles beneath him, sending vibrations up his knees.

He squinted at the grounds. Through the dark blur, he could tell something had happened at the outer gates. Some figures were running towards it, and some were running away.

A strong, eerie wind howled through the air, pulling at his cloak.

The sounds of battle filled the night — shouts, the clash of metal, the heavy stomp of boots. Beast tilted his head, listening, frustration boiling in his chest. He couldn't see. His vision was still blurred, smeared at the edges, useless when he needed it most. So, he tried to make sense of the commotion, tried to catch the words. A lot of confused shouts. A crowd of blurry forms sprinted towards the gates, scattering off into the bushes and flower beds before reaching them. The wind howled louder, a whistling, rushing sound that muffled the shouts of the men.

He had to move. If he didn't leave now, he never would. Whatever was happening down there, it was a distraction. This was his chance. But there was no way he could use the ropes and gear Ink had prepared to scale down the wall. He'd barely been able to hold himself up *before* Valnar beat him down. He couldn't climb down here. He had to find another way out of the city.

Dragging himself forward, he crawled toward the hatch. The ladder loomed beneath him, its rungs too far apart, too much space between them for his battered body to trust. He swung his legs over, lowering himself carefully, but his grip was weak. His descent turned into more of a slump, half-sliding, half-falling into the watch room below.

The stifled screams of the guards greeted him.

Beast lifted his head slowly. The world swam in and out of focus as he blinked, trying to clear the haze that clung to his vision like cobwebs. The two guards were still bound, writhing against their restraints with renewed desperation, the ropes cutting into their wrists as they twisted and pulled. Despite his blurry vision, Beast caught their eyes, wide with terror. They watched him like cornered prey staring at death.

The chamber bore witness to the fiend hound's passage. Streaks of black scorch marks stained the walls, the lingering stench of smoke tainting the air. Even now, Beast could still feel that heat lingering in the air, a fading warmth that made his skin prickle. And yet, for all its rage and ferocity, the hound had left the guards alive. It had torn through this place, focused on its true target, leaving these two trembling men as an afterthought.

The guards thrashed harder against their bonds. Both had gone deathly pale. One had soiled himself — the acrid smell cutting through the burnt stench that still hung in the air.

Beast pushed himself onto his knees with agonising slowness. His muscles screamed in protest, and his vision blurred worse from the effort. His fingers twitched from pain and hatred. He paused there, balanced on his knees, and considered the two men before him.

He could kill them. He *should* kill them. They were bound, helpless, unable to fight back or flee. Even in his current battered state he could easily do it. The guards seemed to sense the direction of his thoughts. They pressed themselves against the wall as if they could will themselves to melt into the stone. Their breathing came in short, panicked whimpers. They shivered as they watched Beast slowly climb to his feet.

The sight he presented only added to the men's horror. What was left of Beast's face was hidden beneath layers of blood-soaked bandages, the fabric stained dark and clinging to swollen, bruised flesh beneath. His hands, wrapped tight in similar cloth, were stained through with fresh blood. His dark cloak hung in tatters around his frame, torn and blackened with soot and ash.

And his eyes...

They could see their path to Farhome in Beast's eyes.

Beast knew what would happen once he killed these two. He didn't understand how, not fully, but he understood enough. He could sense the presence of more fiend hounds waiting by the hole he had torn onto the bottom of that cavern. Waiting to cross. He knew what they needed.

"Death is their passage," Beast said, his voice hoarse. "A *rhoa* leaves, a fiend comes through."

The two men whimpered louder. Beast doubted they understood the value of his discovery, but they were sensible enough to fear the fiendish man talking to himself.

Beast could summon more. A fiend for each corpse. As many as he could kill. He could *take* his freedom.

Hunters always find you.

The familiar words echoed in his head.

"Let them find me," Beast whispered. "Let them find me surrounded by an army of fiends. With fire in their eyes. Let them try and drag me to White Tower."

The guards' muffled whimpers pained his ears. They trembled violently against their restraints. Their eyes were locked on him as he stepped forward slowly. Their terror fed something dark inside him.

Their fear empowered him. Made him feel alive in a way he only felt on the bloodied sands of an arena.

The candlelight flickered erratically, casting dancing shadows that tricked his eyes. The flames seemed to pulse in rhythm with his heartbeat, making everything waver like a fevered dream. He blinked hard, trying to force his eyes to focus properly on the two men cowering before him.

Something about their faces made his stomach twist unexpectedly. Before he could understand why, he saw the resemblance. With his brown hair falling across his forehead and that narrow, freckled face, one of the men looked disturbingly like Ink. Not identical, but the similarity was strong enough to make Beast's breath catch in his throat.

He blinked faster, more desperately now, trying to clear his sight, to see the man as he truly was. But now that he'd acknowledged the resemblance, it was all he could see. The guard's features seemed to shift and blur, becoming more and more like Ink's with each passing second.

Ink's eyes, staring back at him through this stranger's face.

His sight wasn't reliable — he *knew* that — but his gut clenched anyway.

The way Ink had looked at him before he fell. The wide-eyed look of hurt and betrayal...

His fingers twitched, and he found himself stepping away from the bound men.

It wasn't real. Just a trick of his broken sight. His damaged mind trying to torture him with guilt he had no reason to feel. Ink had been about to betray him. He was going to give him up...

"All free men are greedy," Beast growled, but his feet took him another step further from the men. He couldn't shake the growing discomfort that gnawed under his skin.

He staggered towards the stairs. The weight in his chest didn't ease. It only settled deeper, pressing against his lungs. He stumbled down the stairs, his legs unsteady beneath him. His shoulder slid along the cold stone wall for balance, the rough texture catching on his torn cloak. Each uneven step jarred his ribs, and he had to pause halfway down, gripping the wall as a wave of dizziness threatened to send him tumbling. Ink's face still lurked at the edges of his mind like a persistent shadow, but he shoved it away. It didn't matter. What mattered was getting out of here.

The hallways stretched ahead of him. Too bright. He shielded his eyes with the crook of his elbow and kept his head down as he walked, relying more on memory and instinct than sight. His footsteps echoed hollowly in the empty corridors, the sound seeming unnaturally loud in the oppressive silence.

Strangely, he didn't encounter anyone, which was both fortunate and suspicious. After the chaos the fiend hound had unleashed, and whatever commotion was outside the manor, the corridors should have been swarming with activity. The stillness irritated him more than danger would have. It felt wrong.

It would have been easier with the fiends at his side. He should have killed those men. Then he wouldn't have to skulk through these corridors like a wounded, nearly blind, vulnerable animal. With a pair of fiend hounds at his back, their heat and fury clearing his path, no one would dare stand in his way.

But they would also draw attention. He needed to escape the city, not just the manor. Letting the fiends loose would turn every eye on him before he even reached the city gates. This was better, he told himself. Slower, more painful, but better. Maybe it was actually a good thing he hadn't killed those men.

He pushed on, his breath short and ribs aching. The *pemitoin* was still working, keeping his body upright, pushing back the worst of his injuries, but it wouldn't last forever. He had to leave the city before the *pemitoin* wore off and...

He stumbled and barely caught his balance against the wall. *The antidote.*

Once the *pemitoin* wore off, the aftereffects would kill him. He had barely survived the withdrawal last time, and that had been with significant help from

Olira's expertise and constant care. Without the antidote to ease the aftereffects, he was as good as dead.

And Ink had it. The small vial had been tucked safely in his jacket pocket. Now that jacket — and everything in it — lay sprawled on the manor ground outside.

Leaning against the wall, he paused to catch his breath and collect his thoughts. The cold stone pressed against his back through the torn fabric of his cloak. There was no point in escaping if he wouldn't live long enough to make it out of the city. His only option was brutally simple and utterly damning. He had to find Ink's body.

Fuck.

He swallowed against the nausea curling in his throat. There was a painting mounted on the wall directly opposite from him. He could barely make out the details — some hunting scene, he thought. Noble riders on horseback chasing some fleet-footed animal through a stylized forest. The dark brushstrokes blurred together, their red and yellow lines twisting into shapes that reminded him of Ink's war paint. He couldn't look away from it.

Something sat heavy on his ribs. It wasn't like anger or fear. Those had their own bites. Anger was fire in his lungs; fear was cold and suffocating. This was something else, creeping in slow, thickening the silence around him until it became unbearable. It was a lingering thing. He stared harder at the painting, trying to ground himself, but the longer he looked, the more the colours bled together, turning sharp, dark, reminding him of the steep roof above.

He was trying to help you!

Valnar's voice rang in his head.

"No," Beast whispered. Ink was about to betray him. He could tell. He had seen it on his face.

No, he couldn't see shit. His eyes were fucked.

His mind latched onto every word, every shift in Ink's posture, searching, picking it apart, hunting for proof — *undeniable proof* — that Ink had been about to cave. He was *listening* to Valnar, letting him get in his head, letting him turn him...

The wall grew harder against his back, carrying more of his weight.

Do you not feel remorse?

Olira's voice this time.

Remorse makes you human.

I told you, I don't need any more remorse, Ink had said.

Was that what remorse did? Made a man stash ropes and gear on the roof, source *pemitoin* and an antidote, plan an escape? Made him risk his life for a fucked-up man he barely knew?

His throat bobbed. He raised his arms to shield his face from the flickering light.

"All free men are greedy," he whispered through clenched teeth.

Ink's voice answered him.

I'm sorry.

His knees shook violently, and he barely caught himself against the wall before sliding to the floor in a heap. He was bone-deep tired, and he knew with grim certainty that if he sat down now, if he let himself collapse, he wouldn't be getting back up again.

He had pushed Ink to his death.

Ink's face. That look of hurt and confusion just before he fell. Not anger, not hatred, but wounded betrayal.

His throat ached with suppressed emotion, and his vision blurred even worse than before. He had to lower his arms, because his bandaged hands were trembling. Out of exhaustion or something else, he couldn't tell.

"What have I done?" Beast croaked quietly.

He breathed through that lingering weight on his chest. Remorse was proving much harder to brush aside than anger or fear had ever been. It clung to him, refused to be ignored or rationalised away.

But he had to move forward. He had no choice.

He had to face Ink's dead body, take the antidote and—

Alarms rang through the manor.

Beast paused. The fiend hound had been running loose for minutes now. Why were they only now raising the alarm? Or was this about what was happening outside? And where was everyone? He still hadn't seen a single servant or slave since he came down from the roof.

He shoved himself forward, moving despite the protest of his ribs. The distant sounds of fighting reached him through the corridors. More than just one isolated skirmish, the sounds were scattered throughout the manor, breaking out like wildfire in different wings and floors. The entire structure seemed to have erupted into chaos.

Several times, he nearly stumbled straight into a fight and had to backtrack hastily, pressing himself against walls. He didn't know who was fighting whom but the widespread chaos worked in his favour. In the confusion, one more bloodied figure limping through the halls would draw little attention.

The manor's familiar layout was difficult to summon in his fractured mind. Corridors he thought he knew seemed to twist in unexpected directions. He took wrong turns, retraced his steps, searching for a way out. His sense of direction felt as compromised as his vision, leaving him disoriented and increasingly desperate.

Finally, he stumbled into a familiar corridor. He knew it only because he had walked this particular stretch with Valnar so many times, heading to and from the training grounds in what now seemed like a different lifetime. From here, he could make his way towards the watch tower where Ink had fell from.

He started forward, but sudden movement at the intersection ahead made him freeze in place. He pressed himself back against the nearest wall.

A group of armed men were suddenly flung backward through the air, tossed like training dummies by some invisible force he couldn't see. They hit the opposite walls with sickening thuds, their weapons clattering uselessly to the floor. Their hair and clothes rippled and fluttered as if caught in a violent wind, and their bodies crumpled as they landed in twisted heaps.

Before Beast could process what he'd witnessed or think to turn away, someone stepped calmly into the hallway.

The figure was tall and lean, his slender frame giving him an almost fragile appearance. He was dressed in ragged clothes that barely held together. His skin was very pale, like he had been sick, or hadn't seen daylight in a while. Beast couldn't make out the stranger's face clearly, couldn't determine his age or read his expression. But the man's posture spoke of bone-deep exhaustion. His body swayed slightly as he stood there, shoulders slumped with weariness that seemed to go far beyond mere physical fatigue.

When he spotted Beast, the man stilled for a moment. Then, he extended his arm towards him, all five fingers pointing forward. Beast recognised the motion instantly, a chill of dread running through him. He had seen it before. Months ago.

At Brinescar.

On the night of the coup.

This was the same gesture the rogue mage had done when—

Before Beast could force his battered body to move, thick, black ropes shot from the man's fingers like striking snakes. The bindings were slick and unnatural, writhing like liquid shadow but holding like iron chains. They wrapped tight around his limbs with frightening grip, restraining his arms, his legs, coiling around his mouth to silence him.

The bindings yanked him violently off his feet, lifting him as if he weighed nothing. For a moment, Beast hung suspended in the air, his eyes burning and rough as he stared down at his captor through the haze. The man stood below him, his tattered clothes hanging loose on his thin frame. A skeleton of a man, barely held together by flesh and pale skin, and yet he lifted Beast with those black ropes like he weighed nothing.

Then, he flicked his wrist and the bindings slammed Beast against the wall with a brutal force. Pain pierced through his skull. His vision flickered.

Darkness claimed him.

59

OLIRA

OLIRA SAT SLUMPED AGAINST the door, knees drawn to her chest, face buried in her arms. Her throat was raw from yelling. The back of her head still throbbed where she'd hit it against the wall, but the sharp pain had dulled into something distant.

She had stopped crying some time ago.

After Norrol left, she had heard him downstairs, shifting a weight around, probably moving Emberlash to a more comfortable position. Since then, there had been nothing. Just the muffled sounds of the old house, existing against the wind.

Now, something changed.

She heard a soft scuffle from downstairs. Floorboards creaked, followed by a soft knock. And then a louder scuffle that ended with a sharp thud.

Olira lifted her head. Her heartbeat picked up, ears straining for more. Silence stretched for a moment, then the stairs creaked. Light steps. Careful.

Olira shot to her feet, pulse hammering. She turned to face the door, breath coming too fast.

"Norrol?" she asked cautiously.

Nothing.

She swallowed hard as the steps approached to the door, moving more confidently now. The key clicked in the lock. Before the door even opened, she smelled the familiar, acrid scent of leather, sweat, and animal fat. Tannery fumes, clinging to skin and clothes no matter how often they were washed.

Her heart lurched.

Jygan stood in the doorway as the door swung open.

With a strangled cry, she hurled herself onto him. His strong arms caught her instantly, holding her tight against his chest. Olira was sobbing before she could stop herself, her words tumbling out between gasps.

"How did you find me? What are you doing here? I-I thought I was—"

Jygan pressed his chin against the top of her head, holding her for a moment longer before pulling free. He grabbed her hand firmly.

"I'll explain everything later. Let's get out of here first."

Olira nodded and followed when he pulled her toward the stairs. Her legs were shaky but moving. Her mind raced to catch up with reality, thoughts tumbling over each other in a desperate attempt to make sense of what was happening. This was real. Jygan was here. Actually here, not some fevered dream born from desperation.

As they made their way down the stairs, her hand gripping the worn wooden banister for support, she tried to focus on the familiar creak of each step. The sound that had once been mundane now felt surreal, as if she were hearing it through water.

Then she saw Norrol.

He lay crumpled near the hearth, his skinny frame folded awkwardly against the stone, one arm twisted beneath him. The firelight cast shadows across his still face, and for a heart-stopping moment, he looked smaller and more vulnerable than she'd ever seen him. Like a sapling snapped by an unexpected storm. Her legs went rigid, refusing to carry her another step.

"Is he—?"

"He's fine," Jygan said, tugging her hand to keep going. "Just unconscious."

She barely had time to process the guilt that twisted in her stomach before they were rushing outside into the city.

The streets of Calae were quiet, unnaturally so. The usual city noise — the distant clatter of carts, the call of late-night vendors, the murmur of tavern-goers — was muffled in the dead of night, as if the darkness itself had swallowed sound.

Dim lanterns flickered at intervals along the cobblestone paths, their flames guttering in the cool breeze and casting long shadows.

Olira ran beside Jygan, barely keeping pace with his long strides. Her breath came in short, sharp bursts that misted in the night air. Jygan moved like he knew exactly where to go, confident and sure as he turned down narrow alleys, cutting through passages barely wide enough for two people, never hesitating at any intersection.

She didn't speak. She couldn't find the words, couldn't catch enough breath to form them. Her throat burned from the cold air and exertion, each inhalation feeling like swallowing shards of ice. Her mind reeled, thoughts spinning like leaves caught in a whirlwind. Jygan was here. After all this time, through all the despair, Jygan had found her. She was free. She was actually, impossibly free.

They wove through another street, their footsteps echoing softly off the sleeping buildings. The windows were dark, shuttered tight against the night, and Olira found herself grateful for the silence.

Finally, after what felt like an eternity of running, Jygan pulled her into a narrow passageway between two buildings and stopped. The walls pressed close on either side, and she could smell the stale air trapped between the buildings — old urine, rotting kitchen scraps, the musty dampness of stone, and something sour.

"Where are we going?" she asked, her voice barely above a whisper, still breathless.

"Horses are waiting," Jygan said, his own breathing controlled but quick. "We're leaving the city now." He grabbed her hand again, his fingers warm and reassuring against hers, and led her through the other end of the passageway at a fast walk.

"The gates will be closed," Olira said, the practical part of her mind finally beginning to function. "It's the middle of the night."

Jygan didn't answer. His breath plumed out before him in white clouds in the night's chill, and she noticed how his head jerked at every sound — the distant bark of a dog, the creak of a shutter in the wind, the scurry of something small across their path. His tension was infectious, and she found herself listening too, straining her ears for any sign of pursuit.

"By morning, Dienus's men will know I'm gone," she whispered. "They'll search the city, watch the gates."

"We'll be gone by then," Jygan said. "We'll go through the side gate. There's a single guard there. I paid him off in advance."

They turned another corner, and Olira noticed how the streets were growing emptier the farther they got from the heart of the city. The buildings here were different too — less grand, more utilitarian. Fewer homes with their warm, inviting lights, and more old storehouses with their weathered wooden walls and stable yards with their familiar scents of hay and horses.

He had planned this through, every detail carefully considered. How? Her mind was still trying to piece everything together, still catching up with the gift of freedom when she'd given up hope. They neared closer to the city walls, the massive stone structure looming ahead of them.

"Jygan, how did you find me?"

"We've been following you for weeks," Jygan said, his voice carrying a weight of exhaustion and determination. "When I saw the soldiers leaving the house in groups tonight, I knew the house would be weakly guarded. This was my chance."

Olira stumbled slightly over an uneven stone before catching herself, her mind snagging on one particular word. "We?"

Jygan didn't answer right away. Instead, he only picked up the pace, his grip on her hand tightening slightly. They reached the edge of a stable yard, where a small, quiet building stood in the shadows. Three horses were tethered nearby, their forms barely visible in the darkness, saddled and waiting.

Three.

Her heart skipped when she heard her name spoken by a familiar voice.

"Olira!"

Before Olira could react, a small figure shot toward her from the shadows near the horses. Skinny arms wrapped around her waist, nearly knocking her off balance. The breath ripped from her chest.

"Torren!"

Tears spilled down Olira's face before she even realised she was crying. She dropped to her knees, pulling him close, kissing his hair, his forehead, his cheeks. She could barely breathe between sobs, her words a jumbled mess of relief.

"Torren— Oh, Alunwea— I thought... I didn't know! I thought you were—"

She couldn't even finish. She only held him tighter.

"We need to go," Jygan said as he ushered them towards the horses. He helped Torren onto his horse, handing him the reins.

Olira approached the second horse and grabbed the saddle, but before she could mount, she stopped. Tears blurred her vision, and her chest clenched with dread, but she had to ask.

"Is it true?" She stepped back from the horse and turned to Jygan. "Are they dead?"

Jygan hesitated. His hard expression softened, revealing his sorrow. He glanced over his shoulder at the dark streets, eager to move on before having this conversation. But Olira's eyes were haunting. His head sagged.

"I buried Gilann," he said softly. "Behind the hill next to your parents."

The world tilted beneath her. Time seemed to slow down as she fought against an invisible weight pressing down on her chest.

"N-no, he can't be..."

Jygan pulled her into a fierce embrace, gripping her shoulders. She clung to him, sobbing into his chest, her fingers curling into the fabric of his tunic. *Gilann.* She tried to picture him as he was: smiling, laughing, scolding her for being reckless. The way his voice had always been steady, how he had made everything feel exactly the way they were.

But all she could see was dirt covering his body, his name carved into a crude marker.

She blinked hard, pulling away. She had to ask, even though the words were trapped, caught in her throat. She had to know.

"Andar and Kowas?"

Jygan looked away. Olira searched his face, and the grief in his eyes deepened into something worse. A kind of pain that made her stomach drop.

"Jygan?" she whispered. "What happened to them?"

Jygan forced the words out: "Andar and Kowas are enslaved. They were sent to a slave ranch."

The world didn't tilt. It disappeared.

Olira stumbled back. Her breath sounded somewhere between a sob and a gasp. "No."

She couldn't process it. She couldn't see them like that: slave tattoos inked onto their skin, chains around their necks. Andar, fierce and chatty, forced into a void. Kowas, quiet and thoughtful, reduced to nothing.

Her knees threatened to give out, but Jygan caught her. He said something, but she barely heard him. Her mind raced, spiralling into horror and denial. Jygan led her to the horse. Somehow, she found herself sitting in the saddle. The horse moved forward, Jygan leading it, but she barely felt the motion.

All she could see was the slave. Beast. His tattooed neck. The empty look on his face. How he would move around the farm like he barely existed. How he'd carried the weight of his chains even when they weren't visible.

The look on his face when she betrayed him.

And now, her brothers were enslaved. Condemned to the life she abandoned Beast to.

Jygan's low swearing pulled her out of the numb shock that clung to her mind like a thick fog. Blinking, she refocused as he suddenly stopped them in the shadows of a narrow alley. Beyond it, the side gate came into view.

There wasn't one guard at the gate. There were dozens.

Soldiers moved along the walls in organised groups, their armour catching glints of torchlight as they passed beneath the flickering flames. More guards stood clustered directly before the gate itself, spears in their hands. They weren't moving like bored men trudging through another tedious night shift. Their steps were swift and purposeful, eyes scanning the surroundings with alertness. Something was wrong.

"What's happening?" Olira whispered.

Jygan shook his head. "I don't know."

"I thought you said there was only one guard."

"I know."

His jaw clenched as he scanned the scene, his fingers bending and twisting the leather reins. Before Olira could press further, a soldier rushed toward the gate, barking orders. The others responded instantly. They moved into formation and held their spears ready. A group of them dragged an empty cart to serve as a blockade, blocking the street leading to the gate. A pair of guards heaved an iron bar into its slot on the gate, sealing it with a heavy clang. Two archers took their place on the guard watch near the gate.

No one was getting out.

Olira barely had time to feel the hopelessness when hoofbeats echoed through the streets. Someone was galloping toward the gate. A single horse.

A full barricade, with over a dozen soldiers, against a single rider.

A horse emerged at the far end of the street. The hooves struck against the cobblestone streets with no signs of slowing down. The rider slumped forward on the saddle. He was a pale, gaunt man. Nothing threatening about him — nothing that would justify the tension that rippled through the soldiers. If anything, the man looked too weak, barely clinging. Yet, he didn't slow his horse down.

He rode straight toward the barricade.

The soldiers braced, calling out to the rider.

"Halt!"

Olira's gaze flicked to an inconspicuous shape strapped to the saddle behind the rider. A figure bound in black ropes, limps hanging stiffly on either side of the saddle. Bandages wrapped his arms and his head. Something about him made Olira's stomach cold. She couldn't take his eyes off the figure.

"Stop!" the soldiers ordered again. Archers drew their bows and aimed.

Olira held her breath as the rider lifted his hand towards the barricade.

A sudden and unnatural wind howled through the street. The archers loosed their arrows, the bowstrings snapping with sharp cracks. The arrows flew towards the rider, then stayed still in the air for a heartbeat, twitching slightly like birds trying to fly against a strong wind. Their iron points gleamed in the torchlight as they were suspended a few metres from the rider's face.

Then an invisible force slammed through the barricade like a wave breaking against a cliff. A resonant boom rang through the streets. Men flew backward through the air, their shouts of alarm cut short as they tumbled in graceless arcs, their weapons ripped from their hands. The heavy wooden cart that had formed the barricade splintered into countless pieces and tossed aside like twigs.

Olira ducked and shielded her head as debris scattered across the cobblestone street. Her horse reared up on its hind legs with a sharp whinny, its eyes rolling white with fear as it snorted and stamped. She clutched the leather reins with both hands and shouted it to calm down. She barely managed to keep the frightened beast from charging headlong into the chaos. A quick glance to her right showed Torren upright and focused, gripping the reins with more confidence than she expected.

"Get ready!" Jygan yelled. His horse danced sideways, tossing its head and blowing hard through flared nostrils, but he held on.

"For what?" Olira shouted back, but the answer came before he could respond.

The pale rider extended a hand toward the gate. The heavy iron bar sealing it wrenched free and slammed to the ground with a metallic thud. The gates snapped open, swinging wide, and the rider galloped through like a breeze.

As the horse thundered past, Olira's eyes were once again drawn to the bound figure. A cold dread crept into her core.

"Now!" Jygan yelled and kicked his horse into motion.

The remaining soldiers were dazed, scattered by the blast of wind and the collapsing barricade. No one tried to stop them. Olira spurred her horse forward. The three of them crossed the street and rode out into the night, leaving Calae behind.

60

VALNAR

VALNAR WAS SURPRISED TO open his eyes.

For a long moment, he couldn't remember why waking up should have been impossible. Then, as his mind cleared, the state of his body registered all at once. A weak groan slipped past his lips.

He *should* have been dead.

"Lygor," he whimpered.

He would have gladly let go, closed his eyes and let Kiejain guide him to Farhome, but the thought of Lygor dragged him back, fuelled the thin thread of will keeping him upright. He pushed himself up with a ragged breath, groaning as fire licked through his ribs. His vision swam. He had to slow his breathing.

He had to move.

His left cheek and ear burned. His stomach was worse — wet, torn open, his skin stripped by the fiend hound's claws. The wound bled heavily, the heat of it turning his skin clammy. He was losing too much blood. He didn't have much time.

Find Lygor. Make sure he's safe. Then die.

His two-handed sword lay nearby. He reached for it, gripping the hilt with numb fingers. He pushed himself up, biting back the sound that tried to claw its way from his throat.

His room was ruined. Furniture shredded, curtains and bedding burned to ash. The air was thick with smoke, making his throat raw, his eyes water. When he coughed, he nearly lost his balance.

The only untouched part of the room was inside the prayer ring. The fiend couldn't get past the neat, perfect lines. That, and his *dragonscale* sword, were the only reasons he was still alive.

The hound's body was gone. Nothing left but a dark, wet outline at the far end of the room. The remains of the fiend looked like muddy, ashen sludge, thick and clotted but utterly lifeless. No bones. No blood.

Then, there was the smell.

Burnt sugar, thick and suffocating. A scent that might have been pleasant in a fraction of this intensity, but now was overwhelming, rotting in its sweetness. It churned his stomach, bile rising. He had to get out before he collapsed.

The hallway beyond was silent.

Valnar leaned against the wall, dragging himself forward. He left a red trail in his wake, streaks of his own blood smeared across stone. The quiet disturbed him. He had seen men fighting as the fiend chased him. Someone must have heard the fiend, must have seen the flames. And yet, no one had come to investigate. The silence could only mean one thing: another battle, separate from his own, had broken out within the manor. And it had already ended.

Lygor.

The thought consumed him, driving out everything else. Where Beast was, what had happened after Ink fell, it all faded. He had no strength to lift his sword, so he let the tip drag against the floor. The sound echoed down the corridor, the only noise in an otherwise empty house. He felt like the last living thing in the manor.

Two corridors away from the feast hall, he heard footsteps.

Valnar barely managed to raise his sword, gripping it in both hands, but he still had to lean against the wall just to stay upright. In this state, he doubted he could best a maiden wielding a butter knife, but he would try.

The first man to step around the corner was Master Ruzen. Two uniformed men flanked him, both armed, both bloody. They stepped forward when they saw Valnar's blade. Ruzen's eyebrows shot up.

"Sir Valnar?" Ruzen asked, surprised. "What happened to you?"

"Where's Prince Lygor?"

Ruzen jerked a thumb over his shoulder. "Still at the feast hall."

"Lead the way."

Ruzen's momentary confusion shifted to irritation. "I've got business to attend. I don't know if you've noticed, but there's been fighting."

"Yeah, I noticed," Valnar scoffed, then grimaced at the pain. "Take me to Lygor."

"You're perfectly capable of finding the feast hall by yourself."

Valnar pushed off the wall, barely managing to stay upright. He lifted his sword enough to point it at Ruzen. "I'm not letting you get behind me. Lead the way."

Ruzen's men exchanged glances. One of them smirked, amused, but Ruzen didn't. He studied Valnar for a long moment, then shook his head and sighed.

"Fine," he muttered. "Hurry up, then."

He turned, his men falling in behind him. Valnar followed, keeping a careful distance.

The double doors of the feast hall loomed ahead. Another set of guards stood watch, but before Valnar could speak, Ruzen gestured for them to open the doors and he walked inside.

Valnar uttered a silent prayer to Kiejain and followed.

The scent of blood hit him first. Bodies littered the ground. His eyes scanned the dead first, and found Lygor's face amongst the living.

Lygor was talking to Master Naelar. His two purebred beasts stood close behind him. There was no tension in his posture, no immediate danger. Relief crashed through Valnar so hard, it nearly stole what little strength he had left.

Naelar turned, catching sight of them. "Master Ruzen?" he said, puzzled. "I thought you were on your way to oversee the Brocton Keep's capture."

"I *was*," Ruzen grunted, "until I came across Sir Paranoid here."

Lygor's gaze snapped to Valnar. "Where have you been? And where's Ink?" His eyes widened at the blood soaking Valnar's side. His face drained of colour, making him appear younger. "What happened to you?"

Valnar exhaled shakily. "Are you okay?" His voice was hoarse. "I saw men fighting. What happened here?"

"There has been an attempt at Prince Lygor's life," Naelar explained. "Lord Brocton was in on it, together with Prince Dienus Vogros. Master Ruzen led them straight into our trap."

Valnar hardly understood any of that, only that there had been an attempt at Lygor's life.

"Get me a physician!" Lygor said, his voice tight with urgency.

"Master Caerlo is tending to our hostages," Naelar replied.

"*Get him here*!" Lygor growled. "*Now!*"

Naelar's brows twitched upward. Surprise flickered across his face, but he hid it quickly, gesturing for a servant to fetch the physician.

Valnar's head felt too heavy, his vision darkening at the edges.

"What happened?" he mumbled again. His tongue was thick, and his limbs felt like lead. He let himself sink into Lygor's grip.

"Hey," Lygor whispered. "It's all gonna be okay. You'll be okay. Valnar... *where is Ink?*"

Valnar felt like a coward, but he was glad unconsciousness took him before he had to answer that question.

EPILOGUE

VALNAR BIT DOWN ON the leather belt as the blade pressed in.

Fire tore through his side, ripping a raw scream from his throat that barely made it past clenched teeth. His fists twisted in the bedsheets, every muscle locked tight as Caerlo worked with quiet indifference. The scent of scorched skin and fresh salve filled the air. Sweat stung his eyes.

He barely noticed when the belt slipped from his mouth. His jaw hung slack, head sinking into the pillow, breath ragged. Pain dulled just enough to think. Not to move or to speak. Just to survive the moment.

"You should rest, Sir Valnar."

The voice barely registered at first. But then the words settled.

Valnar's eyes snapped open. He pushed himself upright with a grunt, ignoring the fresh wave of pain as it lanced up his ribs. His glare met the physician's calm, unimpressed, slightly nervous face.

"I appreciate the concern," he rasped hoarsely. His face — his burnt left cheek and ear — hurt when he spoke. "But I need to be there."

Caerlo gave a small, measured nod. "As we all do. But the damage was extensive. No sudden movements. No lifting. No fighting. If your dressing tears, it may not stop bleeding next time."

Valnar's jaw clenched. He looked away before he said something he'd regret, purely because the physician had just saved his life and Valnar didn't want to snap at him. He had no intention of bleeding out to death. The thought of dying and leaving Lygor alone in the hands of the manipulative leaders of the Union made him feel nauseated.

His gaze drifted to the weapons rack in the corner. The red *dragonscale* sword leaned against it, no longer hidden beneath the cloth. Light touched the red veins that ran through its black blade, drawing a faint red shimmer from the smooth metal.

"Kiejain's blessing," he muttered.

Caerlo didn't answer. He gathered his tools and just before he left, he added, "I left something for the pain. Try to eat before you take it."

Valnar closed his eyes and tried not to even think about laying back down. He gave himself another two minutes — then another minute, then another one — before he forced himself up on his feet.

He stumbled toward the table by the window, cursing the vast size of the room. It was far more spacious than the one he'd had at Master Vadithas's manor. The space was cluttered with expensive furniture and decorations. By the time he dragged his feet to the table, he was out of breath. He gripped the back of a chair and doubled over, breathing slowly, before lowering himself into the seat.

His stomach lurched at the sight of the food. He clenched his jaw to keep from retching. He had to eat — because he had to survive. He had to live and protect Lygor.

Avoiding both the sight and the smell of the meal, he forced down a few small pieces of boiled potato and a spoonful of plain rice. His face hurt as he chewed. Once he was sure the food would stay down, he ate just enough to feel marginally stronger and counted it as a victory. He drank the herbal mixture Caerlo had left beside the meal, and within minutes, he noticed the pain receding.

A purebred slave entered shortly after. She boiled water for his bath and helped him wash without disturbing the bandages. She worked quietly, eyes down, focused on each task with care. After bathing, Valnar made his way to the dresser and armour racks. Two stands displayed his two sets of armour.

Two distinct lives he'd had. Two choices.

He pulled a tunic from the dresser and let the slave ease it over his head. His eyes drifted to the two breastplates — one bearing Kiejain's black horse with dragon wings, the other Zarall's black-and-gold lion.

He already knew which one he'd wear.

He lifted the breastplate from its stand. The slave buckled it on, piece by piece, until he was fully armoured. He strapped his longsword to his hip and slung the *dragonscale* sword across his back.

Leaving the room, he trudged through the neat, well-kept halls of Brocton Keep. Guards and servants bustled around him, rushing to complete their duties before the ceremony. He recognised several from Vadithas's household. Now they all wore Zarall's colours and coat of arms openly. The sight both pleased and unsettled him.

He made his way to the lower levels and descended the stone stairwell to the dungeons. He passed locked cells without a second glance at the faces inside.

The cell he sought lay two levels below. The corridor was cold but well-lit. At the end of it, two of Lygor's purebred beasts stood guard outside a thick iron door.

The hundred purebreds Vadithas had gifted to Lygor had already acknowledged their new Owner. They only served Lygor. A hundred might not be a dominant force — but they were far from negligible.

These two had been instructed to guard the cell and kill anyone who approached — except for Lygor and Valnar. Not even the Union leaders were allowed near the prisoner. A small but telling sign that Lygor hadn't surrendered entirely to their control. Not yet.

The purebreds stood still as Valnar approached, though the cell they guarded wasn't his destination. He had nothing to say to Prince Dienus Vogros.

He ordered them to unlock the only other occupied cell in the corridor.

Sir Gennald grimaced as the door opened, wincing against the sudden light. A tired groan escaped him as he pushed himself into a sitting position. He was shackled to the far wall, though the chains were long enough to let him lie on the stone floor. He blinked until his vision cleared and focused on the face of his visitor.

"Sir Valnar," Gennald greeted, his warm voice at odds with his unfriendly demeanour. "I was wondering when you'd come."

"Sir Gennald." Valnar nodded curtly.

"I know what you're here to say. I won't deny it."

Valnar scoffed. "Your confession won't earn you any mercy."

"You misunderstand me, Sir Valnar. I'm not denying the fact that I committed treason, but I don't feel remorse either. I'd do it again."

"Then you're a bigger fool than I thought," Valnar spat.

"Because I believed in King Kastian vision for a better Chinderia?"

Valnar stepped forward, anger tightening his chest. "Kastian Vogros is a monster who would stop at nothing to serve his own interests."

"And Lygor Zarall is not?"

"Lygor is a good man," Valnar said. "His heart is in the right place."

"So is King Kastian's."

"Can you say the same for Dienus Vogros? I've heard all about his visits to the pleasure houses. I know what he indulges in."

"And I've heard all about your prince's pastimes."

Valnar growled aloud. Silence settled over the dark cell. His nostrils flared as he stared down at Gennald. A low, guttural sound tickled the back of his throat. Gennald met his gaze evenly.

"There is no greater sin than blind loyalty, Kiejain's warrior," Gennald said at last. "What will you do when you realise Kastian Vogros is not the villain?"

The stone walls suddenly felt close, oppressive. Though it felt like retreating from a battlefield, Valnar backed out of the cell. Dread churned inside him. Gennald didn't laugh or taunt him as he left — only watched him with eyes clouded by pity.

Valnar hurried down the corridor, desperate to leave the cell behind. By the time he climbed the stairs to the first level of the dungeons, his dread had curdled into anger. Sir Gennald would be executed in the morning, before their departure for Euroad. Valnar wished he was strong enough to be the one to perform the execution.

The screams tore through his thoughts. He flinched, startled, then remembered where he was. He told himself he didn't want to know who was being tortured and for what. He turned toward the stairs leading to the courtyard — then paused.

He'd heard the familiar, musical voice of Master Vadithas.

Against his better judgement, Valnar followed the sound down another corridor, toward a large chamber. The screams faded to muffled groans. He smelled burning flesh before he reached the open doors. It reminded him of Beast — how he'd found him at the end of the Fire Breath.

One of the three purebred beasts, selected to replace Beast, sat slumped in a chair. Vadithas leaned over him meticulously. The purebred shivered, fists clenched in his lap. Steam rose from his chest.

Vadithas withdrew the hot iron and leaned forward to inspect the fresh brand. Three symbols now marked the slave's skin, evenly spaced across his chest: a maiden, a rose, and a stallion.

"I'll be with you shortly, Sir Valnar," Vadithas said without turning. He set the iron aside and reached for another from the flames. The end glowed red, shaped like a sparrow.

The purebred braced, holding his breath as Vadithas pressed the brand beside the third symbol. The iron hissed. A strangled sound escaped the slave's throat, but he didn't pull away. His hands stayed on his lap, nails biting into his palms.

Valnar looked away and regretted it immediately.

A second purebred lay face down on a table. Master Caerlo and a pair of house slaves gathered around him. Caerlo worked with calm precision, drawing three incisions across the slave's back from shoulder to hip. The house slaves wiped the blood away quickly for a clear view. Already, the cuts resembled the scars Beast had earned in his fight with the bear. The purebred wasn't restrained. He gripped the table's edges, knuckles white, veins straining on his neck from the effort to will himself still.

"Do you see the difference between a real purebred and that abomination you brought with you?" Vadithas asked, still focused on his work.

The third purebred sat on a bench nearby. The brands on his chest gleamed angrily. Blood trickled from his side and down his back, pooling at his feet. A house slave cleaned the wounds while the slave stared at the floor, his grey eyes vacant.

This one was Beast's half-brother.

A tub of steaming water waited beside him, ready to wash the blood away. Nearby, Valnar spotted a black-and-gold armour set on a rack — and a half mask shaped like a lion's face.

"Aren't they remarkable?" Vadithas said, his voice tinged with admiration. He wiped his hands and turned toward Valnar. "How could we have trusted such a crucial role to a broken purebred?"

He stepped beside Valnar and gestured to the slave on the bench.

"He'll be Lion of Zarall today. But it never hurts to have spares. Don't you agree?"

"Was this your plan all along?" Valnar asked hoarsely. Speaking was a mistake — the stench of burned flesh clawed up his throat. He turned and vomited onto the stone floor.

"No, Sir Valnar," Vadithas replied calmly, following him out. "The plan was Prince Lygor's. We're merely perfecting it."

Valnar wiped his mouth on the back of his hand. The Union had forced Beast into the Fire Breath. That fight had done more than eliminate a problematic slave — it gave them the excuse they needed to reshape Lion of Zarall in their image. Had they always known how it would end? How many steps ahead were they playing?

Valnar didn't trust himself to speak. Instead, he turned and stormed toward the stairs, fleeing toward the promise of fresh air.

"We'll see you at the ceremony, Sir Valnar," Vadithas called after him.

The stench followed him out of the dungeon. It clung to his clothes, to his skin, to the inside of his nose. Even as he walked the keep's upper halls, it lingered, tainting the air.

He climbed the steps in a daze and soon found himself at the doors to Lygor's chambers.

Two purebred beasts stood guard, but they let him through.

Inside, the rooms teemed with activity. Servants and slaves moved quickly to prepare Lygor for the coronation. Masters Naelar and Ruzen were already present, along with Mistress Kyrophe and an older man named Adept Kato.

Adept Kato had joined the Union leaders earlier that morning, taking over from Adept Ziuv, who was also present but stepped aside without resistance, clearly relieved to return the seat to Kato. The man had been attending to an incident relating to the Casters Board of Chinderia at Brinescar. He wore a white robe similar to Ziuv's, its loose cuffs and hems embroidered with intricate red designs. He held himself with regal composure and spoke with clarity.

"Adept Teslaturahel is a third seat mage, but even he can't—" Kato paused as Lygor broke away from the gathering, brushing the slaves aside to greet Valnar.

"Valnar," he said, his young face brightening with relief. "How are you feeling?"

"I'm better, Your Highness." Valnar studied the man he'd protected the last five years of his life. He found only innocent concern and genuine affection in Lygor's expression. But the prince caught the scowl that had crept into his features.

"Valnar, what's wrong?"

The smell of burnt flesh still clung to the back of Valnar's throat, souring every breath. He rubbed his nose, trying to block it out. Sir Gennald's words rang uninvited in his mind.

There's no greater sin than blind loyalty.

He searched Lygor's face. Did he know what was happening below? About the men tortured and mutilated in his name? Of course he did. This was his plan. He would follow through with it.

"Nothing," he muttered, looking away. "I'm just... still a bit tired, that's all."

It felt like he'd fled from three different battles in the span of a few minutes.

The prince laid a hand on his arm, steady and warm.

"Sit down," he said, worried. "Try to take it easy today."

Valnar nodded and moved to the window. He crossed his arms over his chest, leaning against the sill. Eyes turned to him. He met their gazes with his own. He would not back down from Lygor's side.

"Can your Hunters find him?" Naelar asked Kyrophe, returning to their earlier discussion.

The mistress of the White Tower shook her head, her voice flat. "It didn't escape. It was stolen. Therefore, my Hunters cannot track it."

"I can send mercenaries after them," Ruzen offered.

"Tell them to track, not engage," Kato instructed. "Adept Teslaturahel is highly skilled. I'll need a dozen of my mages and a proper ambush."

"Is it true he summoned a fiend?" Lygor asked.

"It was Beast," Valnar said, drawing their attention. He shifted, grimacing as the movement pulled at his wound. "Beast summoned the fiend and commanded it."

"The purebred?" Naelar asked slowly, not bothering to hide his smirk.

"Slaves don't cast spells, Sir Valnar," Kato said. "Though I do admit, it's unusual for someone like Tes to use Darkhome magic. Wait until the Eternal Pillar hears about this."

"I know what I saw," Valnar snapped. "It was Beast."

"If the purebred had that kind of power," Ruzen said, "he wouldn't have lost the Fire Breath."

"We need to notify Kiejain's Army," Valnar said. "There's been a breach, and a fiend was loosed. They need to know."

"And you've expertly taken care of the fiend," Naelar said. "We're grateful you were in the right place and at the right time. No need to get Kiejain's Army involved."

"Absolutely not," Kato joined. "They'll find a way to pin this on the Casters Board."

Valnar didn't waste words on them. He kept his eyes on Lygor, silently urging him to listen to his advice.

To choose him.

Lygor broke eye contact, propping one elbow on his other palm, and studying the embroidery on his ceremonial robe.

Valnar's heart sank.

"How was Ink involved?" Lygor asked.

"We're investigating his connection to the mage," Naelar replied. "If he was scheming with Adept Teslaturahel—"

"He wasn't scheming with anyone," Valnar growled. His stomach tensed as though bracing for a blow.

"Then what was he doing on the roof?" Lygor asked.

Valnar hesitated. The Union leaders watched him closely.

"Beast was trying to escape," he said at last. "Ink tried to stop him and Beast killed him."

He wouldn't let them smear Ink's name. Naelar raised a brow. Valnar realised Vadithas's men would eventually find Ink's gear, if they hadn't already. And there were the two guards Ink had left alive. Still, they must have decided not to disgrace him — for the sake of Lygor's alliance with King Zumnorin of Kaldoria.

Lygor nodded thoughtfully. "I want him alive."

"Your Highness," Kato said, "both the beast and the Adept are highly dangerous. We'd be safer with lethal force."

"I want Beast alive," Lygor said through clenched teeth. His tone left no room for argument.

Adept Kato clearly wasn't used to being overruled. He swallowed his pride and bowed his head. "As you wish, Your Highness."

"Master Ruzen, have you shut down your arenas?"

Ruzen grimaced like he'd been asked to cut off his own arm. "I have, Your Highness."

"Good. Start announcing the return of Lion of Zarall. I want every Chinderian to know we're challenging Kastian Vogros to the Twilight of Infinity."

"Yes, Your Highness."

They continued discussing travel and communications with other lords until Lygor decided he was ready. They left his chambers together. The purebred guards formed a protective square around the prince — two in front, two behind. Valnar walked at Lygor's side. The Union leaders followed behind.

The walk to the grand hall was short. The hall stretched wide beneath a vaulted ceiling, its stone pillars wrapped in black-and-gold banners. Wealth clung to the place like perfume. Traders in expensive robes and nobles draped in velvet murmured in tight circles, but they were fewer than expected. Lining the walls and flanking every entrance stood dozens of purebred beasts in black-and-gold armour.

At the far end, three wide steps led to a raised platform where a single stone chair had been placed. Plain, at Lygor's request. To remind himself and everyone that this was not the throne he was destined to sit. A Pyre from the Chamber of Twelve stood before it, his expensive robes spilling down his feet.

Valnar spotted Lion of Zarall standing behind the chair.

The imposter wore full-plate armour that hid everything but his face. The brands and scars were too fresh to display. A half mask covered the upper half of his face. He stood tall, still, his grey eyes fixed forward. Whatever pain relief they'd given him, it must have been strong. He didn't even sway.

Later, Valnar would remember almost nothing of the ceremony — only that image: Lygor on the stone chair, crown on his head, and the mutilated slave behind him, posing as Lion of Zarall. That image would drown out all the rest.

The new Lord of Calae knelt in front of Lygor, kissed his ring, and pledged his loyalty.

A few weeks ago, when the Union learned that Dienus Vogros had slipped into Calae, Master Ruzen had approached him with a plan to assassinate Lygor. In truth, the assassination plot was bait. The real targets were Dienus and Lord Brocton, who had always been an unpleasant thorn in Union's pocket.

Ruzen had offered them a way to sneak into the manor, promising to open the gates from within and ensuring Lygor's purebreds would be paralysed. But the moment Dienus, Brocton, and started their attack, they were ambushed. Most were killed, including Lord Brocton. Dienus was taken alive. Within hours, Brocton's younger brother, Vayle, had taken his place. Compliant, obedient, and willing to cooperate with the Union, the new Lord of Calae had ordered the soldiers and the city guards to stand down.

It had happened too fast. Too clean. Overnight, the Brocton Keep and Calae were under Union control. The precision of it all made Valnar uneasy.

Young Norrol Heltn and Melton Varius, former squires to Dienus followed the lord. Norrol had been captured in one of Dienus's safe houses. Melton was found vomiting and writhing with stomach cramps during the attack. He had blamed a hostage for poisoning them, but no hostage was ever found.

Lords Heltez Heltn of Fort Heltn and Aelsil Varius of Varibane had already been summoned to collect their sons — after pledging their cities to Lygor. Fort Heltn had nearly a thousand men. Varibane had half that, but they had wealth and shipyards. Both would be formidable allies.

Three cities.

Lygor had arrived with nothing. Now he had three.

All thanks to the Union's scheming.

The Union leaders were next. They knelt before Lygor one by one, kissed his ring, and pledged their loyalty.

When his turn came, Valnar knelt before Lygor without hesitation. His breastplate bore the coat of arms of House Zarall, and his oath spilled from his lips easily.

He took his place behind the prince, beside the purebred.

And endured the lingering stench of burnt flesh that clung to his every breath.

Twilight of Blood series continues in
Fiend of Zarall
Join my newsletter for release updates

ACNOWLEDGEMENTS

Once again, to my husband, Jason, thank you for your compassion and care, and for so often launching yourself out of your comfort zone to meet my needs while I focused on writing, editing, and releasing this book. Mate, I know being married to an author *and* a psychologist can't be easy. You're doing a good job, and I appreciate you.

To my beta readers — Bora, Tamika, Ally, Sarah, and Stacey — thank you so much for your passion and support for this book. All the time you spent writing comments and answering my endless questions has been incredibly valuable. A special thank you to Ally and Lauren for your help with the map. Going through every geographical reference in *Lion of Zarall* and compiling it all made a huge difference when I finally sat down to create the map of Chinderia.

To Bora, for once again being my worldbuilding engineer and fantasy lore expert. I still appreciate those four hours you spent on a video call with me, across time zones, helping me sort through all the tiny, logical details and making sure everything stayed consistent. I'm also sorry for all the times I miscalculated the time difference and texted you at 2am with my "urgent" ideas. P.S. I *will* remember to add page numbers next time, so if you print out the manuscript and drop it again, it's not a total disaster.

To Beast's Launch Team, my amazing street team. You've been such a huge source of motivation. The beautiful graphics you made (those reels even got *me* excited about my own book), posting when I couldn't, and shouting about this series on every platform... I'm truly, utterly, genuinely, crazy grateful to each of you. Thank you.

And to you, the reader, thank you for returning to this story. I'm so grateful you chose to spend your time in Chinderia. These characters have lived in my head for years, and knowing they've found a place in yours means more than I can say. I just want you to know that I care about these characters and if you stick around, I promise it will be worth it in the end.

STAY CONNECTED AND SHARE THE JOURNEY

IF YOU WANT TO follow Beast's journey more closely, join my newsletter. I share exclusive insights, behind the process, and worldbuilding bits and pieces, as well as updates on future releases and excerpts.

By joining my newsletter, you will also get exclusive access to a **Twilight of Blood** short story: **A Taste of Blade and Roar.**

If you enjoyed the book, I'd be incredibly grateful if you left a review on whichever platform you use to share your thoughts. It doesn't have to be long or detailed. Even a quick rating and a few words can make a big difference.

In the blood-soaked pit of the Switchblade Arena, survival is a spectacle, and death is entertainment.

The King's newest gladiator, a young purebred beast raised for the arenas, must earn his place in the merciless head trainer's team by surviving an impossible fight—a Slayer's Pit. But as he steps onto the shifting sands, he discovers the arena offers far more than blood and death. What he finds there will shape the beast destined to become the Lion of Zarall.

Head to www.eddyrose.com and join now

ABOUT THE AUTHOR

EDDY B. ROSE STARTED her writing career when she was in third grade. Her first readers were a small but dedicated group of her classmates who stopped by at her desk at recess to read the next chapter of the story she wrote on a notebook in class, instead of listening to her teacher.

Eddy is a psychologist by day, author by night. She lives in Queensland, Australia with her husband, toddler, and her two German Shepherds (the original babies) Kara and Kal-El. She enjoys getting up at 4.30am in the morning to write.

www.ingramcontent.com/pod-product-compliance
Lightning Source LLC
Chambersburg PA
CBHW061608210726
48287CB00001B/46